HARD CASES

A NEWFOUNDLAND THRILLER

HARD CASES

A NEWFOUNDLAND THRILLER

GARETH MITTON

FLANKER PRESS LIMITED
ST. JOHN'S

Library and Archives Canada Cataloguing in Publication

Title: Hard cases : a novel / Gareth Mitton.
Names: Mitton, Gareth W., 1980- author.
Identifiers: Canadiana (print) 20240427823 | Canadiana (ebook) 20240452305 | ISBN 9781774572177 (softcover) | ISBN 9781774572184 (EPUB) | ISBN 9781774572191 (PDF)
Subjects: LCGFT: Thrillers (Fiction) | LCGFT: Novels.
Classification: LCC PS8626.I88 H37 2024 | DDC C813/.6—dc23

PRINTED IN CANADA

MIX
Paper | Supporting responsible forestry
FSC® C016245

This paper has been certified to meet the environmental and social standards of the Forest Stewardship Council® (FSC®) and comes from responsibly managed forests, and verified recycled sources.

Cover Design by Graham Blair

FLANKER PRESS LTD.
1243 KENMOUNT ROAD
PARADISE, NL
A1L 0V8

TELEPHONE: (709) 739-4477 FAX: (709) 739-4420 TOLL-FREE: 1-866-739-4420

WWW.FLANKERPRESS.COM

9 8 7 6 5 4 3 2 1

We acknowledge the [financial] support of the Government of Canada. *Nous reconnaissons l'appui [financier] du gouvernement du Canada*. We acknowledge the support of the Canada Council for the Arts, which last year invested $153 million to bring the arts to Canadians throughout the country. *Nous remercions le Conseil des arts du Canada de son soutien. L'an dernier, le Conseil a investi 153 millions de dollars pour mettre de l'art dans la vie des Canadiennes et des Canadiens de tout le pays*. We acknowledge the financial support of the Government of Newfoundland and Labrador, Department of Tourism, Culture, Arts and Recreation for our publishing activities. Also, we acknowledge the support of Celebrate NL, a Crown corporation within the Department of Tourism, Culture, Arts and Recreation for its support of arts organizations in the year 2024, Year of the Arts.

To Krista, Piper, and Tommi—the greatest twist in my story, and to chapters yet to come.

If you found a briefcase sitting on a city bus, would you take it?

If you found $50,000 cash inside, would you keep it?

If you could make a million for doing something
truly terrible, would you do it?

Where would you draw the line?

Maroon by the Webb Brothers (2000):
The soundtrack in my mind when writing *Hard Cases*.

1

Newfoundland Standoff

The gun is pointed at my face, and for a moment I get the strangest urge to laugh. If I do, it will be my body's final betrayal. It's already stinging my eyes and soaking my clothes with sweat. I already feel like my bladder or bowels—or both—could give out at any second. All of that would be preferable to a laugh, though. To suggest that I'm not taking Mia seriously.

She's deadly serious, slate-blue eyes unblinking and cloaked in heavy, black mascara to match her black-dyed hair—all serving to make this hundred-pound, nineteen-year-old girl seem all the more sinister. But mainly it's the gun. Held in a trembling hand, rattling, in contrast to that cold, dead stare.

"Give me the fucking money, Greg."

The others are frozen in surprise. They didn't know she had it in her. I know where it's coming from. I get the desperation.

Was this her plan all along?

"Give it to me!" she screams, shrill and loud, in that thick Newfoundland accent I've become accustomed to over the last few months. I'm suddenly aware of how far I am from home. I think of my mum, back over there in England—that other rock floating in the North Atlantic. There are plenty of things she doesn't know about my adventures in Canada, but the events of the past few days certainly take the biscuit.

I instinctively reach out an arm, palm flat, like I'm Darth Vader or some shit. Using the Force to keep her at bay.

"Okay, Mia. Okay," I say.

But it's not a lightsaber in my other hand; it's the leather-bound handle of a briefcase. A matte-green metal briefcase stuffed with the better part of a million Canadian dollars, cash.

"Don't give it to her, Greg," Crispin pipes up, still lying prone on the floor. He props himself up on bony elbows and spits blood from his split lip onto the musty old carpet. "She's bluffing. She's not gonna shoot ya."

"Shut up!" Mia wails, momentarily pointing the gun in Crispin's direction. He tries not to react, attempts to continue with his mind games, but he's not the one holding the gun.

"Yeah, Crisp, shut up," Shelly echoes from her place on the couch in an uncharacteristic whisper, the ever-present hula hoop wrapped around her even as she sits.

"It's not like she didn't shoot somebody already," Scott drones from beside her, eyes bulging large through his jam jar–bottom glasses.

"Give it to me. Now!" Mia screams.

"Okay, okay."

What bloody choice do I have?

I lower my Force hand and bring my lightsaber hand forward, the briefcase rattling as much as her gun.

Everything from that point on happens in slow motion.

Mia's eyes unlock themselves from my own as she lusts after the briefcase.

The gun lowers, just a hair.

Mia reaches her free hand to take the case.

Crisp yells something and there's a yellow blur as Shelly's hula hoop comes down over Mia.

Someone snatches the briefcase from my hand as I reflexively dive backwards onto the floor.

I hear a gunshot—loud and dull in this pokey Long's Hill living room.

As I land, all I see is the tasteless light fixture against the yellowed stucco ceiling caught in a flash of gunfire. I hit hard and my final thought is, *Ew. How gross is it to be lying on this carpet?*

Then all goes black.

2

How We Met

How I met Crispin and the gang is: I moved into this tiny apartment in an old building at the top of Long's Hill.

Wait, back up a year or so. I was in a nightclub in Rochdale. It's a small town in the north of England. The closest big city would be Manchester, and now I tend to tell people I'm from Manchester, but that's not really true. I'm from a tiny village called Shawforth, which is near an average-sized town called Rochdale, which is about half an hour from Manchester.

"Shaw-*forth*?"

I chuckle. She's pronouncing the "forth" like the fourth of July and I love it.

"Well, yeah, but we don't say Shaw-*forth*. We pronounce it Shaw-*futh*."

"Shaw-*futhhh*," she imitates, dragging out the "th" in the cutest possible way.

"Something like that." I chuckle.

She's pretty and I know it's not just the beer goggles, because me and my mates decided to take it easy tonight and drink a bottle of water for every beer, and strictly no shots. It is a school night, after all, and it's easier to pull if you're not shit-faced by ten o'clock.

Anyway, the plan seems to be working, because I clocked this girl from across the room right at the start of the evening and she approached me on the dance floor, so I know I'm onto a winner.

"American or Canadian?" I ask.

"I'm a Newfie." She grins.

"A what?"

"I'm from Newfoundland." She pronounces it New-*fun*-land.

"You mean New-*found*-land?" I say, pronouncing the "found" like in "Lost and . . ."

"Ha!" She smiles, taking a sip of her hard lemonade. "Who's mispronouncing things now?"

And that was how I met Dana, the only Canadian girl ever to set foot in a nightclub in Rochdale, as I would often describe her when retelling the tale to people who would ask me how an Englishman ended up in St. John's, Newfoundland—and that probably wasn't too far from the truth.

We'd met the summer before my final year of university in Preston, England, where she'd moved to be near me. It was a whirlwind romance and we'd both fallen hard—her for an English arts major unsure of where he was going in the world; me for a Canadian woman who, at twenty-four, was three years my senior, cute as all heck, and, well, Canadian, which was a big tick in the plus column from where I was standing.

"Canada is forty times the size of the UK and has about half the population," my crusty old geography teacher had told me and my classmates back in high school. I don't know if that stat stuck with anyone else, but it sure as heck stuck with me. I was a bit of a loner as a kid. I liked my alone time—and that hadn't changed. The idea of all that space. Well, it just seemed like destiny.

* * *

"So, where is she now?" Crispin asks, sitting cross-legged on the musty carpet, shirtless, his long torso inexplicably pale for a guy who spent so much time arsing about in his garden.

"She's home," I squeak, between tokes of the joint that's been circling the living room, before sending a plume of sweet smoke out into the ever-present haze.

I pass the joint to Mint—the mystical puzzle of a girl I'm sitting next to on the beaten old couch. She takes the shrinking doob from me in a careful pinch, and I'm surprised how exhilarating it feels when our fingers momentarily touch.

"Next door? Why don'tcha go get her?" Crispin asks, eyeing me through reddened eyes. He knows I didn't select this place on the couch by accident. I've been fascinated with the American girl since I met her the other day—all glistening ebony skin and perfectly pulled-back dreadlocks. I watch with intoxicated unsubtlety as she places the joint between her lips and takes a pull.

"I said why don'tcha go get her?" Crispin repeats, loud enough this time for everyone to notice the mild undercurrent of aggression. By day he annunciates carefully, his accent some neutral North American, but the more the drinks and the drugs add up, the more the Newfoundland twang begins to come through.

I look at him and smile a drugged-up smile. "Next door but one," I say. "She's in bed. Got work in the morning."

"What does she do?" Mint asks, looking to me as she passes the jay along to Crispin. My heart starts to pound as her big brown eyes look in my direction.

"I'm not exactly sure," I admit, sparking the kind of laughter that response would never generate in a room full of sober people.

"Well, where does she work?" Mint chuckles.

"Fintech? Fin-a-tech. Finatech."

"I know those guys," Crispin says. "The Newfoundland Google."

"Yeah, those are the guys," I say.

"What? They're a search engine?" Mint asks.

"No." I laugh. "They're a tech company. Something to do with helping big banks detect fraud."

"So, what's that got to do with Google?" Shelly pipes up from her place on the giant easy chair in the corner as she reaches to take the joint from Crispin.

"They just call 'em the Newfoundland Google 'cause they got a big office with beanbag chairs and shit," Crispin explains as he reaches his arms aloft in some kind of yoga pose.

"Yeah. And catered lunches every day," I say. Mint raises her eyebrows. "Really. They even have stuff for different dietary needs. Gluten-free. Keto. It's mad."

"Maybe I should apply," Mint says with a quite dazzling smile.

"Maybe we all should," I agree. More laughter.

"I dunno. Kinda sounds like a cult or somethin'," Scott says, waving away Shelly's offer of the last toke of the joint, the shrivelled remains of which she's now holding with a hair clip. She shrugs and finishes it off as Scott continues to use an old rag to clean some kind of power tool, the innards of which lie on another rag on the floor.

"Just another corporate machine trying to keep its cogs in line," Crispin says, now leaning backwards over the couch, making his long torso appear even longer, his hip bones peeping out prominently from atop loose-fitting cotton shorts.

I catch Mint looking at him. Admiring him? A wave of jealousy washes over me. There is something about Crispin. He's kind of lanky, but at six-foot-four his height lends him dominance, and while half the words that come out of his mouth sound like bullshit to me, the others do seem swayed by his charm. If we were a cult, you might describe him as the charismatic leader.

"Mint green. Is that on purpose?" I ask, nodding at the green beads that adorn her dreadlocks.

"It's more a Nigerian thing." She shrugs.

"Nigerian? Mint Bonucci isn't a very Nigerian name."

"My father's Italian. Mom is from Nigeria," she explains.

"And you live in New Hampshire."

"Yes." She smiles that glowing smile.

"And I'm meeting you in New-*found*-land." I emphasize the "found" for comedic effect.

"Yes." She laughs, taking a swig of her beer.

I don't see Crispin approaching, but suddenly he's right there, leaning in between us.

"Mint Bonucci," he says, "a riddle wrapped in a mystery inside an enigma."

3

Metrobum

"It's Churchill," I say before taking a sip of black coffee from my Tim Hortons cup.

Shelly, Scott, and Mint all turn to look at me as though impressed at my knowledge.

"Winston Churchill," Crispin says. It's a statement, not a question—as though adding the first name makes up for him not having made the observation in the first place.

"Are you sure?" Mint asks.

I pick up the note from the countertop of the kitchen island I'm sitting at—on a stool that would appear to have been stolen from a downtown bar—and turn the heavy, expensive paper in my hand. I read the Copperplate type for the fifteenth time.

CLEAN BILLS, NO FRILLS. IF YOU FOUND THIS, IT'S YOURS. NO CATCH. NO JOKE. BUT GET THIS: THERE'S MORE. IF YOU SETTLE A SCORE. THE BULLDOG FROWNS. HIS LIKENESS DOESN'T SUIT. TAKE HIS NOSE, TURN IT UP, PAINT HIM A SMILE. IT IS THE COURAGE TO CONTINUE THAT COUNTS.

"Yeah," I say. "They used to call him the Bulldog. And that quote—it is the courage to continue that counts. That's one of his, I think."

"Real little historian we got here," Shelly says, brushing her hand over my shoulder as she swaggers past. She's a touchy-feely one, Shelly—physical in a way that British girls just don't tend to be.

"Well, he is British," Crispin says in what sounds like a faux English accent.

Shelly continues around the island, twirling as she goes, her copper hair catching in the sunlight, the flowy, near-transparent white dress leaving little to the imagination as it hugs her prominent thighs and neat, bra-less breasts. She's sans hula hoop at the moment but gyrating as ever as she makes her way over to sit on Crispin's lap and kisses him sensually on the lips. I still don't know if they're together or what the situation is. This whole crowd is different from the people back home. More liberal. More free.

"And he is right," Scott says, holding up his iPhone. "Success is not final. Failure is not fatal. It is the courage to continue that counts. Winston S. Churchill."

Scott is the only one of us with an iPhone, though he's not showy about it. There is nothing showy about Scott—a short, slightly pudgy twenty-something with an older man's face coated with a scruffy black beard. His hair is self-shaved, his baggy jeans and short-sleeved T over long-sleeved T at least five years out of date. His thick-lensed glasses always look just a little wonky, which I find strange for a guy who always seems to be fixing things.

Crispin reaches out a long arm and gestures for me to hand him the note in a way I find a little condescending, but I let it go and pass over the piece of paper. He studies it with his usual frown, whip-straight eyebrows arrowing in above his sharp, Nordic nose to accentuate the expression.

"So, what the note appears to be suggesting . . ." He breaks off for a trademark dramatic pause, looking to each of us in turn—his enthralled audience hanging on the edge of our battered couches and stolen barstools. ". . . is that there's more money where this came from." He nods at the open briefcase on the coffee table, which still contains a few neatly bound stacks of fifty-dollar bills, with a mess of loose bills spilling out onto the table and the floor.

How we came to be in possession of a briefcase full of cash is: Shelly has this thing for the cinnamon buns at Rocket Bakery on Water Street.

* * *

"They're some shockin' good, b'y," she says as we pile onto the Metrobus, and she almost catches the driver in the face with her bright yellow hula hoop.

"Oops, sorry, me love," she says, patting the burly, ruddy-faced woman on the shoulder.

"That's all right, me dear. Just don't be hula-hoopin' on the bus."

We all laugh as we grab a seat. People here are so much jollier than back home, I think to myself. Half the bus drivers in Greater Manchester would barely look at you, let alone have a laugh with you. Not that I could blame them, considering some of the undesirables that take the bus over there. But it's not just on the buses. Everything is different here. There's a lighter air. Everyone is more laid-back. Time seems to lose meaning, and I'm beginning to feel like I might never leave.

I'm on first and grab a window seat near the back of the bus. I'm with two women and would normally be more chivalrous, but even after a few months, I'm still a wide-eyed tourist and I want to enjoy the views on this beautiful midsummer's day. Shelly sinks down next to me, casually placing a hand on my thigh, and Mint falls into the seat behind.

The Route 10 Metrobus weaves a wondrous path through downtown St. John's, starting with the descent down Long's Hill—a steep, suitably long, and narrow hill with cars parked almost all the way down one side. Every time I've taken the Route 10, no matter the driver, they've always attacked Long's Hill like it's some kind of bus driver rite of passage, bombing down the street at speeds that turn the colourful houses into a blur of reds and blues, yellows and greens.

I hang onto the seat in front like a kid on a roller coaster as the bus spirals its way down into the city's historic core. St. John's is an old city. The oldest city in North America, as the adverts are keen to remind. It's an old city that grew organically and, as such, it makes no sense. Roads meet each other at inconvenient angles. Heritage buildings butt up against glass and concrete condominiums. Little old pubs poke out from between lawyers' offices, barbers, and boutique clothing stores.

And, oh, the hills.

Long's Hill is only the start of it—kind of like the roller coaster's epic first drop, but the rest of the fifteen-minute ride is where the driver really gets into her groove. She swings the bus right at the sight of the fire engine–red Victoria Hall and bombs down Queen's Road until it gives way to New Gower, a confusion of power lines connecting the hodgepodge houses, bars, fish-and-chip joints, and convenience stores—each building with a colour and character all its own. In the midday sun, the blue-green windows of high-rise hotels shimmer in the distance before the ship-like shape of Mile One Centre—the city's sports arena—comes into view.

A hard left and we're downtown proper. We pass the inconspicuous entrance to the infamous George Street—the street with the most bars per capita anywhere in the world, owing more to the number of bars than to the size of the street—and turn left onto Water Street.

Even here there seems to be an Irish pub for every two or three buildings. There are big banks, fancy shops, wandering folks, and no two structures look the same. Most here are brick, some steel and glass, all snuggled into a seemingly too-small space and punctuated with benches, memorials, and the occasional graffitied wall.

"That's one of Scott's, isn't it, Shell?" Mint says, pointing at a particularly well-crafted piece spray-painted on a brick wall.

"The shark wearing a Hawaiian shirt? Yeah, that's Scott's," Shelly confirms.

"Wow. He's got some talent," I say.

"One of many," Shelly purrs provocatively.

The ride is almost at an end—that part where the roller coaster coasts into home base and everyone gathers themselves and straightens out their dishevelled hair. There's nothing dishevelled about Mint as she hops up to the front of the bus and holds onto the rail near the driver, her dreads jostling for position along her defined upper back, which is on full display thanks to the stringy vest she's chosen for this sunny day.

"Ten seconds to blast off," she says as we pass Rocket and the bus rolls slowly toward the nearest stop, just a little ways past.

"Oh, I can smell da cinnamon," Shelly yelps, grabbing my hand and yanking me out of the seat.

As we make our way toward the front, we pass the only other passenger left on the bus—a shaggy, grey-haired man with a big, bushy beard who I hadn't noticed before. I do my best to ignore the homeless man, but Shelly looks right at him, encouraging him to speak.

"Lovely day out there," he says. His voice grabs my attention. His words are spoken not with the gravel of a thousand repurposed cigarette butts, nor with a particularly thick accent. I'm struck by how normal he sounds.

"It's a glorious day!" Shelly exclaims, making the man smile a smile I can only detect via his eyes, so disguised by frenetic hair is the rest of his face. He's younger than I thought—the hair more salt-and-pepper than full grey, his smiling eyes lined only with adolescent crow's feet.

"Can you spare some change on this beautiful day?" the man asks. That's where he loses me. I turn away as the bus's air brakes sigh and we jolt to a stop.

"Well, I think I can manage that," Shelly says, releasing her grip on my hand and heading over to the man, digging in her colourful, woollen purse as she goes.

She hands the man some change and taps him on the shoulder.

"You have a nice day, now, me ducky," she says. "And don't be spendin' that toonie on hookers and blow, okay?"

Mint chuckles and shakes her head as Shelly makes her way back toward us.

As the bus doors flop open as though they don't really want to, the man calls after us.

"Thank you," he says. "You are good people. Most folks don't even see me."

Shelly looks back at the man with a smile.

"It'll come back to us in kind," she says.

When we disembark, Shelly thrusts her purse at me.

"Hold this for me, would you, handsome?"

She proceeds to hula her way toward the café. Mint and I give her space and walk ahead, past the tiny patio tables that just about offer room to sit with a coffee in the afternoon sun as lunching workers, tourists, and those just lost to the day happen by.

I look up at the sign—an impressive wooden etching of a '50s-style rocket ship and the word Rocket in big, comic book–style letters. The building is old and the door could be the original—the kind of buckled wood that's seen many St. John's rainstorms and survived to tell the tale. It's a door that seems reluctant to let you in, springing back a bit as though to will you back out into the street, but once you're beyond the cranky old door, the place itself is quite welcoming. A young female barista offers a jaunty "Hello" as she rushes to and from gurgling espresso machines.

The café's layout, much like the city it inhabits, makes little sense, housed as it is in a building never meant for this purpose. It's essentially a big house with two large rooms—the one we're in, with its long counter and glass display cases full of sweet offerings, and the one next door, with its delightfully mismatched tables and chairs. Creaky, hardwood floor runs throughout, and the walls are adorned with more of the '50s rocket ships in the form of drawings on the big chalkboards that line the wall behind the service desk, along with other retro spacey offerings, like an old astronaut's helmet and some classic children's toys. Colourfully patterned triangular flags dangle playfully from the ceiling, and high shelves are lined with large food cans from a bygone age.

Mint and I get in the long lunchtime lineup while Shelly—still hula-ing—carries off an animated conversation with some hipster-looking guys just outside, their whoops and guffaws rising and falling in rhythm to the continual opening and closing of the springy old door. They eventually part ways and Shelly joins us, apologetically skipping the line to where we are.

Shelly orders a three-pack of cinnamon buns, with the stated intention that we'll have one each, even though Mint and I both insist we won't eat ours. Mint grabs an oat-milk latte, and I pull together enough change to buy a small dark roast and a ham 'n Swiss sandwich. It's an extravagance and I know Dana wouldn't approve, but I'm starving and the sandwiches here are so much better than up at Tim Hortons.

* * *

"Comes to Canada, gets his first job at Timmy's." Shelly laughs between bites of her second cinnamon bun. The subject of my employment at Canada's foremost chain coffee shop had come up as I'd been comparing the sandwiches to those at Rocket.

"I'm surprised they hired me, to be honest. The woman asked me if I couldn't find anything in my field."

"What did you say?" Mint asks.

"I said I don't really have a field yet, but I really need a job."

The women laugh.

"Mind, now. You'd get a job anywhere with that accent," Shelly says with that trademark cheeky grin, which is just as flirtatious even with a mouthful of dough and sugar.

We all sit in silence for a moment, looking out across the harbour. We're lined up on the harbour wall, legs dangling off the edge, eating our various Rocket treats. I'm using one of the bollards they tie the boats to as a makeshift table for my coffee. Gulls circle and squawk as the water laps rhythmically below. A ship's horn distantly blows.

I chew on my sandwich and look out across the bay. The water shimmers into the distance, the remains of a large iceberg still visible just beyond the Narrows—the suitably named passage beyond which the frigid North Atlantic Ocean unfurls. Either side are two large hills. To the right, Fort Amherst, and to the left its more famous sister—Signal Hill, where Marconi sent the first transatlantic radio message from the iconic Cabot Tower, which sits atop the hill like a tiny crown.

This is the most easterly point in North America—as close as I can get to home without getting wet, as I like to joke.

We sit like that for a couple of hours, chatting on the sun-soaked harbourfront. My phone vibrates a few times, but I ignore it. I'm present with my fun, *liberal*, new-found friends and have no desire for any distractions that will take me out of the moment. Until one does.

"Shit," I say, grabbing my phone out of my jeans pocket. "I've got a shift tonight."

"Don't panic, m'dear. The trusty Route 10 is always a-runnin'," Shelly reassures me.

She's right. The Route 10 does exactly what it says on the front of the bus. It drives Route 10. The same loop, all day, every day. You just have to be standing in the right place when it happens by.

To that end, we hurry back up to Water Street and to the nearest bus stop. Within five minutes the blue and white Metrobus appears on the horizon, slowly ambling its way toward us.

"There ya go, just like clockwork," Shelly remarks.

"Hmm, it's actually ten minutes late," says Mint, studying the schedule.

"Well, they don't call 'er the Route 10 for nudding," Shelly jokes.

The bus pulls up with a hiss and the doors flop open to reveal the same driver from earlier in the afternoon.

"Hello, again," she says as we flash our passes and clomp on board.

"Hello, maid. Still at it, are ya?" Shelly replies, leading the way.

"Oh, you knows," says the driver. Then Shelly stops dead in her tracks, causing Mint and me to almost pile right into her.

"Good Lord!" she exclaims. "It's like we've entered the *Twilight Zone* in here."

I peep past to see what she's talking about. There's no one else on the bus save for the same bearded homeless man from earlier.

"What're ya just riding 'round in circles today?" she asks the man. He shrugs. It's hard to tell, but I think he might be smiling.

"As long as you're not giving Betty up there any trouble," Shelly says. Of course she knows the driver's name.

"Naw, he's good as gold," Betty chimes in as she begins to navigate the bus through the slalom course that is Water Street approaching traffic hour.

We take the erratic movements as our cue to sit down, on the very back seat of the bus this time, so we can all sit together. Shelly takes the window seat and I sit next, with Mint filing in next to me.

"Aw, look at that," Shelly says, hooking her hula hoop over the seat in front and putting an arm around me. "A rose between two thorns."

"I think you mean a thorn between two roses," Mint corrects.

A sharp turn causes me to all but fall into Mint's lap. Not that I'm complaining. Betty appears to be on a mission to get her Route 10 back on schedule and, as Shelly is wont to say, she's *givin' 'er* along the hilly, twisty St. John's streets.

I don't notice Metrobum—for that's what we christened him during our hangout on the harbourfront—disembark the bus, but when we reach the top of Long's Hill, he's no longer there. We're the last ones on the bus, and Mint hits the bell to tell the driver we'll be getting off at the next stop as we begin to make our way clumsily forward.

Betty's just skilfully swinging the bus into position between parked cars when Mint pauses and raises a hand, signalling us to stop.

"Guys," she says. "Check this out."

She shuffles herself aside so we can get a look at what she's seeing. There, on the floor of the bus, jutting out from between seats, is a very sleek, expensive-looking briefcase.

"Ya don't see that every day," Shelly says. And she's right. You don't see a briefcase on a St. John's Metrobus very often. It's not like London or Toronto, where public transport is used by all kinds of commuters. Here, the buses are largely the domain of students, young workers, and average folks needing to get around without a car.

You don't see a briefcase on a St. John's Metrobus very often. And you sure don't see a sleek, minimalist, matte-black briefcase with aluminum trim sticking out from between empty seats.

"What's that?" I ask.

"It's a briefcase. Don't you have those in England?" Shelly replies.

"Not that. That." I point at the farthest corner of the case—the side that's hidden in the shadows between the seats. There's a little piece of white paper or card sticking out from the case. Mint sees what I'm talking about and squats down to retrieve it.

"Are yous gettin' off or what?" Betty shouts, trying to get a look at us in her rear-view mirror. Instinctively I move up beside Mint to obscure the driver's view.

"Just a minute!" I shout back. "What is it?" I ask Mint.

She stands, holding the piece of cardboard, the back side of which is a shock of red and yellow.

"It's a Roll Up the Rim!" Shelly exclaims excitedly. "What a find! Is she a winner?"

Mint is busy reading what's on the other side of the triangular chunk of Tim Hortons coffee cup. She looks at us uneasily.

"What is it?" I ask, before Shelly's curiosity gets the best of her and she snatches the piece of cardboard away.

"Take me," Shelly says, reading the white side of the chunk. "Now don't get excited, Gregory; that isn't a proposition," she jokes. "That's what it says on this 'ere roll-up." She flips the piece of card around, and there it is, written neatly with a Biro.

Take me.

"Yous are gonna have me late to the depot," Betty shouts.

"Be right there, Bets," Shelly reassures.

We all stand there in silence for a moment, debating what to do. I'm sure we all list the options in our minds. Leave the briefcase where it is for someone to discover back at the depot. Hand it over to Betty and explain that someone must have left it behind. Or . . .

"Take it," Shelly says. Mint and I look to each other, back to her.

Shelly rolls her eyes, grabs the briefcase, and squeezes past us, charging off the bus, hula hoop in tow.

"Thanks, Bets! Have a good evening!" she yodels as she jumps onto the sidewalk, and after a moment's pause, Mint and I are following her off the bus and back toward the old house atop Long's Hill.

Mint and I run after Shell, who shoots off like an Olympic sprinter, if Olympic sprinters competed with a hula hoop in one hand and a mysterious briefcase in the other.

We all feel it. The rush of adrenaline. On some level, maybe we all know that what we're doing is wrong. We've taken something that isn't ours. But on the other hand, someone had wanted us to have it. There could be anything inside—and in a place that could be described as a little sleepy, with a new gang of friends who are nothing if not laid-back, this feels like a welcome change of pace.

We barrel through the door and slam it shut behind us. I can't help but laugh along with Mint and Shelly as we make our way past the rickety staircase and along the narrow hallway, ducking right into the living room.

"Ssshh!" says Mint. "Scott's still probably sleeping."

Scott keeps strange hours, often staying up late smoking weed and working on some mad art project, if he isn't out all night with his graffiti friends, spraying up walls in some dark corner of town. This means he's pretty much nocturnal, and this time—about 4:30 p.m. now—is kind of his early morning.

Shelly places her hula hoop against the couch and then sets the briefcase carefully down on the coffee table. She sits down, looking at it. Mint and I follow suit, squeezing in on either side of her, and we sit there for a moment, just staring at this strange, almost alien object, its clean lines and obvious quality a stark contrast to the makeshift, hand-me-down furnishings of the living room.

"Who's the thorn now?" I joke to break the ice.

"Still you," Shelly says without taking her eyes off our prize.

"Maybe we should get Crisp," Mint says.

"Yeah," Shelly agrees. But neither of them move.

Part of me wants to dismiss the idea, ask why we need Crispin, why we don't just open it ourselves. But another part of me is a little afraid. What if there's something horrible inside? What if, by opening it, we're getting ourselves into something we'll regret? Crispin, for all his oddness, is the eldest of the group. He seems to own the house, as far as I can tell, though I have no idea exactly how he makes a living. In any case, I decide that involving him is probably the best move. He's bound to find out sooner or later.

"I'll go find him," I say.

"He'll be in the yard," Shelly tells me. "It's suppertime."

I'm not quite sure what that means, but I don't question it. I hop up off the couch and head back out to the hallway, passing through the kitchen, where the salt-tinged harbour air moves freely—and often at pace—when all the windows are open. And with all the weed smoked in the house, they usually are.

The back door has the tiniest of porches that is a miniature assault course featuring myriad pairs of muddy boots, several pointed gardening implements, and various other knick-knacks ready to trip you up or jab you in the shin if you aren't careful. I manage to navigate it unscathed and open the creaky door to head outside.

I'm greeted with a gust of St. John's wind that punches me in the face as though it has been waiting for me to come out. The yard slopes gently toward the harbour, gravity beckoning it to join a thousand fallen rocks in relinquishing its grip on the hill. Crispin had reassured me that it had all been reinforced years ago and was "sturdy as a Newfoundland woman," but that did nothing to dispel the feeling that we could all slide down there at any given moment in a cloud of dust and rocks.

When I catch sight of Crispin, I stop in my tracks for a moment. He's standing at the end of the yard with his back to the house, shirtless as ever, with his long arms outstretched. Seagulls are all around him—some on the ground, a couple circling above him, and a few more pitched on his outstretched arms. He looks like a cross between Christ the Redeemer and one of the statues from Trafalgar Square—only these aren't pigeons; they're seagulls.

I approach cautiously. Who lets seagulls perch on their arms? They're the rats of the sky.

They're big, too, and a couple of them have already pooped on Crispin's bare arms.

I try to work my way into his periphery so as not to make him jump and cause some seagull-related kerfuffle that might see him tumble to his death over the wind-damaged picket fence at the end of the yard.

"Crisp?" I say, just loudly enough to be heard over the squawking.

Nothing.

As I work my way around, I see that his eyes are closed. There are remnants of some kind of fish dotted about his person and a few reddened patches of skin where the seagulls have taken a peck. In one spot on his upper arm, they've even drawn blood.

I move around to stand in front of him, ducking and waving an arm at a bird that appears to think I might also be adorned with aquatic foodstuffs.

"Crisp?" I say, more loudly this time.

He blinks open his eyes and looks at me, expressionless, as though emerging from a trance.

"Hello, Gregory," he says with just a hint of disdain, before taking in a long breath through his nose and sighing it noisily out of his mouth.

I'm trying my best not to breathe in through my nose, as the smell of fish in the afternoon sun hangs heavy in the air.

He opens his eyes again and looks around as though he's just arrived, having been beamed down from a spaceship.

I sometimes wonder.

He lowers his arms slowly, allowing the seagulls that were perched there to flap away, a couple of feathers circling their way down to the ground, then pulls out a small towel tucked into the elastic of his baggy cotton pants and begins wiping the fish guts and bird poop off his long, narrow arms.

"Larus canus," Crispin says. "One of the most misunderstood creatures that live among us."

“Seagulls,” I say, unsure of what else to do.

“Gulls.” He smiles at me. “Just gulls. It’s tourists that add the ‘sea’ part. And while these particular birds are displaying a gull’s natural behaviour, scavenging along the seashore, human intervention has seen to it that the coastline is no longer the gull’s sole habitat.”

I shift uncomfortably, waiting for an opportunity to tell him about the briefcase.

“Lakeshores, ponds, and—regrettably—parking lots and trash heaps are also common gull gathering grounds these days. We’ve seen to that,” he says as he begins to wipe off the other arm. I detect a pause and think this may be an opportune time to speak.

“We found a—”

“And then we have the audacity to complain when they circle our children at the ice-cream stand or steal our French fries in the Walmart parking lot.” He sniggers.

I take a peek at my phone. I have a shift tonight and am keen to move this along. I want to know what’s inside that briefcase.

“We despise them for the very qualities that make them so amazing,” he continues. “Their resourcefulness. Their adaptability.” He tucks the towel back into his pants and crosses his arms.

“How can I help you, Gregory?”

“We found a briefcase.”

His eyes widen.

“Okay,” he says, and without another word he’s marching back toward the house.

I dodge the one lingering seagull and scurry after him, almost having to break into a light jog to keep pace with his long strides.

We navigate the back-porch assault course, though this time not unscathed as a trowel takes the skin off my ankle, and we head back through the kitchen to the living room.

By now Scott has joined the party, no doubt roused from his slumber by our hurried entry into the house. He sits wrapped in a quilt fashioned from old sheets and clothing—something everyone's nan here seems to make and gift to their grandkids—sipping on a steaming K-Rock mug of coffee.

Crisps seats himself cross-legged on the musty old carpet, leaning in so the case is eye-level on the coffee table. His hands are clasped, two bony, mud-encrusted forefingers poking into his chin as he gathers details. Where we found it. Why we took it. Who saw us. Were we followed?

"Not unless Betty is an awful lot lighter on her feet than I gave her credit for," Shelly jests.

"What if it's a bomb?" Crispin says, his intense eyes fixed on the briefcase.

"Please play again," Shelly says.

We all look at her. She waves the chunk of Tim Hortons cup at us.

"The Roll Up the Rim. It's not a winner."

* * *

I run up the five little steps to our apartment and pause, breathless, for a moment before opening the door. The car's outside and I know Dana will be waiting, looking for an explanation. The apartment is small, so I know there will be no buffer between me and the inevitable interrogation once I step across the threshold. I gather myself and walk inside.

Sure enough, she's in the kitchen, making herself something to eat. She turns and looks at me, saying it all without saying a word. Her thin, dark hair frames her pale, pretty face, neat bangs tickling her sharp eyebrows. Her nostrils flare a little, thin lips slightly puckered, large, brown, doe eyes filled with questions and tinged with hurt. Without saying a word, she asks for an explanation. A shrug and a quick shake of the head do the talking.

"I'm sorry," I say. Her expression asks for more. "I was with Crisp and the gang."

She rolls her eyes and turns her back to me, continuing to prepare her dinner.

"Why didn't you answer my texts?"

Oh, shit. The texts.

"I, um. Phone died," I lie, though it was on its last legs when I checked the time at Crisp's.

She pauses for a moment, her back still turned to me. Since we moved to Newfoundland, we've been drifting, or, rather, I've been drifting away from her, as though the North Atlantic tides are pulling me back, toward the harbour, toward something new and exciting.

Maybe she's thinking that, trying to find the right words to say. It isn't working. This isn't what I signed up for. It's over.

"Don't you have a shift tonight?" is what comes out instead.

"Yeah," I reply. "I need to get a shower."

She lets out a barely audible huff and carries on clanking dishes. I walk up behind her and chance a hug, but she shrugs me away.

"Just. Go get a shower. You'll be late."

I do as I'm told, reflecting on the events of the day as the water runs over me.

They hadn't opened the case. Not before I'd left, anyway. There had been discussion about bringing it to the Royal Newfoundland Constabulary detachment that was just across the street, behind the CLB Armoury—a grand old brick building with flags waving atop its arched entrance. When I'd finally decided I couldn't stick around any longer if I was going to get a much-needed shower before my shift at the Tim's next to the armoury, I'd headed out. On the short walk back to our apartment, I'd felt as though the old armoury—the building itself—was looking at me in judgment, all neat and formal and home to disciplined types in clean uniforms.

Now all I can think about is that neat, uniform briefcase, all sleek and mysterious, like something from another world.

I jump out of the shower and rub myself dry, peeking out from my towel just long enough to see that Dana isn't there anymore. I dress and walk out to the kitchen to find a hastily made sandwich sitting on the peninsula with a note scribbled in Sharpie on a pad of Post-it Notes.

Gone to see Mom. Quiet if you come home.

I feel bad. Deeply, genuinely bad. I know I'm a shit boyfriend. I begin to wolf down the sandwich, which I'm grateful for even though I know I don't deserve it, and finish putting on my Tim Hortons uniform.

As I'm about to leave, I notice black Sharpie ink bleeding through the back side of the Post-it. I pluck the note off the top of the pad and flip it around to read the words on the other side.

Did you really fall in love with me, or just the idea of me?

4

Nouveau Riche

"You're late," says Brenda when I roll in through the door.

"Sorry," I say, dashing to the back room and trying to avoid her disapproving gaze. Brenda is a hard woman. All of five feet tall with a cigarette-shrivelled face and beady brown eyes, her clump of greying-brown hair adhered to her head with a standard-issue Timmy's hairnet. She scares the shit out of me.

"Don't you live just across the street?" she says as I finish putting on my own hairnet and plonk my fetching visor down over top of it.

"Um, yeah," I say as I check the status of the coffee pots. There's a long pause before she speaks again. When she does, it's with her back to me as she wipes over some tables.

"Third time this month," she says.

"Yeah, I know . . ."

"And this is your first month."

I can't think of an adequate reply to that and don't think she really wants one. Those are her last words to me before I get a sharp, short "Goodbye" as she leaves at the end of her shift a half-hour later. Then it's just me and the two other poor schleps stuck with the nighter at the Tim's that sits at the point where Harvey Road and Long's Hill converge. That makes this particular Tim Horton's the first port of call for the downtown party crowd when time is called at 2:00 a.m. and they pile out of the clubs and bars and head up the hill in search of sandwiches, doughnuts, and coffee. Add to that the fact that this is Friday night and, well, there are better jobs and much better places to be.

I cringe at the thought but remind myself that it's still suppertime and for now my temporary place of work is an air-conditioned haven on a warm summer's evening. It's quite a pleasant place at this time of day, when most people are home eating dinner or enjoying a post-work drink on their back deck. It's quiet at the café, with demand for coffee at its daily low and just the occasional single popping in to grab supper for one.

Of course, there are the regulars—a slightly strange but generally harmless man named Tom who stays for hours nursing a large double-double, occasionally requesting that we reheat it in the microwave; a pair of young students availing of the free wi-fi for the price of an Ice Capp. But otherwise, I'm left to keep on top of the coffee rotation (a fresh pot every twenty minutes, the time daubed on the side with a strange, white, gooey pen that I've never seen the likes of in my life before), wipe crumbs off tables, and chirpily serve anyone who happens through the door.

I'm alone with my thoughts, and they drift away from the mystery briefcase for a while and onto my flagging relationship. Maybe Dana was right. Maybe I did fall more in love with the idea of her than, well, her. The idea of moving to Canada. The idea of adventure. She is four years older than me, and at times it feels like she's decades more mature.

It doesn't take long for my thoughts to return to that briefcase, though. All matte black and mysterious, beckoning to be opened.

At around 8:00 p.m. Crispin barrels through the door, the bell signalling his arrival. He's wearing all his trademarks—a thin, somewhat smug smile and a long, dark brown trench coat that, while in no way suitable for the weather, does look undeniably tailor-made for his long, narrow frame. In unison with the fedora on his head, it makes him look like some noir detective or shady 1920s gangster.

"Hello, Gregory," he says, leaning on the counter. He knows I'm desperate to ask, and his eyes encourage it.

"Did you open it?"

"Open what?"

"Come on. Did you open the briefcase?" I whisper.

"What briefcase?" he repeats, loud enough for the half-dozen people in the place to hear, and for a couple of them to turn and look. He just smiles.

"Small dark roast, black," he says. "I need to put a little spring in my step before we head downtown."

"Downtown?" I repeat, noticing Mint, Shelly, and Scott outside the window. They're all dolled up for downtown. Shelly—sans hula hoop—has done something with her hair and is wearing a floral summer dress. Scott is in one of his less grubby but no less out-of-date pairs of jeans and has on a plain black T-shirt. He appears to have had a wash and is, by his standards, dressed up to the nines. But despite Shelly's go-go girl dance number and Scott's excitable thumbs-up, it's Mint who really catches my attention, dreads down and wearing a delightful emerald-green dress with a split that goes all the way up.

"They look excited," I say, pouring Crisp's coffee into a bright red paper cup. He just smirks as I set it down. He loves to have the upper hand.

"Oh, could you double-cup that please, squire? I don't want to burn my fingers."

I grab another cup from the dispenser and slide the coffee into it.

"A dollar sixty, please," I say, prompting Crispin to stand up tall and reach into his trench coat. When his hand emerges, it's clutching the biggest wad of cash I've ever seen. He places it on the countertop and slides it toward me.

I look down at the stack of fresh, clean bills, their pinkish-red colouring making them almost look like Monopoly money on the beige countertop.

"Keep the change," Crispin hisses, with a wink.

"They're fifties," is all I can say in response.

"Yes, they are."

"You opened it?"

"We opened it."

"Jesus," I say, reflexively grabbing the stack as another customer walks in, and shoving it on a shelf under the counter, between the boxes of stir sticks and packs of napkins. "How much?" I ask as the customer approaches.

"What, there or in the case?"

"Both?" I shrug.

"A hundred bills in a bundle, for a total of five thousand dollars right down there by your crotch. Ten bundles in the briefcase, for a grand total of fifty thousand dollars."

The customer is almost upon us, and Crispin has already taken up his double-cupped dark roast and is turning to leave. I feel panic sweep through my body. I don't want to be in possession of five grand in fresh fifties, but I can't very well pull them out from under the counter and toss them at Crisp like the world's most expensive football.

"Since you're nouveau riche and no longer need this shit job, I trust we'll be seeing you downtown?" Crispin shouts back over his shoulder, again loud enough for everyone to hear. I smile awkwardly at the confused-looking customer and try to poke the bundle of bills farther back on the shelf as Amanda—my teenaged boss for the evening—sidles by behind me with a pack of coffee filters.

Crispin wiggles his fingers in a wave as he backs out of the door, the gang's whoops and hollers momentarily audible as they dance beyond the window.

"What can I get you?" I say to the customer, trying my best to hide my smile.

* * *

The next few hours go by at a glacial pace. It's a slow night for a Friday—a result, no doubt, of the clement weather drawing folks downtown to music-filled streets and packed patios.

That's where they are—Crisp, Shelly, Scott, and Mint. Mint, in that gorgeous green dress with the split.

I try to keep myself occupied, but it's no good. George Street is calling and my phone is vibrating with texts from the gang.

Where r u???

Let's partaaay!!!

Don't be a slave to the Tim Hortons industrial complex.

Tell em yer sick!

I can't walk out on my job, I tell myself—5k will only go so far. If I walk out, Dana will kill me.

I sweep floors and serve the scattered customer, checking the wad of cash now and again, which I managed to transfer from the shelf under the counter to a safer spot behind some cups in the storeroom. I try to stay here, try to ignore the vibrations in my pocket, the images in my mind of Mint, dressed in green, flickering in strobe lights. But the pull of those tides is too strong.

"Sick?" Amanda repeats back at me, expressionless as always, chubby cheeks wobbling with every chew of her ever-present ball of bright pink gum.

"Yeah, I don't know what it is. My stomach is just killing me." I see that my act, which I thought dramatic enough to be convincing, yet nuanced enough to be believable, isn't fooling her at all. "And my head," I add, instantly regretting it.

"Well, which is it? Your stomach or your head?" She doesn't blink. She hasn't yet hit her twenties, but her face wears the bullshit-proof look of someone who's lived twice her years.

"Look," I say, "I just don't feel well, okay?" I'm fuelled by the false reassurance of having stuffed the 5k into my Tim's slacks pocket on my last visit to the storeroom.

"Go on wit' ya, then." She shrugs. "It's not like you do anything around here, anyway."

I have neither the time nor the inclination to defend myself. I just thank her, grab my keys from the staffroom, and I'm off into the St. John's night.

* * *

Thankfully Dana isn't home when I go back to change, the apartment still dark, the note still on the countertop. It's after ten and late for her to still be at her mother's, but her whereabouts are hardly my chief concern as I throw on my best party pants and favourite black shirt and try to coax my hairnet-flattened barnet into something resembling a hairstyle.

I chug an India Pale Ale and run down Long's Hill, almost losing my balance on more than one occasion and having to check my stride against the pull of the hill's gravity. It's so easy to get downtown. You don't so much walk or run there as spread your arms wide and fall into its noisy embrace.

I hop onto Duckworth Street and duck down the steep-stepped alley that's home to the Duke—an Irish pub run by a real honest-to-Jesus Irishman named Jerry, who is a massive football fan and has the scarves of a thousand clubs hanging behind the bar. The Duke is one of the gang's regular haunts, but tonight they are pushing the boat out and hanging at the Grapevine—a hip wine bar on Water Street that, on a night like this, will have its front shutters open to the mild night air, the smokers outside illuminated in the red glow of is moody lights.

When I arrive, the gang are already getting ready to leave, Shelly demanding that we find a place to dance. Scott buys me a beer, and I knock it back before following them on to a nightclub. I am swept up in their current, my life before fast becoming some distant shore, "home" a word with no meaning. I am adrift and happy to be that way.

Over at the Sundance, I stand at the bar, being jostled by the crowd, staring at the crisp, impossibly perfect fifty-dollar bill in my hand. It's the first time I've ever held a fifty. Well, technically the second, I suppose. The first time was a couple of hours ago, when I held a hundred of them all at once, but only five of them had made it with me downtown, the rest of them safely tucked between some of my old English football shirts in a corner of the closet I know Dana will never touch.

"Are you just gonna stare at that, or are you gonna use it to buy me a drink?" I hear a voice say from over my shoulder. I turn to see a young woman—the kind youthful enough to require an ID in most bars, but attractive enough not to. She's a little thing with long, dark hair that frames a pale, cute face. She's clutching a pineapple cooler.

"Looks like you already have one," I say. Without skipping a beat or taking her eyes off mine, she raises the cooler to her full lips and chugs what's left of it—which is about half a bottle—down in one.

"Not anymore," she says, trying to keep up the facade of sober coolness while her glazed eyes betray her.

"Same again?" I ask.

Soon we're back on the dance floor, the gang complete again with its newest additions—me, the Brit from three doors down who's gradually becoming part of the furniture, and Mia, the nineteen-year-old mystery girl with an ID to prove it.

The night moves on one song at a time, the beat hammering, the conversations yelled. We dance in stop-motion in the flickering lights, smiles beaming, cares far from this sweltering cocoon of life. The club is packed, the people moving as one great, pulsating mass, the energy and the alcohol flowing through our veins.

We dance for hours, pausing only to squeeze our way to the bar or to relieve ourselves in the cool refuge of the bathroom, with its powerful smell of pee and urinal cakes and the echoey, surreal sounds of drunken youths shouting through a veil of tinnitus and booze. We all dance, together and alone. At times, Mint is in my orbit, turning and shaking dat ass in my direction, occasionally making contact but never sticking around long enough for it to become *us* dancing. I don't know if it's because she knows I have a girlfriend or if she isn't really interested. Neither would surprise me.

Mia dances like a young girl does—aware of her allure and yet a little unsure, slightly rigid, in need of reassurance that yes, she is pretty, yes, she is someone in this world.

You couldn't call the nightclub Shelly's natural habitat, her hippie-like garb and artsy demeanour more suited to a bar like the Fish, where music by bands you probably haven't heard of sends hipsters into jerky, hoppy movements—that is, if they simply aren't too cool to possibly consider dancing. She brings some of those dance stylings to the floor of the Sundance but mixes it up with hula hoop–like gyrations and occasional spurts of closed-eye solos, movements more subtle, hands raised in front of her in an almost protective position. Moments that make you think there is something deeper going on beneath the carefree, fun-filled exterior.

Scott dances like a typical guy who can't dance and wouldn't if he wasn't quite drunk and if doing so didn't give him a chance to sidle up to pretty, sweaty girls wearing very little clothing. He doesn't do it in a creepy way. Scott's harmless enough and most girls can sense it. Mia, Mint, and Shelly all give him fifteen seconds of fame grinding with them, before politely easing themselves away, as do a few other randoms that don't want their girls' night interrupted by some average-looking guy. Scott is a nice guy, and that comes across in his almost apologetic movements. The women can sense he isn't a threat.

Even Crispin, not given to what he calls "dance bars," is throwing shapes, his long limbs lending him the look of some spiny seabird, hopping from leg to leg, spreading its wings to soar. He occasionally winks and points at me with a long finger, still clutching the bottle of India Pale Ale he seems to have been nursing now for several songs.

This is our night and the cash and the drinks are flowing. I've never known a night like it, never felt the pure freedom of having two hundred bones in my pocket and plenty more where that came from sitting at home. I can buy everyone a round—all of us can—each visit to the bar resulting in messy returns to the dance floor as the latest hero carries too many bottles, between strained digits, to the cheers of the bopping crowd.

I could get used to this.

5

Dare Ya

"Churchill Square, probably," Mia says nonchalantly as she enters the kitchen wearing a long, white T-shirt that clearly isn't hers. "Coffee. Thank frig," she adds, shuffling over to the coffee pot and opening a couple of cupboard doors until she finds the one with the mismatched mugs.

She settles on the biggest one she can find—a beige number with faded flowers etched in the side that seems to have somehow survived since the '70s—and pours herself a steaming cup. Without looking at anyone, she blows on it and takes a sip before letting out a long "Aaahh."

The rest of us just watch her in silence and glance at each other. I don't know about anyone else, but I'm experiencing the dissonance of a raging hangover, trying to piece together whose T-shirt Mia is wearing, where she slept last night, and if she just figured out what the clue in the briefcase means.

"Sleep okay, me darlin'?" Shelly says, breaking the quiet.

Mia turns, back leaning against the kitchen counter. The massive mug makes her look like a little girl as she clutches it with both hands.

"Some," she says between sips.

My clogged brain is beginning to put it together. That's one of Crisp's T-shirts. I've seen him wearing it. The little Molson logo that usually sits high on his chest is now hanging sideways from one of Mia's perky breasts. Shelly sounds—not pissed, more . . . disappointed? Mint searches for somewhere to look, while Scott appears somewhat oblivious, now beginning to reassemble what I am thinking is a drill.

Crisp hasn't taken his eyes off the note.

"Churchill Square," he says.

"Ooo, there's a Rocket Bakery there," Shelly says, getting up and stretching her arms long in the air, doing a few twirls on her way to the coffee pot. Whatever it was she was feeling when Mia made her entrance, she seems to have shaken it off.

"And a statue of Winston Churchill," Mint says. She's sitting cross-legged on the tattered easy chair that sits in the corner of the kitchen, fiddling with the beads in her hair.

"Well, it's more of a bust," Scott adds, turning the drill-like thing over in his hand and fiddling with what appears to be a power cord for the device.

"Of course!" Crispin shouts. "The bust at Churchill Square!" He jumps up, note in hand, and begins pacing the room in long strides. Crispin strikes an intimidating figure when he's up and moving quickly.

"I don't remember seeing a bust at Churchill Square," I say. I don't. Though I've only been there a couple of times—once on a Rocket Bakery excursion with Shelly and another time to eat at the Mexican restaurant there with Dana.

"It's not in the square. It's across the street," says Scott, who now appears to have put the power in his power tool and gives it a couple of revs.

"Across Elizabeth Avenue, looking on as though in judgment," Crisp says, still pacing and now waving the note in the air like it's the Charter of Rights and Freedoms.

"What's he judging? The quality of the Rocket's cinnamon buns? 'Cause they are bloody brilliant!" says Shelly, the last part delivered in her excruciating attempt at an English accent.

Sorry, she mouths at me with a wink.

"So, what? This guy wants us to deface the bust of Winston Churchill?" I ask.

Crisp stops dead in his tracks and points a long finger in my direction.

"Exactly!" he says.

"What the frig are you guys mixed up in at all?" Mia yawns before taking another long sip from her giant mug.

"The bulldog frowns. His likeness doesn't suit. Take his nose, turn it up, paint him a smile," Crispin reads from the note as though reciting Shakespeare.

"We have to cut his nose off and paint a smile on him to get more cash?" Mint asks.

"Not just cut the nose off," Crisp replies, marching over to where Mint is sitting and squatting to show her the note. "Turn it up. See here? We'll have to stick it back on, upside down."

Crisp looks up at his audience. Everyone is staring at him, as wide as their hungover eyes will go. Is he really suggesting we should do this?

"A bit of Gorilla Glue would get that done," Scott says, breaking the silence. We've bypassed *should we?* and moved right along to logistics.

"And you got lots of spray paint to paint him a nice smile, don'tcha, Scotty?" Shelly says, now leaning on the door frame, hand on hip, engaged in the unfurling plans.

"What about cutting the nose off?" I ask. "What's that bust made out of?" If you can't beat 'em . . .

Scott's one hop ahead of me, already thumbing his way through a Google search on his phone. He smiles.

"Brass," he says.

"Can you cut that?" Mia asks. She has now joined Mint and Crisp in the corner, looking back and forth between the note and the coffee table with its open briefcase and spilled cash. She's put the pieces together, and a thought enters my mind. Great. We're splitting the spoils six ways now, I guess.

Scott picks up his power tool and slots in the final piece—a sharp-toothed, five-inch blade. He presses the trigger and the reciprocating saw growls to life.

"Yup," he says. "Cuts easy."

* * *

"Wake up. Hey, Gregory—time to wake up."

I open one eye to see Mint's face above me. I flinch as one of her dreadlocks brushes my cheek.

"Sorry!" She laughs.

My mind catches up with what's happening. After the excitement of figuring out the note, my hangover had stepped things up a notch and I'd excused myself to the living room to have a lie-down. I must have fallen asleep.

I'm suddenly hyperconscious of how bad my breath must be, how shit my hair must look. I slide myself into a sitting position, trying to keep as much distance between myself and Mint as I can.

"I must have dozed off," I say.

"Hmm. For . . ." She squints as she calculates. ". . . about four hours."

"Shit." My mind starts playing through the repercussions. I

didn't go home last night. I didn't go home this morning. Dana's going to kill me. Do I have to work today? No.

"Come on," Mint says. "Crisp wants to talk to you."

She stands and leaves the room, looking back at me over her shoulder with a smile.

I sit. I still feel decidedly groggy, but my headache is easing and the nausea is giving way to a raging desire to eat greasy food. I rise gingerly to my feet and see myself in the large mirror that hangs above the long-defunct fireplace.

"Jesus," I say as I rub my three-day stubble and try to ruffle my flattened hair into some sort of life. I turn and head to the kitchen, checking my breath in my hand as I go. I really need to brush my teeth.

When I arrive in the kitchen, it's more akin to a war room. The circular table with the wonky leg has been cleared of the usual ashtrays, empties, and unopened mail and is now covered with an old paper map. The map is so big that its battered edges curl off the side of the table. Salt and pepper shakers, shot glasses, and a couple of Warhammer miniatures from Scott's collection are positioned at various spots on top of it.

Crisp cranes over the map, palms pressed flat against it. He's wearing a pair of glasses I've never seen him wear before, with a safety string wrapped around his long neck.

The others stand around him, looking remarkably together.

"Jesus," I say again.

"Gregory! The final foot soldier to join the fray."

"Well, I'm certainly in Over My Head," I joke. Only Mia gets the reference to the song by The Fray, letting out a small snigger. I guess she's part of the gang now?

"We're going to do it," Mint says.

All eyes are on me.

"So, the only question is: Are you with us, Gregory?"

I look at the ragtag band of drifters before me. A collection of lost souls that the tides have washed together on craggy shores, and that fate has brought a mysterious briefcase full of cash. I don't even need to think about it, or about Tim's, or about Dana, or about home—wherever that is.

"Can I get a shower first?" I ask.

* * *

When I arrive three doors down, Dana's car isn't in the driveway, but everything I own in the world is. That amounts to a battered old suitcase and the backpack she'd bought me when we first decided to set off on our Canadian adventure—complete with Great Britain and Canada patches she'd hand-sewn on for me—which, on closer inspection, are both stuffed with my clothes. There are also a few plastic boxes with various bits and pieces: old books, notepads, and knick-knacks I'd picked up along the way; and an old laptop bag containing my PlayStation 3 and its various peripherals and power cords.

I can't say that I blame her. I've been a crap boyfriend, and this has totally been coming.

I stand for a moment just staring at the small pile that sums up six years lived like a nomad, never staying in one place for very long, never amassing too much—partly because I couldn't afford it, but mainly because I didn't want to feel weighed down. I look at the small pile and I feel exhilarated, freed. Ever since I left my mum's place at eighteen to go to uni, I've been this way. Ever since I got a taste of the world beyond Shawforth, I've wanted to roam, I've thirsted for adventure. And boy, have I found it.

I dig a change of clothing out of the suitcase and leave the rest of the stuff in the driveway. Even though I know she won't have had time to change the locks, and likely wouldn't do that anyway, I'm still relieved when my key unlocks the door. I shower, dress, and have what I expect will be my last look around our little apartment at the top of Long's Hill, with its slightly tree-obscured harbour view and too-small living room. The empty closet in the spare room makes me sad for a moment. This place has moved on from me, and it's time for me to move on from this place.

I search around for a note, but there isn't one. Just the same, pale yellow pad of Post-it Notes sitting on the kitchen counter, her previous note ripped off and discarded with only a few speckles of bled-through Sharpie ink to show that her words were ever there. The Sharpie itself is still sitting on the counter. I take it and write a note of my own.

If it's any consolation, I really did love the idea of you.

I know it won't be any consolation at all.

Scott helps me bring my stuff into Crisp's place. I pull my new landlord aside and ask him if it's okay for me to stay awhile.

"Yes!" he says, grabbing me by the shoulders. "We're going to need you, Gregory," he says slowly. Crisp has a way of being warm and welcoming while at the same time asserting his dominance at every turn. It strikes me that I don't really know him and I don't like being beholden, but right now I have no other choice. I resolve to figure out my living situation in the next couple of weeks. For now, Crisp's den of iniquity will do fine.

I ask him about sleeping arrangements.

"Whatever bed you fall into," he says with a wink.

Shelly tells me to put my stuff in her room for now because it's the biggest. When I make my way up the creaky stairs, I discover four bedrooms and another small staircase leading to a closed attic.

"What's up there?" I ask Mint, who has grabbed a box to help out.

"Not sure." She smiles.

With my worldly belongings deposited into their latest

temporary home, we all gather in front of 69 Long's Hill. It's a typical St. John's summer's day—cool verging on mild with a brisk ocean wind. It's around noon and the morning mist has dissipated, the sun offering a little warmth when it can find its way past the fast-travelling clouds. I take a long breath of salt-tinged air. I've never felt so free.

"Okay," Crisp says, "who's hungry?" We all confirm that we are, with varying degrees of enthusiasm, as Scott holds open the door of the previously owned Toyota Corolla that seems to serve as the house's utility vehicle. It's deep blue, and as unspectacular as a vehicle can be, but seems to be in pretty good nick, save for a few rust spots beginning to emerge around the wheel wells.

Scott had told me that Newfoundland has some of the hardest conditions on car bodywork anywhere in the world, the fast-moving salty air causing rust to form and spread. "In fact," he'd said, while passing me a joint, "car manufacturers will send their vehicles here to test their hardiness." I don't know if it's true, but it seems to make sense.

"Everyone into the Roller," Crisp says, and we all pile in. "Mia, you have the wheel," he adds. While the rest of us are reeling in surprise at this suggestion, the newest addition to our gang grabs the keys dangling from Scott's hand, jumps in the driver's seat, and fires up the engine.

"Shotgun!" Shelly shouts, taking her place in the front passenger seat and expertly arranging her hula hoop so she can secure her seat belt.

"Looks like we're in the back." Mint shrugs. She takes my hand and yanks me into the back seat with her. Crisp pours himself in beside her, having to sit slightly arched with his long legs jammed against the front seats. Scott squeezes in last. Thankfully, there's not much of him.

"To the Square!" Crisp yells, and with that, Mia steps hard on the gas, pinning all of us back in our seats. The Roller's tires scream with surprise as she pulls a stomach-churning U-turn and bombs through the lights at the top of Long's Hill just as they are turning from yellow to red.

"Jesus," I say yet again, as Shelly lets out a loud, "Woo hoo!"

"Sorry, b'ys. If you gets stuck at that light, you're there all friggin' day," Mia says.

Mint's eyes are wide, Crisp just smiles, while Scott looks petrified, white-knuckling the "Oh-my-Jesus" handle.

The Roller blasts onto Harvey Road, and Mia hooks an aggressive right onto Parade Street, flying past the tall, red-bricked fire station and up the narrow road at speeds that could put us into orbit.

"Are we in a hurry, Mister Crisp?" Shelly asks from the front seat.

"Oh, yes, Miss Shelly," Crisp replies. "We don't want to be late for lunch."

With that, Shelly reaches beneath her seat and emerges with a blue police light, which she proceeds to reach out of the window and place on the roof. I see Mia's eyes light up in the rear-view mirror, and just as the Roller begins to emit a loud police siren, she drops a gear and blasts through a stop sign, racing up Parade Street, flooring it through the intersection at Merrymeeting and givin' 'er up Newtown.

Crisp nudges me in the side with a bony elbow. "We needed our wheelwoman, and she appeared." He grins.

"Do you think maybe you should slow down a bit?" I squeal.

"Relax," Crisp says. "There'll be plenty of time for slowing down when you're like them." He motions out of Scott's window at the Roman Catholic cemetery we are now flying past, the elaborate tombstones little more than a blur. "Besides, she's a trained high-speed driver," he says more loudly. "Aren't you, Mia?"

"I was training to be an RNC officer," she yells back as I watch her in the mirror. She never takes her intense eyes off the road. “It didn’t take, but I stuck around just long enough for the driving part.”

With that, she handbrake-turns the car hard right onto Mayor Avenue, where our progress is momentarily hampered by traffic bunched up at a red light. The flashing blue light makes the cars part like the red sea, making way for the police car they assume is coming. The confused looks on people’s faces as they watch a 2004 Toyota Corolla full of young people drive by is pure gold.

Mia keeps her focus on the road, skilfully weaving through the slalom course of cars. Shelly waves and blows kisses. Scott covers his face with a palm and keeps his head down, while Mint, Crisp, and I can’t help but laugh.

Soon we’re through the throng and making haste once again, Mayor becoming Bonaventure in a blur. As we approach the intersection to turn right onto Elizabeth Avenue, Mint spots a cop car stopped at the lights.

“Uh, guys?” she says.

Mia kills the siren and Shelly retrieves the blue light. As we roll up to the traffic lights, it becomes apparent that they aren’t going to turn green in time. Scott continues to facepalm. Mint claws nervously at my thigh. Crisp just wears that trademark smirk, narrow eyes surveying the scene, head twitching, gull-like.

“Just stay cool,” he says.

The Roller comes to a stop right next to the cop car, and we all stare straight ahead. I chance a glance across at the two officers in the front seat of the cruiser. The one in the passenger seat looks right at me.

Shit.

I return my eyes front and grab Mint’s hand tight.

“Wait for it. Wait for it,” Crisp says, still smirking.

We wait for what seems like an eternity until finally the light changes and the Roller moves forth once again. We all breathe and we're all smiles. We got away with one, and that's becoming a habit. An addictive, adrenaline-fuelled habit that longs to be fed.

Mia drives us toward Churchill Square, and as we wait at the light to turn right into the parking lot, we get a good look at our target. Sir Winston Churchill. Or, his head and shoulders at least. Cast in bronze, looking out across the street from atop a black marble plinth beyond a short gravel path flanked with red and white flowers and a couple of tufty shrubs.

"There he is," Crisp hisses.

"How tall do you think that is?" Scott asks with genuine concern.

Lunch is a greasy feed at the Fort Amherst Pub that's conveniently located in the square. Over towering burgers and piles of fries, Crisp dishes out his orders to the team between—and sometimes during—bites, sending little missiles of chewed food arcing across the table.

"Scott, Mia, and I will say here at the square, gathering intel. We'll determine where any security cameras might be located that could see us, the best place for Mia to wait in the getaway car, and the specifics of Scott's facelift for the old Bulldog.

"Shelly, you take the Roller and go pick up some supplies. You should be able to get all of this from Canadian Tire and Mark's Work Warehouse."

Crisp hands Shelly a pre-prepared list of items, scribbled on a battered piece of notepaper in his elaborate, flowing handwriting, which she begins reading from.

"Black turtleneck sweater, black cargo pants, black boots, black balaclavas. Not really my style, Crispy, but I loves a bit of shopping."

"We're gonna look like a cross between a ninja and Steve Jobs," Scott mutters through a mouthful of burger.

Bellies full, we ask for the bill and enjoy the thrill of leaving the waitress a hundred-dollar tip. Back outside, Churchill Square takes on a new guise in the early-afternoon sunlight. It's no longer a mundane parking lot surrounded by a strip mall housing the kind of stores that make you wonder how they ever stay open. Now it's a playground, a puzzle to be solved. A level in a video game.

We stand there, the six of us, at the top of the square, looking across the parking lot, Sir Winston Churchill staring back at us from across the street as if to say, *Go on, I dare you.*

"One last thing," says Crispin. "We're going to need a name."

"How about the Gulls," I say without missing a beat, feeling proud of myself.

"Da Gulls?" Mia says. "Why don't we just call ourselves Da Rats of Da Sky?"

There's a moment of silence as we all wait for Crisp to correct our newest addition. Instead, he chooses to ignore the slight against his beloved seabirds.

"The Gulls it is," he says.

* * *

The ride to the store is much calmer with Shelly at the wheel. She by no means drives like a little old lady, but she doesn't handle the Roller like it's a day out at Daytona.

The shopping itself is a blast. Shelly and Mint model black slacks, turtlenecks, and balaclavas in the middle of Mark's like some militaristic Milan Fashion Week, and we draw a few stares when we take our haul to the checkout.

"We're planning a heist," Shelly says, teasing the teenaged cashier. He just hides behind his long, blond bangs and smiles awkwardly. "That'll be $3,247.55, please."

Shelly proceeds to count out the total in cash, laying down

fifties on the countertop to the wide-eyed amazement of the youth, who looks around for a supervisor.

"Three thousand, two hundred and fifty. Oh, and here's one for you, me ducky," Shelly says, laying a crisp, red fifty to the side of the piles. As the teen tries to figure out what to do with all the cash, Shelly leans in. "To be honest, we already did the heist," she whispers.

Over at Canadian Tire, Mint engages in a long conversation with a lady who is very knowledgeable about reciprocal saws.

"So, it'll definitely cut brass?" she says, holding the thing like one of Charlie's Angels.

"Like a hot knife through butter," says the lady.

"We'll take it," Shelly enthuses, snatching the saw from Mint's hand and throwing it into the cart along with the clanking cans of spray paint.

* * *

When we arrive back at the Square, the Roller's trunk full of our spoils, the other three Gulls are gathered at the foot of the Churchill bust. We park and cross the street to join them.

Crisp stands at the centre of the group, flanked by his lieutenants—Scott to his right, Mia to his left. We file in on either side.

"Did you get the supplies?" Crisp asks without taking his eyes off the Bulldog.

"Yes, sir!" Shelly barks in an awful English accent, giving a sarcastic salute.

"Are we ready to do this?" he asks.

"Yes, yeah, oh sure . . ." we each mutter.

"I said: Are we ready to do this?" Crisp yells.

"Yes!" we all shout in unison.

"Okay, my special seabirds." We all follow Crisp's lead and join hands.

"Gulls on three!" Mia shouts, surprising us all.

"One, two, three . . ."

"GULLS!"

6

Dare 1
Defacing the Bulldog
($100k)

The afternoon is spent planning the mission. Crisp lays it out like a general in his war room, shifting the pieces around another paper map that he's dug up from somewhere—this one detailing Churchill Square and the surrounding area. Scott charges his new reciprocal saw and preps a couple of paint canisters in a duffle bag. Mia is a focused student, listening intently, hanging on Crisp's every word. Mint and Shelly have fun trying on their costumes.

"They're not costumes—they're uniforms," Crisp barks. "It's not friggin' Halloween."

But in some ways it kind of feels like it. We're all about to dress up like Ninja Steve Jobs and head out into the night in search of a very, very tasty bag of treats. But not before we pull a little trick of our own.

We eat supper together in the kitchen, standing around the island. The rickety circular table isn't an option, still covered, as it is, by maps, salt and pepper shakers, and Warhammer miniatures that are supposed to represent us—the gang. The Gulls.

At 8:00 p.m. Crisp calls us all in and goes over the plans one last time. Then he insists we all take a nap. He wants us fresh, and at this point I'm in need of the rest, though the anticipation makes sleep all but impossible. Instead, I end up in Mint's room.

Aside from the bed, her only furniture is a small flatpack desk and accompanying plastic chair, and a couple of bright green beanbags that we fall into. We chat for a while until she decides to lie down for a bit.

"Come lie with me," she says, and I try not to look overeager, even though it feels like I just won the lottery. As I place myself gingerly beside her, she turns back-on to me and snuggles in. I put an arm around her. She sleeps for a while, but I stay awake, breathing in her hair, which has a sweet, peppermint aroma. She certainly lives the brand.

Call time is 2:00 a.m., and Crisp goes around knocking on all the bedroom doors. He starts down the hall, hammering on each door like a drill sergeant gleefully rousing his troops. I hear Shelly complaining, and a sudden wave of concern washes over me. I ease myself off the bed and back my way over to the other side of the room, collapsing into one of the beanbag chairs. I couldn't say why, but my instincts are telling me it would be best not to have Crisp discover Mint and me in bed together, as innocent as the situation might be. I breathe a sigh of relief as he hammers on the door, then passes along without opening it.

In the kitchen there's coffee and a few Tim Hortons muffins. The muffins go untouched, adrenaline suppressing appetite, but at Crisp's insistence most of us do drink some coffee to get the bleariness out of our eyes. We go over the plan one last time, then get into our huddle, hands in for the chant.

"One, two, three, Gulls!"

We do it like we're seasoned vets, like we've been doing this for years, but in reality none of us have so far done anything braver than carry an unguarded briefcase off a Metrobus and party hard with the money inside. This thought hits me as we load into the Roller, the night air cool, the black turtleneck foreign and itchy against my skin. It haunts me as Mia swings the car around to take the route we'd practised earlier in the day, only to get caught at the light at the top of Long's Hill.

"Friggin' light," she mutters, cranking on the handbrake as I only now realize that the Roller has a manual transmission. She flicks the gearshift into neutral, and there we sit, pointing upwards like six monkeys waiting to be shot into space. As the Roller's engine echoes off the colourful row houses and the stately brick armoury across the street, all is quiet in St. John's, its residents sleeping, its windows dark, save for the eternal flame that is Tim Hortons, aglow in the rear-view mirror, serving dead-of-night coffee to those who cannot sleep or just refuse to.

All is quiet within the Roller, too, each of us running through our heads our own little part in this mission of destruction, the full extent of what we are about to do beginning to sink in to our caffeine-addled brains, the implications of what we might be getting ourselves into hitting home. It's terrifying. It's exciting.

"Five . . ." Crisp begins to count down. He's been caught at the light at the top of Long's Hill so often, he has its timing down to a T.

"Four . . ." Mint takes my hand in hers. We exchange reassuring glances and I squeeze her hand tight.

"Three . . ." Scott looks dead ahead, giving a determined nod as he cradles the duffle bag like a precious newborn.

"Two . . ." Shelly's eyes are wide, her lips curved into a nervous smile. She's left her hula hoop behind for this one.

"One . . ." I see the sparkle in Mia's eyes in the rear-view mirror as she eases the gearshift into first and balances the gas and the clutch, a hand poised over the handbrake.

"Blast off!" Crisp says as the light turns green and Mia expertly thrusts the Roller forward in a perfect hill start, pinning us back in our seats as its engine roars in the face of gravity and propels us onward, upward.

Crisp lets out a loud "Woo hoo!" but the rest of us are silent, focused on the task at hand.

* * *

We approach from the back of the square via Rowan Street, Mia guiding the Roller cautiously into the parking lot, which is as empty as we'd all been hoping. She stops by the Churchill Square Mall and tugs on the handbrake, which kills the lights without her needing to stop the engine—something I never knew until now. You learn something every day.

"Time to fly, little birds," Crisp says as we begin to put our plan into action.

Scott hands Mint and Shelly a spray can each and pops the trunk. They both pull on their balaclavas and circle around the back of the Roller, grabbing a small stepladder each. Then they make their way either side of the square, stepping up on the ladders to reach the first two of four security cameras that Crisp and Scott identified as potentially being able to see us. Almost in unison, the two women shake their spray cans and spray green paint onto the camera lenses, the rattling of the ball bearings and the sound of the spray surprisingly loud in the dead of night.

"Wait for it. Wait for it," Crisp whispers, quite unnecessarily, as we have all been very well briefed and know that Mint and Shelly still have two cameras to go before we can advance. Mint pulls out a small lead on Shelly, making her way fleet-footedly along the left-hand side of the square while Shelly takes longer, more cumbersome strides along the right flank. Mint sprays her second camera, hops off the stepladder, and raises both arms wing-like in the air—the pre-agreed signal for "job done." Shelly is just about at the top of her ladder, reaching to spray her second camera. But the can slips from her hand and bounces off the pavement below.

"Son of a . . ." she shouts, probably not as loud as it sounds in the echo chamber of the square. Shaking her head, she clambers down off the ladder to retrieve the can. Just as she bends down, we see car headlights approaching slowly on Elizabeth Avenue.

"Shit," I say as Shelly picks up the canister, her back turned to the road. Mint has already seen the danger and tucked herself away in the shadows of the buildings, but Shelly has her back to the road and is moving at a leisurely Shelly-like pace.

"See it. See it," Crisp hisses through clenched teeth, but as she makes her way back up her stepladder, she's blissfully unaware of what's happening behind her.

The car is getting closer, illuminating the thin line of trees that separates the road from the soccer fields of Elizabeth Park—a line of trees that only parts to reveal Sir Winston's bust in between. Any moment, the car will pass Quintanas Mexican restaurant and Churchill Square will be unveiled for its occupants to see.

"Come on," Crisp implores, his eyes darting left and right, seeking a course of action.

Shelly is up the ladder, mid-spray. The car is almost in view. Suddenly, Mia takes a deep breath and flashes the Roller's lights twice in quick succession. The signal catches Shelly's attention just as she finishes spraying. She looks over toward us. She looks across to search for Mint. That's when she sees the approaching car.

At a very un-Shelly-like pace, she jumps off the ladder, scoops it up, and runs for cover beneath the awnings of Big Bite Pizza. The headlights seem to catch her for a moment just before she ducks into shadow, and we all hold our breath as the car comes into view.

"Lord Jesus," Scott says in his drawn-out drawl.

It's an RNC patrol car.

The Roller's engine ticks over, and Crisp catches Mia's hand as she reaches for the keys.

"It's okay," he says, and he's probably right. Even if they lowered their windows, the cops likely wouldn't hear the idling car all the way at the back of the square from the road. The bigger concern is whether they caught sight of the bumbling Shelly.

The patrol car is moving slowly, and we can feel the eyes of its occupants scanning the square. For a moment its headlights illuminate the Churchill bust, casting shadows across the Bulldog's furrowed features, light blinking off the shiny black plinth. Our goal—so near and yet so far away.

We all stay perfectly still as the patrol car reaches the intersection, where it will either carry on along Elizabeth and into the night, or turn right into the square, its headlights illuminating the Roller in all her rusted, navy-blue glory, along with the four of us, no longer gulls but rabbits with a lot of explaining to do.

The patrol car rolls slowly through the intersection, and when the cops' scan of the square is complete, it gathers pace and disappears out of view.

We all let out a collective sigh and watch as first Mint reappears, followed by Shelly, their arms held wide, Shelly giving a curtsy to punctuate the little victory.

"Okay, Gulls. On with the show," Crisp says. Without missing a beat, Mia throws the Roller into gear, and we make our way across the square.

On seeing the car move, our two spray-can scouts are already off across Elizabeth Avenue, taking their positions just within the treeline either side of the statue. Mia pulls in next to Quintanas, tucking the Roller into shadow, and Crisp gives Scott and me a brief pep talk, hands on our shoulders, giving each of us a sharp slap of encouragement. Scott nods and pulls on his balaclava, hoisting the duffle bag—which looks way too big for him to carry—onto his shoulder, and I follow him across the street.

As we go, I hear the Roller whine its way backwards out of the parking spot. I look over my shoulder to watch Mia and Crisp disappear, as per the plan, back onto Rowan Street. They will circle back around to Elizabeth and lie in wait by Cowan's Optical until they get the signal that Winston's facelift is complete.

Scott and I arrive at the base of the statue, and I collect the stepladder from Mint, her dreadlocks peeking out from beneath her balaclava, eyes wide with nervous excitement. I give her shoulder a squeeze and take the stepladder over to the bust. Scott has already laid the duffle bag down at its base and unzipped it, the thick fabric falling open to reveal shiny paint cans and tools of various descriptions.

I set up the ladder for Scott to climb up. I'm to be the assistant to the surgeon, passing up implements as he needs them.

I watch Scott work—not exactly with surgical precision, but pretty impressively despite a bit of shaking in his hands. He doesn't look much like a surgeon, either, but more like some bizarre frogman with thick goggles pulled over the top of his balaclava. He goes to work on the Bulldog's nose job, and his words to Crisp when we were back on Long's Hill go through my mind as the agitated wasp sound of a reciprocating saw cutting through brass rings in my ears.

He doesn't have a big nose, so I'll have to cut straight up the length of 'er to make sure I have the surface area to stick it back on again after the fact.

He's doing an expert job, even cutting against gravity at an awkward angle, the shakiness levelling out but the effort palpable.

I look around for a moment. I see Mint and Shelly at their posts, keeping a watchful eye on Elizabeth Avenue. I squint to make out the dark shape of the Roller, Crisp and Mia lying in wait. A few orange sparks almost land on me, and my attention is pulled back to Scott and his reciprocating saw, doing their thing on one of my home country's most iconic faces.

For a brief moment I feel a little ashamed. Since I was a kid, Churchill had been a figure I'd been taught to idolize, and here I was helping deface a statue created in his honour. I think about the sculptor and all the hours she must have spent to get his likeness just right. My stomach turns. Wow. We're really doing something criminal here. The thought hits me for the first time. Then Churchill's nose hits me square between the eyes.

"Ow! Shit," I say, rubbing the area through the woollen fabric of my balaclava.

"Sorry," Scott whispers. "Can you get that?"

As I crouch down and begin fumbling around in the gravel for Winston Churchill's nose, I'm vaguely aware of a light in my periphery, followed by a short, shrill whistle. Before I can retrieve the nose, Scott's workboots thud down beside me.

"Come on. Hide!" he says, picking up the stepladder and scurrying around to the back of the plinth.

Panicked, I follow him, the two of us sitting shoulder to shoulder with our backs to the cold marble.

Scott looks at me. Something's not right.

"The duffle bag!" he says, desperation in his voice.

Shit. That was my job.

We'd gone over it in the briefing. In the event of a passing vehicle, Scott would jump down and grab the stepladder, while my job was to take the duffle bag and get behind the statue.

I start to go and retrieve the bag, but it's too late. The car is already creeping beyond the treeline. I lean out just long enough to catch a glimpse of the same RNC cruiser we'd evaded earlier and duck back behind the statue.

"It's the cops!" I say, the sense of impending doom sweeping over me.

"The same cops as before?" Scott asks.

"Yeah, I think so. They must be doing laps."

"What is this, Daytona?"

I put my finger to my lips, imploring quiet, and we stay dead still. Please, God, don't let them see the bag.

It feels like the patrol car is moving at a glacial pace. Did they get out and push?

The engine growls like a stalking lion; the tires crackle along cold asphalt. For a moment I swear I can hear the bleep and hiss of a police radio, though it could just be my mind playing tricks. Did they see it? Are they onto us? Are they radioing it in?

The headlights tickle the trees to my right, and I momentarily catch a glimpse of Shelly, ducked amid the thicket, uncharacteristically unmoving.

It's as though time itself is moving in slow motion. My heart hammers in my chest. This could be it. Game over. And it'll be all my fault.

White lights become red as the patrol car passes by and once again picks up pace when it clears the square. We stay there for a moment, unmoving, afraid to come out in case the lion is still prowling. We listen intently. There is silence save for the faint hum of electrical wires and the distant call of Larus canus.

Scott and I exchange nods, and we spring back into action. He's back up the stepladder, and I manage to retrieve the cold, brass nose from the gravel. I pass it up to him, then open the tube of Gorilla Glue and hold that aloft. Scott makes quick work of daubing the backside of the nose with glue.

Thankfully, the glue is the fast-drying kind. I watch Scott, eyes closed, counting to sixty in his head, every second feeling like a minute, as he holds the nose upside down to the Bulldog's grimacing face.

Satisfied that the nose is set, Scott reaches down, wiggling his fingers at me, and I'm ready with the can of spray paint. He grabs it and gives it a few good shakes before spraying a big, green smile on Churchill's rearranged face. He looks down at me for reassurance. I give a thumbs-up and he tosses me the can of paint before jumping down and grabbing the stepladder.

I stuff the paint into the duffle bag, zip it up, and hoist it onto my shoulder as Scott waves at Mint, who in turn flaps her arms at Mia and Crisp. The Roller groans into life, its headlights beaming on, and Mia lights up the tires as they scream out of the Cowan's parking lot and over to our position by the statue.

As we all rush toward the car, we're surprised to see Crisp jumping out, waving his long arms in the air, a can of spray paint in one hand and an old Polaroid camera in the other.

"Go back!" he shouts, loud enough to make me look around nervously for anyone who might have heard. "Get in front of the statue!"

Everyone realizes what he wants to do, and none of us wants to waste time protesting. Once Crisp has made up his mind about something, there is no going back.

As we gather in front of the statue, Crisp sets up the camera on top of the Roller before striding over to join us. He comes rattling the can of spray paint and passes it to Scott.

"You know what to do," he says.

We all watch as Scott takes the paint can and sprays two words in hot pink onto the black plinth.

Larus Can!

Crisp gestures for us to gather on either side of the plinth and turns to the camera just in time for the flash to fire.

Without another word, he springs back toward the car, snatching up the camera just in time to ease out the photo, which he waves in the cool night air as he bends himself back into the Roller.

We all pile in after him, and once Scott and Shelly—tasked with loading the stepladders and duffle bag into the trunk—are fully in, Mia lights up the tires again and we make our getaway.

Once we're a couple of blocks away from the scene of the crime, Crisp tells Mia to slow down and we remove our balaclavas. The mood inside the Roller is jubilant, the six of us at peak adrenaline as we leave Churchill Square behind, our mission complete. There are high-fives, hugs, whoops, and hollers—until Crisp tells us to simmer down.

"We don't want to draw any unnecessary attention," he says, head twitching side to side, eyes scanning the streets and sidewalks for any signs of life. It's a little after 3:30 a.m. and there isn't any.

Just as Mia hooks a right onto Carpasian Road, a thought strikes me. What about the money?

It's not the first time I've thought about it, but before now there were other things to focus on. The 50k, the riddle to solve, the thrill of falling backwards from the life I had, off the boat of normality and—*splash*—into an ocean of excitement and possibility. But now, squeezed into the back seat of the Roller, the adrenaline beginning to wane and a hint of a headache beginning to set in, I'm starting to wonder.

Was it a trick? Is there even any more money? Or did someone just really want to get a group of young people to do a number on ol' Winston's face?

Before I can give it another thought, Scott pipes up in his trademark drawl.

"Good lord . . ." he says, holding his iPhone in front of his face.

"What is it, Scott?" Crisp asks from the front passenger seat.

"It's the last part of the riddle," he says.

"The part where they tell us where to find the money?" I

ask, the question that had been bobbing just below the surface finding its opportunity to breach.

"Wait—how did they get your number?"

"I haven't the foggiest idea," Scott says, looking disturbed.

"I guess we're dealing with a smart cookie," Crisp says. "What's it say, Scotty boy?"

Scott reads from his phone.

"Well done, daughters and sons. The Bulldog is the happiest he's been in a while. The loot's in the boot behind the first mile."

"The first mile . . ." I repeat back.

"Mile One, baby," Shelly says with a smile, doing a little shoulder shake complete with jazz hands.

"The money's in a boot?" Mia asks, her frown visible in the mirror.

"Could be the trunk of a car," I say. "In the UK we say boot."

I see Crisp's eyes light up.

"Driver, to the Mile One Stadium, if you please."

"Right on," says Mia, stepping on the gas to propel the Roller along Monkstown Road and swinging it right onto Queens.

And this is re-entry. We descend the hill to a downtown suspended in the limbo between the late-night party animals and the early-morning harbour walkers—the children of the night and the adults of the day. We're very much in the former category—the vampires, the nocturnals.

Mia slows the Roller as we approach the Mile One Centre.

"So, what did it say? Behind Mile One?"

"Behind the first mile," Crisp recites thoughtfully.

"Yes, b'y. So how am I gettin' behind it?"

"Pull in here," Crisp says as we pass the concrete block that is St. John's City Hall. Mia does as she's told, pulling into the small staff parking lot between City Hall and the stadium, the Roller's headlights illuminating a single, ruby-red car tucked right at the back of the lot, where the exposed rock of the excavated hill rises to grass and shrubs above.

Mia guides the Roller slowly closer to the car.

"Jesus, is that . . ." I begin to say.

"A red DeLorean," Scott completes my sentence.

"Is that even a thing?" Mint asks.

"It is now," says Crisp. "Pull in here," he says, and Mia brings the Roller to a stop at the base of some steps that reach up to the Mile One Centre.

We all climb cautiously out of the car, any concerns—that there could be someone in the car, that this could be a trap, that we have no idea what we're doing—all trumped by sheer curiosity. I've never seen a DeLorean in real life, let alone a red one.

We're all speechless as Crisp approaches the car. Cupping his hands around his eyes, he peers into the driver's window.

"There are keys in the ignition," he says. We all just look at each other in disbelief as Crisp lifts the catch and opens the door—not outwards, but upwards. He looks back at us over his shoulder with a sly smile. "Gullwing doors," he says.

"Okay, so pop the trunk," says Shelly, sauntering over to the back of the car. Mint chuckles and makes her way to the front of the vehicle.

"Wrong end, honey," she says, waiting for Crisp to pull the release latch before lifting open the long, sleek, stainless-steel panel. "The trunk is in the front of a DeLorean."

We all gather 'round the front of the car and see another sleek briefcase—this time painted red to match the DeLorean—sitting dead centre in the otherwise empty trunk. We watch as Crisp reaches a long arm inside to lift out our prize.

"Feels heavy," he says with a smile.

"Luh," Mia says, pointing inside the trunk. On a piece of the same thick, premium paper that the Churchill riddle had been written on, sitting where the briefcase had been, is another note written in Copperplate type.

BETTER RED THAN DEAD.
TAKE THE CAR. IT'S YOURS.
MAY IT TRANSPORT YOU SAFELY THROUGH TIME.

For a moment we all look at each other and we can't help but smile. Wow. Just wow.

"Shall we take the briefcase back to home base and see what's inside?" Crisp asks rhetorically as he removes the keys from the ignition. "Peppermint, why don't you and Gregory take the DeLorean?" He tosses Mint the keys. "The rest of you—with me in the Roller. Mia, you have the wheel."

"I'd rather have the other wheel," she complains, sounding—not for the first time in the last twenty-four hours—like a sulky schoolgirl.

As the rest of the crew head back to the Roller, I make my way around the DeLorean but stop in my tracks as I realize it's parked mere inches from the rocky wall.

"No way I'm opening a gull-wing door that close to a rock wall," I say.

"Let me move that out for you," Mint says, lowering herself into the driver's seat and closing her door. The DeLorean starts first time, its engine a harmony of deep growl and high-pitched whine—like an aging athlete, happy to be back in the game but slightly pained at having to go again.

Mint eases the car away from the wall and I open the passenger door, sinking into the impossibly low seat and closing the door behind me.

"Where to?" Mint says.

"1985?" I suggest.

* * *

Back on Long's Hill the mood is electric. The rest of the gang took the Roller through the Tim's drive-through on the way back and bought enough coffee and doughnuts to fuel a small army, two Take Twelves sitting on the kitchen island, the rear of one adorned with an attachment holding cups, lids, and stir sticks.

"You knows you've made it when the Take Twelves are comin' out," Shelly jokes before biting into a Boston Cream.

The rest of the Gulls have waited for Mint and me to join them, an odd assortment of seating arranged around the circular table—the old easy chair pulled from its corner, a couple of mismatched kitchen chairs, a red beanbag I've never seen before. The table itself has been cleared of maps, shakers, and Warhammer figurines so that the new, red briefcase can take centre stage.

I grab a coffee from one of the cardboard containers and join the others around the table. We're all seated, save for Crisp, who lurches over the table, long and languid, his perma-smirk almost tearing itself into a full-blown smile.

"Drum roll, please," he says, spinning the red case around and readying his thumb over the clasp.

Those of us in close enough proximity to the table begin tapping our hands on the tabletop. Shelly, reclined in the red beanbag, vocalizes her drum in a high-pitched rolled "R." Scott uses the hard, plastic case of the reciprocating saw—which has found its way onto his lap—as a bongo.

And then Crisp opens the briefcase.

"Well? How much is it?" Mia asks, straining her neck to see inside.

Crisp turns a few wads of cash over inside the case.

"Oh, I'd say . . ."

"What?"

"How much?"

"Come on, Crisp."

"About twice the amount of the last briefcase."

The room erupts into yelps of celebration. Chairs topple, Gulls hug, coffee is spilled. Shelly is doing a belly dance around the perimeter of the room. This continues for a good few minutes until I realize Mint has left the kitchen. Before I can go look for her, she calls out from the living room.

"Hey, guys," she says. "You might want to come look at this."

We all pile into the living room as Mint turns up the volume on the small TV in the corner to see NTV news reporter Toni-Marie Wiseman standing in front of the Churchill bust, with its upside-down nose and bright green spray-paint smile. We all erupt again at the sight of our work on the TV, and high-fives are thrown.

"Ssshh!" Mia hisses as Mint cranks up the volume and a concerned-looking Toni-Marie delivers her report.

". . . this morning as a disturbing act of vandalism was discovered here at Churchill Square. As you can see behind me, the bust of legendary British wartime Prime Minister Sir Winston Churchill—created by the late Canadian sculptor Elizabeth Bradford Holbrook—has not only been attacked with a can of spray paint but has also had its nose turned upside down in an act that . . ."

Another round of whooping and hollering erupts as the TV shows a close-up of Scott's handiwork.

"Very tidy work on that nose, Scotty," Crisp says as he fetches a case of India Pale Ale from the kitchen and begins tossing bottles to people.

Mint sets hers aside.

"It's six a.m.," she protests.

"We're celebrating." Crisp shrugs, taking a swig from his own bottle.

"Ssshh!" Mia hisses again as Scott twists the cap off his bottle and white foam erupts from the top.

". . . resident Bill Parsons was the one who discovered the egregious act on his daily early-morning walk. Bill, can you describe what you saw?"

A senior man with ruddy red cheeks and a flat cap has joined Toni-Marie in front of the statue.

"Well, I was just taking me usual route through the park here at around five thirty and I came upon this monstrosity you see here."

"And this must have come as quite a shock to you."

"Well, yes, miss, it was a shock, yes, a shock indeed."

"Skipper," Scott scoffs before taking a swig of his now-tamed beer.

"Mission complete!" Crisp yells. "Even made the news." He's clearly very pleased with himself as he leaves the room again, chugging back his India as he goes.

"Thank you, Bill," Toni-Marie says as she turns to the camera and her interviewee is awkwardly shepherded away. "A truly shocking and premeditated attack that some are speculating could be a form of protest in light of the recent discovery of mass graves at residential schools . . ."

"Fuckers," Mia snarls, taking a long slug from her dark brown bottle.

"Who? The Catholic Church?" Scott asks. Mia just stares straight ahead as Toni-Marie wraps her report and cues back to the studio.

"She's still so hot," Scott says, feeling the need to change the subject.

". . . security cameras were spray-painted over, and no CCTV footage of the perpetrators was captured, the only clue this hastily painted tag, which appears to read Larus Can . . ."

"It's da gulls," the interviewee says from off-camera, and for a moment we all freeze. “Larus canus is Latin for the common seagull,” he says, and we all breathe again.

“Jesus, I thought skipper was onto us there,” says Scott.

“Ho, ho, ho!” Crisp yells, re-entering the room. “And no, I’m not talking to the three of ye, Shelly, Mia, and my little peppermint candy cane!”

“Oh, Jesus.” Shelly laughs as we all turn to see Crisp wearing a dollar-store Santa hat and fluffy white beard, nursing the bright red briefcase on one forearm and foraging in there with his free hand.

“Merrrry Christmas!” he shouts, beginning to toss stacks of cash to each of us in turn. “Here are your gifts, my children. Ho, ho, ho!”

The fun goes on until we all have three bundles of fifty-dollar bills each and Crisp collapses on the couch with the open briefcase, which still contains another two stacks of cash.

Crisp grabs another beer from the open box on the side table and twists it open. “From now on we’re doing this right. An even split, six ways. That’s fifteen thousand dollars each.” He pokes the neck of the bottle through the small mouth hole in his beard and takes another long swig.

“That’s only ninety k,” Scott says. “What about the other ten grand?”

“Anything we can’t divide without breaking a stack we keep in a kitty for expenses. We’ll use it to pay rent, pay the bills, and for any equipment required for future missions.” Crisp states this as fact, not something open for discussion. No one argues. I’m just happy to have a place to stay rent-free.

“Future missions?” Mint asks. Crisp gives a little wink before taking up a small piece of premium paper like a joint between two fingers and giving it a little wave in the air.

“Another riddle?” Mia asks.

“Another riddle,” Crisp confirms.

Before he can read it, Shelly snatches it away, clears her throat, and reads it aloud to the room.

A PLACE OF FAITH OR ONE OF CRIME? THAT WILL BE DECIDED IN TIME. A PAST THAT CAN'T BE BURIED. A TASK THAT CAN'T BE HURRIED. SEEK OUT THE CROWNING GLORY. A BIG ENOUGH TARGET, THOUGH NO ST. PETER'S. HAVE THE GUTS TO CALL FORTH WINGED ANGELS. LET THEM DROP THEIR FOUL VENGEANCE UPON ITS HALLOWED STEPS.

"Jesus. A past that can't be buried? Sounds like something to do with that mass graves story Toni-Marie was just talking about," says Scott.

Scowling, Mia snatches the note away from Shelly.

"If we're gonna give it to the Church, you can count me in," she says with genuine venom, studying the note carefully. "All the prayers in the world haven't helped me mudder."

"Seek out the crowning glory. What the frig does that mean?" Shelly asks.

"All in good time, little bird," Crisp says, taking back the note. "Business can come later." He folds the note and tucks it into the breast pocket of his loose-fitting white cotton shirt. "Right now I'm thinking breakfast at the Bagel Café, then we hit the shops for a little retail therapy."

Shelly lets out a loud "Woo hoo!" and grabs Mint up from the couch.

"Frig it, I'm starved," says Scott, knocking back the last dregs of his India beer and dropping the empty into the box with a clink on his way out the door.

Mia pouts like the teen she appears to be, despite her protestations that she's twenty-three, but Crisp calms her in an instant with a brush of her cheek, tucking her long, brown hair behind her ear.

"It's okay, little bird," he says softly. "Let's go have some fun. Okay?" She nods and her face softens. He already holds such sway over her. Over all of us?

Mia goes to get ready with the others, and I ease myself off the couch. I'm tired from the beer but wired from the sheer thrill of it all.

Crisp looks as though he's about to say something, when my phone starts to ring and vibrate furiously in my pocket.

"You gonna get that?" he says. I shrug.

I reach into my pocket and flip open the phone, pausing to look at the display. A feeling of dread sweeps over me for a moment as I read the words on the little green screen.

Tim Hortons

"Bollocks," I say to no one. "I forgot. I have a shift today," I say to Crisp.

"I don't think you really need that shitty job anymore. Do you, Gregory?" He eyes the fifty grand that's poking out of my jeans pocket.

I smile and press the little green button to answer the call.

"Hello," I say.

"Is this Gregory?" comes Brenda's voice on the other end, the cigarette growl sounding like a lawn mower played through a PR system on the cheap plastic phone.

"Yes, it is," I say cheerily as Crisp watches on.

"You do realize your shift started half an hour ago?" Brenda rasps.

"Oh, right," I say. "Well, I won't be coming in today, Brenda." Silence on the other end. "In fact, I won't be coming in ever again. Unless I want a large double-double and an Old-Fashioned Glazed, of course!" I have to pull the phone away from my ear and cover the mouthpiece so she won't hear our chuckles.

"Quittin', are ya?" Brenda says after a pause.

"Um, yes. Yes, I am quitting, Brenda."

"And why's that, then?"

I look Crisp in his narrow eyes.

"I found something in my field," I say.

"You know, two weeks' notice is . . ." Brenda begins to say, but I snap the phone shut on that period of my life.

"We gotta get you a better phone," Crisp says, his smirk creeping across his thin face like a crack in porcelain.

We share a laugh and he puts an arm around me as we head out to join the others.

"I hope it didn't bother you too much, Gregory."

"What?"

"Defacing such an icon of your homeland like that."

"Oh, Churchill? Nah. He kinda had it coming," I say.

Crisp almost looks a little disappointed.

"Oh, shit," he says, pausing in the doorway. "TV."

Toni-Marie is still relaying the morning's news in the background.

"I'll get it," I say, almost feeling as though that was the expectation as Crisp smiles and pats me on the back.

I return to the living room and search for the TV remote, which I eventually find stuck down the back of the couch. As I'm about to turn off the TV, something makes me pause for a moment. There's a picture of a man in the top corner of the screen. Mid- to late forties, long, black hair, slightly greying at the temples, pulled back into a ponytail, manicured beard with two lightning bolts of grey either side of his chin. There's something familiar about him. Something in the eyes.

The headline reads:

Local Billionaire Businessman Still Missing

". . . the third week of an investigation into the disappearance of Finatech co-founder Jackson Lorde. Lorde, forty-six, was last seen leaving Finatech's headquarters on July twenty-third. It has since emerged that he sensationally quit the company, selling all his shares to partners and co-founders Justin Lorde and Patrick Bannister. Justin Lorde, who is also Jackson's younger brother, made this emotional plea to the press on the steps of Finatech HQ."

A tall, statuesque man in an expensive shirt and dress pants, tie-less and top button undone, appears on the screen in front of the giant glass-and-metal shoebox that is Finatech's headquarters over near the airport. I'd been there a couple of times with Dana for the lavish gatherings the tech company throws, fully catered for its employees and their significant others. A swarm of press is gathered to hear Justin speak.

"We are asking for anyone with any information pertaining to Jackson's whereabouts to please come forward. We will be offering a cash reward to anyone providing information that leads us to Jackson's discovery, and more details of that will be shared in the coming days. Thank you."

As the flashbulbs crackle and the journalists begin to yell questions, the camera cuts back to the news anchor in the studio.

"A search of Jackson Lorde's three known Newfoundland addresses turned up no evidence, and his estranged wife, Julia, was unavailable for comment . . ."

"You coming?" Mint has appeared in the doorway.

"Yeah," I say, switching off the TV and heading out to join the gang.

* * *

This time, Mia calls dibs on the DeLorean for the day and Shelly calls shotgun. Crisp throws me the keys to the Roller and jumps in the back with Mint, leaving me up front with Scott. I watch Crisp and Mint in my rear-view mirror as much as I watch the road on the way downtown. She seems happy to maintain distance, despite him unfurling a long arm across the back seat and seeming to take up as much room as he possibly can. I catch his narrow eyes looking back at me in the mirror now and again. It's almost like he's looking for a response. Is he doing this on purpose?

Soon we're downtown. It's a Sunday and Duckworth Street is quiet enough that we can park the two cars next to each other on the side of the street, right outside the Bagel Café with its bright red, black-trimmed siding. Breakfast is toasted bagels stuffed with various combinations of bacon, eggs, tomatoes, lettuce, and cheese, with a side of hash browns.

Bellies full and caffeine-fuelled, we head out to explore the clothing stores of downtown St. John's, which are every bit as unique and eccentric as the city itself. Shelly and Mint lead us from one to the next, ducking through alleys I never knew were there and entering doors I never would have thought would lead to a store.

Duran Duran sing about girls on film while the girls of our group put on a fashion show for the ages. Shelly leads the way, this time appearing in a leopard-print jacket, fishnet stockings, ruby red stilettos, and a feathered flapper's headband; next a long trench coat and, well, a broad smile. Not much else, as a quick flash reveals to the group, almost causing Scott's eyes to pop out of his head on springs.

Mint draws most of my attention, highlights including a '60s miniskirt and tight white T, worn braless as the manufacturer intended, and the flapper dress that must have gone with Shelly's headband, all form-hugging and fringed.

Even Mia is coaxed into the action, despite her initial protestations, looking quite lovely in a little black dress and matching flats. She does not "do" heels, but she certainly seems to have gotten Crisp's attention, if she didn't have it before. There's something about her he's attracted to. Something beyond the surface-level youthful beauty. She's damaged, somehow—host to a deep, disturbing angst. That's what he's attracted to.

He, of course, is the star of the show, brightening the day of the Sunday staff by kitting himself out in pinstripe dress pants, loafers, a bejewelled wifebeater, and a pink feather boa—all topped off with a new fedora he's managed to find. He looks like some eccentric sports star at an awards gala.

Scott and I pick out a couple of nice shirts, pants, and pairs of shoes, at Crisp's behest.

"You can't be driving around town in a red DeLorean looking like a pair of skeets," he says. "Cops'll think you stole it."

He's got a point. My wardrobe hasn't received an update since I was back in England, save for a couple of BOGO message T's I picked up at Old Navy. My favourites read All Style, no Content, and I See Your Lips Moving, but All I Hear is Yada, Yada, Yada.

We get a few funny looks as we peel off crisp new fifties to pay for our haul, then we're out the door and heading to our next destination.

"Get yer asses in gear," Shelly yells as she jogs on, leading us back to the cars. She runs like someone who doesn't really run, the flowy, floral dress she's decided to keep on revealing a little too much with every awkward stride. "Avalon Mall's only open till five on a Sunday!"

Born in the '60s, the Avalon Mall has the feel of an aging pop star. She's had a few facelifts, and if you look carefully you can see the wrinkles, but she's still got a lot of go in her. There's something about her. Not like the Village Mall across town, where you can see from one end to the other standing still. The Avalon Mall has a couple of proper levels and enough twists and turns to make it feel like a true destination to visit, rather than just a collection of shops. The Avalon Mall has character.

The Avalon Mall also has a couple of telecommunications stores, one of which we pile into en masse.

"Can I help you?" asks the rather overwhelmed-looking sales associate. He's a short fella with thick glasses, long, mousy hair, and a wispy attempt at a beard.

"We'd all like phones, please," says Shelly, leaning provocatively on the counter. "iPhones. None of this cyborg nonsense."

"I think she means Android," Scott interjects.

"Okay, iPhones. For . . . all of you?" the sales assistant asks.

"Not me. I already have one," Scott says.

"But you could get a newer, shinier one," Mint suggests, giving Scott a playful elbow to the ribs.

"Lead us to your newest, shiniest iPhones, please, oh sage of gadgets and tech," Shelly bellows.

"Right this way," says the sales assistant.

* * *

"These things recognize your face now?" Shelly says with a look of genuine wonder painted across her own.

"Yup. The latest way for Big Tech to gather personal details about you," Scott says before dangling a pizza slice into his mouth and biting off the cheesy tip. "Mine has a fingerprint reader," he continues with his mouth full. "But I don't use it. I just have a PIN. No way they're getting my fingerprints."

"Who? The government?" Shelly asks, her look of genuine wonder now replaced by a look of genuine intrigue.

"The government already has your fingerprints," Crisp says. He's already polished off some kind of vegetarian health bowl and is now leaning back, hands behind head, arms bent back like gull wings as he surveys the Avalon Mall food court.

The six of us are jammed in around two tables, surrounded by shopping bags and tucking into an early supper none of us really needs. A couple of shiny new iPhones lie on the table amid the forest of cardboard containers, single-serve condiments, and branded napkins.

"Not mine, they don't," Scott says.

"They took mine in high school," Mint says thoughtfully, chewing on a pita. "They told us it was in case we got abducted or something."

"See," Scott says. "That right there. That's how they get ya."

"Different government, though, right?" I say, dabbing my face thoroughly to make sure no remnants of my New York Fries poutine are still hanging around. "You grew up in the States, didn't you?"

"This is true," Mint says. "So, I guess I could get away with all kinds of bad behaviour up here." She gives me a wink, the single dimple appearing on her right cheek as she smiles. There's a constant cool calm about Mint. She lives up to her name.

"Well, they got mine," Mia pipes up between nibbles of her A&W Teen Burger. "When I went to juvie."

That gets our attention, and we all wait for her to elaborate. She swallows and looks around at our expectant faces before rolling her eyes and continuing.

"When I was fourteen I skipped school a bunch, did some shoplifting and some other . . . stuff. I was in for about three months, total."

There's silence as she takes another bite of her burger, her face turning as red as the ketchup sachets that dot the table.

"Why did you do those things, Mia?" Crisp asks, leaning in.

"My mom," Mia says. "She's sick, and when my father left, we didn't always have enough food or whatever, so . . ." She speaks fast and then stuffs the burger back into her mouth.

Shelly reaches out and places her hand on Mia's non-burger-toting one. She seems to appreciate the gesture.

"What's wrong with your mom?" Scott asks, oblivious to the tone of the moment.

"MS," Mia says. "Bad. She can't really get around much."

"That must have been very hard for you," Crisp says.

"Yeah, well, still is."

"Your brush with the law. Is that what made you decide to pursue a career as a police officer?" Crisp asks.

"I dunno. Yeah. Maybe."

She clearly wants to get off the subject. Crisp relents and we all sit in silence for a minute or two, finishing our meals and taking in the scene.

The Avalon Mall food court is perfectly laid out for people-watching, a horseshoe of colourful fast-food joints surrounding rows upon rows of tables, each with four seats and barely enough surface space to accommodate a couple of plastic trays. A stained glass skylight and a thousand beaming pot lights make it unnaturally bright. There is nowhere to hide here.

People from all walks of life pour in and out of the heavy metal doors in a constant stream. Families, couples, singles, old folks, kids, and—of course—troops of teens walk the shiny tiled floors and see what takes their fancy. Char-grilled burgers, fried chicken, pitas, Buddha bowls, fish and chips, Chinese, Japanese, Greek. It's all there, and no two family members are forced to eat the same thing.

I slurp on the watery dregs of my over-iced root beer and watch the currents of hungry shoppers flow through. Then I see her, emerging from behind some fake plastic shrubbery, making her way into the food court with her friend Lesley.

"Shit," I say, turning away. "It's Dana."

As one, the rest of the Gulls turn to look.

"Don't look!" I implore, chancing a peek myself. Dana is animated. She looks upset, maybe a little angry. Lesley—a matronly woman who always looks a little sad—seems to be listening, consoling. They rock up to the Japanese place. Dana loves her teriyaki chicken.

"She looks pissed. Must've had her heart broken," Shelly teases.

I glance over again as the two women bring their trays to a table on the other side of the food court. Between the hordes of teens and the plastic shrubbery, there's plenty of cover between us. In any case, they seem too engaged in their conversation to notice very much of anything. I watch them a moment longer. Dana looks really upset. Did I do that? My heart sinks.

"I really didn't think she'd take it this hard," I say out loud, maybe trying to defend myself. "I mean, it's not as if our relationship has been anything to write home about since we got to Newfoundland."

Shelly leans in, a flutter of her eyelashes encouraging me to go on.

"I mean, I know I've been a shit boyfriend, but it wasn't all me. She's been, well, cold."

The whole group is looking at me now, all willing me to share more.

"We haven't had sex in three months, okay?" I blurt out. "And it's not like I didn't want to."

"She is a fetching woman," Crisp says.

Shelly stares at the two women across the food court, her eyes narrowing.

"Maybe it isn't about you," she speculates. "Maybe there's something else going on with Little Miss Doe Eyes over there."

"Ever since she started at Finatech, pretty much," I say, encouraged by this line of thinking—this idea that I'm not a worthless shit who breaks sweet girls' hearts. "I started to see less and less of her. She was always at the office. Always working late."

"Always lounging in beanbag chairs, enjoying her free scoffs," Shelly adds.

I look over at the two women again. Lesley is speaking now—advising, consoling perhaps. Dana glumly chews on her teriyaki chicken. Maybe this isn't about me.

We're all silent for another minute or so. I watch as Dana gives up on her half-eaten food and the two women get up, deposit their garbage, and head off down the escalators. The rest of the gang have finished their meals and are all engaged with their new iPhones, at various stages of set-up and exploration. Crisp breaks the silence.

"Okay, guys and gulls," he says. "If this episode of *Dr. Phil* is over, perhaps we can get down to business." He pulls out the piece of premium paper and slowly unfolds it. "We have a riddle to solve."

Everyone puts down their phones and huddles in as Crisp slides the piece of paper to the middle of the table. We all study the Copperplate text.

A PLACE OF FAITH OR ONE OF CRIME? THAT WILL BE DECIDED IN TIME. A PAST THAT CAN'T BE BURIED. A TASK THAT CAN'T BE HURRIED. SEEK OUT THE CROWNING GLORY. A BIG ENOUGH TARGET, THOUGH NO ST. PETER'S. HAVE THE GUTS TO CALL FORTH WINGED ANGELS. LET THEM DROP THEIR FOUL VENGEANCE UPON ITS HALLOWED STEPS.

"A place of faith or crime," Shelly reads aloud. "Faith meaning religion, I s'pose?"

"A past that can't be buried," I read ahead, my mind instantly flashing back to the news report about the mass graves at the sites of former Indian Residential Schools. "Shit. Are they talking about the Catholic Church?"

"Fuckers," Mia says between slurps of a milkshake that's so big it makes her look like a child drinking from an adult cup.

Scott leans in, trying to keep the momentum going.

"Seek out the crowning glory. A big enough target, though no St. Peter's," he says, a wry smile peeping through his scruffy beard. "They're talking about the Basilica," he says.

"Wha—? How'd you come to that conclusion?" Shelly asks.

"Because the original Basilica is the St. Peter's Basilica, in the Vatican," Scott says slowly and just a little bit smugly.

"Are you sure?" Shelly says, picking up her newly acquired iPhone and thumbing in a Google search.

"Fifteen years of Sunday Mass as a kid. I should be sure," he says.

"I think he's right, Shell," I add.

"Yeah. Sounds right to me, too, and I should know. My mom's a Catholic. For all the good it's done her. Fuckers," Mia adds, slurping the gurgling remnants of her milkshake with the sucking power of a Dyson vacuum cleaner.

"So, what does the next part mean?" Mint asks. She's in the seat next to me, leaning in. "Have the guts to call forth winged angels . . ."

". . . that will drop their foul vengeance upon its hallowed steps." I can't resist taking the opportunity to finish Mint's sentence.

Crisp is unusually quiet, watching on with that perma-smirk and those narrow eyes. It's as though he enjoys watching us struggle to figure it out, in a way that suggests he's figured it out already. I bet he hasn't. Dickhead.

"Yes, b'y. How are we supposed to call forth angels?" Shelly says. "What is this, some voodoo magic thing now? Oh, I always wanted to be a witch!" She beams.

Suddenly, I get a flash of memory: Crisp in the back yard on Long's Hill, the way the seagulls looked so stately with their long wings silhouetted against the afternoon sunlight. I remember the shit dripping down Crisp's arms. I think of London and the statues in Trafalgar Square, covered in pigeon poop.

"Gulls," I say.

"Yes, dear?" Shelly replies.

"No, I mean seagulls. The winged angels. Dropping their foul vengeance. Droppings. Foul vengeance."

"Oh, shit!" Shelly shouts out, jumping up and pointing her finger at me like I just guessed a word in a game of charades.

"What?" Scott asks.

"No, I mean bird shit. Right, Greg?"

"They want us to get seagulls to shit on the steps of the Basilica," Mia says flatly. "Awesome," she adds with the first real smile I've seen on her face.

"And how do we convince a bunch of seagulls to crap on a church?" Mint asks. "Ask them nicely?"

"Gotta have guts," Crisp says, sipping on a green juice.

"Oh, like fish guts!" Shelly yells. She's up now, pacing around the table, drawing glances from other food court patrons.

"Where are we gettin' fish guts?" Mia asks.

All eyes in the group turn to Scott.

* * *

"Like I said, I'll get the fish guts and I'll help you plan it out, but no way am I being directly involved in soiling the steps of the Basilica," Scott says as we walk along the harbourfront.

"Do you fear divine retribution?" Shelly cajoles, delivering the line like a priest on the pulpit—albeit one swirling a hula hoop around one arm.

"The way I see it, there's no way of knowing if there's a God or not. On the off chance there is, I'm not gonna go out of my way to piss Him off," Scott explains.

"There isn't," Mia hisses.

"You don't know that," Scott says. "Nobody does."

"I do," Mia counters.

The four of us are the fish gut retrieval team. Scott's brother, Andrew, said it would take three or four of us to carry the containers of guts back to the car. Mint had an errand to run, so Crisp volunteered to take her in the DeLorean. He always gets the good assignments.

Still, it's another fine summer's morning in St. John's, sun shining, blue skies over Signal Hill, but always with that brisk breeze bringing with it a nip of ocean cool. It always feels salty and fresh here, like the air is doing you some good. Mum would love it.

The fish plant is at the end of the harbour, a good ten minutes' walk from the nearest available parking spot, so we'll have no choice but to cart the fish gut containers by hand back to the Roller. Andrew did say he might be able to avail of some kind of cart or trolley to ease our burden. Please, God.

"So, what does your brother do at the fish plant, Scott?" I ask.

"Half-brother. And chop the heads off fish, mainly, I think."

"Nice work if you can get it," Mia mumbles.

"Oh, hmm, we must be gettin' close now, eh?" Shelly says as a gust of wind carries with it an overpowering smell of fish to our noses.

"Yup. Just over here," Scott says.

The fish plant is a huge, blue oblong with a grey metal roof, and the smell as we approach it is overpowering. We reach a metal door with a wire mesh window, and Scott sends his brother a text. Within a minute a face appears at the window, then the door swings open with a metallic creak, increasing the smell tenfold and causing Mia to gag into her sleeve.

"Yeah, I get that reaction a lot," says Andrew, who is a taller, more muscular Scott with the same jam-jar glasses and a confusion of hairnets covering both his head and beard. His apron is an abstract artwork of fish blood and guts, his bare forearms swollen and defined from a thousand fish lifted, tossed, and gutted.

"Sorry," says Mia. "It's just the smell. I'm gonna go stand over here."

Mia walks away, face in sleeve, leaving the rest of us awaiting our haul.

"There's always one with a fragile constitution," Andrew shrugs. "Four drums of fish guts, is it? Coming right up."

* * *

"I'm tellin' ya, I ain't doin' it," we hear Scott say from the kitchen. His voice is as raised as I've ever heard it, which, considering the cajoling he's been getting from Crisp, might just be as raised as it gets. Even as worked up as he is, Scott still delivers his words slowly and with a drawl, perhaps just a few decibels above his usual level. "I got ya the fish guts, and this is where I get off."

"Scott. Listen to me," we hear Crisp saying, not for the first time. Mint, Shelly, and I are huddled on the couch in the living room, me the thorn between two roses once again, each of them clinging to one of my arms as we listen in on the raging debate. "We need you on this one. It's a six-person operation, just like we planned it."

"I told you, I'm not gettin' involved with anything to do with the Church."

"He's really sticking to his guns," Mint whispers to us.

"I never even knew he was Catholic." Shelly shrugs.

"Jesus, Scotty. When was the last time you went to Mass?" Crisp says.

"That's not the—"

"When was the last time you went to church, Scott? Do you even remember?"

"I am not going to be involved—"

"You're already involved!" Crisp's volume doubles, his words rumbling like thunder, accentuating the silence in their aftermath. "You defaced Winston friggin' Churchill, Scott. You're a part of this. A big friggin' part."

"Crisp, I just can't—"

"I don't wanna hear it, Scott. You're a Gull. We're all in this together. You need to do your bit."

"Or what?"

I feel hands tighten around both my arms, and I swear I can hear the distant call of seagulls outside as we wait for Crisp's response.

"Or you're out. I'll find someone else to take your place."

"Crisp, you can't be bringing anyone else into this."

"Why not? It's a six-person operation, Scott. I'm sure I can find someone who'd like to get a couple of bundles of cash just for keeping guard across from the Basilica. 'Cause that's all I'm asking you to do. Just keep watch. That's all."

Another pause. Crisp lowers the tone and returns to reasoning mode.

"Look, Scott. You did a great job with the first dare. That was all you, man." I can imagine Crisp towering over Scott, a hand on each of his shoulders. That unique mix of friendly and intimidating that Crisp is so very adept at. He's your friend. Your very dangerous friend.

"All I need from you now is to keep watch for five or ten minutes."

Another pause.

"I understand if you can't. I really do. But if you don't, this is the end of the road for you. No more dares. No more cash. I'll find someone else." And there's the twist.

"I don't know what your problem is," we hear Mia pipe up. "It's only a bit of bird shit. Those fuckers deserve worse."

"Whaddya say?" Crisp asks. I can picture him squeezing Scott's shoulders tighter. I'm your friend. Incidentally, I'm also much bigger and stronger than you.

"C'mon, Scott. We really need you on this."

Another long pause.

"Okay, but I'm only keeping watch."

"That's my boy!"

"Ten minutes and I'm outta there."

"We'll have it done in seven."

7

Dare 2
Bombs Away

"So, what's your beef with the Catholic Church?" I whisper to Mia as we crouch in our ninja suits between the trees that line the Basilica's southwest side along Bonaventure Avenue.

"Same as any religion, really. Bunch of bullshit that just gives people false hope and excuses to hurt one another," she says without looking at me.

For a moment the smell of semi-rotten fish guts fills my nostrils and I almost gag. I try to turn my head away from the blue plastic drum with the fishy stains all down the side. The smell is a lot better out here than in was in the car. The Roller's limited trunk size would only accommodate two of the bins, meaning that the other two had to ride in the back seat with Scott and me, Mia driving, and Shelly once again quick to the draw with her "shotgun." Mint and Crisp were to be the eyes of this operation and had gone ahead in the DeLorean to scope the scene.

"Yeah," I say. "You're probably right. But you seem to really have it in for the Catholic Church. Is it because of these mass graves they've been finding?"

It's pretty dark, but there's just enough street light creeping through the trees for me to tell that Mia's scowling at me. She doesn't like to be pressed, doesn't like to talk about herself.

"That's part of it, yeah."

"But not the main part," I suggest.

"No."

She goes quiet for a minute, looking over toward the Basilica and across Military Road as though trying to make out our cohorts, but I sense that she's processing, trying to resist the urge to open up, hoping that some signal to advance the mission will save her from this conversation.

"It's my mom, I guess," she says, momentarily making eye contact but then turning away again. "She prays every day, but it does her no good. Prays for everyone. Me. Her neighbours. My aunts and dat. Maybe for herself a little. She's the one who needs the help. But nobody's listening."

"The MS?"

Mia snorts.

"You don't know what that is, do ya?"

"I mean, I've heard of it . . ."

"Multiple sclerosis. Basically, the immune system attacks the brain and spinal cord. Some people get it worse than others. Mom's got the real bad version."

"I'm sorry."

"Yeah, well, it is what it is, but praying ain't gonna cure it."

I feel a vibration in my pocket.

"This might be our cue," I say, retrieving my phone and looking at the text message.

Get set . . .

I nod to Mia and we both stand, grabbing a white plastic handle each. I hold my phone in my free hand, eyes locked on the screen, waiting for the word.

GO!

We're up, making our way as quickly as possible toward the cathedral, trotting awkwardly along like two people in a three-legged race, bound to each other, the sloshing contents of the bin preventing any sense of rhythm. It looks rather grand to me now—the Basilica—towering above us in the moonlight. For a moment I feel a little nauseous at the prospect of what we're about to do. Or maybe it's the smell of fish guts.

As we approach the steps, statues of saints or some such judging us from above, we see Shelly and Scott emerging from the shadows on the other side. The three-legged slosh-bucket race now has a competitor, and I feel our pace pick up as we try to beat them to the base of the steps.

Shelly and Scott are quicker than we are, though. Mia seems to be struggling a bit with the weight. I hadn't questioned it when she'd volunteered to be one of the bucket carriers, but I did have to disguise my concern when Crisp decreed that I would be partnered with the smallest member of the group.

Shelly has a bit more physicality about her—broad around the beam and sturdy in the shoulders. Plus, she probably has pretty amazing core strength from all that hula-hooping. It helps, too, I think to myself, that she and Scott are closer in height than Mia and me.

In any case, they're winning this race that's really only in my head. The real race is to dump these stinking fish guts all over the steps of the Basilica and get the hell out of Dodge before somebody sees us.

Shelly and Scott are already at the top of the steps, two Steve Jobs ninjas tipping fish guts all over the grey stone slabs. Mia and I have just reached the base of the steps. She has two hands on her handle now as we lug the heavy bin up the steps. I think she might drop it at any second, but we make it to the top and begin depositing our load as per Crisp's plan: one side per team. Start at the top and work your way down. When the bin is empty, go get the second one.

Fuck. The second bin.

In the haze of fish guts and adrenaline, I'd completely forgotten that we have two bins of fish guts, each, to make sure we cover as many steps as possible.

Shelly and Scott are already down the steps and off to retrieve their second bin from the trees on the northwest side of the cathedral.

"Jesus, look at those two go," Mia says between panting breaths.

"I know. They're like an Olympic fish gut carrying team," I say, bringing a rare smile to Mia's face. "You ready to finish the job?"

She nods and we're off, back toward our treeline, moving faster now that our bin is empty, our resolve hardened by the successful depositing of our first load.

We ditch the empty, pause to gather ourselves, and with an exchange of nods, we take up the second bin.

Our progress is quicker this time, our bodies hardened to the demands of the task. We move more like a team despite the sloshing bin's best efforts to throw us off course.

We're still not as quick as "Team SAS," though. They are almost done depositing their second bin by the time we reach the bottom of the steps.

It's me that needs to pause before we make our ascent this time, my forearm seizing up. We plonk the bucket down on the ground, and it's then that I feel a vibration in my pocket. I grab for my phone and instinctively glance up to where I know Crisp and Mint are keeping watch across the street. That's when I see Crisp's long, bony arms waving in arcs in the air. My heart sinks.

Something's wrong.

"Quick," I say to Mia. "Let's get on with it."

If there's a car approaching, we don't have time to run for cover with a full bin of fish guts, anyway, so I figure we might as well lighten our load and ready ourselves for a quick getaway. Besides, I want to see this thing through.

Shelly and Scott have clocked Crisp's waving now, too, and are making their way back down the steps, their bin just about empty.

We exchange nods and I catch a set of headlights out on the road from the corner of my eye as Mia and I hoist up our bin once again.

Except some of the fish guts must have spilled out onto my handle when we set the bin down.

As Mia lifts, my handle slips from my grasp. I lose my footing and the bin tips, the weight of the fish guts creating an unstoppable momentum. I can only jump reflexively back in an attempt to avoid the tidal wave of stinky guts.

The bin thumps against the bottom step. The bright white headlights glimmer. The guts spill all over the stone step just as Scott's foot makes contact. His legs go out from under him and he hits the steps hard, going instantly limp. White lights become blue and red. And we hear the "woot-woot" that is unmistakably the short burst of a police siren.

I freeze for a moment as the police cruiser stops at the bottom of the pathway, and I watch through the stone archway as two RNC officers get out.

I see Mia running back from whence we came and then catch sight of Crisp and Mint. They're all making a run for the cars, which are both parked on the southwest side of the cathedral—mine and Mia's side. The plan had been to throw the empty bins back in the Roller, then for Mia and me to take the DeLorean while Scott and Shelly take off in the Roller, collecting Crisp and Mint from their lookout post across the street before peeling off and heading to home base.

Now, all bets are off.

"Hey. What are ya doin' up there?"

Jesus, it's the cops. They've got flashlights and they've seen us.

I quickly survey the situation. Scott is out cold. Shelly is trying—and failing—to pick him up. My trouser legs and shoes are covered in stinking fish guts. And we're about to get ourselves arrested. Or killed.

"Come on," I say, instinctively grabbing Shelly's hand.

"What are you doing?" she asks as I yank her up from the steps.

She tries to resist, but I pull her with all my might.

"We can't leave him," she says.

"We've got not choice! Do you want to get arrested, too?"

She resists me for a moment, until the cops shout out again, and then she stops fighting and starts running with me toward the refuge of the cars.

We run as fast as we can, the muffled shouts of the cops behind us. I'm half expecting to hear a gun go off. I've never been so scared, never run so fast, pulling Shelly along, forcing her to keep up.

Out of nowhere, the DeLorean appears, lights beaming, engine growling, tires screeching to a momentary halt. We brace ourselves against the hood as tire smoke engulfs us, the acrid smell burning my nose.

"Get in!" Mia shouts from the driver's seat, the passenger-side door flying open.

We race around to the other side of the car and pile in, Shelly landing upside down on my lap as I struggle to close the door.

Before I can get it fully closed, Mia lights up the tires and pulls an aggressive U-turn, sending Shelly and me tumbling over the centre console. As we race off into the night, leaving the police officers in our wake—Scott along with them—Shelly and I manage to arrange ourselves into something resembling a sensible set-up on the DeLorean's single passenger seat, and I finally get the door closed behind us.

Nobody says a word.

I look in the wing mirror and see a solitary seagull circling its way down toward the Basilica below.

* * *

Back at the house, the faces are as long as the hill. When we'd arrived home, Crisp had shepherded us into the house and quickly thrown a car cover over the DeLorean. God knows where he got it. His mood had been as close to frantic as I'd ever seen it, which, by normal-people standards, was still pretty laid-back. All the same, he was serious and clearly concerned that we might be followed or identified.

He'd told us to get changed and put our Steve Jobs ninja suits at the top of the stairs, after which he'd grabbed them and taken them up the narrow, creaky staircase, opened the door with an old key, thrown them in, and locked it again. Except for my trousers, which he'd gotten one sniff of and told me to throw them in the washing machine downstairs.

Evidently, he and Mint had made a run for the Roller when they saw things were going pear-shaped. Now we're all sitting in the living room, curtains closed, with only the pale glow of a salt lamp casting a little light into the room.

"We need to lay low till we know nobody followed us," Crisp says.

Several minutes go by as we all try to process what just happened.

"I hope he's okay," Shelly says, breaking the silence. "He hit his head pretty hard."

"He'll be okay," Crisp says, like it's an instruction.

"The cops were there. They would have called an ambulance, made sure he was all right," I say, trying to convince myself as much as anything.

Another long silence.

"What if he tells 'em?" Mia says, vocalizing what we're all thinking. "About the briefcases. About the money."

"Scott won't say anything," Crisp says sharply.

"How's he gonna explain all the fish guts?" Shelly asks glumly.

"He'll think of something," Crisp insists.

More silence.

"It's not a crime," Crisp says eventually. "I mean, it's not a felony. Putting some fish guts on the steps of some church. It's a misdemeanour at most. They'll hold him overnight, ask him some questions, let him go with a fine."

At that moment I feel my phone vibrate in my pocket, and a couple of others in the room ding.

"Maybe it's Scotty," Shelly says, excitedly thumbing at her phone.

I look at my phone, the thumbprint ID letting me in, colourful icons streaming across the screen. There's a text message from an unknown number.

A little birdie tells me one gull's left behind.

Your reward is planted where you got the guts to go through with it.

Two dares done, one gull gone.

"The money's at the fish plant," Mia says excitedly.

"Great. How are we supposed to get it when we're 'laying low'?" Shelly says, delivering the last two words in a mocking voice and finger quotes.

"I'll go," Mia says.

"I'll go with you," Mint says.

"I'll go, too." The words leave my mouth before I've even thought them.

"No," Crisp says, and we all look to him for a decision. "We don't want to send out a carload. Mia and Mint can handle it."

He tosses a set of keys to Mia.

"Take the Roller. The cops didn't see us take it, so they won't be looking for it. Go straight to the fish plant and come right back. Be quick but don't go flying around. We don't want any more attention from the law."

Mia nods. As Mint rises from the couch to join her, I grab her hand.

"Be careful," I say.

Mint smiles and gives my hand a squeeze before following Mia out of the room.

The three of us sit in silence and listen as they go out the front door, get into the Roller, and head off down the hill.

With Mint gone from her spot between us on the couch, Shelly lies herself down, using my lap as a pillow.

"Wake me up when the news comes on," she says. "Or if you hear anything about Scotty."

I nod as she folds herself into a fetal position and snuggles into my leg.

I'm tired now, too. All the adrenaline has gone, and the exertions of the last forty-eight hours are beginning to tell. My body aches and my eyes are heavy in the inadequate light of the living room.

Even Crisp looks a little fatigued. With the salt lamp illuminating one side of his face and casting the other side in shadow, he looks like the phantom of the opera, long legs folded in front of him on the easy chair, hands clasped in front of his face, index fingers wedged into his top lip. He isn't looking at us. He just stares straight ahead toward the window. He stays like that, still and silent, as my eyes get too heavy and I drift off to sleep.

* * *

I wake up to the theme tune of the NTV early morning news. It takes me a moment to get my bearings. The room is a little lighter now, sunlight beginning to break through a small gap in the heavy curtains and the scattered spots where they are worn through. The TV is bright to my unadjusted eyes as Toni-Marie begins to speak.

". . . another bizarre incident overnight as four people dressed in dark clothing and wearing balaclavas were caught emptying buckets of fish guts onto the steps of the Basilica."

"Hey, guys. We're on!" Mia yells, prompting Crisp and Mint to come bounding in from the other room, followed by Shelly, who I've only just realized is no longer balled up in my lap.

The arrival of Mint makes me suddenly conscious of my appearance. I straighten, wiping drool from the corner of my mouth with one hand and flattening out my hair with the other.

". . . are the scenes as the sun rises over the Basilica, which is now besieged by seagulls, attracted to the building by the smell of the fish guts."

"It worked!" Mia exclaims, and a buzz of excitement moves through the room. I can't help but smile as we watch a flock of the big, grey-white seabirds frantically pecking away at the steps while many more circle above in the morning sunshine.

"Well, obviously it's a great shame that somebody would do this," says the priest, who is now being interviewed at the scene. "The Basilica is a much-loved monument to the people of St. John's, regardless of faith, and this is a very upsetting act of vandalism . . ."

Before he can go any further, a large glob of gull poop splatters down the front of the priest's black cassock.

"Oh, dear," the field reporter says as the priest dabs at the poop with a handkerchief and someone passes a blue NTV umbrella to the reporter from off-camera. The umbrella open and held above them, the interview continues.

"Gulls," Crisp says, looking at each of us when we don't respond. "They keep calling them seagulls," he says, as though his point should have been obvious.

As the interview wraps, the reporter touches a finger to her ear.

"I'm just hearing that another clue has been found in this strange case. A piece of graffiti on the arch leading into the grounds of the Basilica. Can we? Yes, I think we have a shot of this."

The screen flicks to the view from another camera, trained on a section of the stone arch. Sprayed on it in green paint are two words:

Larus Can!

The room erupts with glee once again.

"Yes, b'y," Shelly says, sipping on a big mug of coffee. "How'd ya get the time to do that?"

"We have our ways," Crisp says, winking at Mint.

". . . joined now by Inspector Susan McGuinness. Inspector, the presence of this apparent calling card would seem to suggest that last night's events are linked to the act of vandalism at

Churchill Square on Saturday night. Does the RNC currently have any leads as to who might be behind these incidents?"

Inspector McGuinness is a surprisingly young-looking woman, I'd guess in her early thirties. Her pale, attractive face wears a stern expression, while her shock of long orange hair is pulled back into a tight ponytail.

"Well, we are certainly treating the presence of the graffiti as suspicious, though we can't assume any link between the two incidents. It could just as easily be a copycat, but investigations are ongoing."

"And I understand you already have a suspect in custody?"

It's as though someone turned the heat down ten degrees in the darkened living room.

"Scott . . ." Shelly whimpers.

"That is correct. One suspect was caught attempting to flee the scene when RNC officers interrupted the perpetrators in the midst of their act in the early hours of this morning."

"And is it true that the suspect in fact slipped on the fish guts he'd poured onto the steps and was knocked unconscious by the fall?"

"Oh, wow," Mint mutters. Crisp wears a pained expression.

"I can't speak to any details of the arrest, only that the suspect is currently in custody and being held for questioning."

"And can you give us any details about the suspect?"

"Not at this time. I can't comment on an ongoing investigation."

"Of course. Inspector McGuinness, thank you for your time."

The inspector nods and moves off-camera.

"Another bizarre crime here in St. John's last night and again a mysterious calling card. Once again, Larus 'can' cause mischief, property damage, and no little consternation. Back to you in the studio."

"What if he does say something?" I ask, to disapproving looks from the rest of the Gulls.

"He won't," Crisp says, firmly, before turning and leaving the room, Mia following close behind him.

"Come on," Shelly says. "Gotta get your cut of the winnings." She winks, trying to be her usual carefree self, but she cares about Scott, and I can see the strain in her eyes. She reaches out a hand and Mint follows suit, the two of them pulling me up off the couch.

"My word, what have they been feeding you?" Mint laughs, and we all spill into the kitchen, where the ever-present coffee pot is calling my name and Crisp is counting cash.

"'Ere ya go, gov'nah," he says in his fake English accent as I make my way over to the circular table. No Santa garb this time, though he is wearing a fetching new flat cap that I've never seen on him before. "Thirty grand." He slides six neat bundles of fifties across the table toward me. "Don't say I never do anything for ya."

I give him a thin smile. I think you'll find I was there, too. We all were.

The coffee is a little on the cool side, so I swig down half the contents of my mug and put it on the island before scooping up the bills. This is a serious amount of money, and in light of last night's shit show and Scott's arrest, I feel suddenly compelled to hide it away. Without saying a word, I leave the room and head upstairs, locating my suitcase in Mint's room and burying the bills underneath my crumpled clothing.

I leave the room and am about to head back downstairs when something makes me stop. I walk quietly over the creaking floorboards to the base of the narrow staircase that leads to the attic. I stare up for a moment at the door that Crisp keeps locked, and I wonder what it is—aside from our Steve Jobs ninja suits—that he's hiding away up there. I wonder if he locked the door.

I place my hand on the worn wooden banister, place one foot on the first step.

"Greggy-weggy-oxen-tail!" Shelly's yodelled call from downstairs makes me jump. "Wanna come for a smoke?" she yells.

I take my foot off the step, my hand off the banister.

"Yup, be right down."

* * *

"Wanna make out?" Shelly asks between puffs of her cigarette.

It's not the first time she's asked me, so her candour doesn't come as quite the shock it did the first time. Of course, I had a girlfriend back then, but I guess I don't now.

I consider it for a moment. Shelly isn't unattractive by any means. She's kinda cute with big, brown eyes and a smile with nice teeth—if a little too much gum.

I blow out smoke. She's just not my type, which is a shame. Why can't girls who are my type be so forthcoming?

"Nah, I'm good," I say.

"Okay." She shrugs, in no way perturbed.

They don't make girls like Shelly back in England. I don't think any girl over there has ever asked me if I wanted to make out. (Or "get off," as we Brits would say.) Shelly is a hippie, I guess. Raised by artsy parents. Liberal as all heck. Scott told me that she and Crisp had sex on the hood of the Roller in front of a big crowd of people at a music festival the summer past. Nothing would surprise me.

"Just want something to take my mind off this whole Scott situation," she says.

I take another puff of my cigarette. Well, her cigarette, technically. I hadn't bought a pack in a couple of weeks. In fact, I'd only bought three or four the whole time I'd been in Canada. Dana didn't care for smoking, and I'd tried not to be a smoker just to please her. But I like it. I'm addicted to it, I guess. I should really go and buy my own. It's not like I can't afford it now.

"Wanna walk up to the store?" I ask Shelly.

She nods and we make our way a little farther up Long's Hill toward the convenience store. She's started a second cigarette but didn't offer me one this time. Not that I would have taken it. I'm not much of a smoker-walker—especially when that walk is up Long's Hill. Still, Shelly seems to manage it just fine, distracting her brain with another rush of sweet nicotine.

"I'm sorry about Scott," I say.

"Me, too," she says, in as meek a voice as I've ever heard leave Shelly's lips. The mask is down and she's vulnerable.

"He's smart, y'know," I say, digging for some words of reassurance, perhaps trying to reassure myself. "He'll know what to say. Or what not to say."

She smokes and smiles and gives a nod.

Long's Hill Convenience is a tiny store sitting, as though on a pedestal, on the corner of Long's Hill and Murray, at the intersection that is also home to the Longest Traffic Light in the City. As we reach the red door, I wait for Shelly to take a couple more puffs of her cigarette. She tosses the butt to the ground and stamps it out with the sole of a quirky boot, and we head inside.

I'm grateful that we're the only customers, as the narrow store doesn't allow two people to pass comfortably. I walk up to the little counter space between the haphazard rows of colourful candies, chips, and scratch tickets, and address the cashier—a stocky, older man with an unkempt mess of grey hair and a scruffy beard.

"Twenty Canadian Light and a disposable lighter, please. One of the big ones."

"Colour?"

"Um. Red, please."

The man artfully turns to just where my brand of cigarettes are sitting on a grey shelf behind a black flap behind him, then to the lighters, plucking one out and laying it on the counter next to the cigarettes.

"Oh, and I guess I'll grab a case of India, too, please."

"Little early, isn't it?" the man growls.

"Little judgmental, aren't ya?" Shelly snaps back.

"ID," the man says.

"Okay," I say, pulling my battered British passport out of my jeans pocket and opening it to the photo page. I don't get asked for ID much here—it's maybe about a one in ten shot—but this fella just seems like he's out to make things as difficult as possible. He scowls at me before pointing to a tiny tent sign that's sitting on the counter.

"Driver's licence only, please," he says.

"Oh. I'm visiting from England, so I don't have a Newfoundland driver's licence as yet."

"No licence, no beer," he says flatly.

"Really?" I say, my blood beginning to boil.

"Geez, b'y, here ya go," Shelly says, tossing her licence onto the counter. "And give us a Lotto Max and a 6/49 with everything while yer at it."

The man eyes the ID and goes about printing out the lottery tickets.

"The lottery? Seriously?" I whisper to Shelly.

"You can never have too much money." She shrugs.

The man puts the lotto tickets on the counter and retrieves a big cardboard box of India Pale Ale from the back room.

He rings up the total, and I peel a couple of fifties from the clump of bills I'd stuffed into my pocket before I left the house. The burly cashier shakes his head, and I resolve to buy myself a sensible wallet to carry around all this cash.

"Well, he was a delight," I say as we get outside, the little bell above the door signalling our return to the fresh St. John's morning. "First time I've been ID'd in a while."

"It's those boyish British good looks," Shelly says. "You sure you don't wanna make out?"

I look down at the box of beer, which we are carrying between us, each with a hand inside the little handle-holes on either side of the box. As is the tradition.

"It'd be a little awkward at the moment, wouldn't it?" I say.

"It's only as awkward as you make it," she jokes. "Down here, luh," she says, pulling me by the beer box down a narrow alley between two colourful houses.

"Where are we going?"

"You'll see," she says, leading me to a gate at the back of a house and unlatching it.

"Wait," I say, pulling back on my side of the box. "Who lives here?"

"I dunno," Shelly says. "Come on wit ya."

She pulls me with surprising force into an overgrown yard and stomps around to the other side of the house, where the fence has long since given up the fight to the raging Atlantic winds and laid itself down to rest, the grass and the weeds curling themselves around it and holding it flat to the ground.

We tromp over the fence and squeeze between some old trees before emerging on the other side and stopping dead in our tracks.

"Whoa," I say, seeing now why Shelly has brought me here. We stand at the top of a sheer ten-foot drop, metal ribs poking out through the worn surface of the crumbling concrete wall below. Beyond, downtown St. John's unfurls in the mid-morning sunshine. Its colourful buildings are awkwardly arranged, lending it the feel of some outrageously imaginative toy town. The hodgepodge of buildings is interspersed with green bursts of mature trees—themselves as old as the tales told by the sailors that float in and out of the city's weathered pubs. Beyond, a fishing boat makes its way in through the Narrows, toward the ever-busy harbour, glinting in the same sun that accentuates the rocky contours of Signal Hill and Cape Spear. Cabot Tower is but a dot atop the hill.

"Nice view."

"I love it up here," Shelly says. We place the box of beer down, and Shelly sits herself on the edge of the decaying wall, hanging her legs over the side as though it were nothing. She pats the decaying concrete beside her, beckoning me to join her, and I approach the edge cautiously, lowering myself to sit, trying not to look down.

"Scott and I would sit here for hours when we were kids," she says. "Just fooling around and talking, watching the boats come in and out.

"Sittin' on the dock of a bay," I say.

"Watchin' the tides roll away," Shelly sings, rather well. We chuckle.

I reach back and grab one of the beer box's hand holes, dragging it toward us, bottles clinking. I tear open the box and pull out two room-temperature beers, twisting off the caps and handing one to Shelly. We "cheers" one another and take a drink.

"How long have you known Scott?" I ask as Shelly lights up a cigarette.

"Since we were four or five," she says. "We grew up on the same street, went to the same school. Coupla townies," she says in an exaggerated accent.

"Was he always so . . ."

I search for the right words. Scott's a hard person to describe. She gets it.

"He was a quiet kid," she says. "Fadder wasn't around. Mudder wasn't up to much. Rumour was he was adopted or a foster kid or summin. He'd never talk about it, though."

I've never seen Shelly like this—sans hula hoop and without the performing arts. I can tell she's worried about her friend.

"I'm sure he'll be fine," I say, not sure if I really believe myself. We drink and I ponder the thought for a moment. What will happen? Is the jig up?

"I mean, it's only a bit of vandalism, at the end of the day," I say, trying to talk myself through it as much as anything. "Or, I dunno, 'illegal dumping' or something? Surely that's just a misdemeanour or whatever they call it." I take another swig of lukewarm beer. "Of course, they saw Crispin's tag. 'Larus Can.' I suppose that links him—us—to the Churchill Square, um, incident. But if they didn't see anything, then they can't prove anything, right?"

Shelly nods vacantly.

"And hey," I say. "If we do need to bail him out, it's not like we don't have the money."

"Do you think we should get out?" Shelly asks, seeming a little scared for the first time since I've known her. "I mean, go to the police, or just, I dunno, leave. Leave the house, go get an apartment someplace until the heat cools a little?"

"Shelly Lambert, are you asking me to move in together?"

We laugh and she punches me on the arm and I pretend like it didn't hurt.

"He's manipulative, you know," Shelly says.

"Who, Crisp?" I ask, not really needing to. Shelly nods.

"He has a way of pulling people into him and, well, then it gets hard to get out from under him."

I finish my beer way quicker than I intended. I put the empty back in the box and pull out another, gesturing to see if Shelly wants a second. She shakes her head no.

I twist off the cap and take a swig.

"From what I hear, you've been under him on more than one occasion," I say, trying to lighten the mood. I time it just as

Shelly is taking a swig from her beer bottle, and she spits beer out over the wall.

"Frigger," she says, wiping her mouth with the back of her hand.

"So, what's the deal there? You guys in an open relationship?"

"It's all much looser than that," she says, rolling her eyes.

"He seems to have taken up with young Mia," I say.

"Just the latest in a long line," she says, sounding tired.

We sit in silence for a couple of minutes while Shelly finishes her cigarette.

"What's the deal with Mint?" I finally find the nerve to ask the question that's been on my mind the whole time.

"What's your deal with Mint?" Shelly replies with a smirk, and I feel my face reddening.

"I like her." I shrug. "Like, really like her."

Shelly smiles. "I know." She takes a long swig from her bottle. "I dunno what to tell ya. She's great. Beautiful, of course. But I've known her almost two years and I've yet to see her get involved with anybody."

"Really?"

"Yeah. Not like plenty of people haven't had a crack, y'know, but . . ." She pauses. "She seems to be saving herself for somebody. Maybe it's you, Gregory Masters!" she says, the amateur dramatics returning as she puts on a retro movie star accent and gives me a playful push.

I steady myself. I'm beginning to feel the effects of the day drinking, and I am sitting at the top of a sheer ten-foot drop.

"Maybe it's someone back in the US," I suggest. "When did she come here?"

"The start of the last school term. She's studying psych at MUN. I met her in the States the year before, when I was an exchange student down there."

"I didn't know you were a student."

"Meh, it didn't stick. Made a good friend, though."

We drink some more, both light up a cigarette.

"Who do you think is behind all this?" I ask.

"I dunno," Shelly says. "Gotta be someone with lotsa money," she says—and suddenly something dawns on me.

"Jesus, what about that missing billionaire fella? The Finatech guy."

Shelly's eyes get wide.

"Jackson Whatsisname?" she says, taking a long drag of her Marlboro.

"Yeah. I mean, he's missing, right? And he'd have the money to do whatever he wanted."

"Sure, but why would he want to mess with a bunch of nobodies like us?" Shelly asks. "Sorry—no offence intended."

"None taken," I say. "I have no idea. It might be something worth mentioning to the gang, though."

* * *

We're half in the bag when we get back to the house. It's mid-afternoon and I shouldn't be this buzzed, but the beer will taste even better once it's cool, and the cigarettes are jiving beautifully. The place is quiet when we walk in, but we're not. Shelly's been teaching me old Newfoundland folk songs—apparently she's a walking jukebox full of them—and I've been trying to sing along on the walk home.

"Sods and rinds to cover your flake?" I repeat back to her as we barrel in through the door.

"Cake and tea for supper!" Shelly booms, trying to move me onto the next line. "You should like that. Isn't that what you Brits live on? Cake and tea!" She delivers the last part in her most exaggerated "Queen's English."

"I don't even know where that comes from. Sometimes we drink tea. Sometimes we drink coffee. Sometimes we drink . . . juice or pop. Newfoundlanders are way more obsessed with tea, if you ask me."

"I think he doth protesteth too much!"

We walk down the hallway to the kitchen. It's eerily quiet.

"Hello? Yoo hoo!" Shelly yells, still in Queen mode. We load the remaining few bottles noisily into the fridge and grab a couple of cold ones, twisting off the caps and cheersing once again.

"Where the frig is everyone?" Shelly asks.

"Dunno," I say. That seems hilariously funny, and we both break down in a fit of laughter.

"You sure you don't wanna make out?" Shelly asks. There's a different expression on her face now. The jokey passivity is gone and there's a vulnerability in her eyes. The mid-afternoon sun sends beams through the kitchen window, catching on her strawberry hair as she tucks a loose lock behind her ear. I don't know if it's the beer goggles, but I'm tempted now. I move closer.

"Afternoon, fellow Gulls." Crispin gives us a start, and we back away from one another.

"Hey!" we say in unison, trying—and failing—to look cool.

Crisp seems disinterested, bending between us and taking what appears to be a mason jar full of sludge out of the fridge. He removes the lid, grabs a butter knife from the utensil drawer, gives the thick, muddy solution a stir, and promptly begins to drink it.

"Where were you guys?" he asks.

We begin to talk at the same time.

"We went to the store . . ." I stutter.

"Just hanging at the lookout . . ." Shelly blurts.

Our awkwardness seems to pass Crisp by like a seagull on its way to the dump. His mind is elsewhere. We don't really concern him.

He nods vacantly.

"Cool."

We all sip from our beverages in silence for a moment, and I wonder where he came from. My guess is upstairs, though the stairs tend to creak a warning if anyone is coming down them—and Crisp tends to come down them in a hurry.

"Wanna see the next riddle?" he asks, draining the last remnants of his . . . smoothie?

"Yeah."

"Sure."

We say it in unison once again.

Crisp rinses the mason jar in the sink, wipes his mouth with a napkin, and gestures for us to follow him to the living room.

* * *

THESE SPACES ARE A BLOT ON THE LANDSCAPE.
POKE OUT THEIR GREEN EYES OF GREED.
HAVE THEM LOOK OUT IN FLAMING ENVY.
OVER THE HOUSES, THE HARBOUR, THE SEAS.

"I don't get it," Shelly says, slurring slightly. "How can a space be a blot on the landscape?"

"How can a space have eyes?" I ask, finishing what may be my fifth or sixth beer and laying the empty down on the coffee table.

Crisp sits in his trademark thinking position, hunched over, bony elbows resting on long legs, forefingers pointing into his upper lip.

"Have them look out in flaming envy," he reads aloud. "Over the houses, the harbour, the seas."

"Hey," Mint says as she walks into the living room.

Shelly and I greet in harmony once again.

"Hello, Mint," Crisp says after a beat, not looking up from the piece of paper with the Copperplate writing that sits on the coffee table.

"What are you guys doing?" she asks, seating herself on the easy chair.

"Solving riddles," I say.

"Or trying to, at least," Shelly adds.

"So, we're talking about a space that overlooks the harbour," Crisp says, trying to refocus the growing group.

Mint leans in, studying the words.

"A space," she repeats. "Like maybe a park or a football field?"

"With green eyes?" Crisp asks.

"Maybe that's trees or grass or something," Shelly offers, sipping from the beer she's been nursing since we came in.

"Oh, yeah, that makes sense," Mint says.

I look at her. She seems a little different today. A little flustered, somehow. Where did she come from? I didn't hear the door.

"How can you poke out a tree?" Mia asks as she enters the room. Her hair is still damp from a recent shower.

"Maybe strip off all its leaves?" I offer, but it's mainly the beer talking.

"None of this makes any sense," Shelly decides.

"Well, if everyone else is drinking," Mia says, heading off to the kitchen.

"I'll have another," Shelly shouts.

"Me, too," I say.

"Crisp?" Mia asks as she makes her way down the hallway.

"Not for me, thanks," he says. "Is anybody hungry?" he asks, pulling his attention from the note on the coffee table. "Why don't we get pizza? Let's get pizza."

* * *

The afternoon is whiled away with pizza, beer, and cigarettes. The booze lifts the mood somewhat, but the hole where Scott should be looms large as we wait for the NTV evening news to see if there are any updates on the one Gull missing from our flock.

We're a little disappointed when Toni-Marie only gives the incident a cursory mention, saying that one man in his twenties was detained and is being held for questioning, along with some brief footage of people in coveralls mopping bird poop off the steps of the Basilica.

A larger segment is devoted to Jackson Lorde, his image beamed over Toni-Marie's shoulder. His greying hair is long, pulled back in a ponytail, and he has a scruffy beard.

"A new twist in the story of missing billionaire tech businessman Jackson Lorde today as police have revealed that large withdrawals of money have been made from bank accounts in the MUN alumni's name—accounts they are saying are difficult to trace."

They cut to a press conference, where Inspector Susan McGuinness is addressing a gaggle of reporters.

"She's really got her hands full," Mint says.

"See? They have bigger fish to fry than our friend Scott," Crispin says. "A guy like that goes missing—a guy with money—you can bet they're gonna put all their resources into finding him."

"It is pretty weird, though," Shelly says.

"Maybe he just wanted to disappear. He has enough money. He could have bought himself a new identity," I suggest.

"Or a private island," Mia says.

"He already has a private island," Crisp says. The gang turns to look at him. "Bear Island. It's up around Gros Morne. It's not very big, but he owns the whole thing."

We all wait for Crisp to explain how he knows this.

"I saw it on the news that time. When Finatech got a bunch of funding or something. That's how Jackson Lorde celebrated—by buying an island."

"Must be nice," Shelly says, looking at me over the large mug of steaming tea that she switched to when the day drinking started not to be fun anymore.

"You don't think Jackson Lorde could be funding our dares, do you?" I ask.

Crisp eyes me intently.

"I mean, he'd have the money, of course. Maybe he got bored of being a billionaire with a private island and decided to have some slightly disturbed fun."

Crisp just continues to stare with a slight sneer on his face.

"Or maybe he doesn't like Wilfred Churchill or the Catholic Church," Mia says.

"Winston," I correct reflexively.

"Kinda makes sense that someone who doesn't like our English overlords would be the same person who doesn't care for the Church," Shelly suggests.

"But why us?" Crisp eventually speaks. We look around at one another.

"Well, for someone who doesn't like the English, he's sure giving a lot of cash money to Gregory here," Shelly says with a wink.

"Why not us?" I ask. "A bunch of kids going nowhere with plenty of time on our hands. No offence." The Gulls shrug.

"None taken," Shelly says, pretending to wipe tears from her cheeks.

"We're all pretty lost in the world," I say. "All pretty liberal. Some more than others." I pat Shelly on the shoulder, and she nods in agreement. "Why not us?"

Crisp smiles.

"Why not, indeed," he says.

* * *

It's late when Scott comes traipsing through the door, and Shelly rushes out to meet him.

"Scotty, is that you? Oh, my dear, come on in," she says, ever the mother hen. She closes the door to the cool night and wraps her friend in a bear hug.

The rest of the Gulls gather in the hallway.

"Now, my love," Shelly says. "The golden question: tea or beer?"

"Tea," Scott manages to say, his expression glum. He's still wearing the Steve Jobs ninja outfit, save for the balaclava, which doesn't seem to have made it home with him. He's carrying a few personal effects in a clear plastic bag, and the vague odour of rotten fish hangs in the air. "With a whiskey on the side," he mutters.

"On it," Shelly says. "You go on up and get a shower and, I dunno, burn those clothes? I'll fix you some tea. And a whiskey."

* * *

Out in the back yard, the Gulls huddle around the firepit as Crisp tosses Scott's black pants into the fire.

"I guess we'll have to take another run over to Mark's," he murmurs.

Scott knocks back the second shot of whiskey that Shelly just brought him and goes back to sipping his tea, orange flames dancing in his jam jar–bottom glasses.

All the Gulls sit around the firepit. I'm on an old fold-out canvas camping chair with a mesh cupholder in the arm for my beer. Shelly is wedged into something similar because the "good chairs"—slightly faded orange recliners from Canadian Tire—have been reserved for the recuperating Scott and Our Fearless Leader. Mint and Mia have found an old blanket and are sitting together on it on the ground.

We sit in silence for a while until someone finally plucks up the courage to ask the question that's on everyone's lips.

"So, what did the cops ask ya?" Mia is the one to break the ice.

Scott sips tea, stares into the orange flames.

"The same stuff. Over and over again." The gang waits for him to elaborate. He takes another couple of sips from his floral teacup before proceeding. "Who were you with?" he begins, putting on a subtle impersonation of the interrogating officer, with a serious face and a gruff voice. "Where'd you get the fish guts? Were you involved with the Churchill Square incident? Who were you with? Where are they now?"

"And what did you tell them?" Crisp asks.

Scott turns his head to look Crisp square in the eye, flames still flickering in his glasses.

"Nudding," he says emphatically.

"Nothing at all?" Mint asks.

"I told 'em I was employing my right to remain silent under section seven of the Canadian Charter of Rights and Freedoms," he says, turning back to the fire. "Once twenty-four hours was up, they let me go."

"That easy?" Crisp says.

Scott shrugs.

"Nah, they'll be sniffing around again," I suggest.

"Meh. Bit of illegal dumping. Vandalism. Whatever. They'll probably just stick ya with a fine," Shelly says.

"Sounds like you speak from experience," I say.

"Misspent youth," Shelly replies with a comedic thousand-yard stare.

Scott doesn't appear to be seeing the funny side just yet.

"We got another clue," Crisp says.

"No more clues," Scott replies, almost cutting Crisp off.

"Come on, Scotty. Think about the money. And don't tell me you're not having fun!"

"Fun?" Scott snaps. "This is all just one big joke to you, isn't it, Crispin? Well, you weren't the one locked up and getting interrogated for the last twenty-four hours."

"You want another whiskey?" Shelly asks.

"Yes, please," Scott replies.

Shelly stands, summoning the courage to stand up to Crisp. For all her confidence, she finds it hard to question him.

"Maybe Scott's right," she says. "I mean, what if the police trace the money or something?"

"They're probably unmarked bills," Crisp replies.

"Or what if whoever's doing this is dangerous? What if they want—"

"We're earning the money, Shelly," Crisp says. "By doing the dares. Do the dare, get cash. Don't, and we can all walk away. Quid pro quo. Do or don't. It's a simple business transaction."

"And what about that red friggin' time machine out there?" Shelly continues unperturbed.

"It's a DeLorean," Mia says.

"Yeah, a rare, red DeLorean. What if they saw the car?"

"They didn't see the car," Scott says. "Either car. Never got a good look at 'em in the dark. Heard 'em talking about it."

"Good ol' RNC." Crisp smirks. "There ya go! They got nothing on us. There's no need to worry."

"Well, they know I was there, and I didn't get the impression they were planning to leave me be," Scott says. "So, I'm out."

Crisp lets that hang.

"Anyone else want a drink?" Shelly asks.

We all answer in the affirmative and sit in silence as

Shelly fetches the drinks, Mint hopping up to help her. When they return, we sip away and watch the flames, reflecting on our situation.

We are making lots of money. Having such a close brush with the cops did feel exhilarating. It does seem like we got away with it.

It is kinda fun.

"These spaces are a blot on the landscape." Crisp breaks the silence, all Gulls turning in his direction. He's holding the piece of paper from the briefcase, reading the words aloud.

Mia stands and walks over to where Crisp is sitting. She leans in behind him, her hands resting on his chest.

"Poke out their green eyes of greed," she says, reading the second line of the riddle.

Mint sits up on her blanket, legs crossed, torso long, and says the next line from memory.

"Have them look out in flaming envy."

I take a long swig of my beer, let out a sigh, and read the last line.

"Over the houses, the harbour, the seas," I say. I've committed the riddle to memory, too. It's all I've been thinking about.

Scott and Shelly look at each other, and we wait for their response.

"It's the Rooms," Scott says flatly.

"What?" Crisp asks.

"It's the Rooms," Scott repeats. "'These spaces.' What's another word for spaces? Rooms. And that thing about their green eyes looking over the harbour. They got those big green windows, don't they?"

"Genius," Crisp says. "Genius!" He's up from his orange recliner, arms outstretched like wings. "This is why we need you, Scotty."

"I'm out," Scott says quietly, shaking his head.

"This ingenuity. This lateral thinking. This God-given ability to see that which others are blind to!"

"I'm out," Scott repeats with a little more conviction this time.

"This is why you're a Gull," Crisp continues on regardless.

"I'm not a Gull!" Scott stands up. He's shouting now, and it's like the whole night pauses to listen. "Okay? None of you are 'Gulls.' We're people. Young people that are getting messed with by some crazy person with more money than morals. I mean, who does this? Who makes other people do crazy things just because they have the power to?"

"No one's making anyone do anything," Mia says.

"Really, Mia? You really don't think that's exactly what's happening?"

Mia looks to Crisp and then to Mint, who tries to find anywhere to look but at any of us.

"Everyone here is here because they want to be," Crisp says.

"Yeah?" Scott says.

Crisp shrugs and nods.

"Well, I don't want to be anymore," Scott says, and as though to punctuate the point, he picks up the shot glass and whips it into the fire. He decides to spare the teacup the same fate and marches back toward the house with it.

Crisp looks pained.

"Shelly, was that my St. John's Maple Leafs shot glass?" he asks.

Shelly just lets out an exasperated sigh and follows Scott into the house.

"That was a collector's item," Crisp says, shoulders slumped, staring into the flames.

8

Jane and Her Giant Peach

"Where's he been staying?" I ask, having to raise my voice a little above the indie music blasting out of a nearby speaker.

"His brother's place," Shelly replies. "But they don't get along at all."

"You think he'll show?" I ask. She looks down at her phone and the thread of texts she's been sharing with Scott.

"I hope so."

"Me, too," I say, taking a swig of India Pale Ale from the bottle and taking a look around the bar, largely to avoid the temptation of taking another peek at Shelly's breasts, which, in my defence, are very much intentionally on display, all bound up in leather and forced against gravity's wishes into an eye-catching cleavage.

Not that my eyes are in any less jeopardy of catching sight of a boob or bum elsewhere in the room.

"So, explain this to me again."

"What, burlesque?" Shelly says vacantly as she plays with her phone.

"Yeah. It's not stripping, but it's not exactly a West End musical, right?"

Shelly smiles, placing a hand on my thigh.

"Oh, darling. It is whatever you think it is." She rubs my leg in such a way that, if it were anyone else but Shelly doing it, I would take as a sure sign we're heading to a bathroom stall for a quickie any minute.

In reality she's more concerned with her phone. Waiting for the three little dots to pulsate, letting her know that her friend Scott is typing a reply.

"Don'tcha have burlesque in Great Brittania, hun?"

"Not where I grew up. I mean, I heard about *The Rocky Horror Picture Show*, but I never saw it. To me, Richard O'Brien was just the creepy host of *The Crystal Maze*, randomly playing the harmonica."

"I have no idea what you're talking about, but I'm gonna Google it," Shelly says. She goes back to her phone, and I go back to people-watching.

It seems like most of the cast of *Jane and Her Giant Peach* have gathered in the bar area of the Hall—the creative centre of downtown St. John's. The room is a confusion of men dressed like women and women dressed like men. There are fishnet stockings, there is extravagant makeup, there is plenty of flesh, and even more leather. There's a spider, a worm, and a centipede. I guess there is some degree of reference to the source material.

These colourful characters are mixed in with a varied crowd of spectators, ranging from your standard St. John's hipsters with their man buns and Blundstone boots, to older folks with a few wrinkles on their face but a glint in their eye. I watch one older lady as she quaffs wine and flirts it up with a couple of younger fellas while still managing to look classy. I think about what it must be like to have a person like that as a mother, and suddenly Shelly makes a little more sense. Such freedom.

"He's coming!" Shelly yells, jumping up from her seat, breasts wobbling.

"Who's coming?" Crisp asks, approaching the table with Mia and a round of drinks.

"Scotty Too Hotty!" Shelly yells, doing a little dance number that a passing hipster guy joins in with for a couple of beats.

"Good." Crisp smiles, initiating a "cheers" around the table. Our glasses and bottles clink and we drink.

"Is Mint coming?" I ask.

"That depends on you," Shelly says, literally cupping my actual balls and giving them a jiggle. Such freedom.

"She'll be here," Crisp says with a wink.

* * *

The show itself is a colourful spectacle in every sense of those two words. Loosely based on the Roald Dahl book of a similar name, the basic premise seems to be that Shelly's character—Jane—has a constantly growing, out-of-control rear end, out of which pops a strange selection of anthropomorphic and pretty androgynous bugs. In this version of the story, they all go off to Las Vegas rather than New York City, where they establish the titular burlesque show and become the warm-up act for Britney Spears. All of this happens after Jane's parents are killed by a "giant horn," of course.

It's a bit of a different flavour from the pantomimes I used to attend at the local church as a kid, but it's a laugh nonetheless—and the crowd is very much into it. Shelly steals the show with her ever-increasing orange foam butt and larger-than-life personality.

In another twist from the church pantos, the audience is allowed to drink throughout the performance, and—at our table, at least—the drinks are flowing. By the intermission I'm "half in the bag," as my Newfoundland friends would say. "Feeling no pain" is another one, though that always makes me think of the pain I will be feeling in the morning, or the afternoon, or whenever I wake up from what looks set to be a real marathon of a party.

By eleven that's proving to be the case. The Hall is now a dance club, loud music pumping from the speaker system, the chairs and tables cleared to the side of the floor, which heaves with gyrating bodies. It's warm and sweaty and everyone is close. Some are dressed in leather, a couple are still dressed as part-insect, most are barely dressed at all.

As the night becomes a haze of heat and energy, most of these people fall away and I dance largely on my own. I catch glimpses of my new-found friends—my gang, the Gulls—in and out of the throng. A flash of Crisp's smiling face here, a pinch on my butt from Shelly there. Mia is in full "club mode," her body all fun, her face still serious, long, dark locks tossed hither and thither, tickling the faces of the interested boys and girls. Even Scott, who rolled up just before the show got started, has let down his guard, no doubt with the help of a few India Pale Ales and a few whiskey chasers.

I'm here and yet I'm nowhere. A thousand miles from home and a thousand miles from knowing where "home" even is anymore. I'm surrounded by bodies, but I'm an island, they the sea. I feel so alone.

I think about Mint. I haven't seen her, and it's after twelve now. I text her a couple of times on the way back from bathroom visits, but I get no reply. At one point I yell into Crisp's ear, drawing out the vowels in the hope he will make sense of me above the noise and in spite of the booze.

"Where's Mint?"

He gives me a wink.

"Soon!" he yells into my ear, and I go back to dancing.

When I first clock her, she's with him. It's around one and they're at my six, standing near the entrance where the crowd is thinnest. They're at a pedestal table, squeezed into a corner. They look close, talking into one another's ears.

Are they laughing or do they look serious?

I watch, getting knocked around by the dancing crowd. Crisp pushes one of Mint's dreads gently from her cheek. Their faces are almost touching.

Are they going to kiss?

At the vital moment, a tall, skinny, topless man with sequined pants and a long set of antennae blocks my view. I duck left and then right, trying to see what's going on over by the entrance, but he misinterprets this as a dance move and begins to shake his ass a little too close for comfort.

"Excuse me," I say, easing him aside and squeezing myself out from the crowd.

By the time I catch sight of Crisp and Mint again, they are pulling apart.

Did they kiss? Did I miss it?

They don't catch sight of me until I'm right upon them. I clatter my beer bottle down on the table.

"Hey," I say.

"Hi, Greg," Mint says. I'm expecting them to be sheepish, but they both look completely calm. Mint even seems a little flirty, reaching out her hand and taking mine, rubbing a thumb gently back and forth.

I'm instantly calmed and quite happy to stay that way with her hand in mine. The feeling in this inebriated, uninhibited state is electric.

She takes in a sharp breath and leans forward onto the table, her face coming closer to mine. She must be feeling the energy, too.

Crisp just stands there, smiling, a beer in one hand.

"I hear you've been asking about me," Mint says.

She seems different. Almost hypnotized. Maybe I'm just imagining it.

"Is that what you heard?" I ask.

"Uh huh," she says, leaning in closer, her forehead touching mine, her dreadlocks falling against my shoulders. She takes another sharp breath, her big, brown eyes looking right into mine. Our noses make contact. There's no doubt now.

She's into it.

I touch a hand to her cheek and pass a thumb over her soft, plump lips. She responds by biting down on my thumb, hard enough that—if I wasn't a half-dozen beers and just as many shooters in—might have caused me to retreat. No retreat here. I take the hint and move my hand to her cheek.

Then we kiss.

It's an immediately deep, passionate kiss, the kind you only get when there's fire raging below it. She breathes deep and heavy, clutching my head, kissing harder, deeper.

Just as the room begins to spin, she pulls back, her nails digging hard into my shoulders.

I'm too drunk to really understand what's happening, too drunk to really appreciate the moment I've been dreaming of for the past few weeks. As Mint kisses me softly on the cheek, I try to breathe, try to get my bearings. As I get a little more oxygen to my brain, the room stops spinning and I gather myself a little.

"Come on," Mint says. "Let's dance."

And we dance. All of us dance. Me, Mint, the other Gulls. Boys dance with girls, girls dance with boys, boys dance with boys, and girls dance with girls. The beers flow and the party rages.

My eyes never move far from the flowing form of Mint Bonucci, her toned thighs shining in the lights below a green miniskirt, a white wifebeater doing little to hide what's going on beneath. Braless and gyrating, she's a goddess on the floor—her dreadlocks punctuating the look as they whip through the stifling air.

* * *

The air outside is sweet relief—cool and crisp after the stifling atmosphere of the Hall. It's dark out and quiet, save for the ringing in my ears and the muffled chatter of those spilling out into what remains of the night. Cigarettes are smoked, and the few remaining characters drift away in blue and white taxicabs, leaving only the Gulls, become six again, to figure out our next move.

"Oh, we should watch the sunrise," Shelly suggests.

"Capital idea," Crisp says, swigging from a beer bottle he's brought with him. "Let's go!"

With that, Crisp strides off at pace, and the rest of the Gulls follow. We march down a block to Water Street, the Alt Hotel emerging before us like a big, black Lego brick, its sleek, modern design providing a stark contrast to the heritage buildings that surround it.

"Now, me ducky, where exactly are we going?" Shelly asks. "Because I can't be walkin' far in these shoes."

Crisp heaves his beer bottle toward the harbourfront, the sound of it shattering echoing around an empty downtown.

"Jesus," Scott mutters, his post-arrest skittishness rising up again and penetrating the warm, comforting blanket of booze.

Crisp strides over to Shelly, picking her up into a fireman's lift, and goes about removing her shoes as she screams and giggles, pretending to fight him off.

"Let's get rid of these complicated, strappy foot-vises, shall we?" he says.

Mia and Mint are in raptures. Scott and I just stand back and take in the scene.

"Because we have a hill to climb," Crisp says, placing a now-barefoot Shelly back onto the ground. "Would you like me to carry these, or . . . ?"

Shelly grabs the shoes back from him and gives him a playful shove.

"Wait. What hill?" I ask.

"What hill?" Crisp repeats. "*The* hill, Gregory," he says, arms wide. As he backs away, I squint to see the little, square shape of an illuminated Cabot Tower atop Signal Hill beyond him.

"Oh, frig," Shelly says. "We're not walkin' all the way up there, are we?"

"Perfect place to see the sunrise," Crisp yells into the night, marching ahead.

"Come on," Mint says, wrapping one arm around Shelly and the other around Mia. "It'll be fun," she says, guiding the two forward and shooting Scott and me the cutest grin over her shoulder—one that causes the small dimple on her left cheek to reveal itself and pulls me forward almost against my will.

I'm falling.

"C'mon," I say, tapping Scott on the shoulder, and he's the last to fall in line.

* * *

I've never walked up Signal Hill before, and it's steep. Like, "Oh my God, my lungs are about to explode" steep. But Crisp is leading the charge, and we are pulled in his wake like so many fish caught in the nets of one of the big fishing boats that line the harbour. The boats' silhouettes are strange against the night sky—all awkward shapes and spiny cranes reaching up at the beaming moon.

Beyond the harbour, we sink momentarily into the Battery with its hodgepodge of colourful houses placed at random angles amid the hilly landscape. After that it's all uphill. Oh, sure, it starts tamely enough, with a tolerable climb past the last of the houses that become scarcer the higher you get, like climbers on the foothills of Everest, brave to a point but then left to look up in wonder at what might have been.

As the tilted cube of the Johnson Geo Centre comes into sight, climbers are offered some reprieve as the ground levels out for a short stretch.

"Ever been to the Geo Centre?" Shelly asks me.

"I haven't."

"You should check 'er out. It's not just that wonky building. Most of it's underground."

"They've got the entire solar system under there," Mia says.

"Wow. Sounds cool," I say.

"Nah. The solar system isn't under there," Crisp says. "It's up there!" he shouts, quickening his pace even as the hill begins to steepen once again.

The Gulls screech, and we follow our fearless leader up the steepest part of Signal Hill.

My legs burn. It feels like I'm walking in mud as we wind our way up between the craggy rocks and punkish shrubs, Cabot Tower revealing itself above us.

Crisp turns tour guide, blurting out facts about the hill and its quirky little tower—a building that earns the title "tower" more from the boost of its breathtakingly lofty perch than it does from the size of the building itself.

"That's where Marconi sent the first transatlantic radio message," Crisp regales. I've heard the story a number of times already. When you're a Brit in Newfoundland, Marconi is maybe the second subject to come up after tea. "On the twelfth of December, 1901." He sees the look on my face, which I can't disguise amid the fatigue of the hill climb and the waning effects of alcohol. "But you know that already," he says. "This way."

He leads us away from Cabot Tower along a narrow trail. In the easing darkness I can just about make out a hump of land reaching out into the sea that looks something like the head of the Loch Ness monster.

"Did you also know that this was the site of the final battle of the Seven Years War?" Crisp barks from the front of the line as we crunch along the gravel trail. "In 1762, the Battle of Signal Hill raged on these shores until the French surrendered to. . . .

Anyone?" He turns like a teacher speaking to his class. "Anyone?" he repeats.

"Probably the British?" I say it like a question.

Crisp claps his hands together, the crack echoing off the rocky hills. "Atta boy!" he shouts. "The good ol' Brits, under the command of Colonel William Amherst, who gave Signal Hill its name."

"That explains Newfoundlanders' fascination with tea and cookies," Mint says.

"Tea and biscuits," Shelly corrects in her strikingly accurate impersonation of the Queen.

"Well, we were a British colony until 1949," Scott drones. He's at the back of the queue along with Mia, who seems to be feeling the effects of the hill climb and the alcohol most.

"Just down here," Crisp says, weaving his way down a rocky embankment and disappearing between some tall shrubs.

"Yes, b'y," Shelly protests, stopping to look down at her bare feet, but before she can protest any further, Scott gathers her up like a knight would his princess and carries her down the embankment.

"After you," I say to Mint.

"Yeah, right," she replies. "You go first. That way, if I fall, you can catch me."

"Sounds good to me," I say, instantly feeling like a nerd for doing so.

"You okay?" Mint asks Mia as she catches up. She looks like death warmed over, noticeably pale even in the struggling light.

"Mmm," she responds without prising open her lips, lest a torrent of vomit be released.

"Okay," Mint says, unconvinced. She signals for me to lead the way and I'm off, hopping from rock to rock down the embankment before ducking between the shrubs and emerging with a few scratches on the other side.

"Oh, wow." Crisp has led us to a lookout, beyond which is a sheer drop to the ocean. Suddenly, there's a whipping wind I hadn't noticed before, and I can hear waves crashing against rocks far below. It's as though the few shrubs had created a veil, and now we are exposed to the elements—to the sprawling might of the North Atlantic Ocean.

"Hey, b'ys!" Crisp yells. "Check out me gun!"

Crisp is straddling a large, long-defunct cannon, and I can't help but snigger. Even Scott cracks a smile.

"Well, would you look at the size of that?" Shelly says. Because of course she does. "Mind if I hops on for a ride?"

"If you think you can spread your legs that wide," Crisp jokes.

"You knows me, me ducky," Shelly shouts as she tiptoes her way over. "If there's one thing I'm good at, it's spreadin' me legs!"

"Ain't that the truth," Scott says. He's joking, but he isn't.

Out over the water, dark blue gives way to deep orange, and the peeking sun tickles the tops of the waves, laying out a yellow carpet that leads all the way to the horizon.

Here, where the sun rises first in North America, I might as well be on the edge of the world.

"Look! You can see jolly old England over there!" Shelly yells, legs akimbo as she rides the cannon like a bucking bronco. "Hello, motherland! Is Her Royal Majesty Queen Lizzy available for a spot of tea?"

"Jesus, Shelly," Scott says. He's irritated. I think he'd like to tame her.

"Oh, don't worry," Shelly shouts. "It's four hours later over there. We won't wake her!"

"Three and a half," I say to no one.

"Would somebody be willing to give up their jacket?" I hear Mint ask from behind us. I turn to see her emerging from the shrubs with her arm around a pathetic-looking Mia, who is hunched over, a hand to her forehead. She's visibly shaking, and I realize that it is pretty chilly with the ocean breeze. Between my denim jacket and my beer jacket, I hadn't really noticed.

"Oh, yeah," I say. "She can take mine." I remove the one jacket I'm able to and help Mint wrap it around her. We find an appropriately flat rock for her, and she sits, arms folded on her knees as a pillow for her head.

"Thanks," Mint says, the rising sun catching in her eyes.

I'm falling.

"Is she gonna be okay?" I ask.

"She'll be fine. She, uh, got plenty up back there behind the bushes."

"Ah."

"Yeah, so, watch your step on your way out."

"Thanks for the tip."

She smiles that stunning smile and instantly relegates anything the sun and the ocean are doing to second place.

"Come on," I hear Crisp yell. I turn to see he's off the cannon and helping Shelly down. "Best view's over here."

He walks to the edge of the cliff and turns to look at us.

"Gulls," he says, arms extended to full wingspan. "It's been a hoot."

With that, he springs himself backwards off the edge, disappearing completely, to the shrieks and gasps of the group.

He gives it a couple of seconds for dramatic effect before peeping his head over the precipice with that big Cheshire-cat grin.

"Water's great," he jests.

"You asshole," Shelly yells, jumping down into his arms.

"Asshole is right," Scott murmurs, making his way over.

A shock runs through my body as Mint takes my hand.

"C'mon," she says before turning back toward Mia. "Mimi, you coming?"

Mia shakes her head without raising it from her lap.

"Okay, just wait right there. We won't be long."

"Think she'll be okay?" I ask.

"She'll be fine," Mint reassures me, and we make our way over to join the rest of the gang.

As we approach the edge, the ground seems to fall away, and the wide expanse of the ocean becomes suddenly apparent. I feel my knees go weak and stop dead in my tracks, tugging on Mint's hand.

"What's wrong?" she asks.

"Ah, shit," I say, embarrassed to admit it. "I'm not great with heights sometimes. I mean, it's not really a conscious thing, but when I'm in a high place, I get a bit dizzy."

She turns to me and looks me right in the eye.

"It's okay," she says. "Just look at me."

"Well, that shouldn't be too difficult," I say.

Argh. Nerdy, again.

She smiles, touching her nose to mine. I feel her warm breath on my lips, and my heart races as I think we're about to kiss again, but then she pulls away.

"C'mon," she says, walking backwards, my hands in hers. "Just keep looking at me."

I walk forward and do as she says, never taking my eyes off hers as we approach the edge.

I'm falling.

"Okay," she says, looking back. "I'm gonna jump down. You just keep your eyes on me."

"If you insist."

She lets go of my hands and eases herself down.

"Now, sit and slide your ass to the edge."

I do as she says and dangle my legs over the side before hopping down, never taking my eyes off hers. I lean back against the cold rock and chance a peek. We're on a narrow ledge—no more than eight feet wide. Crisp, Shelly, and Scott are sat happily on the edge, their legs dangling over the side, chatting among themselves.

"You coming?" Mint asks.

"I think I'm good here," I say.

"*What?*"

"What?"

"Gregory Masters. Aren't you going to face your fears?"

I take a deep breath and peek past her to the expanse beyond, and once again the world starts to turn on its head.

"Maybe next time?"

Mint squeezes my shoulders.

"Okay," she says before kissing me on the cheek, turning, and joining the group.

I cling to the rock and watch her join the group.

"Bellissima alba!" she yelps as her dreadlocks dance along her back, and the rising sun gradually turns the four Gulls to silhouettes as a few more begin to sing a morning greeting among the rocks below.

* * *

"There it is!" Crisp exclaims. "In all its post-millennial glory."

We're thankfully far from the edge now, across the parking lot near Cabot Tower, looking back across the city in the early morning light. Despite the height, the lack of a sudden drop and the comforting toy-town appearance of downtown St. John's doesn't have the same unnerving effect on my brain as the last view did.

I've seen this view on postcards in the gift shops. It's a big hill dotted with colour—buildings at this angle and that, a confusion of squares and triangles that somehow manages to look uniform as a whole. If you took any of the many fishing villages that dot the Newfoundland coast—"the bay," as the locals refer to it—and blew them up to city size, this is what they would look like. It's somehow maintained its small-town charm even as its population has risen into the hundreds of thousands.

And there, atop the hill and off to the left, sits the building that Crisp is pointing to. The Rooms is an oddity on the landscape—one of the largest buildings in the city, its exaggerated green windows and simple, shed-like design making it seem somehow disproportionate to the rest. Its yellow walls and burgundy roofs pull the eye away from even the stateliest of St. John's historic buildings—the Basilica itself struggling to catch the eye in the shadow of its modern simplicity.

"I friggin' hate that building," Scott says. He's somehow managed to find another bottle of India Pale Ale from somewhere and is drinking away at it.

"Can we call a cab?" Mia mumbles. She's stopped puking now but is still looking the worse for wear and has seated herself on a bench with her back to the city.

"I kinda like it," Mint says, her arm hooked in mine.

"I think it's all right," I say, which I do, but even if I didn't, I'd probably say it just to agree with her.

"Built in 2005, controversially on the plot of land that once housed the . . ." Crisp leaves it hanging like a teacher waiting for someone in class to complete the sentence.

"Oh! The fire department," Shelly says like an eager student. "And the police station, too, at one point, I believe. Sir."

"Very good, Shelly," Crisp says, leaning into the teacher role. "See me after class for a special bonus."

Shelly puts her hand playfully to her mouth in show of faux shock.

"But before that?"

"Used to be a fort," Scott says. He's got a bit of edge to him right now, like he's a little pissed off. The beer boost appears to have reignited his buzz.

"That's right! A great British garrison, no less," Crisp says, looking in my direction. "Built by the Brits to keep out the French and . . ." He directs his gaze to Mint. ". . . American privateers!"

"Arrr, me mateys!" Shelly screeches, doing her best pirate impersonation.

Mint giggles in my ear, and it's the sweetest sound I've ever heard.

I'm falling.

"Blot on the landscape," Scott says with vitriol in his voice. "That what the note said? It's true. That building is a blot on the landscape."

"Some salty," Shelly says, looking Scott up and down. "Maybe it's time you put down the bottle, me ducky."

Scott seems to interpret this as a challenge and proceeds to chug down the remains of the beer before heaving the bottle out toward the city, the sound of it shattering reverberating off the rocks and sending a clutch of seagulls squawking out into the golden morning light.

"Yes, b'y," Shelly says. "All up in da wind, he is."

Scott strides over to the low wall and steps up onto it, looking out across the city, his sights set on the Rooms.

"Poke out their green eyes of greed," he says.

"Geez," Shelly says, joining Scott atop the wall. "The windows do kinda look like big green eyes, now, don't they?"

"Have them look out in flaming envy," Scott mutters.

Crisp joins them up on the wall.

"Over the houses, the harbour, the seas," he says, taking in a big breath of cool salt air.

"Flaming envy," Shelly repeats. "So, what, they want us to smash the windows and then set 'em alight?"

"Do you know how big those windows are?" Scott asks.

"You okay, Mimi?" Mint asks.

"Can we just call a cab already?" Mia growls.

"She's okay," Mint says to me. "C'mon." She pulls me over to the low wall, and we both join the rest of the gang, standing tall above the City of St. John's.

"They gotta be twenty feet tall," Shelly says. "They're floor-to-ceiling windows—up on the fourth floor. Offering spectacular views of the city, the harbour, and the famous St. John's Narrows," she says in her best tour-guide voice.

"Not gonna break easy," Scott says.

"Oh, that's right, you used to work at the Rooms for a while, hey, Shelly?" Mint says.

Shelly rolls her eyes.

"Yeah. For all of three months. Till missus came back from mat leave and they fired me."

"Gonna need explosives . . ." Scott mumbles.

"I've always found that artsy lot to be a fickle crowd. Not your people, Shell, but those highfalutin artsy types, you know?" Crisp says.

"Well, my manager, *Sandra*, was sure fickle when she was lovely to me for three months, then turned around and booted me out the door with the same patronizing smile on her face."

"Or pneumatics," Scott says.

"So, I suppose if you worked at the Rooms for three months, you'd have a pretty good sense of their security systems." The thought occurs to me, and feeling the building energy in the group, I elect to say it.

"Course, it's not just one big window. It's actually a bunch of small ones," Scott says.

"Pfft," Shelly says. "You'd think they'd have the place locked up like Fort Knox, but it's just a basic alarm system and a retired RNC officer named Ray, who sleeps through most of his night shift."

"It's doable," Scott says.

We all stand in silence for a few moments before Crisp asks the question on everyone's lips.

"So, you in, Scott, or wha—?"

Scott shrugs.

"I'd really like to get my own back on Shitty Sandra," Shelly cajoles.

"And you do hate that friggin' building," Mint adds.

"And I would like to have more of those mad stacks," I throw in.

"Frig it," Scott says with just the hint of a smile. "Why not?"

We are a flock of Gulls standing high on Signal Hill, squawking atop the wall in the early morning sunshine.

"Game on," I say to Mint and then out to the beckoning city. "Game on."

"Can we please just call a goddamn cab?" Mia pleads from somewhere behind us.

9

Checking the Levels

The house on Long's Hill is abuzz with activity. It's less home and more mission control. The kitchen is the war room, the circular table covered with maps, blueprints, and floor plans. Where Crisp gets this stuff is still a mystery to me, but I don't care. Questions can come later.

It's like a drug and we're all hooked again. The last two weeks were pure withdrawal, the whole world on mute. The colourful row houses of St. John's lost their lustre, and it was as though the morning fog never lifted. But now the Gulls are reunited. Now we are back. Now the volume is turned back up, and I've never seen things so clearly. We're going to do a dare—and it's going to be our biggest one yet.

Scott has been more or less living in the small, wind-buckled shed in the back yard for the last few days. Shelly brings him a steady supply of tea as he fiddles with compressed air canisters, rubber pipes, and homemade pistons. The rest of the Gulls go back and forth to the dump, to the scrapyard, and occasionally to Home Hardware and Canadian Tire, bringing back the supplies that Scott needs, along with any and all kinds of glass for him to test his homemade contraptions on. We keep a stiff broom by the shed door and take turns sweeping shattered glass from the shed floor, tossing it into the firepit outside.

When not sweeping up or serving tea, Shelly is consulting with Crisp about the security and layout of the Rooms. Their conversations follow a pretty familiar pattern each time . . .

"So, there are no security cameras along this stretch of hallway?"

"I mean, none that I can recall."

"None that you can recall? Or definitely no cameras?"

"I'm not a hundred per cent certain, Crispin."

"Didn't you work there for three months?"

"Yes, but I wasn't goin' around counting the security cameras!"

And so on.

And so forth.

It seems that the plans Crispin has been able to secure, while detailed, are old, so he's relying on Shelly to remember if anything changed. While that's going about as well as can be expected, her knowledge has come in quite useful, as have her connections. Or, make that, connection.

Ryan Tucker is a weaselly little man of about thirty-five who's always dressed in ill-fitting jeans and a faded plaid shirt and emanates a constant aroma of chemicals and weed. Ryan is a janitor at the Rooms and has been for the last eleven years. Don't ask me how he got the job or, from the tales Shelly tells, how he's managed to keep it, but there it is.

It's a Friday morning when we go for a visit. For whatever reason, Friday mornings are the quietest time—a fact stated by Shelly, endorsed by Ryan, and confirmed by Google. All six of us go to get acquainted. For Mia and me, it's a first visit to the spacious, brightly lit art gallery and museum. The rest of the gang have all spent varying amounts of time at the Rooms. Scott would visit Shelly on her breaks when she worked here, enjoying an overpriced coffee in the fourth-floor café, along with panoramic views of the city and the harbour beyond.

Crisp and Shelly take turns acting as tour guides as we make our way around the grand, open-plan building—itself a marvel of artistry and engineering.

"Know why it's called the Rooms?" Shelly asks, patting me on the bum as we climb the stairs to the second floor.

"'Cause it's roomy?" I offer.

"Back in the day, in the little fishing villages you see all around the bay, they'd have these little sheds, y'see. Simple little sheds with gabled roofs called fishing rooms."

"Ah," I say, genuinely intrigued. "Is that why they designed it to look like big sheds?" I ask.

"Very good!" Shelly exclaims excitedly. "See teacher after class for a special bonus." She winks, playfully adjusting one of her ample breasts and licking her tongue to her teeth. I bet she could teach me a couple of things.

We laugh as our little group passes a much larger group of much smaller humans—a swaddle of kids out on a school trip led by a tired-looking teacher.

"You would have made a good teacher," I say to Shelly.

For a moment the wall comes down, and she looks genuinely touched by the compliment.

"I did like showing people around when I worked here," she says.

On the second floor, we take a little detour to walk through the first exhibit, at Crisp's behest. It's a World War I exhibit, according to the signage at the entrance, memorializing a battle at a place called Beaumont-Hamel. Large backlit displays show black-and-white images of Newfoundland soldiers who fought in the war, while their stories are told on plaques that line the walls. Not that we need to read them with Crisp in our ranks—ever the eager tour guide.

"In August 1914, Great Britain declared war on Germany," he says, pausing at each display to carefully study the faces of the soldiers, sailors, and nurses. "Course, Newfoundland was a British dominion back then, so the call went out to aid the empire. Hundreds of brave young Newfoundlanders answered that call, eager to do their part."

"Wow," I say. "I never realized."

"Resources were limited, and since Newfoundland had no army, nor even any militia, there was a hasty effort to make uniforms. When they ran out of khaki, they had to use navy cloth to make leggings, or 'puttees,' for the soldiers. That's how they got the name . . ."

I pause next to Crisp in front of a large glass case containing a military uniform on a headless mannequin, and I read the sign.

"The Blue Puttees."

He gives a didactic nod and begins to move along again.

"On July first, 1916, Allied forces launched a major offensive in France at the village of Beaumont-Hamel."

"I've never heard of it before."

"It was the beginning of the Somme offensive."

"Oh, right. I remember something about the Battle of the Somme from history class. I probably should have listened more carefully."

"The Allies had hit German fortifications with heavy artillery in the days leading up to the Big Push," Crisp continues as we all make our way slowly along the wide corridor, flanked by soldiers who seem more like people and less like faceless strangers now. "They figured they'd have weakened their defences." He raises an eyebrow.

"I take it that proved not to be the case?"

We walk on again, the other four Gulls following in silence close behind.

"When the Newfoundland Regiment went over the top and charged at the Germans, it was a total massacre. The Germans were entrenched, unhampered, and ready. They mowed down wave after wave of Allied soldiers with machine guns. Within less than thirty minutes, almost the entire Newfoundland Regiment was wiped out. Over 800 brave souls advanced proudly forward that day. Only sixty-eight survived."

"Jesus," I say as the group gathers in front of a huge stuffed caribou with towering antlers. "I had no idea."

"In the tradition of Newfoundland, they were able to regroup and rebuild the Newfoundland Regiment with new recruits. Our soldiers fought in tough battle after tough battle to the end of the war, making their way from France to Belgium. And in another tradition of Newfoundland, that list of arduous encounters was given a name."

"The Trail of the Caribou," I read from the plaque by the side of the majestic beast.

"The caribou became a symbol for the fighting Newfoundlanders, both at home and overseas, along with a reputation for being tough, brave, and skilled."

I look at the hulking caribou, the snow-white fur on its shoulders giving way to darker, brown-tinged fur along its back. Its antlers must be close to four feet tall, rising like some great, symmetrical tree. Its eyes are a vivid mixture of gold and blue, like oil mixed in water.

"It looks so . . . peaceful," I say, to myself but out loud.

"Nudding peaceful about what it represents," Shelly says from somewhere behind me.

"Nudding peaceful about those antlers going up yer arse if you catch 'em in a bad mood," Scott says drably.

"Here we are, Gulls. On our own Caribou Trail. Marching ever forward to glory."

* * *

The third floor is where we find our first target—one of two "green eyes of envy"—the huge multi-panel windows that look out from the big, barn-like structures on either side of the building. This one is accessed via the archives and reference room—a big library full of old books and documents, its perimeter dotted with computer terminals and microfilm readers. Shelly had been right in her assessment up on Signal Hill: the great windows tower a good twenty feet tall.

"Not gonna break easy," Scott repeats his earlier observation, rapping his knuckles against the glass.

"Smells gross in here," Mia says, flaring her nostrils.

"Smells like history." Crisp beams, taking in a huge sniff and sighing it out with a smile.

"Eight panels high, five wide," Scott says, stroking his scruffy beard.

"What are ya thinkin', Too Hotty?"

"Poke out their green eyes of greed," he says, reciting the riddle. "Have them look out in flaming envy . . ."

"Ryan says we can have a poke around on the top floor, then make our way down to the basement to meet him," Shelly whispers conspiratorially, tucking her phone back into her cleavage.

"Jesus, Shelly, do you ever use a pocket?" Crisp hisses.

"I reckon we only need to take out six panels," Scott says, pointing a finger toward the glass and drawing a rectangular shape in the air. "Three up, three across. We take out the six lower-middle panels and we'll have our eye."

"But don't they have to be 'flaming'?" I ask.

Scott turns to me with a smile. "My son," he says, placing a hand on my shoulder as he passes me by, "you're with Newfoundlanders now. We've been startin' fires since we were knee high to a grasshopper."

As we make our way up the final staircase, Scott enlightens us on the science of fire.

"The key to a good fire is layers," he says. "We're gonna need big logs to put at the bottom. A fire this size, we're gonna need a lotta logs. Three or four layers—and wide, too. It's gonna need to be a good six or eight feet at the base to get the size we need so it's visible all across town."

We reach the top of the stairs to find our second target—the next set of windows, which illuminate the wide-open space, the light almost blinding as it shimmers off the impossibly shiny floors.

"My, Ryan's sure been doin' a fine job with that floor polisher," Shelly exclaims. "I wonder if I can get him to buff up me boobies," she says, shaking said boobies in my direction, her phone almost working its way out. I can't help but laugh.

"Then a couple of layers of smaller logs, then sticks," Scott says. "Lots of sticks. We can go out to the woods and get them."

"You getting this?" Crisp asks. Mia plays secretary—tapping Scott's latest shopping list into her phone.

"Couple of layers of dry kindling, then a bunch of newspaper on top," Scott says, moving ahead of the group. He's a Scott-shaped silhouette now, peering out at the spectacular morning view. We fall in beside him.

"Over the houses, the harbour, the seas," Crisp says as we all gaze out.

"It's going to be spectacular," Mint says, shooting me a smile.

"Oops," Shelly says as her boobs vibrate and she retrieves her phone. "Ry-Guy says he'll be ready for us in ten, down in the basement," she says.

We turn en masse and head back toward the stairs, but something catches Mint's eye.

"'Suspense," she reads from the plaque at the entrance to an exhibit room. "Oh, I think I heard about this at school. It's this really cool interactive modern art thing. Let's take a quick peek!"

Before anyone can protest, Mint grabs Shelly by the wrist and excitedly pulls her into the darkened room, the rest of us following on.

"Wow," I say. "This is cool."

The large room is full of colourful glass orbs dangling down at various heights from ceiling, suspended by long, thin wires. Some are as small as a marble, others as large as a softball. Unusually, we're allowed to walk among and through the exhibits—of which there must be hundreds—allowing them to brush off our clothes and swing gracefully through the air. On closer inspection, each orb contains some form of life—fine blades of grass, bright purple flowers, an acorn, kelp, spiders, and ants. Around the perimeter of the room is a forest of giant canvases with paintings of animals—some vibrant with life, others in the throes of death. A giant flock of black birds. A gazelle being slashed to the ground by a pursuing lion. A moose being gutted by an unseen hunter.

"Hey," Shelly says, peering into an orb containing a mosquito. "If we could stick a really small needle into this one, you think we could extract some blood and make a dinosaur?"

"Dino D-N-A!" Scott says in a goofy, southern US accent.

"This is amazing," Mint says, walking through a thick cluster of smaller orbs, her arms outstretched as they brush off her palms and shoulders, swinging gracefully in her wake.

I'm falling.

"A statement about the fragility and fleeting nature of life," Crisp says. "Pretty neat."

"Anyone wanna play conkers?" I say, holding an orb containing a large chestnut. The rest of the gang looks at me vacantly. "Probably a British thing," I say.

* * *

"I don't think chestnuts and conkers are the same thing," Mint says as we all make our way back down the stairs.

God, I love the way she says "conkers," with the drawn-out first vowel. It sounds so much sexier in an American accent.

"I think you might be right," I say. "My mum always told us we must never try to eat conkers because they were very poisonous."

"So, you thread string through them with a needle, then put a knot in it so you've got, like, a mini wrecking ball–type situation?" Shelly asks.

"Yeah. Then one kid lets their conker dangle in the air, while the other kid gets one shot at smashing it with their conker."

"First conker to break is the loser," Crisp says.

"Yup," I say.

"We're gonna need some gasoline, of course," Scott says as we continue our descent. He's opted out of the conker discussion altogether and is still plotting the logistics of the dare. "We want this fire to start fast, burn hot, and go long. Long enough so as someone has to come and put it out."

"Long enough for NTV news to get it on camera." Crisp smirks, getting pulled back into the excitement of the plan.

"And we're gonna need something to contain it," Scott says.

"Rocks or something. Assuming we won't want to burn down the Rooms altogether." It seems as if he may be entertaining the merits of that idea.

"I once had a champion conker that lasted seventeen days," I say.

"Wow. That's one tough nut," Shelly says with a wink.

Scott rolls his eyes. "While you British boys were banging your nuts together, us Newfoundlanders were out in the woods, starting fires and shooting things," he says.

Everybody pauses for a moment, Scott's statement hanging in the air.

"What?" he says. "I was listening."

* * *

Ryan tucks a few loose strands of greasy blond hair behind the ear that isn't occupied by a hand-rolled cigarette and scratches his stubbled cheek.

"We gots ta be quick," he says. "Don't want anyone catchin' yous lot down 'ere." He's jittery, his whole body seeming to have a barely perceptible tremor. He's in constant movement–fiddling with his hair, shuffling his feet–a bag of bones and a bag of nerves.

He shepherds us along the basement corridor, past a supplies room and a small kitchen, where presumably he and the other janitorial staff take their breaks, and on to a set of thick metal double doors. The sign above the doors reads, "Art Storage."

"Through 'ere," he says. I have to listen carefully to pick out Ryan's words. He talks fast and with a thick accent, putting "haitches where there h'are none" and omitting them from where they ought to be.

He unlocks and opens one of the heavy doors. "Go on," he

says, waving us into the pitch-black room and looking nervously up and down the corridor.

As we enter, motion-activated lights plink on and the room is revealed to be large, with various shelves and easels adorned with covered canvases and small sculptures. Toward the back of a room is a towering, multi-tiered shelving unit that runs across most of the width of the room.

"C'mon," says Ryan, who is almost certainly suffering from palpitations by this point as he hurriedly leads us through the room and past the giant shelves.

Once on the other side, the shelving unit is revealed to be just one of three that run parallel to each other. The units appear to be mechanical, with buttons on the side that can be pressed to lower higher shelves for easier access to the various artworks and artifacts that line them.

Scott pauses for a moment, and I turn to see what he's looking at. He seems to be transfixed by a large canvas adorned with a brightly coloured indigenous painting of a bear, its insides made up of all kinds of natural textures.

"Get a move on, would ya?" I hear Ryan say from up ahead.

"Scott?" I prompt.

"Coming."

Behind the third and final shelving unit is a wall running the full width of the room with a single door bang in the middle.

"Geez, b'y," Shelly says. "How big is this place?"

"It runs the full length of the building, pretty much," Ryan says as he unlocks the door. "This room is climate-controlled to maintain the art and dat. Through 'ere's where you'll keep yer gear."

Beyond the door is a garage with a cement floor. The air is cooler and damp in here. Ryan snaps on the lights to reveal a white van with a "The Rooms" logo on the side sitting over to one side of the large space. At the far end is a big garage door with a smaller access door to the side. On the other side is a small shack-come-office space, which Ryan rushes over to and opens up.

"Nobody uses this room," he says as we all peer in over his shoulder. "And as far as I know, I have the only key. I cleared 'er out for ya. You can keep all yer shit in 'ere."

The room is empty save for a small desk with a computer that time seems to have forgotten, sitting dormant underneath a dust cover.

"That'll work," Scott says. "And we'll have access to the garage door to drop stuff off?"

"We'll have to do it at night, but yeah. No one's ever back 'ere save for when there's a delivery—and that's rare. We can figure out timing and dat."

Ryan snaps off the office light and closes the door.

"C'mon," he says. "Let's get da fuck out of it. I needs a smoke."

He leads us to the entrance next to the garage door, pushing on the bar to ease open the metal door.

"Evening of, I'll be the last to leave once Ray gets 'ere. I'll 'accidentally' leave this access door unlocked, so when you gets 'ere, you can just walk on in."

He holds the door open and ushers us all outside. It's a cool, windy day, a fine drizzle in the air.

"Friggin' RDF," Ryan says.

"RDF?" I ask.

"Rain, drizzle, and—not forgetting—fog, me dear," Shelly explains. "It's a Newfoundland thing."

"This door needs a key card," Crisp says. "I assume it's always locked. How are you going to leave it open?"

"Same way I do when I come out for a smoke." Ryan grins, revealing stained and buckled teeth. "With a cuttin'-edge piece-a technology known as a rock." He picks a fist-sized rock up from the ground and jams it in the corner of the door frame, letting the door swing back and catch before closing all the way.

"It's not wired to an alarm or anything?" Scott asks as we wander out into the grey day.

"No, b'y. Besides, I'm gonna cut all the alarms before you gets 'ere."

I pull my denim jacket tight around me and try to get my bearings. We're on the side of the building, at the top of a small service road that leads up a grassy knoll to the garage entrance. Ryan's already retrieved the hand-rolled cigarette from behind his ear and is working on lighting it, huddled next to the building to protect himself from the wind. We all gather around him, doing our best to keep dry, save for Crisp, who is strutting about the hill, arms extended to his full wingspan, breathing in the fresh ocean air.

"I'd offer yas some," Ryan says, suckling on the long cigarette, "but it's mainly just tobacco, and I don't wanna get it wet." He points to the sky as though the wind and the rain are conspiring to ruin his golden moment.

"Don't worry about it, Ry-Guy," Shelly says.

Crisp rejoins the flock, rubbing his recently shaven scalp, the short hairs flicking out a fine spray of water.

"So, no alarms, doors unlocked, cameras will be down, too?" he asks.

"Yup. All of the above," Ryan says between drags.

"In other words, all we have to worry about is Ray," Shelly says.

"Well, yeah," Ryan says. "You're on your own with that one."

"I don't think it'll be too much of a problem," Shelly says.

"It's true what the note said, y'know," Scott says, backing away from the building and looking up at it, fine beads of water forming on the lenses of his glasses. "It is a blot on the landscape."

* * *

The next week follows a familiar pattern. Scott works away in the shed, perfecting the homemade glass punchers that he will use to "poke out their green eyes of greed," or smash the bloody great windows that look out from either side of the Rooms. Crisp and Shelly refine the plans at the circular kitchen table, a constant flow of coffee and cigarettes of various kinds always on the go. The rest of us gopher around as required, finding glass and bits and bobs for Scott and picking up chunks of wood to create our "flaming envy."

"Goin' campin', are ye?" an old fella at Canadian Tire asks us. Mint and I can't help but chuckle.

"Yeah, something like that."

We even take a couple of trips out to the woods, collecting up dried-out twigs and small logs to use as kindling and the upper layers of Scott's perfect fire. We cart big rocks from the beach in metal buckets. Despite Scott's desire to burn the Rooms to the ground, the rocks will keep the fires contained.

By moonlight we fill up the Roller with supplies and ferry them over to the Rooms. The trips fuel our confidence for the big night itself as we effortlessly let ourselves in through the service door that is always reliably wedged open with Ryan's trusty rock each time we arrive. We can even open the garage door and back the car in, unloading our stuff into the small office space. By the last trip the little room is jam-packed with chunks of wood, buckets of rocks, stacks of twigs, and Scotty's nefarious contraptions.

Two days out, Crisp has us all on a strict no-booze, no-weed diet to keep our minds fresh and our bodies ready. Maybe half of us stick to that regime, and even the other three tone it down considerably.

Come the night of the third dare, we are all ready. We nap in the day and prep at the turn of midnight. Call time is 1:00 a.m., and the mission is on.

10

Dare 3
Lighting Up the Rooms
($500,000)

All the gear we need is already at the site, so we are able to travel light. Just like that first dare, which now seems like an age ago, we all pile into the Roller with our Steve Jobs ninja suits on, save for the balaclavas—for now. We haven't dared take the DeLorean out from under its cover since the Basilica job, though nobody has been around looking for it, so we think maybe the cops never saw the car that night after all. Still, best to err on the side of caution, we have all agreed.

We sit in dead silence as we make our way to the Rooms, each of us going over the plan in our heads, each of us with our own important role to play. Crisp, Mint, and I are lugging rocks and wood and building fires per Scott's very specific fire-building instructions. (The layers, and all that.) Shelly and Mia play lookouts. Mia is going to be stationed outside, keeping a perimeter watch, while Shelly is going to position herself near the theatre on the second floor to keep an eye out in case Ray—the aging security guard—decides to wander off from his station at the admissions desk and head up the stairs.

Ray is the only unknown quantity in the whole plan. Ryan has rigged it so the cameras went offline before he left, telling Ray there would be someone by to fix them in the morning. Of course, being without eyes on the whole building might increase the chances of the old fella making a lap of the facility, though Shelly is pretty confident that his dodgy hip will keep him from climbing any higher than the second floor. If he does decide to get adventurous, Shelly will text the rest of the group to let them know that "the eagle is flying." (While we all acknowledged that the use of the code name "eagle" was terribly cliché, Crisp was quick to point out that eagles are a gull's greatest predator. It was hard for anyone to argue.)

We roll up to the garage door just as we have done a dozen times in the last couple of weeks, but tonight it couldn't feel more different. There's an anxiety in the air unlike anything we experienced on our way to the first two dares. Then, it was energy, excitement. Tonight, it's something more akin to existential dread. This is big. Half a million dollars big, assuming the prize continues to double. And we all know it.

Mia backs the car up to the garage door. We all pull on our balaclavas and I jump out, approaching the access door, squinting to see in the dark. The sight of the trusty old rock propping the door ajar is reassuring. Part one of the plan has played out as expected.

I ease through the access door and open up the garage door—a process which seems painfully loud in the dead of night, but that is unlikely to rouse any attention, least of all from Ray the security guard, whose station is way over on the other side of the building.

Mia backs the Roller into the garage, and we all hop out and gather in front of the car. Per the plan, we all check our phones to make sure we have battery life and cell reception, each of us holding our phones aloft in silent confirmation before putting our hands into the circle for a show of solidarity.

The circle breaks and we all get to work with our own particular parts of the plan. Scott and Shelly head immediately through to the art storage area. They will make their way through to the basement hallway and up the stairs to the building itself, propping open all the doors as they go. Shelly will remain at her lookout point on the second floor, while Scott makes his way up to the fourth floor with the first of his pre-bagged glass punchers and a fold-out ladder. Once there he will begin rigging the first glass puncher and await the arrival of the next one.

That's where Crisp, Mint, and I come in. We'll carry the duffle bags containing the glass punchers up to Scott one at a time, since they are so heavy. Once all the duffle bags are delivered, our attentions will turn to the chunks of wood and buckets of rocks for the fires.

As we wait for the signal from Scott and Shelly that they are in position, Mia heads back outside to begin her perimeter watch and I head to the garage door controls. She steps outside and I begin to lower the door. As it's coming down, I notice her freeze.

She's looking at something.

She's looking back into the garage at Crisp and Mint. I follow her gaze to see the two of them in an embrace. It seems like a little more than a comforting pre-dare hug between friends. It seems as though they might kiss if it weren't for those pesky balaclavas.

My heart sinks and I look away, catching sight of Mia's feet, still frozen in the same position as the garage door rattles closed.

I count a couple of beats and see the two of them part in my periphery. I look back and Crisp gives me a nod. I nod back.

I knew something was going on with them. I'm such an idiot.

I wander back over to them and take out my phone. After what feels like an eternity, the phone vibrates and lights up. I read the text.

We're in.

I look up to see Crisp and Mint, again huddled close, both looking at his phone as the message comes in.

That night at the Hall. I knew something was off.

I take a deep breath, try to bury the emotion, and focus on the task at hand.

We make our way to the little office and grab a duffle bag each, my mind immediately refocusing on the plan.

Three bags each. Three runs to the fourth floor. Nine bags total. Then the rocks, then the wood, then repeat for the third floor.

We make our way through the art storage room and out to the basement hallway, the doors satisfyingly propped open by Scott and Shelly, just like we planned it. As we climb the stairs and enter the Rooms proper, I can feel the adrenaline rush through my body.

We're bloody doing it.

Our pace slows a little as we climb the stairway to the second floor. It's as though none of us dare take a breath until we catch sight of Shelly at the theatre entrance. As we emerge at the top of the stairs, she gives us a thumbs-up.

The coast is clear. No sign of Ray.

We march on past the theatre, Shelly giving us a trademark wink as we make our way to the next staircase, halfway up which I already feel the lactic acid beginning to build in my legs. Not a good sign considering we have an even eleven trips to make up and down these steps—some of them with heavier, more awkward loads.

The third level is just a waypoint for now, but there's no time to stop. I follow Crisp and Mint up the final staircase, and we round the corner to see Scott standing at the base of the towering windows. He already has his ladder set up and points at an imaginary wristwatch before giving a shrug.

We need to pick up the pace.

We deposit the duffle bags, and as Scott gets right to work unzipping one and retrieving his homemade glass punchers, I take a moment to look out at the amazing view of St. John's by night, its higgledy-piggledy buildings set against the dark shoulders of the Narrows. It's a perfectly clear night, the sky full of stars, moonlight reflecting off the shimmering ocean.

My attention is drawn back to Scott as he waves me away.

No time to lose.

I turn to see that Crisp and Mint are already approaching the top of the staircase. The two of them appear joined at the hip. I'm like a third wheel on the world's scariest date.

Did he just pat her on the arse?

I try to shake away the thought and refocus, following them down through the heart of the voluminous building. Uninhibited by a heavy duffle bag and with gravity now on my side, I am able to take in my surroundings a little better on the way down. The inside of the Rooms feels massive now. It's dead quiet save for those occasional distant thumps that big buildings make at night, as though they are living, breathing things that have swallowed you into their great belly.

My heart beats hard. This feels like a movie. This is big.

By the time we return to Scott with the next set of duffle bags, he's already got two of his contraptions installed on a couple of the upper windows. They are impressive-looking machines—fist-sized masses of tubes and wires affixed to the windows with large suction cups, each with a small canister of compressed air protruding from the side. Long tubes reach down from each device, coiling like giant snakes at the base of the window. The plan is to run these tubes down to the third floor, where they, along with the tubes from the third-floor window, will attach to some kind of control switch. Once all the glass punchers are attached, a flick of the switch will activate them, and *boom*, the windows on both floors will come crashing down in "glorious unison," as Crisp had described it.

That's going to make a lot of noise.

We're into a rhythm now, fetching and carrying exactly as planned. There's no sign of Ray, as confirmed by Shelly's increasingly theatrical thumbs-ups, which, by the fourth trip up and down the stairs, have become a full-scale belly dance. Things are going swimmingly. Almost too well.

As the repetitive task of lugging heavy crap up the stairs and returning to do it again becomes second nature, I have more and more headspace to analyze the body language of Crisp and Mint. What I'm seeing isn't helping my paranoia. They are behaving like a couple with an unwanted tagalong, and I'm replaying every past interaction in my head. The ones I've had with them. The ones I've seen them have with each other. The things that have been said and done.

That day at the house when Shelly and I returned from our trip to the store and Mia and Mint appeared from upstairs after Crisp. Had all three of them been up there together?

By the time we are on our last run, I'm seething. I feel like I'm being played for a fool, toyed with, laughed at behind my back. Fuck this.

I dump down the box of dried sticks on the third floor, where Scott is installing the last of the glass punchers and Mint is helping Crisp build the second of the two fires.

Mint Crisp. Even the names go together like a delicious chocolate bar.

I'm overheating, sweating profusely in my Steve Jobs ninja suit. My balaclava feels itchy and restrictive. I'm dizzy and breathless.

I need to get out of here.

I turn and head out of the Archives room and make my way over to the railing that overlooks the floor below, pulling off the balaclava and the black turtleneck sweater, dumping them on the floor as I go. I push my sodden hair back and lean on the banister. In my drenched black T-shirt I'm instantly relieved, the cool metal feeling like heaven against my bare arms.

I take a few deep breaths and try to gather myself.

Jesus. We're in the middle of a highly illegal escapade. I need to keep my cool. I need to focus on the task at hand. That, at least, is going well, you'd have to admit.

I chuckle to myself. I'm feeling a little better, and now I can see Shelly on the floor below. She's doing another dance, even more elaborate this time. She's waving her hands in the air like she just don't care.

Shit.

She's waving her hands in the air like she does bloody well care.

She isn't dancing. She's waving. She's panicked. Ray's coming.

She points up and disappears underneath me, heading for the stairs to come up. For a moment, I'm frozen. We talked about this. We talked a lot. Plan A, B, C. There may even have been a D. What to do if Ray was on the move.

We can't go down because he's coming up the stairs from the ground floor. That's why Shelly's heading up. She needs to get to the third floor, where the rest of us are, because soon Ray will be on the second floor, where she just was.

Where he now is.

Fuck.

I'm dizzy again and things move in slow motion.

I see Shelly emerge on my right. Even with the balaclava I can see the terror in her eyes.

We have to move.

But I can't. I'm a caribou caught in the headlights—frozen and waiting for the impact. Much like that helpless creature, I can't see but I can be seen. There are just enough lights left on around the Rooms at night for it not to be dark, and a couple of them just happen to be shining down on good ol' Greg. But as Ray reaches the top of the stairs on the level below, he is cloaked in shadow. I can make him out, but only as a slightly darker blob in among the darkness. A blob that stops. A blob that shouts.

"Hey!"

Shit.

Still, I can't move, even as Shelly gesticulates wildly in my periphery. This is the worst-case scenario. The security guy has seen me, maskless and lit up like a Christmas tree. My brain quickly cycles through all the plans—A through C and maybe D. There was nothing in any one of them about this. Because I've fucked up. Because I didn't stick to the program. Because of Crisp and Mint playing me for a fool.

In a split second, fear turns to rage, and a fresh wave of adrenaline dumps itself down my body like an ice bath. Don't ask me why, but I open mouth and eyes wide and let out a primal scream at the man in the shadows. Then I turn and run, grabbing my sweater and balaclava as I go, to where Shelly is waiting at the bottom of the stairs.

"Go hide!" I growl, pointing up the stairs. "The Suspense room!"

Shelly hesitates.

"Go!" I hiss, and she takes off up the stairs.

I hear Ray. He's still on the level below. I hear the static of his radio before he says something into it.

I spring into action, running into the Archives room, where Crisp and Mint are standing close together—because of course they bloody well are—and Scott is fiddling with the brick-sized unit that houses the switch for the glass breakers.

"We have to go, now!" I scream, and I see everybody's body language instantly change—a clan of calm crooks suddenly turned rigid, poised for fight or flight.

"Where's your mask?" Mint asks.

"Is that thing ready?" I ask Scott, ignoring her.

"Almost," he says, poking away at the mass of tubes and wires.

"We have to do this—now!" I say, and without skipping a beat, I grab one of the gasoline canisters up from the floor and empty half its contents onto the pile of wood.

"I mean now!" I say, pulling a pack of matches from my pocket, lighting one, and tossing it onto the woodpile.

The heat is incredible as the fire ignites with a loud whoosh.

"Scott?" I say. He nods, the fire dancing in his thick-rimmed glasses. He pokes at the unit a couple more times and flicks the switch.

The sound of eighteen high-power pneumatic glass punchers demolishing a hundred square feet of thick glass panels is more akin to thunder than a smashing window. The boom shakes through the walls and floors of the Rooms, followed by the shrill symphony of raining glass.

"The Suspense room," I bark as I rush past Crisp and Mint. "Come on!"

We all rush up the stairs to the fourth floor, where a refreshing, cool breeze greets us.

"It worked," Scott says, allowing himself a moment of self-congratulation as the wind blows in through eight successfully demolished windows on this floor, a ninth splintered with a spiderweb of cracks. The unlit pile of wood lies in wait within a circle of rocks.

We hurry over to the exhibit room with all the hanging glass orbs. Shelly is tucked just inside the door, awaiting our arrival.

"Hide!" I say to her and to everyone.

"Plan Z!" Crisp says, just loud enough for everyone to hear.

Plan Z. I remember now. We had discussed what to do if we got caught on the upper floors with no way to get down. As we make our way across the room, through the inverted forest of hanging glass orbs, Crisp's words about Plan Z echo in my mind.

If we get stuck on the upper floors, we're royally fucked. All we can do is hide and wait it out until there's a chance to make a run for it.

We'd all agreed that we'd better hope it didn't come to that. And we'd all agreed that if it did, the Suspense room, with its confusion of dangling orbs and collection of giant canvases, would be the ideal place to hide in the dark.

It is dark. With the door closed, the only light source is the Fire Exit sign above the door, which casts an ominous red hue throughout the room. It takes a minute for my eyes to adjust. We make our way across the room, glinting red orbs containing dead creatures frozen in time brushing against our skin as we head for the slim sanctuary of the giant canvases.

I end up behind the one with the image of the moose being gutted by an unseen hunter. I can't see it, but I know that it's there. That image, on the other side of the thin layer of wood and canvas that is my only protection from—what? Jesus, I hope that painting isn't too damn prescient.

I take in a stuttered, deep breath and try to reassure myself.

It's just Ray. Shelly says he's, like, eighty years old. What harm can an eighty-year-old do to a bunch of young men and women like us?

But as we hide there in the red-tinted dark, the only sound the wind whistling beneath the door to the exhibit room, another thought occurs to me.

Who was he talking to on the radio? Was he calling for backup? Surely he'll have called the police. And even if he didn't, there are two gaping holes in the Rooms, one of them on fire. Someone's soon going to notice that.

My heart beats hard in my chest, and I feel dizzy once again.

I chance a peek out from behind my canvas. The room takes on an otherworldly quality, the orbs appearing like a thousand red stars against the black backdrop of eternal space. A vacuum with no way out.

I can't breathe.

Just as I think I might lose consciousness altogether, a sound from across the room pulls me back into the moment.

The door is opening.

Ray is coming in.

I hear the static hiss of his radio and the click of the door closing again as he mutters something.

Who's he talking to? The police?

I catch movement out of the corner of my eye, and for a brief moment my attention is drawn to the two figures huddled behind the next canvas over. The canvas with the lion and the gazelle.

One of the figures is unmistakably the tall form of Crisp, his long limbs wrapped around a second figure that is unmistakably Mint, a couple of stray dreadlocks peeking out from beneath the back of her balaclava.

All is silent again for what feels like a much longer time than it probably is. I chance another peek past my canvas and see the door beginning to slowly open again. I feel like it should creak, like that's what a door should do in a movie like the one we're all living right now. But it doesn't. The door just silently opens, revealing the featureless silhouette of Ray the security guard.

He's bigger than I expected him to be.

Ray flicks on a flashlight, and I duck back behind my canvas.

Here we are. Plan Z. The one where we're royally fucked.

I look left and right, catching glimpses of the other huddled Gulls in the beam of Ray's waving flashlight.

"Yous better come on out," Ray says with a thick Newfoundland accent. "Game's over. Police are on their way."

For a moment the flashlight illuminates the canvas with the mass of black birds, full of movement and life and freedom. I think about the party at the Hall and how we danced all night long. I think about the sprawling Atlantic Ocean beyond the rocks of Signal Hill. I think about home—England—all those miles beyond.

I'd rather be there right now. I'd rather be anywhere else right now.

Ray's footsteps come slowly closer, accompanied by the odd rattle of swinging glass orbs contacting each other like giant conkers as the security guard enters the inverted forest.

We aren't the flock of birds anymore—free to fly where we like. We're the moose. We're the gazelle. We're the helpless, hopeless prey.

"Who is that? Who's there?" Ray says, the light of the flashlight spinning around the perimeter of the room.

Jesus. Did he spot one of us?

Then there's a sound that makes my heart stop dead.

C-click.

I've seen enough movies to recognize the sound of a gun being cocked.

"Hey!" Ray shouts. "You just stop right there!"

The sound of the gun being fired in the echo chamber of the exhibit room is deafening.

BOOM!

It isn't like the deep thunder of the shattering windows. This sound is more immediate, more piercing, stabbing into my ears and reverberating through my jaw.

BOOM!

I cover my ears and duck behind the canvas as though it can offer me any protection. Ray has a gun? Why the hell does an eighty-year-old security guard have a gun?

BOOM!

I hear an agonized wail, like an animal slashed along the thigh by a razor-sharp claw, and I can't hide here any longer. I have to get out of here.

I peek around the edge of the canvas to see Ray barrelling toward me. But he isn't wielding a gun. Instead, his arms grasp at the dangling glass orbs all around him as he stumbles forward. He pulls a few of the orbs clean from their moorings, sending them raining down to the ground. He falls forward, face-first, hitting hard. He breathes a laboured breath and twitches a couple of times. I watch as a single glass orb rolls slowly toward me until it stops at the base of the canvas. Then all is still.

In the shocking white light of Ray's dropped flashlight, I see a mosquito suspended in glass. I see a security guard dead-still on the floor. I see vivid red blood slowly filling the canvas of his crisp white shirt. I see smoke rising from the gun that's still held in two shaking hands. Hands that belong to Mia Tobin.

For a few seconds, all is still. Then movement. Crisp is the first to emerge, followed next by Shelly, who must have been tucked behind the canvas with the partially dissected frog.

"Jesus," Crisp says, breaking the silence as he looks down at the slain security guard. Ray's shirt is almost completely red now, and a dark pool of blood is beginning to form around him.

"Is he dead?" Mints asks as she creeps out from behind the canvas.

"I mean . . ." Crisp replies with a resigned shrug.

"Mia? Honey?" Shelly says as she cautiously approaches the young woman, who is still holding the gun in two hands, arms locked in front of her. "It's over, sweetie. Time to put the gun down."

As Shelly gets closer to Mia, she suddenly spins, training the gun on Shelly for a moment, stopping her dead in her tracks. Shelly raises her hands in front of her.

"Mia . . ." she says meekly.

"Lower. The fucking. Gun." Scott says, walking over to stand at Shelly's side.

Mia sniffs and lowers her aim, tucking the gun into her waistband.

I slowly come out from behind my canvas, collecting the mosquito orb in my hand as I do so. Don't ask me why, but I tuck the orb into my pocket and make my way over to join the rest of the Gulls.

Crisp grabs the flashlight from the ground and shines it on the security guard, causing a collective groan from the gang as the full horror of the scene is revealed in glorious Technicolor. Crisp cocks his head to one side.

"That's no eighty-year-old," he says.

He's right. The lifeless, bleeding body on the floor is that of a much younger man, no more than mid-twenties.

Before any of us can say another word, a loud, constant bell begins to ring, and flashing red lights start to flicker.

"Shit," Crisp hisses.

"Fire alarm," Scott says sternly.

"We have to get the hell out of here," I say.

"Not till the job's done," says Scott, pulling on his balaclava. "We've got one more fire to light."

Before I have a chance to ask if he's serious, Scott is on his way out the door.

"Come on," Crisp says, moving toward the door.

"What about him?" Shelly says, looking at the lifeless body of the young security guard.

"There's nothing we can do for him now," Mint says, following Crisp.

Because of course she's following Crisp.

"She's right," I say to Shelly. "We need to get out of here."

I take her by the arm, and we all head to the door. When we get out into the hall, water is raining down from above. It takes my mind a moment to catch up—and then I realize.

The sprinkler system has been activated.

"This gonna be a problem?" Crisp shouts at Scott above the cacophony of loud ringing and cascading water.

"Nah," Scott says as he douses the fourth-floor woodpile with gasoline. "Sprinklers don't reach all the way to the window, and these fires are gonna burn good and hot." He seals the gas canister and collects some random items back into a duffle bag. "We should be good," he says as he casually lights a match and flicks it onto the wood, the heat intense even through the water in the air, as he ignites the pile.

"Okay, let's get the Jesus outta here," Crisp says. And we move, like we've never moved before, down the first of four stairwells that feel like they've had a dozen stairs added now, even with gravity on our side.

Gravity isn't on Scott's side when he slips on a water-slick step and goes down hard, tobogganing down a couple more steps on his behind before he's able to halt himself.

Everyone stops to make sure he's okay. Everyone, that is, except for Mia, who has pushed on ahead of the flock.

"Good Lord, Scott. Have you ever met a set of steps you didn't fall down?"

Scott groans as he climbs gingerly back to his feet.

"Frig off, Crispin," he says, and we are all on our way again—past the Archives room, where our first fire is still raging, and down the next two staircases to the ground floor.

There doesn't seem to be any sign of the police or fire department or anyone else, for that matter, though we don't slow down to do a thorough check. We are full pace in the confusion of fire and water and that incessant ringing bell. We dart along the basement corridor, past the janitor's break room, back through the art storage area, and into the garage, where Mia is already at the wheel of the Roller with the engine running.

Without a second thought, we all do what we rehearsed back at the house on Long's Hill. I head right to the garage door and begin to open it while the rest of the Gulls collect any odds and ends from the little office shack before locking it behind them.

As the garage door rises, I look back at Mia in the driver's seat of the Roller. She doesn't make eye contact, instead staring blankly ahead.

She killed the security guy. And she still has the gun. Where did she get the—

"Let's go," Scott yells from somewhere behind me. I hadn't noticed he hadn't kept up, and I turn to see him running awkwardly toward the Roller, carrying the large canvas with the colourful bear that he'd been admiring when we were casing the joint with Ryan.

"Jesus, Scott," I say.

"What?" He pants as he passes by me. "It spoke to me."

He and the rest of the gang pile into the Roller—save for Crisp, who ducks through the still-opening garage door, shaking a large canister of spray paint as he goes.

"Wait for me outside," he says on his way past.

"Wait for you?" I ask incredulously, but he's already disappeared around the side of the building.

I shrug in the direction of the Roller, but Mia has already hit the lights and I can't see anyone inside.

Once the garage door is opened completely, Mia eases the Roller outside at a surprisingly sedate pace. I hit the button to begin closing the door again and climb into the back seat of the Roller beside Shelly, who buffers me from Mint. Scott is riding shotgun, jammed in with his newly acquired artwork.

"Crisp said to wait for him," I say, expecting protestations, but everyone inside the car is deadly silent, the weight of what's just happened heavy in the air.

"We've come this far. Let him do what he's gotta do," Scott says flatly.

As the engine idles, I notice that Shelly is shaking. I take her gloved hand in mine and give it a squeeze.

I see Mia's eyes in the rear-view mirror. Even through the balaclava she looks cold and focused. She's just here to do a job. Maybe it's the police training kicking in. Maybe it's the sense of assurance that comes from having a loaded gun tucked in your pants.

Scott appears focused but anxious—like he's trying his best to keep calm. He sniffs and cranes to see if he can spot Crisp out in the darkness. He drums his fingers rhythmically on the centre console.

Mint just sits, her head slightly angled so I can't get a good look at her eyes. Her dreads poke out the back of her balaclava and she occasionally picks at her damp clothing, but it's hard to get a read on what she's thinking, what she's feeling.

No changes there, then.

I am a bag of nerves, holding onto Shelly's hand as much for my own reassurance as for hers. My heart is pounding, and I feel like I could pass out at any moment. That or throw up. The balaclava again feels itchy and restricting, even more uncomfortable now that it's wet. I long to tear it off, but the fear of being seen prevents me from doing it.

"This is taking too long," I say, but there is no response from the other Gulls.

Then the sirens start.

They're faint at first. Distant. But getting slowly closer. That unmistakable wailing chorus of not one—but multiple police cars. Maybe even a fire truck, too.

"Guys?" I say.

"Nobody gets left behind," Mint says without looking around.

Would she say that if it was me out there? I wonder to myself.

Still, the sirens get louder. Still, they get closer. Still, we wait.

I'm just about to protest again when the back door of the Roller opens, enhancing the sound of sirens tenfold and pulling the air from the car like a vacuum.

"Let's roll!" Crisp yells as he jumps in, full of the smells of outside and fresh spray paint.

And we do. Just as the surrounding buildings begin to flicker with the red and blue light of approaching police cars, Mia guns it and we make our escape, away from the approaching sirens and down Harvey Road to the refuge of the house on Long's Hill.

11

Fear and Longing on Long's Hill

The heavy atmosphere from the car follows us into the house. Where before, the completion of a dare sparked an all-night celebration, tonight is different. This was big. We were sloppy. And somebody died.

The question of just who died sits on the tip of everyone's tongue, but nobody can seem to find the nerve to ask it, as though if left unspoken, perhaps the event never happened. Maybe we imagined the whole thing.

It sure as shit feels like a nightmare.

Doors are locked, blinds closed, lights low. Six Gulls on an island, each an island now themselves, we sit together but never so apart, in the living room. Some are on furniture, some on the floor. Alone with our thoughts. And Mia. Alone with that gun.

The longer the silence goes on, the more it permeates, taking control, gripping each of us in place, questions we're too afraid to ask out loud cycling through our heads.

What went wrong?

Who did we kill?

Where did the gun come from?

Is it still tucked in Mia's waistband?

There ought to be an interrogation, a debrief, at least a couple of words about what the hell we do next. But there isn't. We're exhausted, drained from the adrenaline dump, bodies aching from the physical toil. We don't know what the consequences of our actions will be, but we do know that only time will tell.

So, we sit here in silence. Some may sleep. I do a little, but never deeply. And then the sun comes up and the TV comes on so Toni-Marie Wiseman can tell all of Newfoundland and Labrador just what we were up to last night.

"A shocking incident at St. John's iconic art gallery and cultural space the Rooms overnight. This was the scene just hours ago as emergency services responded to a call from a night security guard . . ."

Toni-Marie's face makes way for footage of the Rooms with two fires raging in each of its eye-like windows. This was supposed to be our crowning moment—when cheers would ring out and beer bottles would be clanked together as we all revelled in the thrill of completing our most daring dare to date. But all it rouses this morning is a satisfied snort from Scott—the artist behind what will surely become the most famous work the Rooms will ever display—that meets with incredulous stares from the rest of the group that he doesn't even notice.

". . . reports suggest that a security guard was shot and killed during the incident. No details about the identity of the individual have yet been released."

Suddenly, all eyes turn to Mia, who sits staring at the TV, an ice-cold expression etched on her face.

"Who the frig was it?" Crisp asks, breaking the silence.

"Well, it wasn't Ray," Shelly says, her voice hoarse from the crying she's been trying to suppress for the last couple of hours.

"No shit. If it had been an eighty-year-old with a bum hip, none of this woulda happened," Crisp says.

"Maybe you could text Ryan? See if he knows," Mint suggests.

Shelly sniffs and nods, fumbling for her phone.

"Are you sure that's a good idea?" I ask. "I mean, what if the cops trace our messages or something?"

"The phones are burners," Crisp reminds me. "We'll toss 'em soon as we're done here. In fact, give 'em to me now. I'll get a fire going out back. We'll smash and burn 'em. Clothes, too."

A couple of us nod in agreement and begin to hand our phones over as Shelly shakily texts Ryan. Crisp grabs my phone, Scott's, and Mint's.

"Mia?" Crisp says, but Mia just stares straight ahead at the TV as a reporter stands in front of the Rooms, reporting from the scene. "Mia."

She turns to look at Crisp.

"Your phone?"

Mia reaches into her pocket, and I'm sure I'm not the only one who holds my breath for a moment. We watch as she pulls out her phone and hands it to Crisp.

"Thanks."

"What da frig?" Shelly says to no one in particular.

"What did Ryan say?" I ask.

"He says that was Ray."

"Not unless Ray has a time machine," Scott murmurs as Shelly frantically texts back and waits for a response. Then what little colour remained in her face drains away.

"He says it was Ray Junior—old Ray's grandson."

"They couldn't have come up with another name?" Scott asks.

Humour seems to be how Scott deals with stress.

"Does it matter?" Mia snarls. "Old Ray, young Ray. He shouldn't have been there."

Crisp collects Shelly's phone and pokes it into a spare pocket in his cargo pants.

"Where did you get it, Mia?" he asks.

"Get what?" she replies.

Crisp sighs. "That beautiful shirt, Mia. What do you think? The gun."

Mia blinks and looks off to the corner of the room.

"It was in the case," she says.

The rest of us exchange glances.

"The briefcase?" Crisp asks.

Mia nods.

"Wait. Which one?" I ask.

"The last one. From the docks. I opened it and the gun was there, in with the money."

"And you didn't think to tell anyone about this?" Crisp says.

A single tear falls now from Mia's eye, betraying her hard exterior. She wipes it away with her sleeve just as quickly as it appears.

"Well, it had my name on it," she says.

"What? The gun?" Crisp asks.

"Yeah. On the handle. It said 'Mia.'"

Our attention is pulled back to the TV for a moment as the

camera focuses in on Crisp's final contribution—a large, hastily sprayed Larus Can! on the exterior wall of the Rooms—and the field reporter makes the connection for her viewers.

"... familiar calling card on the side of the building here ..."

"Calling card," Scott says with another snort. We all look for him to elaborate. "They're not saying tag or graffiti anymore. They're sayin' it's a calling card. That's what they say about killers."

With that, Mia springs to her feet and leaves the room.

"Jesus, Scott, b'y . . ." Shelly says before grabbing her hula hoop and following the younger girl.

Before anyone can say another word, our collective attention is diverted to a symphony of cellphone chirps and vibrations coming from all corners of the room. The gang's day-to-day cellphones were left scattered around the place, some sitting on the coffee table, some plugged in to wall sockets to charge while we were gone. We each locate our phones to find we have all received the same text message.

And so, the world changes with a bang and a flash. At the top of the hill in the big gun's muzzle is where you'll find the cash.

"Signal Hill, I guess," I say.

"In the cannon," Mint adds.

"I'll get it," Scott says, groaning as he climbs to his feet.

"Get changed first," Crisp says. "Throw your clothes in the kitchen. I'm gonna burn 'em."

"Aye, aye, cap'n," Scott says on his way out of the room, flicking a salute in Crisp's direction.

Crisp, Mint, and I return our attention to the TV.

". . . identity of the deceased security guard has not been released at this time," says the field reporter. "Toni-Marie, back to you."

"Thanks, Shannan. In other news, a development in the search for missing tech billionaire Jackson Lorde. The Finatech co-founder has been missing since sometime last week, with no known contact and no indication of his whereabouts, but today the RNC released a few more details about what they are describing as an evolving and worrying situation."

The screen flicks to footage of Inspector Susan McGuinness, with her stern expression and perfectly pulled-back orange hair, speaking from her lectern to a gaggle of reporters.

"We are able to share today that the circumstances around Mr. Lorde's disappearance are beginning to look increasingly suspicious. Investigations by the RNC have revealed that a large amount of money has gone missing from Mr. Lorde's bank accounts, and certain valuable items have also disappeared from properties belonging to Mr. Lorde."

"Bloody hell," I say, but the other two don't say a word.

"Are you able to share any more detail on exactly what items are missing?" asks a reporter from the crowd.

Inspector McGuinness consults one of her cohorts off-mic and then gives a nod.

"Yes, as well as the money, several items of value are unaccounted for, including a valuable piece of art and a rare car."

"Can you provide any specifics about the artwork or the car?" the reporter follows up. Again, the inspector has an exchange with her colleague.

"Yes, the piece of art is a painting entitled *Family* by the indigenous artist Jeanie Cope. The car is a red DMC DeLorean."

The gathered reporters erupt in a wave of chatter.

"Oh my God," is what comes out of my mouth.

"Huh," is all Crisp can muster.

"Um, sorry, to clarify, that's a red DeLorean. Like the time machine in *Back to the Future*?" asks the reporter.

“That is correct,” says Inspector McGuinness, her stern expression unwavering. “Except this one is red.”

“Well,” Crisp says. “I guess we’ll have to get rid of the DeLorean.” He turns and strides out of the room. “Get changed and bring your clothes out back,” he says on his way out.

Mint turns to face me. “You okay?” she asks.

A wave of emotion runs through me. I’m not sure if it’s the hurt of her sporadic flirtations with Crisp, the travails of the night, or a combination of everything, but tears begin to well in my eyes.

“Hey,” she says, giving me a reassuring hug that I wish would never end. “It’s gonna be okay.”

Is it? Which part?

She kisses me on the cheek and brushes her hand across my chest as she leaves.

“C’mon,” she says. “Let’s get naked.”

I stand there trying to decode her for a moment, trying to figure her out.

It seems like that’s all I’ve been trying to do lately.

As I listen to her climb the creaky stairs, part of me wants to ignore her coquetry and wait till she comes down again. And part of me wants to chase her up the stairs like an excited puppy dog.

Just as the latter compulsion is about to win out, Inspector McGuinness’s last words send a chill up my spine.

“If anybody has seen these items, or if they have any information pertaining to the whereabouts of Jackson Lorde, they should contact the Royal Newfoundland Constabulary immediately.”

I turn to look at the TV to see they have switched to footage of the big, square Finatech building up near the airport. I squint to see Dana among the scattered few employees leaving the building. She is with another woman, who has her arm around her, and she appears to be upset.

Wow. Dana. It seems like a lifetime ago. Maybe I should text her.

I head upstairs, where any faint hope that Mint's words were some kind of invitation are instantly extinguished. She's already changed into some flowy pants and a tight white T-shirt and is standing in the doorway of Shelly's room. When I approach, the two stop talking.

"I just need to get my clothes," I say. They are still in a suitcase in Shelly's room. I haven't found a place to call my own yet, having spent my first few frantic nights at Chez Crisp sleeping wherever I have fallen.

"Of course, my love. Come on in," Shelly says from inside the room. She rises and joins Mint in the doorway.

"We'll give you some privacy. Unless ya wants a threesome," she says, hooking her hula hoop around my neck and giving her hips a little shake.

The tears appear to have dried up for now, and the old act is in full flow. The facade that cloaks the fear.

"I wouldn't say no," I say, trying with all my might not to make eye contact with Mint.

"Ooo! Hear that, Mint Imperial? We're on for later," Shelly says, pinching my cheek as she saunters by.

Mint gives me a smile, that cute little dimple on her cheek making an appearance.

"See you out back," she says.

"Hey, where's Mia?" I ask. You know. The one who just killed a man. The one who still has the gun.

"She's around," Mint says, far too calmly for my liking.

As I get changed, my thoughts are a river—ever flowing, ever changing. Visions of that awful scene at the Rooms. The dead man. Ray Junior. And then Dana, looking tearful out front of Finatech. Dana, who I've known for two years, but who now seems like a distant memory. And on the other hand, the Gulls, who I've known all of a couple of months and now feel like my dysfunctional family.

I decide to text my ex.

You doing okay? (It's Greg.)

She wouldn't know my new number. I never even gave it to her.

I head downstairs and out back to where the Gulls are gathered and the fire is raging. They stand around it like some cult performing a ceremony, staring into the flickering flames. The heat on my face puts me right back there, back at the Rooms, with the fire and the water and all that blood.

I shake away the thought and toss my Steve Jobs ninja suit into the fire.

"I guess we're gonna need new uniforms," I say, aiming for levity.

"We'll pick up some more," Crisp responds, deadly serious.

"I'll go get the cash," Scott says.

Crisp nods.

"I'll go with you," Shelly says.

"No," Crisp says without looking up. "Scotty can handle it on his own. We need to keep as low a profile as possible."

Shelly looks at Scott, who nods in reassurance before disappearing into the house. I can just about hear the front door close and the sound of the Roller firing up and peeling away above the crackle of the dancing flames.

The rest of us stand there in silence for a while, staring at the fire, and I turn the small, glass orb with the mosquito in it in my pocket. I assume that, like me, no one else can get that nightmarish scene from the Rooms out of their minds, either. But, again like me, nobody seems to have an appetite to talk about it just yet. The group feels fractured now. There is distance between us—physically and figuratively. Each of us an island. All of us, save for Scott—gone to fetch the spoils of our crimes—and Mia, still conspicuous with her absence.

Then a sound from somewhere behind me makes me jump.

C-click.

My sleep-deprived, trauma-addled brain interprets this as the sound of a gun being cocked, and I'm instantly on my toes, body poised to run for cover. Except we're out in the yard and there is no cover—except for the little old shed, which won't provide much protection from a gun-wielding crazy person.

All of this goes through my head in the couple of seconds it takes for my brain to register what's actually going on.

The sound was not that of a gun being cocked, but of the latch on the little white gate that provides entry to the back yard being unclasped. And it isn't Mia coming through. It's two strangers dressed in black suits and long, black trench coats.

Maybe a gun-toting teen would have been preferable.

"Beautiful morning for a fire, Mr. Hobbs," says the shorter of the two men, who has the look of a don from a mafia movie—a stocky character with a muscular face, beady little eyes, and greying black hair. There's an Irish tinge to his accent.

"Indeed it is, Mr. O'Hare," replies his cohort—a huge hulk of a man, at least six-foot-five, with a square jaw and sandy hair in a short military style. His voice is as gruff and deep as his frame suggests it should be, the accent a standard Newfoundland drawl.

We all stare in silence as the larger man—Hobbs—carefully closes the gate behind him and the two of them approach us.

"This is private property," Crisp says, holding his palms out in front of him and prompting O'Hare to stop, reaching out an arm of his own to prevent Hobbs from advancing any farther.

"Well, we do apologize. Don't we, Mr. Hobbs?"

"Most profusely, Mr. O'Hare."

I try to swallow and almost choke, my throat is so dry. I grip the glass orb in my pocket tightly.

"What do you want?" I find myself asking, some primal desperation washing over me.

"Just to ask a few questions," O'Hare says, lowering his arm and adjusting his jacket.

"About what?" Mint asks.

"About your friend Scott, for one," O'Hare says.

"He isn't here," Shelly says.

"We know. We just saw him leave, didn't we, Mr. Hobbs?"

"In a hurry, Mr. O'Hare," the big man replies.

What the hell is with these guys? They don't seem like cops.

"Look, Scott answered all the cops' questions down at the station—" Crisp says.

"Oh, we're not with the police, are we, Mr. Hobbs?" O'Hare says with a snicker.

"Far from it, Mr. O'Hare," Hobbs replies with an unnerving smile.

O'Hare takes a couple of steps closer, the orange flames dancing in his dark little eyes.

"Nice fire," he says. "Strong burn."

"It's all in the layering, Mr. O'Hare" Hobbs says.

"That is the key, Mr. Hobbs," O'Hare says without taking his eyes off the flames.

These guys are onto us.

"Hey—did you hear about what happened over at the Rooms last night?" O'Hare asks. "Terrible business. A man died, so they say."

"Not to mention the egregious property damage, Mr. O'Hare," Hobbs adds.

"You young pyromaniacs wouldn't happen to know anything about that, would you?" O'Hare asks.

"We don't know what you're talking about," Crisp insists.

"Hmm. And what about your little fish-gut-dumping incident over at the Basilica? Did young Scott put you up to that?" O'Hare asks as Hobbs makes the sign of the Cross and shakes his head.

"We weren't there," I say.

"Of course you weren't," Hobbs says, looking right at me.

These guys are dangerous.

"I'm afraid I really must insist that you leave," Crisp says. "You're trespassing, and if you don't go, I will be forced to call the police."

"Well, we wouldn't want the police coming over here, would we, Mr. Hobbs?"

"Oh, my goodness, no, Mr. O'Hare."

"Not with all that cash hanging around," Hobbs adds with a sneer.

"Please. Leave," Crisp says, moving toward the two men.

I grip the glass orb so tight that I think it might shatter in my palm.

"No need to get aggressive," O'Hare says, holding up his hands in a show of submission. "We were just on our way out. Weren't we, Mr. Hobbs?"

"Things to do, people to see, Mr. O'Hare," Hobbs says, cracking his knuckles loudly.

With that, the two turn and head back toward the gate, followed at a cautious distance by Crisp, the rest of us filing in behind him to make sure the men do, in fact, leave.

When they get to the little gate, the big man opens it cautiously and lets his friend go through. Then he steps daintily across the threshold himself before gripping the gate in both hands and effortlessly tearing it from its hinges, tossing it at Crisp's feet.

"More firewood," he says with an icy calm.

Crisp looks back at us, I think just to make sure we have his back, before continuing to follow the men along the side of the house and out to the sidewalk.

As we round the corner, O'Hare is standing by the red DeLorean, pulling up the dust cover to peek underneath.

We all freeze.

"Looks like an unusual vehicle," O'Hare says before carefully patting the corner of the dust cover back in place. "Yours?"

"No," Crisp says.

"No," O'Hare hisses. "Come along, Mr. Hobbs," he says, climbing into the driver's seat of a sleek black SUV. "We've kept these fine young people long enough."

Hobbs squeezes himself into the passenger seat as O'Hare fires up the engine and winds down the windows.

"Perhaps we'll see if we can find our boy Scott," he says loudly before pulling away and heading down Long's Hill.

The four of us stand there on the sidewalk and watch the car disappear into downtown St. John's.

"What the hell was that about?" I ask, my heart hammering, the dizziness from the night before returning. I rest my hand on the wooden siding of the house to steady myself.

"I don't know," Crisp says, turning to look at the covered DeLorean. "But they know about the car. We'll have to do something about that."

"And they know about the money," Mint says. We all look to her. "They mentioned about there being lots of cash around," she explains.

"She's right," Shelly says. "They did."

Crisp puts a hand to the back of his shaved head. "They could have been fishing for information," he says.

"Or they could know about the money," I say.

"Maybe we should go to the police," Shelly suggests.

"No," Crisp snaps.

"But what if they come back?" Shelly asks, shakily lighting a cigarette. "Dey already tore off da gate. Next time dey might tear off our heads," she says, without the use of her lips, the cigarette lodged between her teeth.

Prompted by her lead, I light a cigarette of my own and take a long drag. My thoughts are racing.

I'm scared.

"Maybe she's right," I say. Crisp glares at me through narrow eyes. Et tu, Brute? "I mean, if we fess up now, we could limit the damage. And who knows what those guys are capable of?"

"No," Crisp says, looking from Gull to Gull. "We've come too far to turn back now. We don't need to be afraid of Andre the Giant and Paul Bearer."

"I think it was the Undertaker who hung out with Paul Bearer," I say.

"Point is, we're young. We're strong. We have resources."

"Crisp is right," Mint says. Because of course she does. "We're in too deep. You do remember that we killed a man last night?"

"Technically, *we* didn't do anything of the sort," I say.

"Now, Gregory. You know the pact. All Gulls as one. What Mia did, she did to help us. She did it because she's one of us." Crisps walks over to me and grabs me by the shoulders. "Gregory. We're all in this together. Scott has gone to fetch a briefcase containing half a million dollars. The money's doubling with every dare. A couple more and we'll all be set for life!"

He has a point. I don't want to do jail time, and the money could change our lives.

"When all this is over, we can go anywhere we like," he says. "In the meantime, we can handle a couple of aging lackeys."

"Sure we can." We all turn to see Mia leaning at the corner of the house.

She must have come from around back. How long has she been listening? Long enough to hear me suggest we throw her under the bus?

"Especially since we still have a gun," she says before disappearing back into the yard.

We all let that sit for a moment before Crisp breaks the silence.

"It'll all work out just fine," he says, giving me a final, reassuring tap on the shoulder before heading back toward the yard himself.

Mint blows air through her lips as though letting the pressure of the situation ease out like the air brake of a truck, then she follows Crisp around the back of the house. Because of course she does.

Shelly and I are left out front to finish our cigarettes. We speak no words. She just smiles a resigned smile, and I try to offer a reassuring smile in return, though I'm not sure how convincing it is. We speak no words, but our faces speak volumes.

We're in it up to our necks, and there is no turning back now.

As I'm taking my last drag, I feel my phone vibrate. I flick my cigarette butt into the street and fish the phone out of my pocket. It's a text from Dana.

I've been better. You?

I peer down the street. I think I can see her car outside the apartment.

You home now?

Yeah

Can I pop over?

Sure. Bring beer.

I check the time on my phone. It's not quite ten thirty. On Monday morning.

I guess she isn't going to work today, then.

K. There in 10.

I tell Shelly I'll catch up with her later, and she hesitantly rounds the house, heading back to the impromptu bonfire out back. I make the climb to Long's Hill Convenience, grabbing a case of India Pale Ale and a pack of smokes before lugging the beer back down the hill, past the house and the smell of the fire. It's another crisp, sunny St. John's morning, and the sun feels good on my face.

It'll be nice to be out of that house for a while.

Just a few short steps farther down the hill, I arrive at the place I used to call home. I ring the doorbell. The little curtain twitches back, and I see Dana's face peering out at me. She looks scared, like she's been crying. She unlocks the door and opens it.

"Come in."

I do, and I'm surprised to see the place is a bit of a mess. Nothing compared to the constant chaos of my new-found home, but untidy by Dana's exacting standards. Her coat is tossed over the back of the couch. There are a few dirty dishes by the sink. Papers litter the usually bare coffee table.

"You've been smoking," she says as I dump the case of beer on the breakfast bar.

"Yeah, I just had one . . ."

"You smoke now?" she asks rhetorically, tearing into the beer box and pulling out two beers. She hands one to me, and we both twist off the caps. "You're changing," she says before taking as long a swig as I have ever seen Dana take from a beer bottle.

If only you knew.

"Wanna sit?" she asks, making her way over to the couch.

"Sure," I say.

"Bring another one," she says, holding her beer bottle aloft.

I grab two more Indias out of the case and join her on the couch.

"There's another box of your stuff over there," she says, nodding at a small cardboard box on the floor. "Just a few bits and pieces I found lying around."

"Thanks," I say.

"I was seeing Jackson," she blurts before plugging her mouth with the beer bottle.

"What?"

"Jackson Lorde," she says after another long swig of beer that may or may not be the cause of the tears once again forming in her big, doe eyes. "He's one of the owners at Finatech. I was seeing him."

"The fella who's missing?" I ask.

The tears are definitely not being caused by the bubbles as they stream down her cheeks. Still, she manages to chug the remainder of the beer and twist open the second one.

"How long has he been gone?" I ask.

"A little over a week now," she says, breaking into a jerky sob. "I'm sorry."

"No, hey, it's okay," I say, giving her a hug.

"I mean, it's not like things were going well between us," she mumbles into my chest.

"Wait. How long were you seeing him?"

"A couple of months," she says.

"A couple of months?" For a moment I'm indignant. That makes sense. We hadn't had sex for ages.

"I'm sorry," she repeats. "I wanted to tell you, but it never seemed like the right time. You were always up at that house at the top of the hill doing God knows what."

"Two months," I repeat. I'm shocked, but I don't have time to dwell on it. And it's not as though I've been an angel.

"You just kept pushing me away. Then you would disappear for hours on end—whole nights, even. What was I supposed to think?"

"Do you have any idea where he went?"

"All you talked about—when we did talk—was your new friends up the hill."

"Dana, have you heard from him?"

"And I know you have a thing for that Mint girl."

"Dana, has he been in touch with you?"

"I mean, I'm not surprised. She is beautiful—"

"Dana," I say, louder now. "Have you heard from Jackson Lorde?"

She shakes her head and wipes tears away with her sleeve.

"We were supposed to meet for dinner," she says. "He never showed up. He didn't return my texts." She looks a little drunk now. She never was much of a drinker. "I didn't sleep with him," she says. "I mean, I wouldn't have. Not while we were still . . ."

"I know. It's okay."

"Did you . . . did you cheat on me with that Mint girl?"

"No."

"Promise?"

"She kissed me the other night at a party, but never before you kicked me out," I say. "Anyway, I think she's into Crisp."

"The lanky guy?"

"Yeah."

"Some women have no taste," she says.

"Thank you," I say, and I mean it.

We share a resigned smile.

"Be careful with that crowd," she says. "They seem like a bit of a shit show."

"Yeah," I say, taking a swig. You could say that.

"I'm worried about him," she says. "Jackson. He's a busy man. I mean, he has a lot of responsibilities with work, and . . . well, with his family."

"He's married?"

"Separated."

"Kids?"

"Two. Finnian is four, and Lorean is six." She smiles. "They're good kids."

"Lorean? That's unusual."

"Yeah. Jackson loves his cars. He named her after the DeLorean. You know, like in *Back to the Future*."

"Yeah." I'm dizzy again. There isn't enough air in the room. I drink more beer in the absence of anything better to do.

"He owns two, actually. A silver one and a red one, which is very rare, apparently."

"I would imagine." I have to lean into the back of the couch to steady myself, focusing to slow my breath.

"So, hooking up with the boss. Good career move." I say the words not to hurt her but to fill space, like keeping the conversation going will help me cling to consciousness as my heart hammers in my chest and I feel the blood draining from my face.

"It wasn't like that," she says defensively. "We got talking at a Finatech party."

"The one with Sam Roberts?" I ask. Finatech were known for throwing elaborate private parties with high-profile musical guests, and I remembered Dana talking about this one.

"Yes," she says wistfully, as though remembering happier times. "I couldn't believe he was talking to me. He could have his pick—and not just of the girls in that room."

"Well, he is a billionaire," I say.

"And good-looking."

"And kinda old," I snap. Getting defensive again.

"He's only forty-two."

"Only?"

I can see from the expression on Dana's face that I'm doing myself no favours going down this road. I need to be gathering information, not antagonizing her.

"Sorry," I say.

She rolls her eyes and wipes away a fresh tear.

"So, about a week ago you are supposed to meet Jackson for dinner and he stands you up."

Dana nods.

"When did you last hear from him?"

"That morning," she says. "He told me he'd made reservations for the evening and where to meet him. It was out of town. He was trying to keep it low-key, I guess."

"And then nothing?"

"Nothing," she says, staring emptily out of the window.

"Did he tell you what his plans were for the day?"

"It was last Sunday," she says without looking away from the window. "He said he might be out of cell range because he was going fishing with his son."

"His son? Didn't you say Finnian was only four years old? Isn't that a little young to go fishing?"

"I thought the same thing, but I didn't question it. I figured maybe he just liked to get him out in nature, you know . . ."

"Is there anything else? Have you been to his home?"

"No. I think he has an apartment in the city, but I don't know where it is. He owns a number of properties."

"Of course he does." The jealousy again.

"He has a cabin in the middle of nowhere. It's on an island, I think. And his wife, Melissa, she got the family home in the divorce. It's a big place on a lake in the East End. She still lives there with the kids."

"What about his office?" I ask.

She looks back to me as though the thought had never occurred to her, as though the question sparks some small glimmer of hope for a moment.

"He has one. At Finatech. But I suppose the cops will have been through it already." I see the hope drain from her face again. "If there had been anything useful there, I'm sure they would have found it."

I shrug.

"Depends what they were looking for," I say.

She frowns at me, her eyes imploring me to elaborate.

"I mean, you might find a clue in there that the cops could have missed. Because you knew him. You know . . ." I smile, attempting to lighten the mood. ". . . really knew him." I give her a playful nudge.

"Stop it," she says, batting my hand away, a smile sparking on her face for the briefest of moments, then fading like a flanker cast loose from a fire.

"Could be worth a try, I suppose," she says, taking another swig of beer.

"I could go with you," I suggest.

"You?"

"Yeah. I mean, just for moral support. We could go in after hours. Tonight, maybe? You have a key, right?"

She sniggers.

"If by key you mean an app on my phone that automatically triggers the doors when I get within three feet of them, then yes, I have a key."

"Well, excuse me," I say theatrically, sparking another flanker smile.

"Okay," she says after a beat.

"Okay?"

"Meet me here at eight. We'll go over in my car."

"Okay."

"And don't drink any more today. You can drive," she says before slugging back the remainder of her India, putting the empty on the coffee table, and snatching the half-empty bottle from my hand.

"Okay, then," I say.

"Now, piss off back to your new friends. I have work to do." She gestures to the high-end laptop sitting next to the empties on the coffee table.

"No longer welcome. Got it," I say, standing to leave.

"Gregory," she says from the couch as I'm halfway through the door. "Thank you."

I smile and close the door behind me.

* * *

Long's Hill is cloaked in a midday sun that is actually providing some warmth for a change. The air feels weird, I think to myself as I climb the hill toward the house, then I realize it's because it's still. The standard St. John's wind, which is known to blow pretty much constantly—and often from multiple directions at the same time—is conspicuous with its absence. Long's Hill itself seems unnaturally quiet. No neighbours coming and going. No cars idling at the Longest Traffic Light in the City. It's strangely, unsettlingly calm.

I see that the Roller is once again returned to its spot in front of the house, its front wheels turned customarily in toward the curb—a trick Scott uses to prevent it rolling all the way down to Gower Street in the event that the parking brake fails against the aggressive gravitational pull of Long's Hill. As I get closer, I see that the back door of the car isn't fully closed. I perch my butt against it and sink my weight back to close it.

That's weird. The front door of the house is ajar, too.

Instinctively, I look up and down the street, searching for any sign of—well, take your pick—that black SUV, those two terrifying men, a cop car, Jackson friggin' Lorde himself. Nothing would surprise me.

I listen for a moment in the stillness. It remains eerily quiet with just the occasional swish of a passing car up on Harvey Road and the distant squawk of a seagull.

Then I hear the voices. Raised voices, coming from inside the house.

I feel the blood pumping through my temples and take a deep breath to ward off the dizziness again. Then—slowly and cautiously—I approach the front door and ease it creakily open.

It's dark inside compared to the bright afternoon sunshine. The hallway and the stairs are cast in shadow, and there's an uncommon stillness about the place.

I listen for voices. When I hear none, I pull the front door closed behind me with what seems like an inordinately loud clunk. I see movement ahead from within the kitchen, then there are more muffled voices from behind the closed door of the living room to my right.

Then I see that the movement in the kitchen is Shelly. She must have heard me close the door. She's been crying. She looks scared. She shakes her head at me and gestures—*shush*—before returning to what she was doing, stuffing handfuls of cash into a briefcase.

I watch her for a moment, frozen to the spot. It's a new briefcase. Green, to match the envious eyes of the Rooms.

It must be the one Scott went to retrieve from Signal Hill.

My brain begins trying to piece things together.

She's putting all the cash from all our dares into the one, new briefcase.

She finishes stuffing the briefcase and closes it up with trembling hands. Then I hear deep, thudding footsteps. The living room door flies open, and Mia bursts into the hallway. I reflexively jump back against the door and raise my hands when I see she's pointing the gun right at me.

"Whoa!" I say.

"Get in there!" she yells, gesturing to the living room door with the gun. "Get in that fucking room!"

"Okay, okay," I say as the walls around me begin to warp and my heart just about bursts from my chest like a Giger alien.

As I shuffle over to the open door, I see Shelly standing in the entrance to the kitchen. She's visibly shaking, the matte green briefcase in her hand. Inside the living room, Crisp, Mint, and Scott sit with gloomy looks on their faces.

"Is that thing full?" I hear Mia ask. Shelly mumbles something in response. "It's all in there? All of it?" Mia screams.

"Yes," I hear Shelly say meekly.

"Get in there. Get in that room!"

Shelly stumbles into the room as though shoved in the back on her way.

"Sit down," Mia barks at me, again waving the gun in my direction. I do as I'm told, sinking down on the couch next to Mint and Scott. Crisp sits cross-legged over by the old tube TV.

"Put the rest of it in there," Mia instructs Shelly, gesturing to the few stray bills that lie scattered on the coffee table and the musty old carpet. Shelly opens the briefcase on the table and begins gathering up the bills.

As she does, Crisp shifts his position, unfolding his legs and propping himself up, hands on the carpet behind him.

"Don't frickin' move!" Mia yells, noticing the movement. Crisp wears that trademark sly grin, as unflappable as ever. He looks like he's planning to do something.

Mia trains the gun back on Shelly.

"Hurry up!" she yells as Shelly gathers the last few bills into the briefcase and clasps it shut again with trembling hands.

"You don't need to do this, Mia," Crisp says.

"Shut up!" Mia yells. "You shut up!"

Crisp is up on his knees now, long arms reaching out in front of him like a hundred-metre sprinter in the blocks. He's definitely planning to do something.

"It's normal for gulls to fight one another," Crisp says as Shelly conducts the world's worst Easter egg hunt, digging down the backs of chairs and underneath the couch to scrape up every last bill, per Mia's instructions. "They're a lot like us. Most of the time they act like they can't stand each other. They squabble over food scraps. They posture to display their dominance. They even eat each other's eggs."

Crisp's voice is steady and calm, somehow commanding attention even amid all this chaos. It's as though his voice is in our heads—a placid narration detached from reality.

"But for all that, they can't get away from the fact that they're social creatures. There's an understanding among gulls, an uneasy peace, and a strict code of status and seniority."

"Over there, on the TV stand," Mia yells at Shelly, trying her best to ignore Crisp's words.

"You see, deep down, gulls know they need each other. Even with all that tension and rivalry, they know when to band together. When eagles swoop down from above, or foxes penetrate the colony, they take flight as one, screeching, diving, and shitting all over their collective enemies like a well-oiled machine."

"Good. Now give it 'ere," Mia says, lowering the gun and extending her spare hand to take the briefcase from Shelly.

"At the end of the day, gulls know who their friends are," Crisp says, continuing his detached monologue, gimlet eyes narrowing with focus.

"Why are you doing this?" I find myself asking Mia.

"You knows why," she says, the question clearly piercing her armour, her voice cracking. "My mom. She needs treatment out in Toronto. She needs the money. You lot'll just piss it away. But she needs to go to Toronto. And now I need to go to Toronto, too. Because . . . because I killed that fella at d'Rooms."

As her hands lower and her grip weakens and her rage gives way to despair, it is as though time itself slows in the house on Long's Hill. All sound is pulled from the room, save for the last line of Crisp's monologue, delivered in steady, dulcet tones.

"But what gulls do best, what truly makes them prosper and persevere, is that they never, ever pass up an opportunity to swoop and claim their prize."

With that, Crisp springs into action, popping up from the floor and using all his length to swan-dive over the coffee table and rugby-tackle Mia. But for all the poise Crisp demonstrates in his words, this does not translate to grace in his movements, and he only manages to knock her sideways into the couch.

The shunt causes the gun to go off, the sound of which is very different from how the shots sounded at the exhibit hall at the Rooms. There, it was like an echoing thunderclap. In this more intimate setting, it is more like a dull thud cranked up to eleven, reverberating through my bones.

Crisp yelps and falls backwards, then I see my chance. The green briefcase is at my feet, and instinctively I grab it and jump up from the couch. But Mia is blocking my path to the door as she squirms to right herself, the gun still looming large in her undersized hand.

I'll have to go around.

That's what my brain decides, and I go for a lap of the coffee table with the intent of escaping out the front door and legging it for all I'm worth down Long's Hill and far away from here.

But by the time I round the coffee table, Mia is up.

I stop dead in my tracks.

"Give it to me," she says through gritted teeth, and I'm suddenly aware of Crisp whimpering on the floor to my right. He seems to be holding his leg, but I daren't look. I daren't take my eyes off Mia. She's pointing the gun right at my face, and for a moment I get the strangest urge to laugh. If I do, it will be my body's final betrayal. It's already stinging my eyes and soaking my clothes with sweat. I already feel like my bladder or bowels—or both—could give out at any second. All of that would be preferable to a laugh, though. To suggesting to Mia that I'm not taking her seriously.

She's deadly serious, slate blue eyes unblinking, black mascara tracing the memory of tears down her pale cheeks.

"Give me the fucking money, Greg."

Was this her plan all along?

"Give it to me!" she screams, shrill and loud, in that thick Newfoundland accent, and I'm suddenly aware of how far I am from home. I think of my mum, back over there in England—that other rock floating in the North Atlantic.

I instinctively reach out an arm, palm flat, like I'm Darth Vader or some shit—using the Force to keep her at bay.

"Okay, Mia. Okay," I say.

But it's not a lightsaber in my other hand—it's the leather-bound handle of the briefcase. A matte green metal briefcase stuffed with the better part of a million Canadian dollars, cash.

"Don't give it to her, Greg," Crispin pipes up, still lying prone on the floor. He props himself up on bony elbows and spits blood from his split lip onto the musty old carpet. "She's bluffing. She's not gonna shoot ya."

"Shut up!" Mia wails, momentarily pointing the gun in Crispin's direction. He tries not to react, attempts to continue with his mind games, but he's not the one holding the gun.

"Yeah, Crisp, shut up," Shelly echoes from her place on the couch in an uncharacteristic whisper, the ever-present hula hoop wrapped around her even as she sits.

"It's not like she isn't capable of shooting someone," Scott drones from beside her.

"Shut up," Mia hisses.

"In fact, it's becoming a bit of a habit. A hobby, even," Scott says before Shelly gives him a sharp elbow to the ribs.

"Give it to me. Now!" Mia screams.

"Okay, okay."

What fucking choice to I have?

I lower my Force hand and bring my lightsaber hand forward, the briefcase rattling as much as her gun.

Everything from that point happens in slow motion.

Mia's eyes unlock themselves from my own and lust after the briefcase.

The gun lowers, just a hair.

Mia reaches her free hand to take the case.

Crisp yells something and there's a yellow blur as Shelly's hula hoop comes down over Mia.

Someone snatches the briefcase from my hand as I reflexively dive backwards onto the floor.

I hear another gunshot—loud and dull in this poky Long's Hill living room.

As I land, all I see is the tasteless light fixture against the yellowed stucco ceiling caught in a flash of gunfire. I hit hard, and my final thought is, *Ew. How gross is it to be lying on this carpet?*

Then all goes black.

12

Everybody's Searching for Something

"Well, we gotta figure it out soon if this thing has to go down tomorrow night. I mean, what if it calls for a lotta prep?"

"How much prep can it call for if it's tomorrow night? Surely he would have factored that in."

The voices are muffled as I blink open my eyes, but I can make out the words plain as day. I sit up on the couch and feel a sharp pain at the back of my head. I reach back to find that my hair is sticky with semi-dried blood and wet from the damp cloth that now lies, itself stained with blood, on the couch. On the musty old carpet there's a small patch of what I can only assume is more of my blood, along with a few more specks on the other side of the coffee table that must have spilled out of whatever wound Crispin sustained in the melee.

"Well, it is gonna be worth a million dollars if the money keeps doubling like it has so far. Maybe he's making it more difficult for us now."

"More difficult than what we just went through?" Mint says incredulously.

I'm up on wobbly legs. There's no one else in the living room, so I head toward the voices in the kitchen. As I approach the living room door, I notice a bullet hole in the wall that is now a peephole into the hallway beyond.

"Jesus," I say to myself as I head out the door.

"Who is *he* exactly?" Shelly is the one asking.

"Wha—?"

"You keep referring to our mysterious benefactor as *he*. Does that mean we've decided it's this Jackson Lorde character?"

"Yeah, it is," I say as I enter the room.

"Oh, you're up," Shelly says, instantly switching to Mother Hen mode. "Now, don't be wobblin' around or you'll do yourself a mischief. Sit down here, luh."

She guides me to the easy chair in the corner that she herself just vacated, moving aside her hula hoop to accommodate me. The rest of the gang wait for me to finish my thought.

"The red DeLorean. It's too big a coincidence, right?" I ask.

"Right," Crisp says. He's sitting on one of the wooden chairs pulled back from the circular dinner table, one long leg outstretched, his heel resting on an upturned metal bucket. He's wearing only his tighty-whities, with a thick, pink robe wrapped around him and a cup of steaming tea in his hand. Mint sits at his side, dabbing a small cigar-shaped wound on his upper thigh with a wet cloth.

That's right, I think, dabbing the back of my head with my fingers to make sure no blood is continuing to escape. Take care of your boyfriend. Don't worry about me.

Soon enough, I'm being tended to myself, as Shelly finds another wet cloth and perches herself on the arm of the easy chair.

"Tilt your head forward, honey," she says, dabbing my wound. I suck air through my teeth. "I know it hurts," she says.

"And what about those two men who came here today?" I ask.

"What men?" Scott asks.

"Ah, right, Scotty doesn't know about our gate-hating visitors," Crisp says, blowing on his tea.

Shelly catches me eyeing him.

"You want some tea, sweetie?"

"Yes, please."

"Okay. Hold this to your head," she says, pulling my hand up to the damp cloth before heading over to the stove to boil the kettle.

"Two men came here today," Mint explains. "They were dressed all in black and drove a black SUV."

"Lord geez, was it Will Smith and Tommy Lee Jones?" Scott asks, almost causing Crisp to spit out his tea.

"Not quite. Misters Hobbs and O'Hare," he says.

"Well, what did they want?" Scott asks.

"They were asking about you," Shelly says with a look of concern as she pops a tea bag into a large mug.

"Me?" Scott looks alarmed.

"Yup," Crisp says, his expression more serious now.

"Well, what, were they cops?"

"Said they weren't," Mint says.

"They didn't look like cops," I point out.

"Didn't talk like cops, either," Shelly says, leaning on the island.

"Frig," Scott says, looking around as though the walls are watching him. "I gotta get outta here."

"We might all have to get outta here," Crisp says, drawing the attention of the whole group. "This place is getting too hot," he adds, blowing on his tea.

"Where's Mia?" I ask, my body suddenly going rigid as I remember the reason why I was knocked unconscious and Crisp has a bullet wound in his thigh. A wound that Mint continues to tend to.

The rest of the group look between each other sheepishly.

"She's in the attic," Crisp says.

"And the gun?"

"It's safe," he says in a tone that suggests the conversation is over.

"What are we gonna do with her?" I ask, but I am answered only with silence as Shelly brings over a cup of steaming tea in a St. John's Maple Leafs mug. She passes it to me and perches herself on the arm of the easy chair, once again dabbing my head with the wet cloth.

"Do we have a new clue?" I ask, eyeing the open green briefcase on the kitchen table and taking a sip of what might possibly be the most delicious cup of tea I've ever tasted.

"Yeah, and it's a doozy," Scott says excitedly, all talk of imprisoned teenaged girls and mysterious men in black suddenly forgotten.

Crisp smiles and reaches out a hand for Scott to pass him the latest notes, which he reads out for the room.

THREE DARES DOWN AND TWO TO GO
NOW, TO THE GULLS' MOST FEARSOME FOE
AT THE HOME OF THE GOOSE WHERE THE HAWK TAKES FLIGHT
TAKE ITS LEGS, CLIPS ITS WINGS, TOMORROW NIGHT

"Tomorrow night?" I ask, suddenly aware of how weary and groggy I'm feeling.

I don't know if I have it in me.

"Exactly," Crisp says.

"So, where's the home of the goose?" I ask, to which nobody replies. Clearly they've already had this conversation and gotten nowhere.

"Well, where does a goose live?" I ask, sipping my tea. "The park, maybe?"

"Could be," Mint replies. "But which park?"

"Bannerman?" I suggest.

"Bowring has the duck pond," Shelly says as she tries to find a spot on the wet cloth that isn't stained with my blood.

"Not a whole lotta hawks down at Bowring, though," Scott says. "Plenty of little old ladies power walking. Not so many hawks taking flight."

"Maybe he's not talking about a real hawk," I suggest. "Maybe it's code for something."

"Well, I should hope so," Shelly says. "Because no way am I gettin' involved in any animal cruelty."

"Right, 'cause we only hurt humans," Scott blurts, instantly regretting it.

For a good few seconds, the only sounds in the room are Crisp and me sipping our tea.

"So, what are we going to do with Mia?" I ask.

* * *

The attic door creaks open, and I stand on my tiptoes to see past the Gulls on the steps ahead of me. I'm as eager to see just what's inside the mysterious little room at the top of the stairs as I am to see what kind of state Mia is in.

The answer to question number one is that the narrow room is painted all white with the same age-old stucco ceiling as can be found throughout the rest of the house. On either side the walls are lined with floor-to-ceiling shelves that house all manner of interesting paraphernalia. There are old file folders full of documents and maps. There are jars of what appear to be various kinds of marbles and beads. There are ornaments, many of them depicting birds and other animals, some of which look antique. There are even a number of what appear to be large paintings propped up next to each other and carefully wrapped in age-weathered dust covers.

Where did Crisp get all this stuff?

There is even a selection of tools and implements—any one of which would have been very useful to Mia in order to cut loose her binds but, alas, the answer to question two is that she is in no state to make use of them, tied, as she is, to the rusty-but-robust radiator that's dead centre of the back wall.

We all stare at the girl like kids trying to get a look at a wild animal in the zoo. But the fight appears to have left this particular beast, head down, pale cheeks streaked with the dark lines of mascara-laden tears. She's been gagged with some duct tape and an old dishcloth.

Crisp walks into the room and retrieves a toolbox from one of the shelves, pulling out a folding knife and opening out the blade.

"I'm gonna cut you loose," Crisp says, waving the knife in front of Mia's face. "Don't do anything stupid. Everybody's here. We're not gonna hurt you. Just relax and hear us out and everything will be fine. Okay?"

The girl gives a shallow nod before Crisp goes about cutting the zip ties off her ankles, then the ones attaching her hands to the old radiator. As she rubs her reddened wrists, he folds the knife away and removes the gag.

"There. You want some water?"

Mia nods and Crisp holds out a hand, prompting Scott to enter the little room with a small plastic bottle of spring water. He takes the top off and hands it to Mia, who takes a few shaky sips before collapsing into a whining sob.

"Now, look. We know you've been through a lot with your mudder and all, and the past few days have been kinda crazy. But when a baby gull turns on her elders, well, that only ends one way. You're outta the flock, Mia."

Mia whines, prompting Shelly to step forward and console her.

"Come on, now. Everything's gonna be okay," she says.

"I'm sorry," Mia squeaks, curling into Shelly's motherly embrace.

"Ya killed a feller," Crisp says. "But you were only acting out of self-defence. His name was Ray Junior," he continues, looking out the door at the rest of us. "His name was Ray Junior," he repeats. "His name was Ray Junior." We all just stare blankly back at him. "Just me, then."

Mia continues to sob into Shelly's bosom.

"Okay, look," Crisp says, removing a thick envelope from his pocket. "Here's fifty grand. Gather up your mother and head to Toronto. Or somewhere close, anyhow, because Toronto is expensive. This'll be enough for you to get set up, at least. Get a job. Maybe enrol back in the police. That'd really be suckin' it to 'em, now, wouldn't it?" Crisp taps Mia playfully on the shoulder with the envelope but only receives a scowl back in response.

"Disappear. Forget about all this. You're still young. Start a new life." Crisp stands and tosses the envelope on the floor in front of Mia.

"Fly free, little bird," he says as he leaves the room, squeezing past us and off down the stairs.

We all just stand there staring for a moment until Shelly shoos us away.

"Geez, by's. Ya want some popcorn or wha—? Give her some space, would ye?"

With that, we turn and make our way back down the stairs.

We mull around for a while, the gravity of the situation dawning on us.

One of our own killed a man. His name was Ray Junior.

Now she's been cast from the group. And if one Gull can be cast out from the flock, any of us could be.

Mint deals with the dish mountain that's been gradually piling up at the side of the sink. Crisp turns his attention to the bloodstains on the carpet—literally the first time I've seen him clean anything in the house since I got here.

"You have to blot," he says, as though he's known this his whole life and it's not something a scary-looking bearded man from Idaho just told him in a YouTube video. "Can't be rubbin'. Rubbin'll only spread it."

I stand in the living room doorway, keeping an eye on the muted TV to see if the news will come on and if we'll feature, but it's just *Wheel of Fortune* for the moment. I check my phone and see that there's somewhat of a frenzy over it all in the local media. Images of the Rooms with its fiery eyes are played in loops, one up close from across Harvey Road, another from some hill to the west, and then the money shot from the distance of Signal

Hill before the sun had come up, the building cast pale against the city lights, the fires glowing like two devil's eyes in the darkness.

The image shifts to a shot of those two words, scrawled across the side of the building, this time with a little M-shaped seagull, the way our art teacher taught us to draw them in primary school.

Larus Can!

Then there's a shot I haven't seen before: an interior showing the aftermath of the fires. Smoking embers doused with water. Crime scene tape flapping in the wind at the doorway to the exhibit room.

I find myself clutching the glass orb in my pocket tight in my hand once again, so tight that it might fracture in my palm.

Then Mia and Shelly come creaking slowly down the stairs. Mia is still sniffling, head down. Shelly is carrying an RNC bookbag filled with the bits and pieces that had migrated their way over to the house from wherever Mia lived before she met us, just a few crazy days ago.

Mia heads straight for the front door and opens it, a mild draft blowing through the wind tunnel that is the hallway. Shelly hands her the bag and gives her one last motherly hug.

"You take care, now, okay?"

Mia manages a nod and turns to leave.

Just then, Scott comes barrelling down the hallway.

"Mia! Mia, hold on," he says, stopping the young girl in her tracks. "Here," he says, holding out another envelope thick with cash. "Ten grand won't get you far in Toronto."

Mia tentatively reaches out a hand and takes the envelope, even managing a thin smile through the tears. And then she is gone.

I notice that Crisp has appeared beside me in the doorway. He squeezes reddened water from a cloth into the same metal bucket that had been his footstool an hour earlier and gives Scott a look as though he's the guy who just left a tip after he'd paid for the whole meal.

"Who wants some Ches's?" Crisp asks. "My treat," he shouts as he makes his way back along the hallway.

* * *

We all devour the Ches's fish and chips, washing it down with watery soda from oversized paper cups, and sit around the kitchen table in relative silence.

As she slurps the dregs of her soda noisily through the plastic straw, Shelly turns the note from the green briefcase in her spare hand.

"Goosey, goosey gander, where shall I wander," she says to herself. "Upstairs and downstairs and in my lady's chamber." She looks up at us. "Goosey, goosey gander," she says, this time to the group, holding the piece of paper aloft.

Crisp is the first to clue in.

"Genius!" he exclaims, hopping up from his chair and almost tipping over the tableful of fish-and-chip wrappers and soda cups. He makes his way around and gives Shelly a big kiss on the cheek, to which she flutters her eyelashes and pretends to be overcome.

Crisp snatches the piece of paper from her hand.

"Goosey, goosey gander!" he exclaims. Mint is the next to make the connection.

"Gander," she says. "As in the famous airport."

"'At the home of the goose, where the hawk takes flight,'" Crisp recites. "The hawk must be an airplane . . ."

"That's going to take off from Gander Airport," I say, finally arriving at the party. "So, where is Gander Airport, exactly?"

"Lord geez, honey," Shelly says with a snigger. "How long have you been in Newfoundland now?"

The rest of the group start chuckling, too, as Shelly jumps up and puts one foot on her chair like Captain Morgan. "And have ye never heard of *Come From Away*?" She begins clapping her hands and launches into a musical performance.

"On the northeast tip of North America, on an island called Newfoundland, there's an airport," she says in a rough, aggressive voice. "It used to be one of the biggest airports in the world, and next to it is a town called Gander."

The monologue turns to song as the rest of the Gulls begin stomping and drumming on the table, sending soda cups toppling and chip wrappers flying.

"Welcome to the Rock if you come from away,

"You'll prob'ly understand about half of what we say.

"They say no man's an island but an island makes a man,

"Especially when one comes from one like Newfoundland."

For the next line, the whole group joins in, singing out in unison.

"Welcome to the Rock!"

Then Crisp takes over that way Crisp does, chanting loudly and rhythmically, the rest of the group following his lead, all of them dancing around the kitchen.

"I'm an islander, I am an islander! I'm an islander, I am an islander!"

This goes on for a good minute or so before Crisp grabs me by the shoulders.

"Gander Airport, Gregory! The flock is flying north."

The excitement becomes a bit of a party for the next hour or so, bottles of India being passed around the room. Solving—or at least part-solving—the riddle has re-galvanized the group, even as six become five. I accept a beer but only take a sip, questioning whether drinking is such a good idea after a knock to the head and with Dana's words ringing in my ears:

Don't drink any more. You can drive.

I don't know whether she said that because she doesn't like driving in town or because she worries about my drinking.

Probably a little bit of both.

After a while the party mood calms and Crisp is back to planning mode.

"It's about a three-and-a-half-hour haul up to Gander," he says. "So, we'll leave in the morning. No big rush, maybe around nine when everyone's up and showered. We'll grab a breakfast sandwich over to Tim's and hit the road. Gander has a Canadian Tire and a Mark's, so we can re-kit out there." He looks around the room with those narrow eyes and that thin smile. "Game on, Gulls."

Eventually, everybody drifts away. Crisp, Mint, and Shelly head to the living room to watch *Wheel of Fortune* and *Jeopardy!* while Scott wanders off upstairs. It's coming up on eight and I have a date to keep, so I throw on my denim jacket, empty out my old bookbag, sling it over my shoulder, and head for the front door.

"Where ya goin'?" Scott's voice gives me a start as I'm halfway out the door. I turn to see him standing at the top of the stairs. I have to squint to see that he appears to be polishing some sort of ornament with a rag.

"Oh, I, uh . . . I have a date," I say.

"Yeah? What's the bag for?"

"Uh . . . pockets in this jacket are shit, so I threw my wallet and phone in there."

"Huh. Well, don't be up canoodlin' all night," he says. "Gander town in the mornin'."

"Yeah, no, I won't."

"Don't wanna upset the boss, right?"

I assume he's talking about Crisp.

"Right. Wouldn't want to do that."

"See ya later, Greg."

"Yeah, catch you in the morning."

I close the door behind me and head out into a fresh St. John's summer evening, walking the short distance to Dana's apartment. Her white Jeep Cherokee is sitting outside, and I smile. She'd always wanted a Jeep, and it had been a gift to herself when she landed the coding job at Finatech.

I ring the doorbell and the door opens almost immediately.

"You're late," Dana says.

I look at my watch. 8:14 p.m.

"Well, fifteen minutes or so, I guess."

"You were only coming from three doors over," she says. "Come on. You're driving."

And now I remember why I broke up with her.

She locks the door and hands me the neat little bunch of keys, pausing before I can take them from her.

"Let me smell your breath."

"Seriously?"

She shoots me a look that confirms without question that she is, in fact, serious. I open my mouth wide and breathe.

"You're chewing gum," she says, rolling her eyes.

"Is that not allowed, either?" I ask.

We're falling back into the old routine.

"You better not have been drinking," she says, pressing the key fob to unlock the Jeep's doors before jamming the keys into my palm and climbing into the passenger seat.

"Scout's honour," I say, squeezing into the driver's side and starting the car before adjusting the seat so I can move.

"I forgot you like to drive with your face pressed against the windscreen," I say.

"I forgot you like to drive lying down," she retorts.

The old routine.

We make the short drive to Finatech—a big grey block of a four-storey building out by the airport with a big red logo emblazoned on the side. There are no other cars in the large parking lot as I pull into a spot close to the entrance and kill the engine.

"Ready?" I say, detecting hesitance in Dana's eyes.

She takes a deep breath.

"Okay, yeah. Let's do this."

We get out of the Jeep and approach the big double doors that are set into a glass column reaching the full height of the front of the building, behind it a staircase visible from the outside that zigzags all the way up to the top floor.

As we get close to the door there's a high-pitched chirp as the little red LED turns green. Dana slaps the big square button to open the door, shepherding me inside.

I wander toward the elevators to the right but feel Dana's hand tugging me back.

"We'll take the stairs," she says, going on ahead of me. I look up at the open staircase and begin to feel the fatigue of the past few days creeping back into my bones.

"Of course we will," I sigh, following along after her.

Two large sets of stairs separate the floors, each with a red sign indicating the floor we're on. As we climb I feel rather exposed in this glass column, in the bright glow of the fancy dangling light fixtures.

"Not very inconspicuous," I wheeze. Dana doesn't acknowledge the complaint.

By the time we get to the fourth floor, I'm horribly out of breath and horribly unable to disguise the fact.

"Good grief, Gregory. You really ought to lay off the smokes," Dana says, the little chirp greeting her as she approaches the entrance.

She opens the door and we step inside. The space is completely open-plan with rows of uniform desks and identical red office chairs. Each workstation has a monitor and jacks for people to plug in their laptops. The floor is grey carpet with an unfussy pattern of slightly darker grey. All of this is just about visible in the meagre illumination provided by hundreds of dimmed pot lights that line the ceiling.

"So, where is Jackson's office?" I ask.

"Why are you whispering?"

"I don't know."

"This way."

I follow Dana past the banks of desks and monitors to the far end of the space, where there's small library behind glass walls.

"Why is it that even modern libraries are spooky as shit at night?" I ask. Dana doesn't answer. She never was one for a rhetorical question.

We make our way past the library and to a door, but we're greeted by a minor note and a flashing red LED.

"I guess you don't have security clearance for Jackson Lorde's office," I say. "Too early in the relationship, I suppose."

If looks could kill, the one Dana shoots me would have stopped my heart on the spot. She brushes past me and makes her way back around the other side of the library.

"Where are you going?" I ask. This time my answer comes in the form of a happy chirp from the library door. I follow Dana inside and past the rows of books—an intimidating selection of coding bibles and business theory tomes—until she reaches the farthest shelf.

"What are we doing here?" I ask. I'm still whispering. We are in a library, after all.

Dana gives me a "just watch" look and proceeds to pull three identical copies of Simon Sinek's *Start with Why* off the shelf before pushing a little hidden panel that springs open to reveal a keypad. She keys in eight digits, and the whole bookshelf sinks back into the wall with a loud clunk. Dana leans her back against it and pushes the secret door open as she looks me right in the eye.

"Not *too* early in the relationship," she says.

"Blimey," I say as I follow her inside. "It's like an Indiana Jones movie. If Indiana Jones movies were made by computer nerds."

The office is reasonably small and sparsely decorated with just one painting hanging on the wall—a vibrant, colourful piece of indigenous art depicting a soaring eagle, within it a deep red sunset with silhouetted trees and smaller flying birds that second as the details of the eagle's feathers and wings.

The painting looks out of place in the otherwise stark and clinical office. Everything else is very much in its place. A computer monitor and a docked laptop are the only things on the desk, and the chair is tucked in neatly. A matte-white storage cabinet sits with its doors and drawers neatly closed, and nothing adorns the top of it except for a small model jet plane, itself matte white. The place is immaculate.

"Who is this guy—Marie Kondo?" I ask.

"He likes things to be neat and tidy," Dana replies as she examines the painting. "Maybe you can learn something."

"Yeah, like how to be anal-retentive."

I join Dana in front of the painting. It is a fabulously detailed work of art.

"This is indigenous, right?" I ask. "Is he into that kind of thing."

"He likes art," Dana says. "He's into all kinds of things."

"I bet he is."

Dana ignores me and looks around the room, shrugging. "Look around, I guess," she says.

I start with the shelving unit, trying the drawers and doors. All are locked, even though I don't see any discernible keyholes. All except for the last drawer I try—a small drawer down at the bottom of the unit, which slides open with the kind of smooth ease that only comes with very expensive furniture. Inside there's something wrapped in a piece of colourful, floral cloth. I pick it up. The cloth is old and smells musty. I unwrap it to reveal a thick, wooden picture frame with intricate carvings of shapes that look vaguely from nature—leaves and shrubs and branches. Inside the frame is a picture of a young white man and an indigenous woman wrapped in a colourful shawl. I squint and hold the picture closer. The woman is holding a tiny baby in her arms. The picture is a little blurry, but the couple look happy, standing on the top of a hill or mountain with a valley falling away in the background.

"Found something," I say, rising to stand.

"What is it?"

"A weird old picture." I examine the man more closely. I've only seen pictures of Jackson Lorde on the news, with his beard and long, pulled-back hair. This guy has short hair and is clean-shaven, but it could be him.

"All the desk drawers are locked," Dana says with a sigh, making her way over. I hold the picture out so she can see it.

"That's Jackson," she says breathily.

"Are you sure?" I ask.

"Yeah, it's him."

"You can tell that? Even without the Jesus beard and the man bun?"

"It's him," she says. "I'd recognize those dreamy eyes and that hot bod anywhere."

"Easy, now. So, who's the woman?"

"I don't know."

"It's not his wife?"

"Who? Melissa? No, she's bimbo blonde and half his age."

"So, around your age, then?"

Dana delivers a sharp elbow to my ribs.

"Ow. And what about the baby?"

"I don't know," Dana says, taking the picture from me. She examines it closely for a moment. "Where is this?" she asks rhetorically.

"Newfoundland, for sure," I say.

"Looks familiar, but it's kinda blurry," Dana says.

She flips over the picture frame and looks at me as though for permission.

"Crack it open," I say.

She eases back the fasteners and carefully removes the piece of cardboard.

"Huh," I say, seeing the handwriting scribbled on the back of the photo. "Jacks, Jeanie, and little . . . what is that? Laura? Lanna?"

"I can't tell. But it's not Finnian or Lorean."

Dana hands me the photo and the dismantled frame.

"There's a date here, too," I say. "June 29, 1997." Dana shrugs. "He would have only been about twenty," she says before moving on to examine the rest of the room.

"Guess I'll just pop this back together, then," I say as she rechecks all the other doors and drawers in the storage unit that I've already checked.

I take a snap of the front and back of the photo with my phone before reassembling the frame, wrapping it carefully in the colourful cloth, and placing it back in the drawer.

I see that Dana is looking at the model jet plane.

"Is he into planes, too?" I ask.

"Not particularly," she says. "But he does own one."

"Of course he does."

She picks up the model jet and turns it in her hands.

"Maybe if everyone owned their own jet, we could destroy the planet by next Christmas," I say.

"Well, the company owns it, I guess," Dana says distantly. "Him and the other partners."

"Ah. That makes it okay, then."

"They're flying out in it tomorrow night, actually. The other partners—Justin and Patrick. They're heading to New York to talk to Nasdaq about a possible buyout."

"What—*the* Nasdaq? As in the stock exchange? That Nasdaq?"

Dana nods.

"Jackson should be with them. Or they should be with Jackson. He's the real brains of the operation. Without him they'd never have gotten this far. Now they'll be taking all the plaudits while Jackson is . . ." She tails off, tears forming in her eyes.

"Hey," I say, placing a hand on her shoulder. "We'll find him."

This guy obviously means a lot to her.

As she places the model jet back on the storage unit, I notice an insignia marked on the side. I snatch the model up and look at it closely.

"*Hawk 1*?" I say, my eyes widening.

"Yeah. That's the name of the plane," Dana says. "Why?"

"Dana, where are they taking off from?"

"I don't know. St. John's airport, I assume."

"Not Gander?"

That sparks something.

"Oh, wait, yes, you're right. When they came back from Dubai last month, it was too foggy to land in St. John's, so they diverted to Gander and drove in from there. I remember Jackson saying they wanted to check out some sites in central, so they were going to keep the plane there and fly out to New York from Gander. Justin and Patrick are there now. But how did you . . ."

"I, uh. I think they mentioned something about it on the news," I lie. I know she can tell when I'm lying, so I quickly put the model back on the storage unit and head over to the desk, rechecking the drawers she's already checked—still very much all locked—and attempting to change the subject.

"Isn't it a bit strange that he didn't take his laptop?" I ask, opening it up, tapping on the space bar, and getting a password screen.

Dana shrugs. "He probably has about a dozen of them, so not necessarily. Greg, how did you—"

Before she can finish her sentence, we are both stopped dead in our tracks by a bright light shining in through the window from below.

"Get down," I say.

"Why?" Dana asks, quite legitimately considering we're way up on the fourth floor.

"I dunno. That's just what they usually say in the movies."

Dana rolls her eyes and walks over to the window.

"There's somebody down there," she says, now with a little more tension in her voice. "Two weird-looking guys and a big black SUV. They're right next to the Jeep."

"Hobbs and O'Hare," I say.

"Who?"

"I'll tell you later," I say, folding the laptop and shoving it into my bookbag.

"Are you stealing that?"

"I'm borrowing it. Come on."

We retrace our steps out of Jackson's office and through the secret door, closing it behind us and returning the books to the shelf.

"Is there another way down?" I ask.

"Yes, there's another staircase on the back of the building," Dana says. "But how are we going to get past them?"

"We'll figure that out when we get there," I say. "Show me where the stairs are."

Dana rushes ahead, out of the library and down a narrow passageway at the back corner of the floor. She eases open a heavy metal door to reveal a stairwell. Dimly lit, this one lacks the grandeur of its counterpart on the front of the building, but if it will get us out and past the gruesome twosome, it's all right by me.

As I start down the first set of steps, I notice that Dana has stopped behind me at the top of the stairwell. I pause and turn to see her holding her phone in front of her face. Before I can say anything, I hear a voice come through the speaker-phone.

"911, what is your emergency?"

"I'm at Finatech off Torbay Road. Some men are harassing my friend and me. Please send the police. I think they might be dangerous."

Before the operator can reply, Dana hangs up.

"What are you doing?" I ask, but Dana just charges on past me down the stairs.

"Come on."

I begin to follow, but I'm not done with my remonstrations.

"You called the police? Dana, we just broke into Jackson Lorde's office."

"We didn't break in. We walked in. I'm an employee, re-member?" she says as we descend through the floors.

"Yeah, but I stole his laptop."

"No," she says as we continue down. "You just borrowed it."

She pauses to give me a little wink before continuing on down.

"Jesus, Dana. You don't know what these guys are like."

"No, but you're going to tell me all about it as soon as we get the hell out of here."

We finally reach the ground floor and make our way down another long corridor that leads to another heavy metal door with a push bar. Dana leans her back against it and waits for me to catch up.

"Okay, here's the plan," she says, taking charge of the situation. "This door brings us out on the side of the building. It's dark on this side and well away from those two goons in the parking lot. We stick to the shadows and make our way over to Canadian Tire on the next parking lot. It should still be open, so there will be people around. We'll call someone to come pick us up."

"What about your Jeep?" I ask.

"I can come get it tomorrow." She shrugs, almost looking a little excited now by the adventure of it all.

"Ready?" she says, leaning back on the door and heading out into the night before I can form a reply.

I wedge myself in the doorway and grab her by the arm.

"What if they see us?" I'm whispering again.

"Then we better hope the St. John's RNC are quick to answer their 911 calls," she says, shaking her arm loose and setting off along the side of the building on her tiptoes like some cartoon cat burglar.

I follow her lead as she steps off the path and behind a small line of shrubs that run between the two giant parking lots. These buildings are pretty new, and the immature bushes don't provide much cover—not that this seems to be hindering Dana's progress.

She looks back at me with a smile as we clear the side of the Finatech building and begin making our way across the patchy grass toward the bright, inviting lights of Canadian Tire. Adrenaline pumps through my body. We're almost home free.

Then a bright light flashes in our faces, stopping us in our tracks.

"Going somewhere?" comes the familiar, raspy voice of Mr. O'Hare. As he lowers the flashlight, I can make out the ominous silhouette of the stocky little man and his towering partner, Mr. Hobbs. Dana grabs my hand.

"Canadian Tire," I say. "Need anything?"

As my eyes adjust, I can make out O'Hare's beady eyes and bitter little smile.

"No, I think we have everything we need," he says. "Don't we, Mr. Hobbs?"

"I believe we do, Mr. O'Hare," the big man gruffly replies.

"See, they do this little routine where they call each other by their surnames all the time," I say to Dana. "Isn't it just darling?"

Dana scowls at me. She already has the sense that these two aren't to be messed with.

"We're glad you enjoy it, aren't we, Mr.—" O'Hare stops himself. "Just get over there. We'd like a little word."

He nods his head toward the white Jeep and the black SUV back over on the Finatech parking lot.

"Oh, I always try to use little words when I'm talking to you fellas," I say, prompting Dana to squeeze my hand in protest as we start walking.

The parking lot feels huge, the walk to the two vehicles long. It's so flat and wide open—and yet there is no sign of any RNC cruiser. It's funny, I think to myself. I've spent the last two weeks trying to evade those things, and right now I long to see that white car with its red, yellow, and blue go-faster stripes and crown of flashing lights.

I laugh to myself as we approach the Jeep.

"Something funny?" the big man asks.

"You mean apart from your haircut?" I ask, instantly regretting it as he shoves me hard into the side of the car.

"Argh. Dammit," I say, rubbing my arm.

O'Hare signals for Dana to stand next to me at the side of

the Jeep. I can hear her breathing, stuttering and shallow. She's frightened.

I'm shitting bricks, too. The goons just cranked up the stakes. They aren't messing around.

"What's in the bag?" O'Hare asks.

"Just . . . stuff," I say.

"Whose stuff?" Hobbs asks.

"My stuff," I say.

"Open it," Hobbs barks.

"No," I protest.

"He wasn't asking," O'Hare says, and with that the big man spins me around, rips the bookbag from by shoulder, and lays it on the hood of the Jeep.

"It's my laptop," Dana says, prompting a glare from Hobbs as he pulls the sleek aluminum slab out of the ragged old bag and places it carefully on the hood. He opens it up and is faced with the same password screen I'd seen back up in Jackson's office.

"Anything else in the bag?" O'Hare asks. Hobbs shakes his head. "Search their pockets," he barks. For the briefest of moments I catch a look in Hobbs's eyes that suggests he's fed up with being ordered around by his diminutive colleague, but the stone-cold glare quickly returns and he does as he's told. He rounds the Jeep and grabs me by the shoulder.

"Turn around," he says. Not that I have much say in the matter as he spins me around and shoves me hard into the side of the car.

"Bend over. Spread your legs."

"You mean like you do every day for your sugar daddy over there?" I say, instantly regretting is as he delivers a hard punch to my ribs, knocking the wind out of me as Dana lets out a shriek. I use my palms to brace myself against the car as he kicks the inside of my ankles to widen out my stance and then begins to frisk me.

Shit. He's going to find my phone.

He makes his way up my legs, patting my thighs and arse pockets.

"Don't get too excited, sweetheart," I manage to wheeze.

The comment clearly strikes a nerve as he stops his pat-down to grab me by the hair.

"It figures you like it rough," I say, prompting him to slam my face hard into the car.

I hear Dana remonstrating as the world turns blurry and my eyes water in response to the sharp pain in my nose. I can taste blood, and I start to get the feeling that if I don't shut up this could end really badly.

But then, through the haze, I see those flashing red and blue lights, accompanied a moment later by a quick blast of a police siren.

The big man immediately pulls me to my feet and spins me so that my back is resting against the Jeep. I blink his stern-looking face back into focus as he murmurs to me.

"Stand up straight. And clean up that blood."

He hands me a white handkerchief from his pocket, and I hold it to my stinging nose, tipping back my head in an attempt to stop the flow.

From the other side of the Jeep I hear the police cruiser roll to a halt and two doors opening and closing.

"What's goin' on here, then?" a male Constabulary officer asks.

"Good evening, Officers. Thank goodness you got here in time," says O'Hare.

"Come around to the front of the vehicle where we can see you," says a female officer. "All of you."

"Wipe it up," Hobbs hisses at me as I struggle to stop the blood trickling from my nose. Dana and O'Hare make their way around the Jeep as the big man continues to keep vigil over my self-treatment.

"Come on," says the male officer. "Right now, please."

I shrug at Hobbs and stuff the bloody handkerchief into my jeans pocket. The bleeding seems to have stopped for now, though I'm sure the bruising is already beginning to show beneath my eyes.

Hobbs grimaces and reluctantly makes his way to the front of the Jeep. I follow along behind him.

"That everyone?" the female officer asks.

"Yes, Officer, it's just the four of us."

"We received a 911 call," says the male cop. "Wanna explain to us what's going on here?"

"These men are harassing us," Dana says before O'Hare can get another word in. "And they assaulted my boyfriend."

The officers look at me.

"Is this true, sir?"

"I, uh . . ." I'm hesitant to say yes. If these guys are capable of busting up my nose in a public parking lot, what might they be capable of if they get us somewhere more secluded?

"We are security for Finatech," O'Hare says, gesturing to the giant red logo on the side of the building. "These little crooks broke into the building and were about to make off with an expensive piece of company hardware."

The officers see the open laptop sitting on the hood of the Jeep.

"Stand away from the vehicle," the female officer says, heading over to inspect the laptop and bookbag.

"These guys aren't security," I say, unable to help myself. "They're a couple of two-bit heavies."

"We're gonna need to see some ID," the male officer says.

"Certainly," O'Hare replies, retrieving what appears to be a sleek metallic card from his breast pocket and presenting it to the officer. He examines it carefully.

"You, too," he says to Hobbs, who produces a metallic card of his own.

"Just a second," the male officer says, returning to the cruiser with the two cards.

The female officer finishes checking the bookbag and taps the space bar of the laptop, bringing up the password screen again.

"It's my laptop," Dana says. "I work here. At Finatech. I'm a coder. A programmer."

"ID," the female officer says. "And you," she says to me. We do as we're told, and she looks back and forth between the IDs and the two of us.

"Okay," she says, handing back our IDs. "If it's your computer, log in."

Dana freezes.

"I'm sorry?"

"You said this is your laptop? So, put in your password and log in."

Dana looks at me and at the computer.

"Okay," she says, slowly approaching the hood of the Jeep.

She stands in front of the screen for a few seconds, her trembling hands poised above the keyboard.

"She won't be able to put in her password because the computer isn't hers," O'Hare hisses.

The officer looks at him and then to me, squinting in the confusion of moonlight and headlights.

"What happened to your nose?" she asks me.

Out of the corner of my eye, I'm sure I can see Hobbs cracking his oversized knuckles.

"I—"

"I told you. He was assaulted by this pair of sleeveens," Dana says.

"I fell," I say. "I tripped and I fell."

The officer eyes me suspiciously before returning her attention to Dana.

"Remember that password yet?"

Dana doesn't take her eyes from the screen.

"I changed it recently. Just making sure I get it right."

I hear the sound of the police radio in the background, then the jangly walk of the male officer returning from the cruiser.

"IDs check out. Mr. Hobbs and Mr. O'Hare. Employees of Finatech." He hands the metallic cards back to the two men. "Now, how are we doing over here?"

"Miss Riley here is about to enter her password to prove to us all that she didn't steal this computer," the female officer says.

Suddenly, all eyes are on Dana as her quivering hands hover above the keyboard.

"Well. Carry on, then," the male officer says.

Dana takes a deep breath before tapping away at the keys, little asterisks steadily populating the grey box on the middle of the screen. Then she hovers her finger over the Enter button.

"Dana . . ." I start to say, but before I can finish, she brings her finger down on the button, setting a whirling circle of pulsating little lines swishing around on the screen as all the St. John's night air is sucked away into the vacuum of space.

And then the screen flickers to reveal a very tidy desktop with just a couple of folders neatly arranged in the bottom left-hand corner.

"There," Dana says, managing to sound impressively matter-of-fact. She turns to face the group. "Can we go home now?"

* * *

The relief inside the Jeep as we tear down Portugal Cove Road is palpable.

"How did you know the password?" I ask Dana, who is at the wheel this time.

"How did you know the goons?" she replies.

"I guess we have some things we need to talk about," I say.

On the short car ride from Finatech back to Long's Hill, I tell her everything. I tell her about the briefcases, the cash, the dares. Our previous brush with Jackson Lorde's heavies. Even Mia and Ray Junior. And the gun. She remains silent, but the look on her face says it all. She's completely amazed that I could get myself into so much trouble in just a couple of weeks, and as we pass the Basilica Cathedral of St. John the Baptist, it's as though old Saint J himself is looking down on me in judgment.

We pull up at the apartment and she kills the engine, a silence descending on the inside of the Jeep the likes of which I've rarely known. I wait to hear what she'll have to say. I'm expecting, *You have to go to the police.* Or, *How could you be such an idiot?* Maybe even, *Go back to England and forget all about this.* But she doesn't say any of those things.

"I'm coming with you," is what she actually says.

"What?"

"To Gander."

"Dana, you can't just—"

"If you don't let me come, I'll go to the police. I'll tell them everything you just told me, and you and your friends will go to jail."

"I mean . . . I'll have to check with . . ."

"Crispin? Your fearless leader? Grow up, Gregory."

I recoil from her words like a turtle retreating into its shell. Dana always did have the ability to chastise me like a mother might a naughty child. She's way more mature than I am.

"What time are you leaving in the morning?"

"Around nine. We're gonna grab breakfast at Tim's and then—"

"I'll be there at eight. Do not leave without me. Now, get out of my Jeep."

She snatches up the bookbag containing Jackson's laptop and slams the Jeep door. I do as I'm told and jump out the passenger side.

I make my way to the back of the car and watch as she unlocks the apartment door.

"So, how *did* you know that password?"

"Lucky guess," she says before disappearing inside, locking the door behind her.

And so I'm left, not for the first time, to battle Long's Hill's fearsome gravity, making my way up toward the house—a place I'm beginning to wish I'd never crossed the threshold of in the first place.

I open the door and walk into the hallway, my eyes drawn to the bullet hole in the living room wall. Then I notice another hole in the wall. A bigger hole revealing exposed wiring underneath. I close the door and hear rummaging coming from the kitchen. As I make my way past the living room, I peer in to see that the old tube TV has been taken apart, it's insides scattered across the coffee table.

Instinctively, I grab the glass orb in my pocket as I make my way quietly into the kitchen.

"Crispin?" I say.

"Ow!" he yelps as the surprise of my voice causes him to jump from his position, crouched and half inside the unit under the sink, banging his head before popping up and glaring at me.

"Shit. Sorry," I say as he rubs his head a few times, but his expression soon shifts from scowl to smile as he makes his way over to me.

"Gregory! You're home." He beams, giving me a big hug with those long, skinny arms.

He emerges from the hug and grabs me at arm's length by the shoulders.

"Ah, Gregory. It's so important to have people you can trust."

As he gives my shoulders a squeeze, I look around the room. There are several holes in the walls, and the light fixtures are no longer attached to the ceiling, instead dangling with a gentle sway by their wires. Pots and pans are strewn all over the table and floors.

"Crisp. What's going on?" I ask.

He shakes his head and puts a hand to his chin.

"Hmm. Can't trust anyone, Gregory. They have eyes on us—I know it. Cameras, y'know? But tomorrow morning we're outta here. We're outta here and they won't be able to spy on us."

"Who? Hobbs and O'Hare?"

"Nah, they're just the muscle. But whoever's in charge—whoever sent them. They're smart, Gregory. They think they can catch us out. But we're smarter!"

"Crisp—"

Before I can speak, he grabs me by the shoulders again.

"You're my number one, Greg. You hear me? You're my number one."

"Okay . . ."

"The car gotta go," he says, his expression turning dead serious.

"The car?"

"The DeLorean. It's too hot. Like this place. It's a beacon that'll lead them right to us. We get rid of it tonight, okay?"

"Get rid of it?"

"Just you and me," he says, whispering, leaning his head to eye the hallway for anyone who might be listening in. "No one else. You head upstairs and get some sleep. Sleep in my room. I set up an air bed on the floor. Don't mind no one else—they're all sleepin', anyway. You go on to my room and get some shuteye. We leave at three a.m., okay?"

"Okay," I say, resigned to the fact that arguing would be futile.

"Okay. On ya go," he says, fair shoving me into the hallway. "And don't set an alarm," he says. "I'll be up in a few."

Up in my makeshift bed, I drift in and out of sleep for the next few hours, occasionally hearing some banging and sawing from downstairs. I'm pretty sure Crisp doesn't enter the room until three o'clock sharp, when he rattles me to wake.

"Gregory? It's time."

* * *

There's a chill breeze and a damp mist in the air as we peel the cover off the red DeLorean. Crisp balls the cover up and attempts to toss it over the worn white fence and into the yard, but it catches on the broken gate, which falls pathetically to the ground.

"The DeLorean's final voyage," he says, throwing me the keys. "She's all yours, Gregory."

Crisp opens the gullwing passenger door and lowers his long frame awkwardly into the low-slung car, and I climb into the driver's seat. It takes a couple of attempts, but eventually the car coughs into life, the engine settling into that harmony of deep mechanical growl and high-pitched whine.

"Where to?" I ask. "1985?"

"Nah, b'y," Crisp replies. "Signal Hill. Current day."

I press the gas and we begin our descent down Long's Hill.

"And if you see any cops . . ." He pauses. "Well, let's just hope we don't see any cops."

"You really think they have the house bugged?" I ask as we coil our way down Church Street and onto Duckworth, the DeLorean's brakes squealing in complaint.

"Could be," Crisp responds. "House is too hot. Car is too hot. St. John's is too hot right now. It's good we're getting out of town for a while."

The mist turns to a fine drizzle as we make our way along Duckworth Street, past the pubs and restaurants and lawyers offices, and into the narrowing streets of the Battery. I have to turn on the DeLorean's wipers as moisture begins to gather on the windshield. They do half a job at clearing the water, creating arcing streaks across the glass.

"Where'd you get to before? Scotty said you had a date?"

"Yeah." I shrug, unsure of how much to reveal to Crisp about our mission to Finatech and our run-in with Hobbs and O'Hare.

"What, she not appreciate your advances?" he asks, eyeing me carefully in the intermittent street light.

My nose.

I glance at myself in the rear-view mirror. It's subtle, but you can see the bruising beneath my eyes.

I'm gonna have to come clean.

"My date was with Dana," I say.

"Your ex?" he asks.

"Yeah."

"Well, that explains the nose, then. Newfoundland girls are feisty, Gregory. I tried to tell ya."

For a moment I consider running with it and saying that Dana bopped me one for being such a crappy boyfriend.

"I'm surprised you're seeing her again," he says before I have a chance to speak. "I thought you were sweet on Mint."

A thousand responses run through my head. *Would it matter if I was? It looks like Mint is pretty sweet on you. What the hell is going on with you two, anyway?*

I take a breath and grip the wheel of the DeLorean tight. The fleeting illumination of the street lights has given way to the ominous dark of a cloud-covered night as we begin our ascent of Signal Hill, its gravity pinning us to our leather seats. The drizzle has turned to rain, and I have to crank up the speed of the car's unwilling wipers.

"Dana's coming with us," I say. He's going to find out when she shows up on our doorstep tomorrow morning, anyway.

Crisp considers this for a moment.

"Is she cool?" he asks.

"She's smart," I say. "And she helped me figure out what we have to do in Gander tomorrow evening."

"This evening, technically," Crisp says, never one to let an opportunity to correct someone pass him by.

I look down at the clock on the DeLorean's digital dashboard. 3:26 a.m. Damn, the DeLorean's dash is cool.

"Right," I say as we curve our way up the hill, the rain rattling noisily off the car's steel body panels.

"So? What do we have to do?"

"The hawk, whose wings we have to clip. It's *Hawk 1*—Jackson's private jet."

Crisp chuckles to himself. "Fascinating." Then his expression turns to one of consternation. "Wait. We don't have to bring it down out of the sky, do we?"

"I think the point is more to stop it taking off," I say.

Crisp shrugs. "Scotty'll figure somethin' out."

We arrive at the summit of Signal Hill, the DeLorean's wipers doing their best to bat away the incessant rain.

"Go on up past the tower," Crisp says.

I drive the DeLorean slowly to the other side of the empty parking lot.

"Down there," Crisp says, pointing to a gap in the wall that leads to a grassy patch in the shadow of Cabot Tower.

I drive the DeLorean off the pavement and onto the soft grass.

"Go right on to the edge," Crisp says.

I do as he says, stopping the car with a creak just a few feet from the edge of what appears to be a sheer drop.

"Kill the engine," Crisp says, pulling a clump of latex gloves out of his pocket and handing a pair to me. "Put these on."

"Are you sure about this?" I say as I put the DeLorean's growling, whining engine out of its misery, the rattling rain taking over as the dominant sound.

Crisp doesn't answer. He pulls a rag out of another pocket and begins wiping down the DeLorean's dash, door handles, and centre console before passing the rag to me.

"Fingerprints," he says, as though it needed an explanation. "Make sure you get the steering wheel and that. Anything you touched."

Crisp opens his gullwing door and steps out into the night.

"Meet me outside when you're done."

I finish wiping down the car's interior surfaces and climb out, becoming instantly soaked in the torrential rain.

"She's a real beauty," Crisp says. "It's a damn shame."

He gestures for me to join him as he makes his way around to the back of the car.

Okay. I guess we're really doing this.

In unison, we heave the heavy mass of stainless steel forward until gravity begins to do its thing, the weight of the red DeLorean pulling it away from us. We stop ourselves just short of going over, too, as the slippery grass gives way to even more slippery rocks.

The cliff is too sheer for us to see the DeLorean's descent, but a couple of crashing sounds call out from below to signal its battering journey to the whipping waves below. As we peer down into the abyss, it's too dark to make anything out, but it would seem that the car is now lost to the sea.

"Well," Crisp says. "Easy come, easy go."

He takes a couple of long strides backward, away from the edge, before reaching into his belt and pulling out the gun.

I jump at the sight of the weapon.

"What are you gonna do with that?" I ask, sounding just as scared as I feel.

"Oh, shit, sorry," Crisp says, lowering the gun. "I just wanna get rid of it. I hate guns. No more of that shit for the Gulls. That's not what we're all about."

I look out at the lighthouse over on Cape Spear. I think about my family all those miles away, across all that raging ocean.

"What are we all about, Crispin?" I ask.

"Not death. Not killin'," he says. "It was never meant to come to that. That's where we draw the line. Here," he says, making his way toward me. He spins the gun around in his hand, offering me the handle end.

"You have the rag. Wipe it down, and you do the honours. Toss the friggin' thing into the sea."

I pull the rag from my pocket and use it to take the gun. It's a murder weapon, and I don't want to touch it.

It's heavy. Heavier than I thought. I wipe it over carefully as Crisp tries—and fails—to light a cigarette in the teeming rain.

"Jesus," he says, looking around. "Friggin' rain. I'll meet you over by the tower." He turns, pulling his trench coat pointlessly around him. "Give it a good toss, now," he yells back at me as he strides away.

I hold the gun in my hand for a moment, feel its weight. As Crispin walks away from me, back turned, toward Cabot Tower, the thought crosses my mind. I could kill him. I could point the gun, squeeze the trigger, and end him right here. I could throw his body over the edge and into the ocean, along with the DeLorean and the gun. Nobody would see. Nobody would hear. Nobody would ever know.

I could end this.

I do point the gun. I raise it up in front of me, close one eye, and aim it right at his head.

Then I lower it back down, not quite ready to use it, but not quite ready to part with it.

I reach my spare hand into my pocket and feel the glass orb

inside, clutching it tight in my hand. I tuck the gun into the back of my pants, pulling my shirt over the top of the handle. For a moment I think about tossing the orb over the side, but I don't want to part with that, either.

Crispin needs to see me throw something.

He's almost at the tower. I see his lanky frame, pale in the sodium lights.

Before he reaches the shelter of the tower, I pick up a vaguely gun-sized rock from the ground. As he turns, I hold the rock aloft. He gives a nod as he lights his cigarette, and I toss the rock with all my might over the edge and into the sea.

As I turn back to look at Crispin, he blows smoke and gives a little round of applause. I tap the gun, its cold metal muzzle jamming into my arse cheek, and I make my way over to join him.

"Crispin?" I say, lighting a cigarette of my own.

"Wha—?"

"How are we getting home?"

Crisp swallows, eyelids flickering as the rain comes down in torrents, before shooting me a resigned smile.

"I guess we're walkin'," he says before striding off back toward the road as though it were the most natural thing in the world.

13

Take a Chance on Chance Cove

At around 8:00 a.m. I head outside for another cigarette. I don't feel particularly proud that it's my third or fourth of the day already, but having arrived home soaking wet a little after five, there didn't seem much point in trying to go back to sleep. I'd grabbed a warm shower and brewed up a pot of coffee, enjoying a couple of hours alone in the house on Long's Hill.

I'd sat at the end of the back yard, wedged between the buckled trees, and watched the sun rise over old St. John's. They call it the City of Legends, and on this summer morning it had lived up to the name, a deep red sky casting a stunning hue over the jelly bean houses, hodgepodge buildings, and the bobbing boats in the harbour beyond.

As I'd looked out over the shimmering ocean, I had recalled that saying: "Red sky in the morning, fisherman's warning." It was a variation on the one I'd grown up with back in England, where instead of fishermen, it was shepherds who should heed the warning of a red dawn.

I just hope that red DeLorean sank right to the bottom of the Atlantic, I had thought to myself as I'd chugged down luke-warm coffee.

For cigarette four—or five—I head out of the front door instead. The mystery of the red sky has given way to a golden glimmer, the peace of the golden hour replaced by the steady buzz of a waking city. As I step outside, Long's Hill is a roller-coaster ride of commuting citizens, most approaching its peak and hoping to Jesus their brakes hold out on the steep decline, others click-click-clicking their way to its summit, fighting its gravity with everything their engines have to offer.

I light my smoke and take in that golden first puff—the only one that's really enjoyable, the nicotine addiction immediately satiated and the remainder of the cigarette mere fuel to keep me chugging through the next hour or two until the addiction demands feeding once more.

"A smoker, now, are ya?" The familiar voice reaches up to me from lower down the hill.

I turn to see Dana striding toward me, defying the hill's gravity with long, purposeful strides, breathing unencumbered by the toll of toxic smoke.

I'm still mildly embarrassed to be caught smoking in front of Dana. She never did like it, and for a while I was able to reduce my habit to a near-non-existent level, sneaking one here and there when she wasn't around. Then she wasn't around at all, and the sneaking was no longer necessary, the habit drawing me in one draw at a time until I was up to half a pack a day—and much more when drinking was involved. Which was often. It didn't help that money had become no object in the past few weeks.

"Early as always," I say, taking a puff. Too late to hide it now. And besides, it's not like we're together anymore.

"Well, I didn't want to miss the boat," she says, breathing just a little heavily as she reaches the house, keeping a good two metres' distance and making a face at the smell of the smoke. She's carrying the medium-sized of her three backpacks, which she lowers to the ground and leans against the house, before doing so herself. Arms crossed, she glowers at the Roller.

"We're not going in that, are we?" she asks.

I breathe out smoke and watch as the old blue Toyota Corolla emerges from the cloud. I hadn't given it much thought, but since we pushed the red DeLorean off Signal Hill, we are back down to just the one car again, and it will be a pretty tight fit now that the gang is back to a six-pack.

Before I can say anything, a large, silver Range Rover comes in hot over the crest of Harvey Road and screeches to a halt barely an inch from the back of the Roller. I reflexively flick my cigarette to the ground and prepare to run, but then I see Crisp's trademark smile peering out at us from the driver's seat.

He exits the vehicle and makes his way around, using the key fob to make the sleek SUV chirp and flicker its lights.

"D'ya like her?" he says as he approaches us.

"Did you steal that?" Dana says, eyes wide.

"What? No," Crisp says, looking offended at the suggestion.

"Dana, Crisp; Crisp, Dana. I think you guys have met before. Dana's going to be joining us on our trip to Gander," I say.

"The new sixth Gull." Crisp beams.

"It's not quite the fifth Beatle, but I'll take it," Dana replies.

"British reference!" Crisp yelps. "I guess you lived over there for a while, eh?"

"Yeah." Dana shrugs.

"British car, too!" Crisp says, tossing the keys up in the air and catching them again.

"Actually, I think they make them in China these days," I say, which seems to legitimately hurt Crisp's feelings. "Dana will be a great asset to the group," I say, still feeling the need to justify her inclusion. "She knows Jackson . . . intimately."

"Oh, stop," she says.

"Well, despite the palpable sexual tension, welcome aboard!" Crisp says before tapping me on the shoulder. "Get packed, Greggy boy. Almost time to hit the road."

"Packed?" I say, the thought having at no point occurred to me, even after seeing Dana's pre-trip preparation. She chuckles to herself and rolls her eyes at me.

"What? If I need more clothes, I'll just buy some."

"Right. With Jackson's money."

"With my money. Hard-earned, in keeping with the rules of the game."

"Oh, that's cute. He thinks this is a game."

"You know what I mean," I say, lighting another cigarette, more to spite her than because I actually want one.

"I managed to open one of the files on his laptop last night," she says.

I raise an eyebrow in response.

"It was encrypted, but I cracked it."

"And?"

"There was just one document inside. A Finatech memo from the other partners—Justin and Patrick—addressed to the board, stating their concerns that Jackson's actions could jeopardize the planned sale of the business to Nasdaq."

"Blimey. What was he doing to deserve that?"

"Jackson never wanted the business to be sold to investors outside of Canada. He wanted to keep Finatech here and use Atlantic Canadian talent as much as possible."

"I take it the other partners didn't see it that way."

Dana shakes her head. "I don't think anyone could have anticipated the growth of the business. Justin and Patrick said it's gotten too big and it's time for Jackson to let go of his idealistic vision of a Newfoundland company on the world stage."

"But he wasn't going to budge?"

"No. And without the buy-in of all three partners, no Nasdaq deal."

"So, what, you think they did him in or something?"

"Well, it's awfully convenient that he would disappear just a couple of weeks before they were due to fly to New York and seal the deal."

"That's where they're heading on the company jet tonight."

Dana nods. "And with Jackson out of the picture, the two of them might just have the power to sell his empire to the highest bidder."

"His empire? I thought they were equal partners."

Dana snorts. "Maybe when it comes to counting the profits, but Finatech was always Jackson's vision. He's the real brains of the operation. Patrick is nothing more than an average coder who made the right friends in university, and as for Justin . . ."

"Family," I say through a cloud of smoke that a sudden gust

of St. John's wind carries in Dana's direction. She wafts it away and coughs dramatically.

"Sorry," I say, tossing the remaining half of the cigarette I never really wanted onto the ground and grinding it into the sidewalk under my sneaker.

The dizziness is back again, and I'm not sure if it's all the smoke inhalation or the gravity of Dana's story. Then it occurs to me.

"None of this explains the briefcases and the dares, though," I say. "If Jackson Lorde is captive or, well, you know . . . worse, then it's pretty unlikely he's writing haikus and sending a bunch of kids on a wild goose chase for cash rewards, right?"

Dana shrugs. "Maybe all this has nothing to do with Jackson."

"Who, then?"

"Morning, darlings! What a beautiful day for a road trip!"

Shelly is a post-shower ray of sunshine as she bursts out of the front door and immediately begins swirling her hula hoop around those generous hips, still-wet hair turning her white T-shirt transparent enough to cause Dana to search for another place to look.

"Hiya, Shell," I say. "Have you met Dana?"

"Not officially," Shelly says.

"Dana, Shelly; Shelly, Dana," I say. "Dana's going to be joining us on our next adventure."

"My dear," Shelly says. "Do you even know what you're gettin' yourself into?"

"I have a sense of it," Dana replies.

Shelly smiles, working the hula hoop skilfully up to her arm and twirling it there while she spins herself around 360 degrees.

"Oh, nice wheels," she says as she clocks the new Range Rover. Then she suddenly stops her twirling and gyrating, grabbing the hula hoop in her hand.

"Where's the DeLorean?" she asks.

The one part of the story I didn't tell Dana about.

She immediately looks to me for an explanation, but before I can offer one, the rest of the gang begins spilling noisily out of the house.

Introductions are made, the new Range Rover is admired, and we all pile into the opulent rig. I'm in the back next to Dana, who has Scott and Shelly to her left. Crisp has taken the wheel, and Mint has called "shotgun"—because of course she has. All present and as correct as we'll ever be, we make our way across Harvey Road to the Tim Hortons drive-through.

"Go ahead wit yer order," comes the monotone voice of the bored teen through the tinny speaker. We order up a laundry list of coffees, breakfast sandwiches, and a multitude of baked goods, to audible sighs from the other end of the speaker.

When we roll up to the window, we are greeted—in the loosest possible sense of the word—by Amanda, my ruddy-faced, gum-chewing, teenaged former boss, her face locked in its one expression, which can best be described as "utter contempt and apathy for the world and everyone in it." The look is only enhanced when she clocks me in the back seat of the Range Rover.

"Gregory," she snarls. "You never turned up for your shifts last week. Or the week before that."

"Oh, right," I say. "That's because I quit."

Amanda chews on her ever-present ball of gum, eyeing the fancy Range Rover and the motley crew aboard it. She blows and pops a large pink bubble.

"Must be drugs," she says as Crisp pays for our breakfasts on the debit machine.

She pulls the machine back into her window and tears off the receipt.

"And this is for your trouble," Crisp says, handing Amanda a fifty-dollar bill.

Her eyes light up and she almost spits her gum out of the window.

"Definitely drugs," she says, stuffing the bill into her back pocket.

* * *

As we peel out of old St. John's, the sense of relief inside the Range Rover is palpable. Gone are the sleepless nights in the claustrophobic confines of the house on Long's Hill, traded for bright sunshine, the wide-open Trans-Canada Highway, and an eclectic selection of tunes pumping from the vehicle's impressive speaker system. Even Dana seems to be relaxing into the adventure, requesting a song or two and singing along with lustre.

We are young and free again, our hair blowing in the wind through the Range Rover's cracked windows. The memory of the Rooms and Ray Junior has been left behind, along with Mia and her itchy trigger finger. Even the smooth surface of the glass orb in my jeans pocket does more to reassure than rekindle. We are out of there now. We got away with it.

I try to ignore the hard edge of the gun when it occasionally digs me in the ribs from its place in my inside jacket pocket. *You're just trying to spoil my fun.*

As we launch into the final chorus of "Wonderwall," I notice Mint's eyes narrowing in the passenger-side wing mirror. In fairness, I've been looking at those eyes in that mirror for much of the first hour or so of the drive. So far, they've been largely lit up with fun and joy, but now there's something else in there. Concern. Anguish. Fear.

"Crisp," she says, hitting the touch screen to turn off the music. "How long has that car been following us?"

Shelly continues to sing a good few seconds after the music has cut out before realizing that something's going on.

"Wha—? What car?" she asks.

"Don't turn around," Crisp hisses, looking back at us in the rear-view mirror. "It's Hobbs and O'Hare."

"Good Lord," Scott says, ignoring Crisp's instruction and turning around to look out of the back window. "Who the hell are these guys?"

"They work for Finatech," Dana says. "They're Jackson Lorde's heavies."

"This *is* something to do with him, then," Mint says.

"Looks that way," I answer as I squint to see the unmistakable black SUV in the mirror, rolling along ominously behind us.

"Well, what are we gonna do about it?" Shelly asks.

Crisp takes his eyes off the mirror and scans the roadside to get his bearings, just as we pass a sign letting us know that the next exit leads to a place called Chance Cove.

"Take a chance on Chance Cove," Crisp says, depressing the accelerator and putting the Range Rover's considerable power to good use.

I watch in the mirror as the black SUV follows suit, speeding up to keep the distance between us minimal. I glance over at the speedometer as it climbs.

140 kph

150 kph

160 kph

"Crispin?" Shelly whimpers from the back seat.

"Better hang onto those 'Oh-my-Jesus' handles," Crisp says. "And check yer seat belts."

I do as I'm told, making sure I'm buckled in and reaching for the handle above the door. I feel Dana grab my hand as every Gull in the car tenses up, like we're one giant muscle bracing for action.

170 kph

180 kph

The engine whines, the exit fast approaching, the black SUV racing to keep pace.

"Crisp," I say. "Don't you think you better—"

At the last moment, Crisp yanks the Range Rover onto the exit ramp, tires squealing in protest, as he wrestles it back under his control and we race off down the ramp.

For a moment there is no black SUV in the rear-view mirror and I think Crisp's last-minute turn may have caught them out and sent them off up the highway. But then there is another, much more pronounced screeching of tires from somewhere behind us, followed by a visible cloud of tire smoke, and then that cursed black SUV, wobbling onto the ramp before righting itself and arrowing down toward us.

"Shit," I say.

"They're still back there," Shelly adds.

Crisp doesn't reply. He just carries on down the narrow, country road, slowing the speed of the Range Rover from "insanity" to "mildly reckless" with the black SUV responding in kind. He gambles at a stop sign, rolling on through it, the SUV rolling right on through as well.

"Um . . . maybe this wasn't such a good idea?" Scott says, giving voice to what everyone else was probably thinking as we cruise along one Main Road.

If this is the "main" one, I'd hate to see the side roads.

"It's fine. We used to come here all the time when I was a kid. I know this place like the back of my hand," Crisp says, as though his prior knowledge helps our plight at all.

According to the green sign amid the roadside shrubbery, we are six kilometres from Chance Cove. We roll along in silence, Main Road dipping and curving, the cold ocean occasionally peeping at us between the thick bushes, the black SUV following along as though tied to our tail by a piece of string.

After a few minutes the landscape begins to open up, and we drive among small houses dotted along the rugged coastline.

"Maybe we could knock on one of these doors," Dana suggests. "Ask someone for help."

Crisp doesn't respond. He just keeps on driving, a little too quickly, always keeping check on the black SUV in tow.

A few more minutes down the road, Crisp slows the Range Rover and turns onto a dirt road, rattling along until the treeline drops away and the great North Atlantic Ocean sprawls out in front of us. The road is now barely a road at all, just two tire grooves carved into the landscape, the Range Rover bouncing capably over water-filled potholes as the rugged coast reaches out to the ocean on all sides, a single bonsai-looking tree perched in stubborn isolation on the brink of the rocky cliffs.

Without word or warning, Crisp brings the Range Rover to a sudden stop, the black SUV slamming on its brakes and sliding to a halt just inches from our rear bumper. I can just about make out the two men in the dark vehicle now. The short, stocky O'Hare is in the driver's seat, his tall and broad cohort, Hobbs, at his side.

Crisp revs the Range Rover's engine a couple of times.

O'Hare answers with a couple of revs of his own.

"You're definitely gonna need those 'Oh-my-Jesus' handles this time, Gulls," Crisp says, a knowing smile on his face.

Once again, we all tense as one, Dana's fingernails digging into my hand.

"It's gonna be o—" I go to say, but before I can finish my sentence, there is a great roar of the Range Rover's engine, its tires spinning for a moment before grabbing onto the rocky ground and propelling us forward at what feels like warp speed.

Like six monkeys waiting to be shot into space.

My head is pinned to the backrest, and I feel Dana's weight against me as Crisp violently yanks the Range Rover to the left and goes full off-road, bouncing and rattling along, heading straight for the bold bonsai that sits way too close to the edge of the cliff.

My knuckles turn white as I grip the handle above the door, the Range Rover hammering along, the black SUV in full pursuit, a shaky spectre in the rear-view mirror.

"Crisp?" I yell as the tree grows and grows in front of us, nothing beyond it but sheer, rocky, watery doom.

"CRISP!" I scream, and the others scream, too, as the Range Rover shoots past the tree and the black SUV gives chase.

As the edge approaches, Crisp gives the Range Rover one last yank to the left, but it does no good. We go over the edge at speed and for a moment we are flying, weightless. We are six monkeys blasted into orbit, and my final thought—that we are without a chance in Chance Cove—almost makes me laugh out loud.

We are flying. We are weightless. Until we aren't. Until the impact, sending a shock wave the likes of which I've never experienced through every bone in my body.

We bounce and bobble and shake and my brain tries to process what's going on. Then it all stops, our bodies jerking forward as one before falling back into our seats. My head is spinning and the silence is deafening. It takes me a moment to scan my body and make sure everything is in one piece. It is. I turn my attention to Dana. Shaken, but seemingly uninjured, as are all the others.

Then I see something flying by us out of the side window.

It's the black SUV of Hobbs and O'Hare, drifting surreally through the air before disappearing below us. The sound of buckling metal and shattering glass is louder than I would have expected, until I realize that the front passenger-side window of the Range Rover has been shattered with the impact.

I expect to see the orange glow of an explosion, just like in the movies, but there is only that heart-stopping sound of a car hitting rocks.

And then there is nothing.

"Is everybody okay?" Crisp asks, rolling his shoulder a couple of times.

"I'm bleeding," Mint says flatly.

I do another quick scan of myself. No blood. No significant pain. No limbs pointing in the wrong direction. Just a bit of pressure on my chest from where the seat belt dug in when we hit.

I release the belt and lean forward over the front passenger seat to see what's going on with Mint. Crisp is already picking the tiny beads of glass from the shattered window off her clothes.

"What happened?" I ask. "Are you okay?"

"She's fine," Crisp says. "A piece of the glass must have cut her just above the eyebrow there. It doesn't look too serious.

I take off my denim jacket, being careful not to let the gun drop out of the inside pocket, then pull off my T-shirt, tearing it at the seams and ripping a large strip of fabric away. I clump it up and hand it over to Mint.

"Here, hold this to the wound," I say.

"Thanks," Mint replies, taking the fabric and placing it gingerly to her eye.

"It won't have cut her," says Scott, matter-of-factly.

"What?" I ask.

"Car windows are made of safety glass, designed to shatter into small pebbles on impact. So, it won't have cut her, per se. One of the beads may have nicked her eyebrow."

"Jesus, Scott," Crisp says. "So, it *nicked* her eyebrow. What's the difference?"

"Probably about a dozen stitches." Scott shrugs, releasing his seat belt.

Suddenly conscious of my naked torso, I pull my jacket back on and inspect the rest of the back-seat passengers.

Shelly has a thin smile on her face, her eyes wide.

"You okay, Shell?" Scott asks her.

"Yes, b'y," Shelly replies. "All in one piece."

"C'mon," Scott says, opening the door. "Help me inspect the damage."

"Okay," Shelly says, jauntily, taking off her seat belt and following Scott out of the Range Rover.

She must be in shock.

"Is nobody going to mention the fact that those two men just plummeted to their death?" Dana asks. Her doe eyes are wide, and she seems to be shivering a little.

"Well, I was hoping they wouldn't," Crisp says as he clears the last of the glass from Mint's lap and carefully unclasps her seat belt.

"Dana, I . . ."

She fixes her wide-eyed gaze on me.

"Or that we almost just died? That we just went over the side of a cliff and I thought we were going to die?"

"We were never going to die," Crisp says. "I told ya, I know this place like the back of my hand."

Dana gives an incredulous snort. "Right, yeah, well, you might have shared your little plan with us before driving us off the edge of a cliff!"

"Dana, it's all right. We're all right," I say.

"What the hell have you gotten yourself into? Who have you gotten us involved with?"

"Hey, we are here, you know," Crisp says.

"Come on," I say, unfastening Dana's seat belt. "Let's just get some air, yeah?"

I open the door to a gust of fresh, coastal Newfoundland wind and a chorus of gull-song.

"Careful out there. There's not a lot of clearance," Crisp says as I climb out of the Range Rover and coax Dana to follow. "Making my evasive manoeuvre all the more impressive," Crisp mutters under his breath. I'm not sure if he catches my "just leave it" expression.

Out on the side of the cliff, it's hard to deny that Crisp's manoeuvre was rather impressive. Well, either that or just plain lucky.

The Range Rover is lodged on a narrow ledge jutting out from the cliffside, no more than a couple of car widths wide and a half-dozen car lengths long. Behind, the rock dips in a smooth curve—almost like a man-made little road down to the ledge. To the front, the ledge ends at a flat cliff wall, which the Range Rover came to a rest about three feet away from.

"How are we not dead?" Dana asks, sticking to the back of the ledge, as far from the sheer drop as she can get.

"Because of my Evel Knievel–level driving skills," Crisp says as we all inspect the scene.

"Didn't Evel Knievel ride a motorcycle?" Mint asks.

"Didn't Evel Knievel break every bone in his body trying to jump over a fountain?" Scott adds.

"Well, I scouted it out on a bike," Crisp says, drawing questioning glares from the group. "When I was a kid," he says. "Me and my buddy used to ride our bikes down the dip there and dare each other how close to the edge we could get before we hit the brakes."

Dana shoots Crisp her best "are you friggin' serious?" look.

"I mean, that was probably foolhardy, lookin' back. Came in awful handy today, though." He grins.

Dana will never understand Crisp. They might as well be from different planets.

"Well, nothin' seems to be leakin'," Scott says as he straightens himself after having a look underneath the Range Rover. "This tire's busted, though. Got a spare?"

"I assume so," Crisp says. Scott shrugs and opens the trunk, locating the spare and taking out a tire wrench.

"That's it?" Dana calls out from her position at the back of the ledge. "Let's change the tire and act like nothing happened?"

"Dana . . ."

"Isn't anyone going to look over the side?"

We all pause for a moment and look out toward the cliff edge. Then Scott tosses the tire wrench back into the trunk and strides to the edge of the cliff, peering over.

"I think it's pretty safe to assume they're dead," he says, prompting a gasp from Dana. "Did you want to take a look for yourself?"

Dana shakes her head, her hand to her mouth, tears forming in her eyes.

"Okay, then," Scott says, striding back over to the Range Rover. "Let's get this tire changed."

"I'll help," Mint says, making her way over.

"No," I protest. "You should keep pressure on that wound. I can help."

"Do you know how to change a tire?" Mint asks.

"Well, I mean, I . . ."

She smiles that glittering smile, the cute little dimple appearing on her right cheek.

"Look," she says, pulling the clump of bloodstained T-shirt fabric from her eyebrow. "The bleeding has stopped. I'm fine. And I know how to change a tire."

I can feel my face flushing red.

"Thank you for this," she says, gesturing to the bloody fabric.

"Hey, it's the least I could do."

She chuckles and gives my shoulder a squeeze.

I'm falling.

As she makes her way over to help Scott, I see that Shelly has gone to console Dana, while Crisp is now standing at the edge of the cliff, taking a look at the wreckage below for himself. He stands, tall and slender, beyond him endless ocean, squawking gulls circling all around.

I cautiously approach him, stopping a few feet from the edge.

"How bad is it?" I ask.

"Pretty bad," he says without looking back.

"No chance they survived, then?"

He considers this question for a moment.

"Nope," he says bluntly.

"Right," I say. "Did you talk to Scott about the whole *Hawk 1* thing?"

"Didn't get a chance before we left," Crisp says, turning to face me. "We'll go over it when we get to Gander."

As Crisp stands there now, he looks tired for the first time since I met him. In this moment, the effervescent energy is gone. Semi-silhouetted against the midday sky, his eyes are cast in shadow, lacking that usual sparkle. Our charismatic leader looks forlorn, as though the weight of a climbing death toll weighs heavy on his shoulders. I had thought he might be behind it all, that maybe he was a trust-fund kid with nothing better to do than send his friends on a crazy goose chase for all that cash he could never spend.

He doesn't know anything. He's along for the ride, just like the rest of us.

Suddenly, something catches Crisp's eye and he becomes animated again.

"Would ya look at that!" he shouts like an excited child, pointing at one of the seagulls circling close by. "He's got a crab in his beak. Ya see it?"

I squint against the sun to see what he's talking about. The bird does indeed have a surprisingly large crab wedged in its beak, the legs and pincers dangling helplessly out of the sides.

"He's gonna crack it!" Crisp yells.

"What? With his beak?"

"Nah, too tough. What he'll do is, he'll fly up real high, then he'll drop the crab onto the rocks far below to shatter the shell. Then he'll swoop down and help himself to the delicious meat inside."

"No shit," I say.

"Go on, drop it!" Crisp yells at the bird. "Smash it! Crack it!"

Rarely have I seen such glee in a grown adult as I do in Crisp when the gull opens its beak wide, letting the crab fall before diving down beyond the cliffside after it.

"Woo hoo!" Crisp yelps, and for a moment I think he might fall down to the rocks below, too, such is his unbridled enthusiasm. He cranes to look over the side and watch the scene play out below. "Come see, Gregory. Come take a look at this."

"Um, I think I'm good," I say, suddenly beginning to feel a little queasy.

Too many things falling off the side of cliffs.

"It's just nature, Gregory," he says without looking back. "Nature in all her glory."

I back away from the clifftop of death and turn to see how things are progressing with the Range Rover. Scott and Mint already have the old, muddy tire off and are working to affix the fresh new one. I circle the Range Rover and assess the damage. The front bumper has come off altogether, and some of the panelling along the bottom is cracked. Mint's window is the only one that bought it with the impact of our crash landing, and the wing mirror on the passenger side hangs loose from a confusion of wires like a war-beaten cyborg's eyeball.

"You think we'll be able to drive it?" I ask Scott as he holds the new tire in place while Mint cranks the tire wrench.

"We'll find out," Scott replies.

I watch for a moment as Mint capably tightens the wheel nuts, her defined arms shimmering with perspiration in the midday sun.

Still falling.

I check on Dana—still shaken—and Shelly—still putting a jolly spin on the situation despite it all—and then I survey the scene. The narrow ledge isn't wide enough to perform a three-point turn. It might have been had we been driving the Roller or even the DeLorean (though neither of those vehicles would have been likely to survive the impact), but in the Range Rover, physics was not on our side. The embankment Crisp and his childhood friend had diced with death riding their bikes up and down—while their parents were doing I'm not sure what, exactly—and that the Range Rover had jumped entirely on the way down was certainly surmountable for the rugged all-wheel-drive SUV . . . if it were pointing in the right direction.

Mint gives the wheel nuts one last solid torque, and Scott removes the jack.

"There," he says, wiping his hands on what remains of my T-shirt. "Good as new."

I look at the beat-up three-hour-old Range Rover, and at the hill behind it, which looks steeper with every passing minute.

"And how are we getting back up there, exactly?" I ask.

Scott and Mint look to the hill and at each other. Dana looks full of consternation. Shelly just smiles and gives me a wink.

"We reverse!" Crisp says cheerily, striding over from the cliff edge—this episode of *The Nature of Things* apparently over—and climbs straight into the driver's seat of the Range Rover.

We all hold our breath as he goes to start up the car.

With a triumphant *v-vroom* the SUV starts first time and Crisp gives the engine a couple of good revs, grinning broadly from beyond the mud-speckled windshield.

"We reverse," I say with a shrug and head to the back of the vehicle.

"We reverse," Scott says with a shake of his head, himself climbing aboard. "Because there's frig all else we can do."

Mint opens the front passenger door and picks the remaining few glass beads off the seat.

"Did you want me to sit there?" I offer.

"Trying to take my shotgun?" she teases, giving me a playful dig to the ribs.

"Hey—you can't blame a boy for trying," I say.

"Your seat's back there," she says with a smile.

"Yeah, yeah," I say, trudging to the back door. "Enjoy the new air conditioning feature," I add, pointing to the missing window.

"Hey, I like feeling the wind in my hair."

Dana and Shelly are the last to hop aboard, and as all the doors slam shut, I get the feeling that I've just climbed on board the world's worst roller coaster—the one that sets off backwards and has a dodgy safety record.

"Okay, buckle up," Crisp says. "I can't because I have to look behind me and the back-up camera appears to no longer be functional, but the rest of you should put on your seat belts."

Scott peeks past me at the looming drop.

"Honestly, Crispin, I don't think seat belts will make a whole lotta difference if you shag this up."

"Okay. Ready? On the count of three."

I feel Dana's hand grip mine again.

"One . . ."

I reach for the "Oh-my-Jesus" handle.

"Two . . ."

Every muscle in my body tenses.

"Three!"

And with that, the Range Rover's wheels squeal into life, spinning in place momentarily before gripping the rocky surface and pushing us all forward in our seats. There are some audible gasps as our restraints dig in, in the same spots they dug in during the impact. The reversing Range Rover whines in protest as we begin to ascend the hill arse-foremost. Crisp battles with the steering wheel as the vehicle veers wildly, first left and then right, toward the cliff edge. The wheels appear to find purchase just at the wrong time, almost shooting us clean over the side, but Crisp is able to correct its course and we bumpily climb the rise backwards, the whole world coming back into view as the Range Rover levels out and we back hastily away from the edge.

"Well, praise be to Jesus," Shelly says, and even Dana manages a relieved smile.

We sit there motionless for a few moments as we collectively take a breath.

"Right," Crisp says. "On to Gander town, then."

14

Come from Away

Gander is strikingly flat compared to St. John's, and it strikes me that this makes sense for a town known around the world for its airport. I haven't seen the musical *Come From Away*, which tells the story of Gander's part in the events of 9/11, but I'm familiar with the story of how airplanes were diverted to the little airport and the residents of Gander showed that renowned Newfoundland hospitality to people going through the trauma of that time.

Another striking feature of Gander is its lack of ocean. They say it's in "central" Newfoundland, but looking on the map, it's more to the east, though not far enough to be "on" the coast. It is about halfway up the island, though, vertically speaking—a three-and-a-half-hour drive from the capital city that's been my home for the last year or so.

Gander lacks the cheeky upstart quality of St. John's, though an abundance of mature trees gives it a homey, inviting quality. As Crisp drives the beaten-up brand-new Range Rover around its streets "to get our bearings," it quickly becomes apparent that the town grew out from the airport. Gander is a sleepy assemblage of suburbs and strip malls with all the trademark big box stores—your Walmarts, your Dollar Stores, and—lucky for us—your Mark's Work Warehouse and Canadian Tire.

"We'll check into the hotel, get ourselves something to eat, and make some plans for this evening," Crisp says. "We can come back out to gather up supplies after."

Our home for the duration of our stay will be the Albatross Hotel, which sits on the side of the Trans-Canada Highway, conveniently located between a Jungle Jim's and a Tim Hortons for all our culinary needs. The Albatross would be a pretty standard roadside motel, save for the dramatic peaked roof that adorns its main building, though I'm pretty certain Crisp chose it purely because it's named after a seabird.

We dump our stuff and head over to Jim's for a much-needed scoff. It's after two at this point, and everyone's starving. I order up a burger and fries, my own cliffside nausea now having been replaced by raging hunger.

"Okay," Crisp says through a mouthful of loaded nacho chips, "so here's the deal."

He goes on to fill the gang in on the details of the dare, explaining that our "hawk" is in fact a private jet belonging to Finatech.

"Jesus, we're not gonna bring down a plane, are we?" Shelly asks as she nibbles on a Caesar salad like a hamster.

"Not bring it down," I say, dipping a fry into a mound of ketchup. "Stop if from taking off."

"Look at the phrasing," Crisp says, pointing to the now-crumpled piece of paper from the green briefcase. "'Take its legs, clip its wings.'"

"So, how do we stop a jet from taking off?" Mint asks between bites of her turkey club sandwich.

"Dana has a thought about that," I say, and all eyes are trained on the newest Gull.

Dana studiously finishes chewing her mouthful of whatever vegan rice bowl situation it is that she ordered up before speaking.

"Well, I just think that the bit about taking its legs probably means puncturing the tires," she says.

"But couldn't 'clip its wings' be a hint at how they want us to handle this, too?" Crisp asks, flashing Dana one of his "sexy" smiles. The man is incorrigible.

"Well, unless you know a way of getting access to the plane and then figuring out a way to damage the wings, I'd be inclined to take that part as a turn of phrase rather than an instruction," Dana says. She doesn't intend for it to sound as mean as it does—Dana is just wicked smart and sometimes doesn't have much of a filter.

"Dana's a pilot," I say, and she looks a little embarrassed. "I mean, she knows about planes. She was in the . . . what is that called?"

"The Air Cadets," Dana says.

"Not to be confused with a space cadet," Scott jokes as he works on his fish tacos.

"I just think the safest way to stop a plane taking off is to puncture the tires before it gets up enough speed to achieve liftoff," Dana says. "Assuming we don't want to kill any more people."

The comment casts quiet over the table for a moment, the only sounds clinking cutlery and background chatter.

"Puncture the tires it is!" Crisp exclaims as though it were his idea.

"And how are we gonna do that?" Scott asks.

"Shame Mia wasn't still around," Mint says. "Maybe she could have gotten a hold of one of those spike strip things the cops use to puncture car tires."

"Airplane tires are too thick," Dana responds, seemingly enjoying the opportunity to correct her. "Those things are designed to create slow punctures in car tires. They wouldn't get near rupturing an airplane tire."

"How thick are we talking?" Scott asks, the cogs already turning.

"I'm not sure. Pretty thick. Tough, too. Though the side walls are a lot thinner."

"Interesting," Scott says.

"What are ya thinkin', Scotty?" Crisp grins.

* * *

"You can't just buy a bear trap, though, can ya?" Shelly asks as we drive back into town.

"No," Dana says. "Because they're inhumane and barbaric."

"Some people say that about Scotty, don't they, Scotty?"

"I'm not condoning the use of bear traps to trap actual bears," Scott says. "I'm just saying that the mechanics of it would appear to be useful for puncturing an airplane tire."

"How's that, now?" Shelly asks.

"See, a bear trap is essentially like a jaw with two sets of big, sharp metal gnashers on either side, like this," Scott says, demonstrating with his two hands held in front of him, his fingers curled to represent said gnashers. "There's a pressure pad in the middle, so when Winnie the Pooh steps in the middle of it—clank! The jaws slam shut, trapping him in its grasp."

"Poor Winnie," Mint says with a grimace.

"So, if we could make a bear trap big enough and then lay it in front of the airplane's tires, it would bite into those weak side walls Dana was talking about and puncture the tire."

"Genius!" Crisp beams.

"And you think you can make a bear trap that big in the next . . ." I check the time on my phone. ". . . eight or so hours?"

"With the right equipment, yeah," Scott says in his casual, almost lazy manner. "We should probably get on with it, though."

"Think you can get what you need at Canadian Tire?" Crisp asks.

"I should think so," Scott replies.

"Okay, here's the deal," says Crisp. "Canadian Tire and Mark's are on the same lot. Scotty, you take Dana, since she knows what she's talking about, and Shelly, 'cause, y'know, she's Shelly." He gives Shelly a wink through the mirror, and she blows him a kiss in reply. "Grab what you need there. Greg, Mint, and I will hit up Mark's and buy us some new uniforms."

"Uniforms?" Dana says incredulously.

"Steve Jobs ninja suits, to be exact," I say.

"That's right," Crisp says, examining Dana in the rear-view mirror. "What are you, beautiful? About a four?"

Dana rolls her eyes. Could it be that Crispin Summers finally met a woman impervious to his charms?

We roll into the parking lot and split up as Crisp had prescribed. Once again, we have to endure the judgmental glares of a Mark's Work Warehouse cashier as we purchase our black cargo pants, turtleneck sweaters, and balaclavas.

"We're puppeteers," Crisp says to the middle-aged man. "Y'know, with those glow-in-the-dark puppets." The man rings us in without saying a word. "We have to disappear into the background." The cashier bags our gear. "Otherwise, it ruins the whole illusion." He gives Crisp his receipt. "For the children."

Back at the Range Rover, Scott is loading up the trunk with a smorgasbord of metal bits and bobs, springs, nuts and bolts, portable lights, and new power tools.

He looks like a kid on Christmas morning. If that kid was also a crazy inventor.

We all jump back in the mangled SUV and head to the airport "for reconnaissance."

The famed Gander International Airport is two runways and a modest terminal building set in a large field with a parking lot. In stark contrast to the hustle and bustle of London Heathrow, which I had flown out of just a few short months ago, and even the relatively modest St. John's International, it is almost eerily quiet. Save for the occasional takeoff and landing, there is very little activity and few people coming and going. If you were going to try to puncture a plane's tires, this would be the perfect airport at which to do it.

It isn't hard to locate our target. *Hawk 1* is a Cessna Citation X—according to a quick Google search—decked out in red and white Finatech livery. Handily, it has "Hawk 1" emblazoned clearly on the side. Dana was able to pull the flight plan from Jackson's computer, so we know that Justin and Patrick plan to take off for New York at 9:45 p.m.

"Bingo," Crisp says. "That's our bird."

We circle the airport, searching for a weak spot—an access point to the runway where we're unlikely to be spotted. We find just the place on the west side of the runway, where a service road runs off Garrett Drive, the only obstacle a rather unimposing gate sealed with nothing more than a thin chain and a padlock.

"That's our way in," Scott says as we creep slowly by like a carful of curb-crawling weirdos.

We hatch the rest of our plan while performing a few more laps of the airport. We'll bust open the gate with Scott's shiny new bolt cutters and deposit Scott—along with all his bear-trap-building supplies—in the field to the west of the runway. He'll construct the contraption right there on-site.

"Aren't you going to need power?" I ask.

"Nah," says Scott, piecing together a newly acquired drill. "Everything I bought is battery-operated." He gives the trigger a squeeze, the drill whining and whirring into life. "And I picked up plenty of batteries."

"So, he builds the bear trap and . . . what? We somehow put it on the runway when the jet is taxiing?

"Nah, no good. Can't do it when the plane's moving slow," Crisp says.

"What? Why not?" I ask.

"Well, think about it," Crisp says. "If we try to roll up and put a bear trap in front of a taxiing plane, they'll see us coming and they'll just hit the brakes. It'll never work."

"So, what exactly are you suggesting?" Dana asks.

Crisp is so glad she asked.

"We wait till the jet guns 'er. Then we race ahead of it and drop the bear trap from the back of the Range Rover."

Dana laughs. "Clearly you can't be serious." She looks around at the rest of the group for reassurance that he isn't. She gets none. "Oh my God, you are serious."

"Will we even be able to get ahead of it?" Mint asks. "I mean, how fast does a plane need to be going before it takes off?"

All eyes fall on Dana. She shakes her head, not quite believing she's having this conversation.

"Technically it is possible. A small jet like that can take off at anywhere from about sixty to a hundred knots."

We all look at her for clarification. She does the math in her head.

"About seventy miles per hour."

I nod along, but the rest of the group still isn't getting it.

"So, around a hundred and ten kilometres per hour," Dana clarifies.

The gang mumbles and nods in agreement.

"Well, Crispin had the Range Rover up to about one-sixty out on the highway," Scott says.

"Yes, b'y," Crisp says. "She's got da guts in 'er."

15

Dare 4
Grounding the Hawk
($1,000,000)

As I pull on the black cargo pants and turtleneck sweater, my heart begins to race. It feels good to be getting back in uniform again. It really is like a drug. The adrenaline. The thrill of doing something outside of the law—and, crucially, getting away with it. The promise of money. More money than I'd ever dreamed of before.

One. Million. Dollars.

That was the prize on offer for this little gig—one that for me amounted to sitting in the back of a speeding Range Rover and helping to lower a giant, homemade bear trap out the back of the tailgate onto a runway to burst the tire of a private jet belonging to a couple of tech billionaires.

Nothing to it.

I look around my little hotel room to see what else I'll need. I pause for a moment to watch the cars and trucks passing along on the Trans-Canada Highway from the not-so-dizzying heights of the Albatross Hotel's fourth—and top—floor.

The sun is going down. It'll be dark when we get to the airport. Just as we planned.

I grab up the glass orb from the side table and turn it in my hand, examining the little mosquito suspended inside.

"Dino DNA," I say in a thick southern US accent. I chuckle to myself and slide the orb into one of the many pockets of my cargo pants.

I pull on my brand-new black boots and stuff the balaclava into another of my many pants pockets. Then I grab my denim jacket from the back of the easy chair. As I do so, the gun falls from the inside pocket and hits the floor with a loud thud. I perform a dance move from Swan Lake, as though amateur ballet would save me from a bullet in the event the thing did accidentally discharge. Thankfully it doesn't, and I retrieve it from the carpeted floor.

I hold the gun in my hand, and for a moment nothing seems real.

I'm holding a gun. A gun that killed a man. A gun that killed Ray Junior. I'm holding a murder weapon.

I feel the weight of the matte black weapon in my hand. It seems to be getting heavier.

Bzzzz!

The sound of my phone vibrating on the table makes me jump, and I almost drop the gun again.

"Jesus," I say before putting on my denim jacket and sliding the gun back into the inside pocket.

I grab the phone and read the text from Crisp.

My room. It's time.

When I arrive in Crisp's room, Shelly and Mint are already there. *Quelle surprise*. Dana stayed with Scott, quite literally out in the field, the gang figuring that her superior knowledge of airplanes made her the best candidate to help Scott put together his Cessna-tire-bursting contraption.

"Okay, jackets on," Crisp says. "We want to look as inconspicuous as possible until we get out to the car, okay?"

Mint and Shelly pull on their jackets and fasten them up.

"We'll go out in pairs, two at a time."

"Greg and I will go first," Mint says before Crisp can bark any more instructions. She grabs me by the hand and pulls me toward the door, the contact making my heart beat harder than the falling gun had just a few minutes earlier.

"Okay, yeah," Crisp yells after us as though it were his idea. "Shell and I will give it ten minutes, then we'll be down."

Mint pulls me along, out the door, down the narrow hallway, and to the Albatross Hotel's single elevator. She hits the call button and looks at me with that smile.

"Excited?" she asks me.

About what? I think to myself. The life-or-death mission we're about to embark on, or the prospect of being alone in an elevator for thirty-some seconds with you?

"Very," I say. It'd be true either way.

Maybe it's the adrenaline. Maybe it's some deep-seated concern that this time we might not all make it out alive. Whatever it is, my mouth starts saying things that my ears can hardly believe.

"Mint, what's the deal with us?" I ask just as the elevator arrives with a real ding of an actual bell.

She takes both of my hands in hers and pulls me into the tiny elevator.

Before the door is fully closed, she pulls me to her, the sensation of our bodies touching sending electricity coursing through me. And then we kiss. A perfect kiss in every way, except that it doesn't last nearly long enough.

Ding!

We're still locked to each other when the door reopens.

"Ah," I hear a shaky voice say from out in the hallway. "Young love."

We turn to see a senior couple waiting to board the elevator—she a tiny little lady with a big smile on her face, he a tall older gentleman searching for a place to look.

Mint takes my hand and leads me out of the elevator.

"Excuse us," she says to the older couple.

"Not at all," says the lady. "That's nothing compared to what I plan to do to Albert once we get back to our room."

Mint and I laugh out loud as the saucy older lady and her now red-faced husband disappear behind the closing elevator door.

"Think that'll be us one day?" I ask.

"Let's just focus on surviving tonight first," Mint replies.

As she leads me out into the lobby, I can hardly feel my legs.

I'm falling.

The lobby is brightly lit and relatively impressive for a roadside hotel just outside of Gander, what with that peaked roof and glass-panelled entrance. We try to look as casual as we can as we pass by the front desk, the concierge—a beaming young brunette lady—wishing us a good evening.

We are almost at the door when something catches my eye on the TV behind her.

I stop dead in my tracks, Mint shooting me a puzzled look. She follows my gaze to the headline on the screen.

Red DeLorean found on rocks off Signal Hill

Mint gasps audibly.

"So, that's where the DeLorean went," she says.

"Yeah," I whisper. "But it was supposed to disappear into the ocean, not get wedged on the rocks for all to see."

I stride over to the desk.

"Can you turn that up, please?" I ask the brunette lady, who goes from beaming to mildly perplexed at the request.

"Oh, um, sure," she says, trying to locate the remote among the myriad drawers and shelves. She finds it and turns up the volume just in time for us to catch Toni-Marie Wiseman delivering the end of the report.

". . . no sign of anyone inside, the RNC are set to recover the vehicle and conduct a thorough search for clues and fingerprints. While it is still unconfirmed, speculation has been rife that the vehicle might be the missing red DeLorean of tech billionaire Jackson Lorde—himself still unaccounted for, more than two weeks after his sudden disappearance. While the rarity of the vehicle would suggest this to be a strong possibility, police are refusing to speculate, stating only that investigations are ongoing."

"Thanks," I say to the confused-looking front desk lady, who simply smiles and wishes us a good evening in the exact same bright and breezy way she did when we first passed through the lobby, as though her internal computer were free now to go back to running its usual routines.

Mint and I jump in the back of the Range Rover together, and my mouth starts doing that thing again.

"So, what's the deal with you and Crisp, then?"

She considers the question for a moment.

"It's just . . . he's fun, but not relationship material."

"Right." And am I? She sees the question in my eyes.

"Look, we're young," she says. "I like you. Let's just see where it goes, okay?"

"Yeah, totally," I say, trying to be as nonchalant about it as she is. But I'm not. I want you. I need you. I'm falling in—

"A pair of star-crossed lovers," Crisp says as he opens the driver's door and squeezes his lanky frame into the vehicle. He can even make a luxury SUV look like a tight fit. He flashes us that narrow smile in the rear-view mirror as Shelly hops into her shotgun seat, hula hoop and all. I'm not sure if he knows the rest of that quote, but we read *Romeo and Juliet* in high school and I know it doesn't end well. We instinctively pull away from one another.

"Okay," Crisp says as he fires up the Range Rover and rolls toward the Trans-Canada Highway. "Time for a flock of Gulls to pick up a bear trap and stop a hawk from taking off."

"There's a sentence you don't hear every day," Shelly says.

After a quick Tim's stop, Crisp enters the airport parking lot from the east side, checking to make sure the getaway car is in position. We'd figured the Range Rover would be too hot after we pulled our stunt, so the plan is to hop into a new vehicle and burn the Range Rover. Crisp had picked out a brand-new Nissan Pathfinder in "Super Black." "Big enough to carry the flock, gutsy enough to get us out of a jam, and unassuming enough not to draw attention," as he'd put it.

Content to see the black SUV sitting in wait where we'd left it, he circles around to Garrett Drive, over on the west end of the airport, steering the Range Rover off the road and over the field toward the waiting Scott and Dana. Dana sits crossed-legged on the thick blanket and couple of cushions Scott had picked up to provide them with some degree of comfort during their time in the field, but she looks anything but comfortable as she blows into her hands and pulls her jacket tight around her slender frame.

Scott, on the other hand, stands proud in the beams of the lights he'd purchased at Canadian Tire, his latest contraption sitting on the ground by his feet. The homemade bear trap is a mean-looking mass of sharp metal teeth and thick springs. As I carefully climb out of the Range Rover with the cardboard tray of Tim's coffees in my hand, I think to myself, *I don't want to get anywhere near that thing.*

"Hey, Greg. Gimme a hand to get this thing into the truck, would ya," Scott cheerily requests.

So much for not getting anywhere near that thing.

"Right. Yeah. Just gimme a second."

As the rest of the gang jump out of the Range Rover to get a better look at the contraption, I make my way over to a frozen-looking Dana.

"Doing okay?" I ask. She just looks at me incredulously. "Brought you a coffee," I say, popping the cardboard cup from the tray and passing it to her.

"Thanks," she says, peeling back the little tab on the plastic lid and taking a sip, coffee dribbling down her chin. "Jesus, are they ever going to come up with a better design for these lids?" she asks.

"Probably not," Scott says, gratefully taking his coffee from the tray.

Crisp gives a long whistle as he examines Scott's handiwork. "Not bad, Scotty Too Hotty!" he says as he drains his Tim's cup, crushes it in his hand, and tosses it onto the field. "Is it gonna work?"

Scott seems to take this as a challenge and picks up a thick tree branch from the ground, jamming it into the centre of the bear trap and causing the mean-looking teeth to slam shut, shattering the branch in an explosion of splinters.

"Dammit, Scotty," Shelly remonstrates as she attempts to wipe spilled coffee off the front of her turtleneck. "A simple yes woulda sufficed!"

Scott shrugs.

"Better to leave it closed while we're transporting it," he says, giving me the eyes to help him carry it to the Range Rover.

"No shit," Mint says as she sips on her beverage.

"But if anyone does have to reset it, use a stick or somethin'," Scott says. "Just push against one of the jaws. Too dangerous to be doing it with your hands."

"We'll keep that in mind," I say. I sink the remainder of my lukewarm coffee and toss the cup before squatting to help Scott lift the bear trap.

"One, two, three," Scott says, and we lug the contraption toward the tailgate that Crisp has just opened. It's clumsy but not as heavy as I expected. A comfortable weight for two people.

We slide it into the back of the Range Rover and begin deconstructing Scott and Dana's makeshift workstation, putting the lights, blanket, and cushions in the vehicle. Then we all climb aboard.

"Okay. Everyone know what they're doing?" Crisp asks. We all nod and mutter affirmatives. "Okay, hands in," he says, and we stack hands. "Gulls on three. One, two, three, Gulls!"

With that, Crisp fires up the Range Rover and we go about executing the plan we hatched back in Jungle Jim's.

We make our way back to Garrett Drive and head up the dirt access road, passing through the gate with its chain and padlock, which the bolt cutters make light work of. Crisp kills the lights, and our balaclavas are pulled back on as we roll up behind a small cluster of trees just off the west side of the runways.

Scott jumps out, with a pair of high-powered binoculars—another of his Canadian Tire purchases—strapped around his neck. Following a brief sojourn to the back of the car to reset the bear trap, he heads over to the treeline to take up his position. Dana gives me a peck on the wool-covered cheek. "Be careful," she says before joining Scott. They will be our scouting party, making their way on foot across the parking lot to the Pathfinder, giving the rest of us more room to manoeuvre inside the Range Rover, and positioning Scott at the wheel of the getaway car for a smooth exit out of Gander. Scott is also our eyes for this part of the operation, crouching among the trees with Dana at his side, watching for Justin and Patrick approaching *Hawk 1*.

The rest of us arrange ourselves per the agreed plan. Shelly maintains her shotgun position alongside Crisp at the wheel. Mint and I fold down the back seats of the Range Rover and crouch together, either side of the nefarious contraption. We will be the muscle—it will be our job to lower the trap out of the back of the speeding Range Rover and onto the runway, with the help of a long strap that runs underneath it.

And there we wait, like the coiled springs inside our trap, full of nervous energy, stretched to our limits, just waiting to go off.

"What time is it?" I ask from the back of the Range Rover.

"Almost time," Crisp says coolly.

The anticipation is agonizing. My balaclava feels warm and itchy. I'm just beginning to feel dizzy again when we get the signal from Scott.

"It's time," Crisp hisses, and he fires up the Range Rover, pulling slowly forward to the edge of the treeline.

In the distance I can just about make out the figures of a few people walking across the tarmac to the red-and-white private jet, climbing the stairs on the side, and disappearing into the belly of the plane.

Scott and Dana scurry by, giving a wave as they go, and a chill runs up my spine as I hear the scream of the plane's jet engines powering up.

Oh, shit. It's time.

As the plane begins to taxi, the Range Rover mirrors its movements, Crisp creeping the SUV slowly forward, off the dirt and onto the asphalt.

"Time to fly, little bird," he says, softly patting the steering wheel like he might a newly hatched gull chick.

The plane swings around and for a moment is headed right for us. We tense as one, hoping that the pilot doesn't spot the Range Rover sunk back in the shadows. We breathe again as the jet veers off to our right and points itself east before rolling to a stop.

"Hold onto something," Crisp says. Mint and I crouch, bracing ourselves against the sides of the vehicle. Shelly grabs her "Oh-my-Jesus" handle. Crisp revs the engine. Mint takes my spare hand in hers.

The jet engines scream to life once again.

The plane begins to move.

Crisp floors the throttle of the Range Rover, and we are almost propelled out of the back of the vehicle as its wheels screech and we fly forward from a cloud of burned tire rubber.

The Range Rover is up to full speed before the jet is out of the blocks, and we are almost alongside it before it begins to move.

"Careful," Shelly says, hearkening back to the plan hatched in Jungle Jim's.

We want to make sure the plane is moving before we get ahead of it. We don't want to be spotted and have the pilot abort the takeoff before we can get the trap laid.

Crisp eases off the gas a little and waits for the plane to lurch forward. As soon as it does, he hammers on the gas again, and we are in a straight race with the Cessna.

We fly along beside the jet at breakneck speed.

"Okay, door!" Crisp yells, prompting me to open the Range Rover's tailgate. When I do, the noise is incredible, causing me to reflexively reach for my ears before my brain realizes the stupidity of that action and instead sends my hands grabbing for whatever piece of car interior they can hold onto.

Just when I think the Range Rover has no more acceleration to offer, Crisp finds some, slamming the pedal to the metal and causing the engine to reach a pitch I've never heard a car hit before.

We pull ahead of the jet, getting some good yards between ourselves and the front of the plane.

Mint and I grab an end of the strap each and take the weight of the trap.

"Ready?" I yell. Mint nods. I don't think she hears me over the roar of engines, but her eyes seem to get my meaning.

"I love you!" I yell. This time she doesn't grasp what I'm saying, her eyes squinting in confusion. I just nod, and we return to hefting the trap to the back of the car.

We kneel at the back of the speeding Range Rover and begin to slide the trap toward the edge of the tailgate, but just as we are about to lower it over the side, the deafening scream of the jet's roaring engines drops several octaves and the plane immediately begins to fall back from the Range Rover.

They've spotted us.

I don't know if it's the sudden change in the plane's speed that disorients us or if Crisp eases off the gas, but both Mint and I stumble, the bear trap clattering to the floor of the SUV and somehow discharging. I right myself just in time to see that Mint has fallen toward the back of the car. It feels as though Crisp hits the gas again, and I watch in horror as Mint is sent flying toward the opening.

I dive forward and manage to get a hold of her leg just as her head disappears out the back. Even above all the noise, I hear her scream, and I pull with all my might to get her back aboard the Range Rover.

I try to look her over in the middle of all the mayhem. She is clearly in pain, but her head appears to have escaped injury. I feel warm, slick blood, and she holds her arm. I pull her to me, away from the back of the car, away from the roaring jet. Only her safety matters now.

And then, out of nowhere, I see the yellow flash of Shelly's hula hoop, followed by Shelly herself, squeezing between the front seats and into the back of the car with us. I hold Mint tight and watch as Shelly eases open the jaws of the bear trap with her hula hoop before grabbing up both sides of the strap and single-handedly lowering the trap out the back of the tailgate.

She falls back into the car and tears off her balaclava, giving me one of her trademark flirty winks.

There's an explosion of air and rubber as the plane's front wheel hits the trap and it discharges exactly as planned, its sharp metal fangs biting into either side of the tire's walls and shredding it to pieces.

It's a large piece of tire rubber that flies forward off the jet and right into the back of the Range Rover, smashing into Shelly's head and buckling her neck at a sickening angle.

In the quickest of moments, she goes limp and rolls out the back of the Range Rover, bouncing off the asphalt and under the sparking remains of the jet's front wheel.

Her yellow hula hoop lies where she just was, shaking and alone on the floor of the car.

Jesus. Did that just happen?

The Range Rover seems to slow, and the plane's tires are screeching now as it barrels toward us.

I turn to see Crisp's eyes wide in the rear-view mirror as he, too, tries to process what we just saw.

"Crisp!" I yell. He doesn't hear me.

The Range Rover slows.

The plane bears down.

"Crisp! Gun it!"

Suddenly, Crisp comes back to reality, and just as the nose

of the plane is about to ram the back of the Range Rover, he floors the gas and we peel away from the screaming bird.

I pull Mint tight to me and watch as the plane veers to one side and eventually comes to a rest, one wing almost touching the ground.

Take its legs. Clip its wings.

"Hold on," Crisp says, and we brace as he guns it straight through a gate on the east side of the airport and drives the Range Rover to where Scott and Dana sit waiting in the black Pathfinder.

Crisp beeps the horn a couple of times on his way past and the Pathfinder speeds away, falling in behind us as we head out toward the highway.

16

Lost to the Flames

I feel the heat on my face and watch as the Range Rover succumbs to the flames. Mint and Dana stand either side of me in silence on the dirt side road we'd found about twenty minutes up the highway from Gander. My hand rests on the bright yellow hula hoop, which I rock gently back and forth against the ground.

Somewhere behind us, Scott and Crisp talk in raised voices.

"What was she doing in the back of the car?" Scott asks for the third or fourth time.

"She went back there to help, Scott. I told you."

"So, why didn't you stop her? Huh? Why didn't you try to stop her, Crispin?"

"I was a little busy trying to outrun a speeding jet plane, Scott."

"No, no. This wasn't supposed to . . . this can't be happening!"

Scott's feet crunch in the gravel as he paces back and forth, his words becoming muffled as he puts his face in his hands.

What's that thing about the phases of grief? Scott seems to be experiencing them all at the same time.

"No," he says, over and over again. "No, no, no. Not Shelly. Not Shelly . . ."

"Scott. We all loved Shelly. Everybody loved Shelly."

"No. You didn't know her like I did! You didn't know her from a child. You didn't grow up with her, Crispin . . ."

Scott's voice cracks, and he begins to sob uncontrollably. I hear both the women beside me begin to sniffle. Instinctively, I lean the hula hoop against my leg and take a hold of each of their hands.

"What about her mother?" Scott says. "Poor Mrs. Lambert. She's gonna be distraught. We have to let her know."

"No," Crispin says.

"We have to let her know, Crispin. We owe her that, at least!"

"We can't risk implicating ourselves right now, Scott."

"Oh, Jesus," Scott says, cupping his hands to his face once again. "And what about a funeral? Oh, man, her body's just lying there on that cold runway," he sobs. "We gotta get her body, Crisp! We gotta give her a proper funeral!"

"Scott. Scott? You're not making any sense. You're not thinking straight, buddy."

Suddenly, Scott stops his pacing. I half-turn to watch him in the headlights of the Pathfinder. He stands facing Crispin, the two of them silhouetted like two samurai about to face off in a duel.

"Maybe I should end this, Crispin. Maybe it's over."

"Scotty, you're emotional right now—"

"Am I? Well, maybe that's all right, Crispin. Maybe that's

how normal people are. Maybe if you were capable of showing a little emotion, we'd all be a lot better off."

Scott strides right up to Crisp, facing him down—his boldness making up somewhat for the fact he has to arch his neck to look up at the much taller man.

"It's all just a game to you, isn't it?"

Crisp doesn't answer.

"This isn't a game!" Scott yells, sending spittle flying into Crisp's face. "This was never a game!" he shouts before backing away and taking a couple of breaths. "It's more than that," he says, quieter now, his voice heavy with fatigue.

He turns toward us and takes in the scene. Me, the two women, the burning Range Rover. The orange flames dance in his thick, jam jar–bottom glasses as he stares at us, expressionless.

Then he makes his way toward us, his feet crunching on the gravel. My body tenses as he gets closer.

I feel the weight of the gun in my inside jacket pocket.

Scott strides closer.

I let go of Mint's hand and reach my hand into my jacket. I feel the cold steel of the gun.

Scott stops in front of me and stares me right in the eye. Except I can't see his eyes. All I can see is those orange flames dancing and flickering in those jam-jar glasses. Two great, fiery chasms where his eyes ought to be.

Scott reaches out and grabs the hula hoop from my side, yanking it away from me like it's a memory I don't deserve, and he storms back toward the Pathfinder, climbing into the front passenger side of the black SUV and slamming the door hard behind him.

Without words, we follow him to the car, the three of us brushing silently past Crisp and getting in the back. I sit in the middle. The thorn between two roses.

Crisp is the last to join us, getting in the driver's seat.

We all sit there in silence for a moment as the flames begin to die down.

"Shelly was—" Crisp begins to say.

"Don't," Scott interrupts. "Just don't."

Before anyone can say another word, our phones beep and vibrate in unison, and we take them out to see a new message from our mysterious benefactor.

The flock is culled, friendships torn.
One dare remains in the hills of Gros Morne.

"What?" Dana asks. "Is it another message? Is it from him?"

I turn my phone to show her.

"No specifics this time," Crisp says. "About where the million dollars is."

"'Cause that's what's important," Scott hisses. "The money."

"Well, if money wasn't important, would you still be along for the ride?"

"I told you. It isn't about the money. It's more important than that."

"What, do you want revenge?"

Scott stares Crisp in the eye. "Like you would never understand."

"Could you guys just cut it out?" Mint snaps.

"Bear Island," Dana says, cutting through the tension.

"What?" I ask.

"Jackson has an island off the west coast, close to Gros Morne. It's called Bear Island."

"He has an island?" Mint asks. "Like, he owns an island?"

"It isn't a very big one," Dana says, a mite defensively.

Scott scoffs.

"I mean, it isn't on any maps, but he told me how to find it."

"Think you can take us there?" Crisp asks.

"Yeah, I think so," Dana says.

"Then that's where we're heading," Crisp says. "It's about time we got us some answers."

He starts up the Pathfinder, and we make our way shakily back out to the Trans-Canada Highway.

17

Up the Coast

The drive to Gros Morne is four hours spent largely in silence. Gone is the "carpool karaoke" of journeys past. Gone is the lightness, the unbridled freedom and joy. Gone is the sweetest and kindest member of our little clan, her bright yellow hula hoop sitting at Scott's side, tapping on the passenger window occasionally as if to remind us of all we've lost.

I've never felt more lost. As we stop in at Deer Lake to gas up and relieve ourselves at the twenty-four-hour Circle K, I've never felt so far from home. It seems like an age since I saw the ocean, and there's something about seeing the ocean that I find calming. Like there's an end to all of this. Like England still exists just across those waters. Like there's still hope I'll see my mother and my family again.

"On up the mountain," Crisp says, with none of his usual vigour, as he climbs back behind the wheel of the Pathfinder. "I brought snacks," he says, depositing a plastic bag that's overflowing with chips, bars, and cans of soda onto the centre console. "Help yourselves."

I can't remember when I last ate. Jungle Jim's back in Gander? I have little appetite now, but my head is starting to ache, so

I fish a bag of all-dressed Ruffles out of the bag and try to force a few of the chips down. This seems to remind the rest of the crew that they haven't eaten in a while, either, and they gradually retrieve their own snacks out of the bag.

We also haven't slept for a while, but there has been no suggestion of stopping to grab some shut-eye from any of the gang. Since the airport—since Shelly—it's as though time has lost all meaning. Had I been aware of the kind of roads we would need to navigate as we made our way up the Great Northern Peninsula from Deer Lake toward Gros Morne, I may have had cause to question the wisdom of tackling the drive in the dead of night with nothing to fuel us save for chips, candy, and energy drinks—all of which Crisp is gorging himself on copiously as we wind our way upwards.

I say upwards. In reality, the roads are a rally fan's wet dream of sharp turns, steep climbs, and exhilarating drops that invite you—against all better judgment—to let gravity take control and slingshot you into the next sweeping corner.

Crisp is a wide-eyed picture of concentration, seemingly enjoying the challenge of keeping the Pathfinder on its path and out of the ditches—and occasional dramatic drops—on either side of the winding road.

Sat dead centre in the back seat, I get a premium view of the dark and desolate world beyond the windows, backlit by the fullest of full moons on this clearest of nights and highlighted in the stark white beam of the Pathfinder's LED lights. For me, it's a white-knuckle roller-coaster ride, and no Red Bull nor Monster Energy is required to keep my eyes peeled and my senses on high alert.

Seemingly, the journey has the opposite effect on the two women sitting either side of me—the sensations of being rocked back and forth, of falling and being caught, coupled with the multi-pitched hum of the vehicle's engine, serving to lull them both to sleep. I stare at myself in the rear-view mirror, my face ghostly white and with their heads resting on either of my shoulders. On the one side, the super-smart, highly practical woman who'd plucked me from a bar in Rochdale and brought me across the ocean to a world I could never have imagined. On the other, the equally smart but doubly mysterious woman who I simultaneously feel I've known for years and yet know nothing of at all.

Oh, God, I think to myself. I'm in love with them both.

No sooner have I had the thought than the whole world is changed. Gone is the rhythmic climbing and falling, gone is the singsong hum of the Pathfinder's engine straining and coasting. In their place is the screech of tires locked into a hard brake, like an unwelcome alarm clock sounding before the sun has had a chance to rise.

En masse, we are flung forward, the shock enhanced by the pain of seat belts digging into those same tender spots created when Crisp had jumped the Range Rover onto the mountainside ledge back in Chance Cove.

The screeching stops, and so does the Pathfinder, the sudden shift of momentum slamming us hard into our seats.

Amid mumbles and groans, I look up and momentarily think we might all have died. For there, beyond the windshield, glowing in the bright white headlights, is some kind of otherworldly beast. It is pure white with great, curving antlers protruding high from its head. It stands perfectly still, night-black eyes staring blankly yet intently back at us, piercing into our very souls.

"Jesus. Sorry, b'ys," Crisp says, snapping me back to reality. "Friggin' caribou."

As I blink, I see that it isn't just one giant, white, horned beast but a whole herd of them.

"Caribou?" I ask. "They look like albino reindeer."

"Technically, they are reindeer," Dana says, rubbing the back of her neck. "Their coats turn white in the winter. It's unusual to see one that white at this time of year."

"It's an omen," Scott says glumly.

"It's no omen," Crisp counters. "It's a friggin' traffic jam, is what it is."

He beeps the horn, which sounds loud in the relative quiet, as though the sound bounces off the sides of unseen mountains.

"Come on!" Crisp barks. "Outta the way, ya big white bastard!"

The lead caribou stands his ground for a moment, seemingly unperturbed by the sounding klaxon, even as the rest of the herd pick up their pace and scurry across the road to the refuge of the woods.

"He must be the leader," I speculate, peering out from between the Pathfinder's front seats into the great beast's vacant eyes.

"He's the devil, is what he is," Scott mumbles.

"Come on!" Crisp shouts, leaning hard on the horn. "We're a sitting duck here if a transport truck comes along."

Giving zero frigs and in his own sweet time, the great white bull waits for the rest of his herd to pass and then casually turns before sinking away into the darkness of the treeline.

* * *

Gros Morne is a place that reminds you how small you are. How young you are. How brief. How insignificant.

As we make our way up the coastal road, a vast blanket of ocean sprawls out to the left of us. In stark contrast to the angry, pounding waves that battered the rocks of Signal Hill, the water here is almost mirror still.

To the right, two monolithic, flat-topped mountains tower in the hazy distance, serving as giant curtains, parting to reveal the rising sun. Fractured golden rays beam out from the mist. The scene is surreal, and my senses struggle to assess the scale of the giant, beckoning fjord.

"Amazing, isn't it?" Dana says, giving me a start. I hadn't realized she was awake as I'd leaned over her to get a better look. "That's Western Brook," she says. "Those mountains were carved out by a huge glacier during the last ice age. Anywhere from ten to twenty-five thousand years ago."

Dana is a fountain of knowledge—especially when it comes to her beloved Newfoundland.

I say nothing, entranced as we pass the mountains by—at speed and yet slowly, their distance and size almost seeming to slow time, the curtains appearing to overlap as the Pathfinder strains to leave them behind.

Just as Western Brook sinks away in the rear-view mirror, I feel my phone vibrate in my pocket, as a couple of the others' phones ding and chirp.

A new message from our mysterious . . . benefactor? Tormentor?

We all look at our phones in unison.

A boat awaits in the shallowest bay
Take her out and make your way
East, past the islands that everyone knows
To discover the bear where nobody goes

"Well, more instructional than cryptic this time," Dana says as she peers at my phone.

"Except, how are we supposed to know which bay is the shallowest?" Mint asks.

"Simple," Crisp replies. "We'll get wee Scotty to walk out into the water and see which one he can stand up in without drowning."

"Oh, I see. It's a short joke," Scott drones from the front passenger seat. Crisp gives him a playful punch to the shoulder, but he doesn't seem to appreciate the humour.

"Well, there's a bay called Shallow Bay," Dana says.

All the car's other passengers turn to her in unison while Crisp eyes her through the rear-view mirror.

"In fact, it's about twenty minutes up the road."

A chill shoots up my spine. Twenty minutes. Until now, our destination had been ambiguous, a mystery. And this had been a place where time was measured in centuries. The immediacy of twenty minutes is jarring. I reach into my pocket—not the one with the gun this time, but my jeans pocket for the smooth, reassuring surface of the glass orb. I squeeze it in my hand—so hard I think it could shatter.

Shit just got real again, and you can feel it inside the car. The rest of the journey is spent in almost total silence as we rumble over a metal bridge in St. Paul's—a tiny town of dotted houses where fishing boats bob in the gently lapping early-morning waves. We pass a gas station with a surprisingly modern-looking sloped roof, and I see Crisp look down at the Pathfinder's fuel gauge.

"We nearly there?" he asks Dana.

"Yes," she replies. "Next left, I believe."

He steps on the gas again and propels us ever closer to our final dare. To our destiny.

Trees flicker by outside the window, and I can hear my heartbeat hammering in my ears.

"Just here," Dana says, and Crisp slows the car before making a left where the sign says "Cow Head."

We drive down a long, narrow road with trees lining both sides, the occasional cabin peeping out and a couple of four-wheelers randomly parked off in the dirt. I smile at the sight of sheep grazing in a field. Back home, sheep are everywhere, but these are the first ones I've seen since arriving in Newfoundland. As we round a corner and houses start to appear, I think of Mum and my sister. As the ocean once again comes into view, a sudden overpowering urge rises in me to run to it, to swim, to cross it, to leave this place and return to the comfort of home once again.

I grip the glass orb even tighter.

Cow Head itself is an idyllic little fishing town with white houses dotted about. If the great mountains we'd passed on our way in were created by colliding continents and carved by glaciers, then this is where the ice flattened the land, removing all obstacles and allowing the landscape to unfurl into beckoning ocean.

As we arc around to the centre of the town, those shadowy mountains reveal themselves once again in the distance—a looming, distant presence in the struggling morning light.

But it's the ocean that pulls us forward, past the two-storey house that serves as the doctor's office, past the little white church and its small, neatly arranged botanical garden, past the beige corrugated box that serves as the town store, past the motel and the theatre.

"The theatre!" I find myself saying out loud. "I knew I'd heard of Cow Head. Shelly told me about it. The little town with the theatre."

"She had a stint working up here," Scott says glumly, and I realize that my enthusiasm is horribly out of place.

"Sorry," I say, not explaining for what and not having to.

The memory of Shelly rides with us the rest of the way, her yellow hula hoop tap-tapping against the window as we follow Dana's instructions and trundle along the potholed, tree-lined dirt road that lies at the conclusion of the town.

As we emerge from the trees, the whole world widens. The potholed road comes to a loop around a tufty oval of grass with room for parking on either side. As we bobble our way in, a large blue pickup truck passes us in the opposite direction, slowly creeping past. Two hard-looking men stare at us from the truck. The driver—a slim fella with mid-length greasy hair and prominent crow's feet—gives us a nod with a stone-faced expression.

As Crisp parks the Pathfinder, I see sand whipping around in the sharp morning breeze. There's only one other car, parked at the far end of the lot, as we disembark and I take a deep breath of salty sea air. I thought the air in St. John's was fresh, but this is a whole other level.

"Where now?" Mint asks.

"The beach is that way." Dana shrugs, pointing at a gravel path leading off toward the ocean.

Crisp has already hopped the low fence and is relieving himself behind a small cluster of bushes on the other side. He peeps his head around, and both women grimace at him.

"You do realize there are bathrooms right there," Mint says, pointing past him to the small building that sits adjacent to a kids' playground.

"Well, if you gotta go, I'd suggest you get on with it," Crisp says as he gives himself a shake.

Mint, Dana, and Scott all go in to use the washroom, leaving Crisp and me standing on the path. I don't feel the need to go, which is surprising considering I'd ended up chugging a couple of energy drinks on the drive.

Crisp stands with his hands in his pockets, the wind whipping at his face.

"You still got the . . ." He takes one hand out of a pocket, extends a finger, and gives a wink as he mimics firing a gun.

I push my elbow into my side, feeling the edge of the gun's handle hard against my ribs.

"How did you . . . ?"

"I can tell the difference between a gun and a rock, Gregory." He chuckles. Then his tone shifts. "Give it to me," he says.

It isn't a request. It's an instruction.

I hesitate.

He scoffs.

"You ever fired a gun, Greggy boy?" he asks.

I shake my head.

"My old man loves his guns. Had his own shooting range set up out back of the old house. He'd gather up any old shit he could find for targets. Bottles, cans. He even had a few of those cardboard cut-out people with the targets on 'em. You know the ones."

I nod.

"He used to get pissed off when I hit 'em better than him." He looks at me with that thin Crisp smile. "If things get hairy where we're going, do you really wanna be the one holding the gun?"

I take a deep breath of salty ocean air and look out toward the water. Then I reach into my jacket pocket and hand Crisp the gun.

He's just about done concealing it in the back of his waistband when the washroom door opens with a loud creak and the two women re-emerge, seemingly getting along well, chatting away, comforted by each other's consolation.

Just as they rejoin us, our phones buzz and chirp again.

"Another message," Crisp says.

Follow the horseshoe to the end
Your watery chariot is just round the bend
Jump in, start her up, and head due east
Twenty minutes to Bear Island—the home of the beast

Just as we finish reading it, Scott reappears from the bathroom.

"Two women got outta the bathroom before you, Scotty," Crisp says. "The hell were you doing in there?"

"I had to take a dump," Scott says as he makes his way over.

"Well, I did ask," Crisp mutters as Scott notices that we're all engaged with our phones. "What's going on?"

"Another message," I say.

"Really?" Scott asks, pulling his own phone out of his pocket and taking a look.

"Horseshoe?" I ask no one in particular.

"The beach," Dana says. She's huddled with Mint, looking at her phone. "It's a white-sand, horseshoe-shaped beach."

"I guess we're going for a walk on the beach," Crisp smiles. He puts his phone away and makes like he's adjusting his trousers, but I know he's making sure that the gun is secure.

Something about Crisp with a gun makes me nervous.

He leads the way as we walk along the path toward the beach, the gravel gradually disappearing below a layer of fine, white sand.

"The home of the beast?" Mint says. "Does that sound a little ominous to anyone else?"

"It's called Bear Island," Dana says. "Maybe our riddler is just referring to the eponymous bear."

"There better not be any friggin' bears on that island," Crisp says as we climb a couple of steps onto a wooden platform with a couple of benches—a stopping-off point allowing tourists to change from path mode to beach mode, or vice versa.

We gather on the platform and take in the view of Shallow Bay. Just as Dana had described, it is a beautiful, big, horseshoe-shaped white-sand beach that arcs off to our right, waves lapping rhythmically back and forth, staining the white a deep beige in the growing morning light. Gulls circle and squawk overhead as though in a fanfare to our final adventure. The moment isn't lost on Crisp, and nor is the opportunity to say a few words. He turns to face us, leaning his back against the wooden railing, eyes squinting against the whipping, sandy breeze.

"And so it has come to this," he booms. "Five Gulls on a sandy beach, set to storm forth and take on the ocean in search of a foreign land. We've lost some of our flock along the way." I catch Scott's head drop out of the corner of my eye. "We've endured mutiny in our ranks. But still, we stand strong. Still, we have our resolve. And always we will have each other." He looks around at each of us like a proud father. "Onward, Gulls. Fly forth!"

With that, he kicks off his loafers and tosses them onto the beach before springing over the railing and landing with little grace on the white sand below. I wonder if anyone else sees the butt of the gun peeking out of the arse of his jeans as he rights himself. Then he collects his shoes and backs off toward the water, long arms held wide.

"Larus can!" he shouts, his words carried along the beach by the breeze.

The rest of us take off our shoes and use the steps to get down onto the beach, following the waterline toward the next waypoint on our dot-to-dot adventure.

Crisp strides ahead. Scott lags behind. Mint seems to be off in a world of her own, clearly enjoying the sensation of the salt water and the dampened sand between her toes as she walks on just ahead of Dana and me. So strong is the wind now that it lifts her dreadlocks into the air. They glimmer like rays of sunshine in the golden morning hue.

"I get it," Dana says.

"Get what?" I ask.

"She's lovely. Smart. Funny. More than a little mysterious. How could you not go for that?"

"Who—Mint?" I ask, trying and failing to act aloof.

"I know how it is with you, Greg. This is more than a kiss at a party. You fall fast and you fall hard."

I look at her, an apology hanging on my lips.

"It's okay," she says, though there's hurt in her eyes. "You feel too much," she says. "It's your gift." She pauses. "And your burden."

I wipe a tear from my eye that I can easily attribute to the sand being whipped into my face and not—you know—all those feelings.

"And what about your Jackson Lorde?"

"He isn't my Jackson Lorde!" Dana protests.

"But you'd like him to be?"

She shrugs. "I just hope he's okay."

"You think he's on that island?"

"I guess we're going to find out."

We walk in silence for a few steps.

"Why don't you go catch up with Mint?" Dana suggests.

I look at her to make sure it's really okay.

"Go on!" she insists. "I'll drop back and make sure Scott is doing okay. He's suffered quite the loss," she says, and we both glance back at him as he shuffles along the beach, head down, still wearing his sneakers.

"Dana," I say. "I . . ."

She shakes her head and raises a finger in the air. Her eyes are glazed with tears that wish to part.

"Don't," she says. "Go catch up to Mint."

She stops and I walk on, picking up my pace to catch up with the woman ahead of me.

"Hey!" I say.

"Hi, Greg," she replies. "How's Dana? Are you guys ready to patch things up?"

The question almost takes my legs out from under me. Oh, no. Does she think that I want to get back with Dana?

"We're done!" I protest, a little too insistently.

She smiles that perfect smile, the little dimple making a brief appearance.

"I mean, it's over. We're just friends now."

"Okay," she says, and we walk on a little farther. "So, if you're just friends," she says, eventually breaking the painful silence, "why did you let go of my hand when you saw Scott was bearing down on us?"

Jesus. Did I do that? Back at the burning Range Rover? Yes, I did, but . . .

"Only because I'm right-handed," I blurt.

"I see," she says. "I guess that makes sense. So, you needed your right hand to reach into your left inside pocket, because . . ."

Oh, shit. Does she know about the gun?

"I was . . ."

I got nothing.

She digs a playful elbow into my ribs, and that smile appears once again.

"I know about the gun, Greg." I'm at the same time embarrassed and strangely relieved. "The damn thing was poking out of your jacket half the trip here," she says.

Dammit. Maybe when I nodded off to sleep that time?

"Where is it now?" she asks, her bluntness catching me offguard.

"It's, uh . . ."

"You don't have it," she says. It's a statement, not a question.

"No," I say. "I gave it to Crisp."

"I see," she says thoughtfully. "Well, hopefully he doesn't have to use it."

We walk the rest of the way in silence as the whole conversation plays in loops in my head.

Does she think I'm an idiot who can't hide a gun?

Does she think I'm untrustworthy because I tried to?

Does she think I'm weak for giving the gun up to Crisp?

Tall, carefree, charismatic friggin' Crisp . . .

Before I can form any words to say or questions to ask,

Crisp calls out from up ahead. His voice is muffled—carried in all directions by the whipping wind—but I catch the key words.

"... the boat!"

I squint to see him dancing about excitedly. Beyond him, there's a sleek-looking red and white motorboat tied to a small wooden dock.

By the time Mint and I get there, Crisp is already in the boat, now holding up a sleek briefcase. It's brown this time.

Brown like a bear?

Brown like all the shit we're in?

Then I notice the name of the boat, emblazoned on the side in a delicate script.

Hawk 4

How many personalized vehicles does this guy have?

"This is it, Gulls. This is the big one!"

He's like a child on Christmas morning, eyes aglow with excitement. There are no signs of grief over Shelly. There are no signs that he's barely slept. He's running on energy drinks, ego, and adrenaline.

Mint and I climb aboard the boat. It's compact but luxurious, with plush white-leather seating that wraps around a small, triangular table. There's even a fully-stocked minibar in the corner and red cushions scattered about.

Crisp lays the briefcase on the little table and pops open the clasps.

"Whoa!" he says, pulling a captain's hat out of the case and turning to Scott and Dana, who are just arriving on the dock. "Who's gonna be the skipper? Scotty, you knows how to drive a boat, right?"

Scott helps Dana aboard and then climbs aboard himself, shrugging in response to Crisp's question.

"Here you go, then!" Crisp tosses Scott the captain's hat. He fails to catch it, retrieving it from the leather seat where it lands and placing it at an angle on his head before giving the world's least enthusiastic salute.

"Cap'n Scott, reporting for duty," Crisp says, saluting in return.

Scott makes a beeline for the minibar, taking out a miniature bottle of Scotch and draining it in one before tossing the bottle overboard and grabbing another one.

"Go easy on the loony juice, there, Skipper," Crisp says.

"So, what else you got in there?" Mint asks Crisp playfully. Flirtatiously?

Crisp brings a pinky finger to the corner of his mouth and grabs a stack of cash out of the case.

"One. Million. Dollars," he says in his best Dr. Evil voice, before tossing the stack of cash at Mint and proceeding to toss a stack at each of us. "And . . ." He pauses for dramatic effect. "Another love letter from our mysterious benefactor."

Scott finally pipes up for the first time since the Range Rover bonfire.

"He writes us. He gives us money. He must really love us," he says as he examines the boat's controls, a half-empty miniature of Scotch poking out of the cupholder to the side of the steering wheel.

Crisp examines the piece of paper, just waiting for somebody to ask. I'm the one who bites.

"What does it say?" I ask.

"It's just a number," he says.

"What kind of a number?" Dana asks, rising to join Crisp in looking at the card.

"A PIN, maybe?" Crisp speculates. He holds the paper so she can see it.

97 06 29

"Or a date," Dana suggests. "Written year, month, day."

"Ninety-seven," Crisp says. "Six would be June, so . . . June twenty-ninth?"

Something about that date feels familiar to me.

"Wait," I say. "Say that again."

"June twenty-ninth, nineteen ninety-seven," Crisp clarifies.

Where have I seen that date before?

Then it occurs to me.

"The photo!" I exclaim just as Scott starts up the boat.

"Buckle up, people. We're heading west . . . to Bear Island." The last part is said in some kind of weird accent. I think he was going for "pirate." I think he's feeling the effects of that Scotch. I hope he's in a fit state to drive this damn boat.

"Crisp, get the rope?" Scott requests, and Crisp unfurls the thick white rope from the dock.

"Good to go, Cap!" he yells with another salute.

The power of the boat seems to take even Scott by surprise, his captain's hat blowing off as we are propelled away from the beach with a guttural roar of the engine.

"Whoa, there!" Scott says as we all right ourselves. "Sorry, me hearties. She's got plenty of wind in 'er sails, does this one!"

Definitely "pirate."

He gets to grips with the boat, and soon we are jetting along, bouncing only a little across the relatively calm waters.

I bring up the snap of the photo Dana and I had found back in Jackson's office and study the people in it for a moment—a young Jackson, an indigenous woman named Jeanie, and the dark-haired baby.

Dana has made her way back over to me, and I'm the thorn between two roses again, Mint and Dana squeezed either side of me on the white leather seats to get a look at the photo.

"Where did you get this?" Mint asks.

"At Jackson's office."

Hearing that, Crisp joins us, too, squeezing himself close to Mint—because of course he does—and using his length to peer in at the picture with us.

Scott appears blissfully unaware, standing at the wheel of the boat with his re-secured captain's hat, singing loudly with a miniature bottle—of what appears to be vodka this time—raised in the air.

"I's the b'y that builds the boat," he sings with gusto but woefully out of tune. "I's the b'y that sails her!"

"Who is that? Jackson?" Crisp asks.

"Yeah, it's definitely him," Dana says.

"I's the b'y that catches the fish . . ."

"Who's he with?" Mint asks.

"I dunno," I say, swiping to the snap of the backside of the photo, "but her name seems to be Jeanie." I pinch and expand my fingers to zoom in on the scribbled writing.

"And brings 'em home to Liza!"

"Jacks, Jeanie, and little . . . Laurie?" Crisp says.

"That's not Laurie," Mint says, squinting. "Looks more like . . . Lara?"

"And look at the date," I say.

"June twenty-ninth, nineteen ninety-seven," Crisp reads out loud.

"Same date that was written on the note in the briefcase," Mint says.

"Huh," Dana says.

"What?" I ask.

"Wanna see something even stranger?"

"Stranger than this?" Crisp asks.

Dana pulls out her phone and shows it to us.

"Look at the date," she says.

"Well. Would you look at that," Crisp says as we all stare wide-eyed at the screen. I finish his thought.

"Today is June twenty-ninth."

"It could be a coincidence," Mint says after a beat.

"Land ahoy!" Scott yells from the front of the boat. "Come see, me hearties!"

If he is going through all the stages of grief, this must be the "get piss-loaded and drive a ridiculously overpowered boat" stage.

With a combination of intrigue and concern that we might hit said land, we all make our way to the front of the boat. Crisp and I fall in behind Scott, gripping the boat's own version of "Oh-my-Jesus" handles—a couple of shiny chrome bars adjoining the neat little roof to the sides of the boat—as he steers the boat onward. The two women clamber over to the front of the boat and lie themselves down on two of the three plush leather sunbeds that adorn the bow.

"Alas, these lands are not our final destination, me laddies," Scott says, still keeping up the pirate thing as he guides the boat with surprising skill between two small islands that appear to be little more than rocky bumps in the ocean, covered in hardy little trees. He opens a compartment beside the steering wheel and pulls out a pair of fancy binoculars, having a peep through them and adjusting a dial on the side.

"That be our destination," he says before handing me the binos. I look through them in the direction he'd had them trained and see another island off in the distance. It's larger than the two rocky bumps we've just passed between, but small nonetheless.

"Is that a . . ."

"Swanky billionaire's home on his own private island?" Scott says. "Aye, lad. That it is."

The home is indeed swanky. It appears to be made from shipping containers. One of those fancy architectural jobs you see on Pinterest. It's two storeys of rectangular prisms adjoining at what ought to be impossible angles, one of them overhanging a huge wooden deck, appearing as though on the brink of falling down onto the carefully arranged patio furniture below. Floor-to-ceiling windows abound, and there appear to be lights on, dotted about the place. Of course, the whole thing is a striking combination of red and white. Very "on brand."

"Take a look," I say, handing Crisp the binoculars.

"Hold onto your butts, people!" Scott shouts. "Bear Island, here we come!"

Mint and Dana scream out from the front of the boat as Scott guns 'er and we bounce along the ocean waves, the island growing ever larger in front of us.

As we approach, the sun has completed its rise behind us and bathes Bear Island in golden hues, those floor-to-ceiling windows becoming shimmering mirrors reflecting an oil-painting-worthy scene of ocean, land, and distant mountains. We pull up to a dock, and Crisp jumps out to moor the boat as one by one we clamber out to join him. Scott is the last out of the boat, killing the engine so that the only sounds are the gently lapping waves and the squawks of the ever-present seagulls circling overhead.

We all take a moment to get our bearings. The island is small, the dock reaching out from a white-sand beach dashed with pebbles and lined with kelp. The stunning home is set back about a hundred feet, that grand wooden deck inviting in weary sailors with promises of a comfy evening in front of the great, stone firepit, drinking cocktails and having a laugh with all your rich, rich friends.

But there are no friends here now. No stories by the firepit. No laughter. Instead, there is an ominous stillness about the place, its interior mysterious and impenetrable, its windows reflecting back only you and the paradise left behind. Like it doesn't want to let you in. Like it's warning you to stay away.

"So," I say. "What now?"

It's Scott who steps forward, toward the beach, taking in the billionaire's holiday home and chuckling to himself with a shake of his head. He pauses to finish the miniature he's holding in his hand before tossing it onto the beach and half-turning to look back at us, the sun on his glasses obscuring his eyes, like there is no soul to find in there anymore.

Something broke in Scott, back in Gander. Something in him died. Or something came alive. I don't know which is scarier.

"Well, let's see if there's anyone home," he says flatly before waddling off toward the house.

As we begin to follow him, I feel someone grab a hold of my hand. I look up to see that it's Mint. I squeeze her hand tight as we make our way toward the house.

We step up from the rocky ground onto the smooth wood of the deck and weave our way between patio furniture of a quality far superior to anything I've ever seen inside a home before. We arrive at a large glass door with no discernible handle.

"Is that even a door?" Crisp asks, pushing against the glass and attempting to pull at the narrow metal frame.

A little LED light flashes—seemingly from within the glass itself—as we look at the maybe-door.

"What was that?" Mint asks.

"Huh," Dana says. "Could be some kind of facial-recognition device embedded in the glass."

"Of course it could," I say.

"Gotta be a way to override it," Scott says, cupping his hands to his face and trying to get a look inside the building.

I step forward to carefully examine the frame of the door. It's all so sleek and uninterrupted with anything as ghastly as a keyhole. Then I notice something. Just to the side of the door there's a panel—almost seamless and painted the same red as the rest of the house, but a panel all the same.

"Here's something," I say, instinctively pressing my finger against the panel. With a satisfyingly solid little click, it depresses a few millimetres, then opens up smoothly to reveal a small touch screen. I tap the screen and a full-colour Finatech logo animates before giving way to a keypad.

"We need a code," I say.

"Numeric?" Crisp asks, leaning in to look at the touch screen.

"Well, we do have a six-digit PIN," Dana points out.

"The date from the photo," Mint says.

"Do it in the order in the text message," Crisp suggests.

I pull my phone out of my pocket, bringing up the last text we all received.

97 06 29

I go to input it, then pause.

"What if it isn't the right code?" I ask. "What if it sets off an alarm or something?"

"We should have enough time to get away before the cops get here," Scott says scornfully.

I look around. Trees, ocean, seabirds. He has a point.

"Okay," I say, again raising a finger to the screen. "Here we go."

"Don't frig it up," Scott helpfully suggests as I tap in the six digits.

97 06 29

I type them in like that, in sets of twos. Like a date written backwards. The twenty-ninth of June, nineteen ninety-seven. The date on the photograph. The date in the text message. Today's date.

The thought sends chills down my spine as the whole touch screen turns green and a pleasant chirp accompanies the subtle sound of an electronic lock releasing its grasp on the door.

"Okay, c'mon," Scott says. He's more bullish than usual, his personality skewed someplace where intoxication and grief intersect.

He's on a mission. He could be dangerous.

He reaches out a palm, but before he makes contact with the door, it senses his hand and opens of its own accord, inward, inviting us to enter.

Scott does just that, moving forward with little regard for what might be on the other side. The rest of us cross the threshold more tentatively, the silence of the room feeling ominous and claustrophobic as the automatic door closes behind us, taking with it the gull calls and the waves.

It's quiet in here. Too quiet.

Inside, the colour scheme goes off-brand. Stark white remains the base, but gone is that vivid red, the large, open living room punctuated with tasteful wood tones. The walls are uninterrupted save for a large, colourful piece of indigenous art in the centre of the far wall depicting a bear, its body filled with a woodland scene, its limbs with abstract natural textures—wood grain, waves, and petals. There's a bar area with a sink and cooktop integrated, and the large, flat-panelled storage units keep any clutter hidden from view. A pair of painfully stylish pale-brown leather loungers sit by a bulb-shaped metallic wood stove that hangs impossibly from the ceiling.

"Nice place," Crisp says.

"I mean, it's no Long's Hill, but I could put up with it," I say, aiming for levity but hitting only silence.

We fan out and look around the room. There is little here to betray its owner. The couple of cupboard doors and drawers I try are locked. Decoration is minimal. One of those miniature tree things you are never sure are real or fake. A couple of tasteful bowls with nothing in them. No photos. No books or mugs left lying around.

"It doesn't feel very lived-in," I say, with nothing coming back save for the room's mild echo.

There's a wrought-iron staircase, spiralling to the overhanging shipping container above, demanding exploration. Mint must catch me eyeing it, as she grabs my hand again and pulls me toward it.

"Come on," she says, yanking my arm and leading me over to the staircase, releasing me to charge on up it.

I stop at the bottom for a moment and watch her wind her way up above me before following her, leaving the heavy, foreboding feeling of the living room behind for the childlike fun of the corkscrew ascent.

When I arrive on the second level, Mint is a slow-moving silhouette against an enormous, single-pane window. The room is completely devoid of noise, its smooth floorboards covered in the centre by a large, perfectly circular grey rug. More flat-panelled storage units line one wall, the other left bare. It's as though the owner never got around to decorating in here. Or they wanted nothing to detract from the view.

And what a view.

As I join Mint at the window, I look out past the beach and the bobbing boat that brought us here. Breakers flicker against the two islands we passed, beyond them the horseshoe of Shallow Bay's white-sand beach. Little white houses dot the mainland, beyond them thick, lush forest. In the background, flat-topped mountains appear like a watercolour painting, layered in varying shades of grey. All of this below the biggest, bluest sky.

"Wow," I say.

"Yeah," Mint agrees.

I take her hand in mine as we stand in silence for a moment, breathing in the scene.

I don't even notice Crisp and Dana coming up the stairs until his phone chirps from somewhere behind us—Mint's, too—and my own vibrating in my pocket.

As though pulled out of a dream I don't want to wake up from, I take out my phone and read the message aloud.

Like the view? Take it; it's yours
But first, one more task, below, down two floors
Find him, bind him, bring him up on the hill
When he's gone it's all yours—and a cool twenty mil

"'Him'?" I say as we turn to face our cohorts. "Who's *him*?"

"Twenty mil," Crisp says.

"And what was that part about binding?" Dana asks. "Lemme see that."

"Twenty friggin' mil," Crisp says as Dana strides over toward Mint and me, placing herself between us to get a look at my phone.

"And he's giving us the house?" Crisp says, squinting out at the view beyond the three of us with that ever-present smile.

"That's the part you're focusing on?" Mint asks. Crisp shrugs, for once looking a little perturbed, and turns his attention back to his phone.

We all try to digest what the message might mean. I try to flip it and adjust it in my mind, try to make it not mean what I think it means.

"Jesus," I say. "What exactly is it that they want us to do?"

"Well, there's only one way to find out." Scott's voice gives us all a start. We hadn't heard him climbing the spiral staircase. He isn't all the way up. Just his head peeps up from between the confusion of black wrought iron, the reflected sun obscuring his eyes once more. "I found the basement," he says in monotone before disappearing down below once again.

"He's getting weirder and weirder," Crisp says matter-of-factly before turning to follow. "C'mon, Gulls. Let's check it out," he says as he clanks down the metal staircase.

Mint, Dana, and I exchange glances. Mint takes my hand and begins leading me toward the staircase. But before we reach it, I feel Dana grab me by the arm, pulling me back.

"Gregory," she says. "What if it's Jackson? What if he's . . ."

"It'll be okay," I say, trying to sound as convincing as possible. But I'm starting to think that none of this is what it seemed.

What if this hasn't all been the game of a bored billionaire? What if somebody kidnapped Jackson? What the hell are we going to find down in the basement?

"Come on," I say, taking Dana by the hand.

As the three of us spiral down, those words spin in my mind.

Find him. Bind him. When he's gone . . .

Gone where?

Suddenly I'm warm again. As we step off the staircase, the room whirls around me. I can't breathe.

"Through here," Scott says flatly. He's on the far side of the room, standing in a now-open doorway. He turns from us and heads down a wide hallway.

I focus on my breath, try to stay strong, try to stay conscious.

Crisp shrugs and walks on after Scott. Even his super-cool veneer is wearing thin. There's concern in his eyes, trepidation in his steps.

Dana, Mint, and I follow on, through the doorway, down the hall with its smooth panelled walls and seamless frosted-glass doors. We emerge in a large, modern kitchen with tiled floors to see Scott standing in another doorway, behind him a large, black-tinted glass door with no discernible handle. We pause as Scott slowly removes his glasses. He looks so different without them on. His eyes are narrow and intense with black rings the whole way around. He looks like shit. He looks like he hasn't slept in weeks.

He smirks at us before turning to face the door, two little red LED lights flickering beneath the surface of the glass before turning green. There's a chirp, followed by the subtle sound of an electronic lock releasing its grip. The door sinks back an inch, and then the glass panel slides smoothly into the wall, revealing a staircase leading down to the basement.

"Down here," Scott says without looking back. And he sinks slowly away.

We all stand dead still for a moment. My heart is pounding in my chest, in my head. I make a conscious effort to control my breathing.

"What the frig was that?" Crisp asks, breaking the silence between us.

Dana looks at me with terror in her eyes. Mint seems calmer, wide-eyed and smiling. In shock, maybe?

We all try to piece together what we just saw.

The door recognized Scott's face. How did the door recognize Scott's face?

"Is he . . ." Dana starts to ask. "Is he in on it?"

We all look at the staircase beyond the doorway. A soft light emanates from below, inviting us, beckoning us to see what's down there.

I look to Crisp. For once he's speechless, directionless.

"Well," I say as I peer down the stairwell, trying to make out any details, feeling my heart pounding in my chest. "If he is . . . are we sure we want to go down there?"

"We have to," Dana says, the fear in her eyes suddenly turning to resolve. "We have to know what's really going on here."

She takes a step toward the stairs but stops in her tracks at the sight of two figures emerging from below. We all freeze as two men slowly make their way up the stairs toward us.

"'Scuse us," says the first of the two—a tall, wiry, middle-aged man with greasy, chin-length hair and a cigarette tucked behind one of his ears. We all step back reflexively, and I see Crisp reaching into the back of his belt—for the gun.

"Comin' through," says the second of the men, also tall and lean—younger, with a buzz cut and shifty eyes. He could almost be the other fella's son.

They walk between us and we part like the Red Sea. As they make their way down the hallway toward the living room, the older of the two calls out without looking back.

"Go on down," he says. "He's waitin' for yas."

The younger one stops and turns to face us.

"And don't try to leave," he says, brushing back his unbuttoned plaid shirt to reveal a gun poking out of his belt, its black shape stark against his white wifebeater. "If ya do, he told us to go ahead and kill ya." He smirks, and the two head through to the living room, the door closing behind them.

We're all frozen to the spot. I count my breaths and try to stay calm. In for four, out for four. In for four, out for four. I look out of the kitchen window, hoping to see ocean, searching for the reassurance that home is still there—somewhere across the waves, no matter the miles. But I can only see trees. And then the shape of the tall, wiry man, who takes the cigarette from behind his ear, lights it, and stares in at us for a moment as he takes a long drag.

There's nowhere to run, I think to myself as he disappears momentarily behind a cloud of smoke, only to reappear, even more sinister than before.

"Jackson could be down there," Dana says flatly.

"Yeah," I say. "But who's in charge? Jackson or Scott?"

"There's only one way to find out," Mint says, striding toward the stairwell and sinking down a couple of steps before half-turning back to face us. "You coming?" she asks, before trotting casually down the rest of the steps. We watch as she is illuminated momentarily in the soft light at the bottom. Then she disappears into a room off to the left.

My heart hammers in my chest as my brain tries to reconcile everything that just happened.

"Come on," Dana says, grabbing my hand and yanking me toward the stairwell. I don't resist. I follow her down, down, into the darkness, toward the light. As we reach the bottom, I look back up to see Crisp's lanky frame, still standing motionless at the top of the stairs.

Isn't he going to come down? He has the gun. He friggin' took it from me!

Dana pulls me into the light of the basement, down a short hallway and into a large, open room. It's an artist's studio, full of colourful paintings, mainly indigenous, but some still-lifes, realistic animal paintings, and the scattered portrait. There are so many paintings. Piles of them, on shelves, on easels, even laid about on the floor at the perimeter of the room.

There are more paintings here than at the Rooms, I think to myself.

In the centre of the space there's a large island with shelves and cupboards filled with painting supplies, its surface dotted with papers, brushes, and pots.

Mint is standing near the island and looks back at Dana and me as we enter the room. Beyond the island, at the far end of the room stands Scott, hands in pockets, staring at us from the shadows.

Next to Scott is a man sitting in a chair, a large light trained directly on him. His legs are bound with zip-ties, his hands seemingly bound behind him. He's been gagged with a paint-speckled rag, and a little bit of dry blood is visible around his nose and on his lip. There are a few drops on his sweat-stained white dress shirt, too, the collar of which is unbuttoned a couple of buttons down. His long hair hangs messily around his bearded face as he tries to make us out beyond the glare of the light.

"Jackson!" Dana shouts.

The man mumbles something in reply. He looks gaunt and tired, a pale shade of the beaming billionaire we'd all seen on TV. But it's him nonetheless. Jackson Lorde. Finatech CEO and the richest man in Newfoundland.

"Come on in," Scott says. Dana and I stay frozen near the doorway, her hand tight in mine.

"What have you done to him?" Dana asks.

Scott looks at Jackson, seeming almost confused by the question.

"What have I done to him? That's a bit rich, eh, Jackson? Not as rich as you, of course," he says, giving the bound billionaire a playful punch to the shoulder that actually seems to hurt him a little. Probably because he's already bruised underneath his shirt.

"It's you," I say out loud, as though hearing the words will cause them to make any sort of sense. "You've been behind this the whole time?"

Scott's face breaks into a smile for a moment. He's proud of his work. But then something occurs to him.

"Where's Crisp?" he asks.

I half-turn to see if he's emerged in the doorway behind me. He has not.

"Where is Crisp?" Scott repeats, louder this time, as he pulls a gun from one of the shelves and points it casually in our direction. I grip Dana's hand tighter as the colours of the paintings begin to blur into one another, the room turning on its axis. I count my breaths. Four in, four out. Four in, four out.

"He's still upstairs," Dana replies meekly before I can find the words.

"You," Scott hisses, pointing the gun at Dana. "Get over here. Stand by the island."

She pauses for a moment, then starts to make her way forward, taking me with her.

"Not you," Scott barks, training the gun on me. "You go shout up to Crisp and tell him to get down here."

I give Dana's hand a squeeze, then let it go, instinctively raising my hands in front of me as I back toward the entrance.

"Stay where I can see you," Scott says.

I back into the little hallway and crane to see up the stairs. I can just make out Crisp's long legs at the top of the stairwell.

"Hey, Crisp," I say. "Scott wants you to come down here."

Crisp lowers himself to his haunches and talks quietly.

"Is Jackson Lorde down there?"

"Yeah."

He reaches for the gun in the back of his belt. I shake my head.

"Just, maybe . . . just come down and join us, okay?" I say.

"What's taking so long?" Scott shouts. "Tell him to get the frig down here."

"Scott has a gun," I say as quietly as I can. Crisp seems to get the message. He takes a look around, most likely to see where the two skinny heavies have gone, then he rises up before slowly making his way down the stairs.

"Just keep calm, okay?" I whisper. "He's not right in the head. Don't do anything . . . heroic."

Crisp nods.

"What are you whispering about?" Scott yells. "Get the frig in here right now!"

We enter the room together, Crisp's expression giving nothing away as he casually scans the room and takes in the sight of the bound and beaten Jackson Lorde.

"Oh, look," Crisp says. "It's the fella off da television."

"Over here by the island," Scott demands.

"Looking a little rougher than in his profile pics, though," Crisp mutters as we do as we're told, making our way to join the others by the island, the sight of Jackson becoming all the more vivid in the dazzling light. He's a strikingly handsome man with piercing blue eyes, and even in this sorry state he gives off an aura of calm and intelligence. Super-rich. Super-handsome. Composed in a jam. I can see what Dana sees in him.

"So," Crisp says. "What are we doing here, Scotty boy? Got yourself a situation going, eh?"

"Shut up, Crisp," Scott says, waving the gun in his general direction. "This isn't your time to talk anymore. This is your time to listen."

"We're all ears," Crisp says with a shrug, the unflappable cool returning.

"Well, you've probably all figured it out by now," Scott says. "I am the puppet master. I'm the one who's been pulling all your strings."

"Puppet master." Crisp sneers.

"Yeah, what of it?" Scott snaps.

"No, I mean, it makes sense. I just thought you would have gone with something a little . . . more original."

"Like, the Ventriloquist?" I suggest, hardly believing the words are leaving my mouth.

"Yeah, but then he'd have to shove his hand up all our arses," Crisp says.

"Fair point. Wouldn't want that."

"Oh, what about the Riddler?" I say.

"Oh, yeah, 'cause of all the little rhymes he's been writing this whole time," Crisp says. "He's good at it, too. The Poet, even . . ."

"Wouldn't be a stretch," I say, noticing a little smile in Jackson's eyes.

"Shut up!" Scott yells, waving the gun and taking a couple of steps toward us. "You shut your smart mouths up! I'm in control here. I'm the one holding the friggin' gun. One more word and I will end you!"

"Like ya did Shelly," Crisp says without skipping a beat.

Scott lets out an anguished cry, cocking the gun and pointing it across the island, right between Crisp's eyes. He stands there for a few seconds, teeth gritted, gun hand shaking, before pulling away and swiping painting supplies off the island, jars of muddy water smashing to the floor. "Shelly wasn't meant to die. She was never supposed to be in the back of that goddamn car," Scott screams, his voice beginning to crack.

"In control, huh?" Crisp mumbles. Mercifully, Scott doesn't hear.

I know what he's trying to do. He's trying to get Scott emotional, off-guard. But he's playing with fire.

I shoot Crisp a glance to cool it. *Wait for the right time. Don't do anything heroic.*

He seems to get the message.

"Why have you brought us here, Scott?" Dana asks. "Why are you doing all this?"

Scott's chest heaves, and a grin returns to his face. He likes this. He likes that we're getting back to his narrative. He likes the limelight, feeling like he's the one in control.

"Why?" Scott says. "Why am I doing all of this?"

This is what he's been waiting for. This is how he rehearsed it, so many times in his twisted mind.

He strides over to Jackson and yanks the gag loose. Jackson takes a deep breath and spits threads from between his lips.

"Tell 'em," Scott says. "Tell 'em who y'are."

"I'm Jackson Lorde," he says.

"No, no, no!" Scott yells, clipping the man around the head with the handle of the gun as Dana's hand grips mine once again and she gasps at the violence. "They know who you are. Tell them who you are in relation to me."

Jackson closes his eyes and takes a moment to steady himself—from the question or from the pain, I'm not quite sure. He opens his eyes again, staring right at us.

"I'm his father," he says.

And it occurs to me.

"You're the baby in the picture."

The others look at me, piecing it together.

"Nineteen ninety-seven," Dana says. "The dates work out."

"A year before he walked out on us to go study in London," Scott says. "Did you know that he didn't have two nickels to rub together back then? My mother had to raise money selling her art so that he could go."

"Your mother?" Crisp asks.

"The woman in the picture," Dana says, tugging on my hand, prompting me to reach for my pocket. As I make the move, Scott trains the gun on me again. I quickly raise my hands in the air.

"I'm just grabbing my phone. To look at the picture."

Scott nods for me to continue.

I reach my hand into my inside jacket pocket, but instead of the phone, I feel the smooth, hard surface of the glass orb with the mosquito inside.

I'm pulled back to the Rooms, to when the orb rolled across the floor. To when Ray Junior lay in a widening pool of blood. I shake away the thought.

"Wrong pocket," I say. Scott nods again for me to check the other one.

I pull out the phone and call up the picture. Jackson, baby Scott, and an indigenous woman named Jeanie. Scott's mother.

"She was an artist," I say out loud, and I look about the room at all the magnificent, colourful paintings.

"Yeah. This is her work," Scott says with pride in his voice. "A portion of it, anyway. The stuff this piece of shit didn't give away to the Rooms or all his rich friends." Scott points the gun at Jackson's face, causing him to recoil.

"That's why you took the painting from the Rooms," I say. "It was one of hers."

"Just taking back what's rightfully mine," Scott says.

"But your mother lives up on Lemarchant," Crisp says.

"And what about your brother?" I ask. "The guy at the fish plant."

"Stepmother," Scott says. "Stepbrother. Y'see, Jackson here never came back to us after he left for London. He came back to Newfoundland but not to us. Too caught up in his new life, with his new friends. Too obsessed with starting his tech company and building his empire. Then my mom, Jeanie, she got sick. He made her sick."

"She had a rare heart condition," Jackson protests.

"Died of a broken heart, more like," Scott snarls before moving over to some of the covered paintings.

"Look at this," he says, pulling the dust covers off the canvases to reveal several paintings featuring Jackson. A portrait looking right into his piercing blue eyes. Him walking on a trail, her hand reaching out in the foreground as she is left behind. Jackson naked, in an embrace with a female figure formed of wispy shadows, blowing away from him in the wind.

"He was the love of her life, but to him she was nothing. We were nothing!" he screams, striding back over to Jackson and delivering another punishing blow to his chin.

This time Jackson yelps in pain, fresh blood dribbling from his lip.

"Stop it!" Dana pleads, making to go toward them. I grab her arm and pull her back.

"I was just a kid myself," Jackson says, his eyes tearing up.

"Goddammit, we were so young when you came along. I never planned to leave her, to leave you. But life, it just happened."

"It just happened," Scott growls, teeth clenched, spittle shooting out as he gets close to Jackson's face. "It happened, all right. It happened for you. It happened without us!"

"Jeanie, your mother, she wouldn't talk to me after I left. I wanted to see you. I tried, but she wouldn't let me. I wanted to be part of your life, but she got cold, callous."

"Don't you talk about her like that!"

"She wanted to create a rift between us. She wanted to hurt me."

"She wanted to protect us from you and all your filthy lies!" Scott screams before delivering a hard front kick to Jackson's chest, sending him, chair and all, toppling over backwards onto the hard floor.

"No!" Dana screams, this time shaking loose from my grasp and running over to where the fallen Jackson lies groaning on the floor.

"A million bucks," Scott murmurs as he shrinks back into the shadows, his big, jam jar–bottom glasses like two great white eyes staring out from the dark. "That's the price he landed on. That's how much he figured it would cost to buy me out of his life. To buy my silence. One million dollars, deposited to me, taxes paid, on my twenty-first birthday."

"We have to get him up," Dana says, holding Jackson's head in her hands. He seems to be semi-conscious and struggling to breathe. "Scott, we get that you're hurting, but this has gone too far. We have to cut him loose."

"And then just bury the past. But this time the graves were just a little too shallow, Daddy dear."

"Scott!" Dana yells as Jackson lets out a disturbingly guttural gurgle.

Scott glares over at Dana and his choking father.

"Yeah, right," he says, emerging back into the light, almost in a daze. He opens a drawer in the island and takes out a pair of child's safety scissors, tossing them on the floor next to Dana.

"Cut him loose. Just the legs. Hands stay bound or I'll shoot you."

Dana retrieves the scissors and gets to work cutting the zip ties around Jackson's ankles, the child's scissors struggling to chew through the hard plastic.

"Time to go, anyway," Scott mumbles. "Time to go for a nice, long walk. I'm sure we could all use a little air."

Dana has Jackson's bonds free and helps him to a sitting position. He spits blood onto the floor, gradually getting control of his breathing again.

"Get him up," Scott commands, pointing the gun at Dana.

"Jesus, can you give him a moment to—"

"Up!" Scott yells at full volume, the gun shaking in his hand.

"Okay, okay," Dana says, helping Jackson to his feet.

"Gotta get out of this basement," Scott says, now back to mumbling again. "Too stuffy. Too dark. There's a whole National Park out there, for God's sake."

He waves Dana and Jackson on with a flick of his gun.

"Go on, go on. Up to the kitchen."

The two move past him and beyond the rest of us by the island, Dana helping the still-dazed Jackson to walk on wobbly feet.

As they make their way toward the doorway, Scott begins to follow them, and I feel Crisp come and stand beside me.

I look up at him, and he gives me a wink.

Oh, shit. He's going to do it. He's going to do something "heroic."

Before I can protest, he pulls the gun from his belt, using all his length to reach over and pistol-whip Scott on the back of the head, sending him tumbling face-first to the floor. He hits with a sickening crunch, and his own gun is sent flying among the stacked canvases at the side of the room.

I watch, frozen to the spot, as Crisp stands over the prone Scott with his gun pointed right at him.

"Game's over, buddy," Crisp says.

Before I can inquire as to whether he rehearsed that line in his head, my legs are suddenly swept out from under me. I hit the floor hard, the impact sending shock waves through my entire body.

As I struggle to catch my breath, I watch through bleary eyes as Mint appears, holding a gun, and raises it to Crisp's shaven head.

"Drop it right now," she says, "or I swear to God I'll paint your brains all over that canvas."

The last thing I see before the darkness consumes me is Crisp letting his gun fall to the floor and the little shadow of the tiny dimple on Mint's cheek.

She's smiling, I think to myself.

And then all is black.

18

The Finest View of Western Brook

I come around to the sound of a boat's engine and muffled voices. I can feel the wind on my cheek and taste salt in the air. Then comes the sense of motion—a gentle bobbing and swaying that my half-conscious brain can't reconcile. Then comes the unstoppable wave of nausea, bubbling in my stomach, forcing me up off my back. My brain computes that I'm on a boat and guides me to the side just in time for me to vomit into the churning water below. I cling to the cold metal railing, trying to gather my senses, trying to stop the world from spinning. Then I hear laughter.

I wipe my chin and turn to see the two skinny heavies. I'm at the bow of the boat and they are both reclined on the loungers, each clutching a Blue Star beer in their hands. The older one is still smoking a cigarette.

"What's the matter, b'y? Didn't bring yer sea legs?"

He flicks his butt over the side and places his thumb and forefinger between his lips, letting out a piercing whistle loud enough to carry over the engine noise.

"Sleepin' Beauty's awake out here," the man yells. "And he's lookin' a little pasty."

"Like a little English pastie!" adds the younger one.

The two of them have a grand laugh at that one, Blue Star spilling liberally onto the deck.

The nausea wells up in me again, and I'm forced to drape myself over the railings once more, despite the protestations of what remains of my pride. I retch a few times, until my stomach aches and my throat burns, but little more comes out. The two hyenas continue to laugh it up behind me.

I wipe my eyes, the fresh ocean air blowing in my face, and I try to get my bearings. There's no sign of the two little islands we'd passed just off Shallow Bay, nor of the horseshoe-shaped white-sand beach itself. To my right is endless ocean. To my left is rugged land.

We're heading along the coast. But to where?

Then I see it, in the distance, looming in a thin cloak of mist, huge and ancient. The great, flat-topped mountains of Western Brook, overlapping in varying shades of grey like a muted watercolour painting, dark and ominous. The boat arcs inland, the change in movement making my head spin again, but I'm getting accustomed to the motion now and am able to keep control of my senses.

"Where are we going?" I ask, turning to direct the question at the two skinny heavies. But it is intercepted by Mint, who has climbed up to the bow in response to the greasy one's whistle.

"We're going for a hike," she says with that smile, with that dimple.

I lean back against the railing and try to piece together what happened back in the basement. Crisp's heroics. Me, falling. Mint with the gun.

"You swept my legs," is what comes out of my mouth.

"Technically, it was a throw, not a sweep. Judo lessons since I was eight. Thanks, Mom and Dad."

"She kicked your arse," says greasy, the two of them laughing away as they each crack open another beer.

"You hit pretty hard," Mint says. "Is your head okay?"

It's only with the mention of it that I become aware of the pain in the back of my head. I reach my hand back and feel dried blood in my hair, a couple of rubs locating the cut underneath and cranking the pain up from dull to searing.

"Ow," I say, pulling my hand away and examining the streak of fresh blood on my fingers.

"It's just a nick," Mint says. "You'll live."

"Maybe we should call his mummy to come kiss it better," comes the chatter from the peanut gallery, in a terrible faux-English accent this time.

"Shut the fuck up or I'll shoot you," Mint says cheerily to the men, who immediately quieten down.

As the boat turns, the glare on the windshield clears and I can see Scott at the wheel, one of the lenses of his jam jar–bottom glasses now a shattered spiderweb.

"So, you and Scott . . . ?"

"Me and Larus," Mint corrects me.

"Larus?"

"Larus Lorde," she says. "Son of Jackson Lorde and Jeanie Cope—the famous Mik'maq artist." She pauses. "God rest her soul."

I shake my head and try to come to terms with what's happening.

"So, Larus Can . . ."

"Was Scott's idea. Crisp's whole seagull obsession came from Scott. He planted it. Crisp is so easy to manipulate. The man hasn't had an original idea in his life."

"This whole time, you and Scott have been playing us. And you . . ." The thought occurs to me. ". . . you've been stringing me along, stringing Crisp along, playing us off against one another."

"Yeah. Sorry about that," she says, biting her lip.

I watch as the boat nears the shore, the rocky beach getting closer and closer, the layered, flat-topped mountains looming in the background.

"Was any of it real?" I ask. "I mean, did you feel anything for me?"

She pretends to think about it for a moment, but I already know the answer before she gives it to me.

"Sorry, honey. I don't think it's going to work out between us." She leans in close so I can feel her dreadlocks on my shoulder, her breath on my cheek. "Besides," she says. "I don't think you're really over your ex."

She kisses me on the cheek before turning back toward Scott—toward Larus. I swear I can see a smirk on his face through the glass as she gracefully lowers herself back beside him at the boat's wheel.

"Drink up, boys," she shouts at the skinny heavies. "Time to go for a little walk."

"Yes, ma'am," the older one mutters, giving a salute with his beer bottle before chugging back the remaining beer and tossing it into the ocean with a loud belch.

“She’s hot,” the younger one mutters to himself as he clinks his empty back into the box.

Suddenly my thoughts turn to Dana, and I leave the b’ys behind and clamber into the main body of the boat myself, albeit far less gracefully than Mint had. She’s now draped around Scott, who looks to have grown a couple of inches from just having her there as he skilfully steers the boat toward a small make-shift dock jutting out from the rocks.

I make my way to the stern of the boat, where Crisp and Dana both sit looking pale and forlorn, with a now slightly more lucid Jackson Lorde, who appears to be fastened somehow to the seat. I cling to the railing as the boat slows and bounces on the waves below, trying my best to stop the nausea from returning.

Get me off this bloody boat.

Crisp, Dana, and I exchange no words, only nervous glances, as the older skinny heavy jumps onto the dock and the younger one tosses him the rope to moor the boat.

Scott kills the engine and makes his way toward us with Mint by his side, now holding a gun that looks very much like the one I’d given to Crisp.

“We’re all going for a walk now,” Scott says. He seems more subdued now, like the alcohol has moved past the fun stage and hangs heavy on his eyelids. “Everyone’s going to behave themselves. If you do, you’ll find it a pleasant hike, though it will be challenging in places.”

As though on cue, Mint pulls a duffle bag from under one of the seats, unzips it, and takes out several small bottles of water, tossing a couple to each one of us.

“You all have two bottles of water. Stay hydrated. It’s going to be a warm day, and I want everyone to make it to the top.”

“The top of what?” Crisp asks.

Scott squints into the distance through the one good jam jar–bottom he has left and raises his hand to point.

"The top of that," he says, and we all follow his gaze to the looming mountains of Western Brook Pond.

* * *

The hike is long and punishing, crossing a couple of rivers where the water is as high as our hips, making the rest of the travail a squidgy, uncomfortable experience. In places the trail is barely a trail at all, reduced to a two-foot-wide mud pit with untrimmed trees clawing at our faces as we plow our way through. The two heavies lead the way like a couple of gangly Sherpas, utterly unfazed and seemingly unimpeded as they push relentlessly on.

At one point we have to traverse a near-sheer incline of fine shale that trickles and bounces off protruding rocks that we have to cling to, in order to prevent a snakes-and-ladders-style fall to right back where we started. Few words are spoken, and when they are, they are met with short shrift from our short-tempered host.

They have the guns. We don't. They have the power. We don't.

Beyond the shale hill we emerge at a clearing with nothing to separate us from a long fall and a sudden death. Were the situation different—were we not prisoners held at gunpoint, were my head not throbbing, were my socks not soaked and my sneakers not slashed by the unforgiving terrain—the view would be stunning. Below us, the world falls away. The long, deep-blue pond snakes between interlocking flat-topped mountains, recalling the meandering path of the age-old glaciers that carved their memory indelibly into the landscape. Trees uncountable reach up the sides of the great, rugged rock giants, while narrow waterfalls cascade in narrow streams in the seeming slow motion that such scale creates.

"Pissing Mare Falls," says the older skinny heavy, dumping his backpack down on the ground and taking out a beer. "What?" he asks, aware that everyone is glaring in his direction. "That's the name of it." He twists off the bottle top and takes a swig of beer. "Don't shoot the messenger, sexy," he says, playfully raising his hands in the air and ogling Mint.

Mint smiles at him. He shoots her a wink. Then she pulls out the gun and shoots in him the face, shattering the beer bottle in an explosion of suds and brain matter.

Dana lets out a scream, and my guts finally give in on me again as I heave up a sad little splatter of water and bile.

"Shut up," Scott says, quietly at first. But then Dana screams again, and he yells at Mint to "friggin' do something about her."

Mint strides over to Dana and grabs her by the hair, pointing the still-smoking gun directly in her face.

"Shut your screeching mouth or I swear to God you're next," she says. Dana nods, tears streaming down her face.

Mint shoves her over toward Crisp and me.

"Now, take a seat. That was just the warm-up," she says, nodding at the murdered man. "Time for the real show to begin."

Crisp, Dana, and I look to one another, trying to process what the hell is happening.

"Sit down on the goddamn rocks," Mint yells, pointing with her gun at a collection of large rocks jutting up along the side of the clifftop. We make our way over and try to find the flattest ones to sit on.

"You," she barks at the remaining skinny heavy, who appears to be in a state of shock, staring wide-eyed at his fallen comrade. (His fallen father?) "Hey, you redneck little shit, wake up," she yells, getting his attention. "Bring Mr. Moneybags over to the cliff's edge." The man just stares. "Do it now!" she screams, pointing the gun in his direction.

After another glance at the faceless remains of his buddy, the man leads the still-bound Jackson Lorde over to the edge of the cliff, just a few feet from where we are sitting.

"She's friggin' crazy," Crisp whispers to me.

"Totally insane," I agree.

"Complete murdering psychopath," Dana growls.

"Did you . . . did you . . ." Crisp gives me a suggestive look. "With her?"

"No. You?"

"Nah. I mean, not for want of trying."

"Bullet dodged," I say, drawing a look of ire from Dana. "Poor choice of words," I concede.

"That's right," Mint shouts at the skinny heavy as he and Jackson reach the cliffside. "Just a little closer. Right to the edge." The two men shuffle toward the cliff's edge, hoping she'll tell them to stop.

"That's our gun, isn't it?" I whisper to Crisp.

"I'm afraid so," he says.

"They took our phones, too," Dana says.

It hadn't dawned on me to check, but now I do, feeling at my pockets, careful to not be seen.

She's right. No phone.

"They took them when you were unconscious," she says.

I finish checking my pockets, just to be sure, when I feel something deep down inside the lining of my denim jacket. I can't help but let out a little chuckle.

"What?" Dana asks.

I half-turn to make sure Scott and the newly minted devil woman don't see me as I reach down into my inside pocket and locate the little tear in the stitching. I delve down deeper until my fingers come in contact with a hard, smooth object—a cool glass sphere that I retrieve and clutch in my hand.

When I'm sure Scott and Mint aren't looking, I peel back my fingers to give Crisp and Dana a little peek at the glass orb, the little mosquito suspended inside.

"Well, it's not a gun or a phone, but it could give someone a nasty headache," Crisp murmurs.

"Stop!" Mint yells, causing us all to jump in unison.

Shit. Has she seen us looking at the orb?

"Right there," she says.

Nope. She's too consumed with positioning two men at the edge of a giant cliff.

"That's perfect," she says, her hands raised in front of her like a movie director framing a scene, the gun still clutched in one of them. "Now," she says to the remaining skinny heavy. "You, move away from Scrooge McDuck."

The man starts to move away from the edge of the cliff.

"No!" Mint yells. "Not this way. Stay at the edge. Just move to the side."

The man follows her hand signal and shuffles carefully along the edge of the cliff, being careful not to trip on the uneven surface.

"A little farther," Mint instructs.

The man shuffles a few feet more.

"There!" Mint shouts. "Hold it right there," she says. The man does as he's told. "That's perfect," she purrs, her free hand held palm-out toward him as though she were a superhero with this man under her sway.

She enjoys this. She enjoys the power.

"That is perfect," she repeats, before pointing the gun at the man and taking careful aim.

He just about has time to glance over at his dead friend one more time, a look of resignation etched on his face. Then the gunshot echoes off the mountains, the man's head snaps backwards, and he tumbles over the edge of the cliff.

Dana squeals again, burrowing her head into my shoulder.

"Warm-up complete," Mint says, puckering her lips and blowing on the tip of the gun.

Jackson stands with his back to the cliff, his hands tied behind his back, his head hung low. He looks tired, like his legs might give out at any moment, like a strong gust of wind could take him over the cliff's edge to join the skinny heavy—body dashed on the ragged rocks below.

Scott now makes his way over, positioning himself in front of us and just a few feet from Jackson. He glances over at the dead man and then at us.

"They couldn't be trusted to keep their mouths shut," he says.

It's a warning.

He clears his throat and looks thoughtful for a moment.

"I've rehearsed this in my mind so many times," he finally says. "Thought about the words I would say. But it's all gone blank now.

"This," he says, pointing at Jackson. "This is my father, Jackson Lorde. I'm Larus. Larus Lorde. I know—surprise, right? You thought the whole Larus Can thing was Bird Boy's idea over here." He nods at Crisp. "But no. It was my little message to the world. A message to say that the little boy who wasn't good enough to be the son of the great Jackson Lorde, well . . . he's the one in control now."

"Larus, please." Jackson finally speaks.

"Ah, he speaks. Already pleading." Scott removes a gun of his own from his belt and gestures for Jackson to shush. "You'll get your chance.

"Do you remember this spot, Dad?" He spreads his arms wide and spins slowly around, a full 360 degrees, breathing in the majesty of the scene. "Do you recognize this place, Jackson Lorde?"

Jackson lifts his head and looks around.

"We came here with your mother," he mumbles.

"Louder so the group can hear," Scott insists.

"We came here with your mother, Jeanie."

"Ah, yes, that's right," Scott says. "This is the place from the photo." He looks over at us for the first time since we arrived on the mountaintop. "You got that picture there, Mint, my darlin'?"

Mint swaggers over and pulls my phone out of her pocket, bringing up the picture before handing it to Scott.

"There we are. A young Jackson Lorde and Jeanie Cope—a couple of years your senior, all the same—and little baby Larus."

"Larus Can," Dana says aloud.

"Yeah. That was his idea," Crisp concedes.

"See, now, dearest Dad here thought that Larus could not. Once he flew the nest, so to speak, and made new friends, and met new women, and made more and more cash, Mom and I were no longer worthy of his time, of his love, isn't that right, Dad?"

Jackson shakes his head.

"It wasn't like that," he says, prompting Scott to stride over and slap him hard across the face, causing the man to sink to his knees. We all hold our breath as he threatens to lose consciousness, swaying precariously on the cliff's edge in the stiffening breeze.

"That's exactly what it was like," Scott yells, accentuating every word before composing himself to continue.

"Three of us in the picture," he says. "So, what, was the camera on a timer, or . . ."

Jackson grimaces and mumbles something.

"For the group to hear!" Scott yells.

"Charlie took it," he says, glancing over at the dead skinny heavy lying prone on the ground, his greasy hair matted with blood.

Scott looks theatrically over to the body and back to Jackson.

"Oh, the two of you knew each other?"

Jackson says nothing, his chin dropping to his chest.

Scott again strides over, grabbing Jackson's long hair this time and yanking his head back violently.

"Tell them who he was!" he demands.

"He was my childhood friend," Jackson shouts before breaking down. "He was my friend . . ."

"Right," Scott says, releasing Jackson's head. "He was your friend when you were growing up around the bay, but then you got all rich and famous, and you didn't bother to stay in touch with him anymore. Are we beginning to see a theme here?" Scott looks over at us, his one visible eye wide and manic, the other clouded behind fractured glass.

"It didn't take much to convince him and his nephew to keep you prisoner in your own basement. It's amazing what a bit of money can buy. Though he resented you so much, he probably would have done it for free."

Jackson appears to be sobbing now, head down, chest jerking spasmodically.

"You couldn't buy me, though," he says. "He tried, you know," he continues, addressing us now—his witnesses, his audience. "One million dollars, plus interest, of course, put aside for me in a trust fund paid out on my twenty-first birthday. Pretty generous, you might think, right? Except Jackie Boy here is worth billions and, y'know, a billion is, like, a thousand million, so, relatively speaking, I'm just the shit on the bottom of his expensive shoe, the unfortunate mishap he made as a young man, something to be bought out and forgotten about."

Jackson shakes his head and Scott paces in circles for a few moments, rubbing his head with his hand.

"He let my mother die," he says eventually.

"No," Jackson protests, throwing gasoline on Scott's fire once again.

"You let my mother die," he screams at the top of his lungs, shaping to kick Jackson over the edge but stopping just short, leaning down to shout in his face. "You let her die, you son of a bitch!"

"I paid for her treatment."

"It wasn't enough! Money wasn't enough!"

"She was sick, Larus. She had a congenital heart defect. It wasn't curable."

"She died of a broken heart! She said it. She told me that. You broke her heart and no doctor would be able to fix it. She told me that on her deathbed!"

Jackson kneels, sobbing at the cliff's edge.

Scott cocks the gun and points it at Jackson's head.

"No!" Dana shouts.

He likes that, taking it as encouragement, looking over with a menacing smile, trigger finger twitching.

Then he lowers the gun.

"No, no. You are correct. We have to do this right." He's manic now, excitable. "Why don't y'all come over here and join us?"

We look at each other, hesitant.

"Come on, don't be shy, get over here," he says. "Now." He points the gun in our direction.

Dana, Crisp, and I get to our feet and make our way over to the edge.

"Line up right there," Scott says. "That's right. Good."

The wind is really picking up, and while I try to fight the urge, I can't help but take a peek over my shoulder. Big mistake. The drop is mind-boggling, the ground opening up into a great, glacier-carved abyss below, nothing but jagged rocks giving way to deep waters. The world begins to spin, and I feel Crisp's arm on my shoulder.

"Careful," he says, and I face inland again. Not that the news here is any better. We are lined up alongside the beaten-down Jackson Lorde, our backs to the abyss, facing a madman and his psychotic girlfriend—both armed—on the edge of a cliff.

"I shoulda stayed in England," I mutter.

"Too late for that now," Crisp whispers. "But we gotta do something if ya ever wanna see England again."

I squeeze my arm against my denim jacket and feel the hard glass orb against my ribs.

"Yeah," I say.

"What the frig are you two whispering about?" Scott growls, sauntering over to me and pointing the gun in my face.

"I was just saying," I reply, "I shoulda stayed in England."

Scott chuckles, lowering the gun for a moment.

"You know what," he says. "You really should have."

He taps me on the head a couple of times with the butt of his gun.

"Gregory Masters. Washed ashore from the motherland. The land of our colonial masters. Helped us cut off old Churchill's nose to spite his face. Do you ever wonder, Gregory, what Newfoundland would have been like if your lot had never set foot on these shores? I know I do."

He moves along the line to Crispin.

"And Mr. Crisp. Our fearless leader. Always cool, always in control, always gets the girl. Well, not this time. You did your bit, though. With your little speeches and your big charisma. We couldn't have done it without you."

Crisp doesn't speak. He just maintains that trademark Crisp-thin smile until Scott moves along the line.

"And Miss Dana," Scott says. "Know how I knew you'd help old Greggy boy here connect the dots?" Dana scowls as Scott gestures to Mint. She walks over to join him and takes Dana's chin in her hand.

"Because our Englishman is still in love with you," Mint says as she squeezes Dana's cheeks hard until her lips pucker. "Can't really see why, though. You're a bit of an anal-retentive plain Jane, if you ask me."

Dana swipes Mint's hand away.

"Who asked you?" she hisses.

Mint chuckles.

"Feisty, though."

"Last and most certainly least, Jackson Lorde. *Dad*," Scott says as he makes his way over to the still-kneeling Jackson.

"You shot for the stars, I'll give you that," he says. "But like Icarus, you flew too close to the sun." He pushes Jackson's head back with the muzzle of the gun. "And like Icarus, you will fall, fall, fall. Down to the earth."

Then, there's a loud sound. Not the gunshot we are all bracing for, but a loud, piercing squawk as, from nowhere, a huge seagull emerges from over the cliff's edge, almost striking Jackson's head with a great wing.

Scott jumps back.

Jackson slumps forward.

We all just about have a collective heart attack as the flapping bird circles around us, close to us, screeching and squawking like it's possessed.

When the initial shock passes, Scott begins to laugh, just a little at first, then breaking into a full belly laugh.

Mint starts laughing, too, bent double like the last loose screw in her twisted mind has finally popped its threads.

Then Crisp starts laughing right along with them.

Dana looks at me, unable to grasp what's going on, but instinctively I start laughing, too, forcing myself at first, but then taken over by some complete system failure of emotion. I laugh, for real, uncontrollably. Crisp laughs. Mint laughs. Scott laughs, stumbling about the cliff's edge, gun in hand, stumbling over to me, his head mere inches from my chest as the seagull circles and squawks above.

"A gull!" Scott exclaims between guffaws. "The Gulls!" he yells, spreading his arms wide before buckling over again in rapture.

We laugh.

And the gull circles.

We laugh.

And the gull squawks.

Then Crisp yells out.

"Smash it! Crack it!"

And I dip my hand into my jacket pocket, feeling the smooth, hard surface of the glass orb with the little mosquito inside. I take it in my hand, pull it out.

And with all the might I can muster, I swing hard, smashing the orb into the side of Scott's head with a sickening crunch that seems to echo off the mountains.

And the laughing stops.

Scott's twisted, shattered glasses fall to the ground as he twitches and lurches toward me.

I jump aside.

And he falls, face-first, off the cliff.

"No!" I hear Mint scream, but before I can turn to face her, I'm being rugby-tackled to the ground. A gunshot rings out and I hit the ground hard, all of Crisp's weight landing on top of me.

Things go blurry for a moment, and when they come back into focus, I wish they hadn't.

I see Mint's form reshaping itself from smudges of colour.

She's pointing the gun right at me, and I'm pinned. I can't move.

I'm done for.

As she squints one eye and takes aim, I see the telltale little dimple appear on her cheek as her dreadlocks dance in the wind.

She's smiling.

And then . . .

From nowhere, Dana appears in view, holding a large rock in the air, bringing it crashing down with both hands onto Mint's head, sending her falling to the ground.

"Take that, you crazy bitch!" Dana yells.

I see Mint's gun hand twitch.

Then all is still.

Dana helps wrestle Crisp off me, and I manage to hoist myself to my knees.

Then I see the blood trickling from Crisp's mouth.

"Jesus, Crisp . . ."

He lies on his side, smiling that same thin smile.

"Remind me never to call you a plain Jane," he says to Dana.

"It was the 'anal-retentive' part that really got to me," Dana replies.

We can't help but chuckle momentarily, but then Crisp coughs and more blood spills down his chin. Still more blood is gushing between his fingers, from the gunshot wound in his abdomen, which he clutches with both hands.

"Put pressure on it," Dana says, but the blood continues to gush, and Crisp's face gets paler and paler as he drifts away before our eyes.

All I can do is hold his hand and be there. Then I realize.

He took a bullet for me.

"Crisp. You didn't have to—"

"Nah, it was nothing, Gregory. You would have done the same for me, right?"

I watch as his eyes glaze over.

"Right," I say, not knowing if I believe myself.

"Gulls may squabble, gulls may fight. But at the end of the day, they look out for one another," he says. Then his grip goes weak, and he's gone.

The seagull that's been circling lands by his side and pecks for a moment at his shoulder before stopping to stare at us. Then it takes off with a great flap of its wings and powers itself higher and higher until it is lost in the light of the midday sun.

"Bye, Crisp," I say, carefully closing his eyelids.

Then I catch a whiff of something foul. The odour of rotting fish—emanating from Crisp's shirt. Carefully, I pinch the fabric and peek inside his breast pocket.

"Fish," I say.

"That's what attracted the seagull," Dana says.

A groan from Jackson pulls our attention to him, and Dana rushes over to his side.

"Jackson! Are you okay?"

I make my way over, too. He's in bad shape, bloodied and bruised, slumped over on his knees, but he's just about lucid.

"My hands," he manages to say, and I find a sliver of rock with an edge sharp enough to gnaw through the zip ties, which have left ligature marks so deep that there is blood on his hands.

We help him into a sitting position, supported by a couple of the larger rocks, and Dana locates a dropped bottle of water for him to drink.

"Now," Dana says. "How are we gonna get off this goddamn mountain?"

"I can help with that," Jackson mumbles. "Find me a phone."

Dana and I look around but find no phones have been dropped. We look at one another as we approach Mint's body.

"I can't," she says, turning away from Mint's motionless body, clearly still in shock over what she's done. What she had to do.

I nod.

I can relate.

I do my best not to look as I crouch and rifle through Mint's pockets. I locate three phones, one of which is mine.

We bring the phone over to Jackson.

"Are you gonna call air rescue?"

"Nah," he says. "This'll be quicker."

* * *

Hawk 2 is a sleek helicopter in the standard Finatech red and white livery. We huddle to protect ourselves from the dust it kicks up as it approaches from between the mountains.

Jackson was right. It did get here quickly.

Inside, blood becomes smeared on white leather seats, and Jackson's own medical team gets him on an IV before tending to Dana and me.

I hold her hand and she holds onto Jackson's. We'd talked about taking a helicopter ride through Gros Morne. It was on our bucket list. But having come so close to death among these great rocks, the stunning views hold little interest. Instead of looking out the window, I look to my palm, turning the little glass orb with the mosquito inside, flaking dried blood off it with my fingernail.

19

Gone but Not Forgotten

London is loud compared to Newfoundland. Like someone turned up the volume on the world.

"Canada is forty times the size of the UK and has half the population," my crusty old geography teacher had told me and my classmates back in high school. I felt that during my time there. That sense of space.

But in a strange way, London is comforting. The people, the smells, the noise. It's bustling and vivid where Newfoundland was quiet and stark. Where before I longed for that peace, to escape all the noise, now it's the quiet I fear.

Blood on the rocks is more shocking than blood on the streets.

I don't understand all the people going around wearing headphones. I want to hear the sounds of the city.

Maybe it's a kind of peace that they seek. Peace in a place that can't offer any.

I check the time on my phone and peep out from the bus shelter to see the red double-decker approaching through the pelting rain.

I climb on board and settle into my seat for the commute home. The bus is busy but lightens its load with every stop. I sit and watch the city pass by through the dirty, rain-streaked window, pushing my elbow into my side to feel the reassuring sensation of the glass orb pressing against my ribs.

One stop away from where I get off, a rough-looking man a couple of seats in front of me rings the bell. He stands, and, before the bus comes to a halt, he half-turns to look at me.

Did he wink at me?

He puts up his hood and disembarks.

No sooner has the bus set off again than my phone vibrates. I pull it out to see a text message from an unknown sender.

Back once again in London town
But no need to pout, no need to frown
We're still on an island, we can still have some fun
Check the case 'neath the seat for a dare and a gun

Acknowledgements

Thanks to Jerry Cranford and the team at Flanker Press for believing in the book and treating it with care and attention.

Thanks to Pete Farmer—always the first editor (and critic) of anything I write. I will always appreciate your eye, your honesty, and your friendship.

Thanks to Krista Burton for seeing my vision and helping to bring it to life. I love the way you see the world.

Thanks to my beagle buddies, Duke and Dallas before him, for being my early-morning writing partners.

Thanks to anyone who's ever spent time reading something I've written, particularly to those who have offered words of encouragement or constructive criticism. I hope you will continue to pick up my work in the future. Feedback is always welcome.

Thanks to Mum for giving me those storyteller genes and to my high school English teacher, Mrs. Ashworth, for telling me I had the writing ability to craft novels one day. A simple sentence uttered to a young person can make an imprint that lasts a lifetime.

Gareth Mitton is a writer originally hailing from Rochdale, northern England, who has been living in Atlantic Canada since moving across the pond as an adventurous twenty-something in the early 2000s. His 2020 debut novel, *Pedestal* (Engen Books)—a science fiction story—was lauded by the *Miramichi Reader* as ". . . an admirable first novel, an innovative leap from the genre's first-gen."

Gareth is a published essayist, blogger, and author, whose short story "Watcher"—a 2017 ScreenCraft Cinematic Short Story semifinalist—was featured in Engen's 2019 anthology, *Dystopia from the Rock*.

In his "day job," Gareth is an advertising creative director and copywriter with over two decades of local and national campaigns to his credit.

(*continued*)

Hard Cases sees a return to his first love of fiction writing, with more novels set for publication in the near future.

Gareth lives in St. John's, Newfoundland, with his partner, Krista; stepchildren, Piper and Tommi; and beloved beagle, Duke.

Gareth is a big advocate and supporter of Beagle Paws Rescue and encourages you to please support the cause of mistreated and neglected beagles. Please visit www.beaglepaws.com to learn more.

You can follow Gareth in the following places (and he loves it when you reach out and say hi!):

Website: garethmitton.com
Insta: instagram.com/garethmitton/
Facebook: facebook.com/gwmitton
X (formerly Twitter): @GazMit
Amazon Author Page: https://www.amazon.ca/Gareth-Mitton/e/B087QKV1B3/ref=dp_byline_cont_pop_book_1

HARD CASES

A NEWFOUNDLAND THRILLER

Visit Flanker Press at:

www.flankerpress.com

https://www.facebook.com/flankerpress

https://twitter.com/FlankerPress

https://www.instagram.com/flanker_press

http://www.youtube.com
/user/FlankerPress